15

CIRCLE OF BETRAYAL

Close Enough to Kill Series - Book One

JACQUELINE SIMON GUNN

This book is a work of fiction. Except for brief references to true crime cases all names, characters and events are from the author's imagination. Locations are used fictitiously. Any similarity to actual persons, living or dead, is purely coincidental and not intended by the author.

ISBN: 1518788211
ISBN 13: 9781518788215

For my family,
And in loving memory of my mother...

"The meeting of two personalities is like the contact of two chemical substances: If there is any reaction, both are transformed." C. G. Jung

Prologue

Prison is a place where your room has bars instead of a door. The steel closes behind you, and locks keep you contained, trapped from any sort of free choice. Within this confined space called a cell, your toilet and bed are next to each other, the stench causing nausea for months until that odor becomes your norm. Then one day you realize that you no longer smell anything strange.

In prison, you are basically stripped of your freedom. Your life is now under the direction of strict rules and authoritarian humans. At night there are sounds that come from other cells that initially cause terror, but that you eventually get used to. You practically invite the noise because without it, you are left alone in a silence so empty and painful it could kill you. But there is another sort of prison, one which there is no escape, not even with the temporary respite of work duty, lunch and dinner breaks or time in the court yard. This prison isn't a place, but rather a state of mind where your own thoughts and feelings keep you trapped, hindering your ability to feel free. There is a loss of volition over your choices, making you a victim of your own private nightmare.

It's hard to imagine, I suppose, that you can live in such a psychic prison — a psychological hell filled with seething emotions and barely contained impulses — that you just can't find a way to free yourself. Kadee would not have understood this until she actually found herself there. Held captive by the grip of secrets, lies and obsession that had become her life, prison became an unwelcomed but familiar home; a place that she had only imagined from reading books and watching movies; a place that became irresistible, taunting her to stay no matter how hard she tried to leave. For almost a year that's how she lived, self-tortured in that place. The tragedy that freed her was akin to a theatrical performance, evolving slowly with unbelievable turns ending in murder.

It was hard to explain; it was something she wondered if even her psychiatrist understood. The feeling of being so imprisoned in your life, so trapped that the only thing you know is to act. Often, you can't even think; you just act in a frenzy, a hurried tactic to rid yourself of feelings for which you can find no words to describe. This is the pain that causes some people to jump off a bridge, others to commit unthinkable acts toward another, and still others not to remember the unspeakable acts they had done.

And in this emotional prison, Kadee looked back on that brisk late October morning when she serendipitously met Noah. It was one of those perfect autumn mornings when the sun was bright, lighting up the whole sky; the air had that touch of crispness that made you wrap a long sheltering sweater around you.

It was one of those invigorating fall mornings where the infinite cloudless sky made anything seem possible.

Then suddenly, anything was.

Kadee's friends tried to warn her about Noah. They tried to help her. They would say he wasn't good for her, that they didn't trust him. Something was off. Kadee knew they were right, but she loved him. So she tried to ignore the truth. At first she wouldn't listen, she was still that strong, independent woman, the type that liked to forge out on her own, the one who rarely took any advice despite the veneer of polite listening. But when it came to Noah, she couldn't listen. Trapped by the power of her own feelings for him, she couldn't hear the truth.

It is amazing how much can change in a year. Or how much influence one relationship can have on you. You can see yourself one way at the beginning, or can be a certain way in the beginning—self-reliant, self-assured, confident—then at the end you are so broken, your identity so shattered, that you can't even remember who you were when it started.

Then, of course, there was the murder. The salacious headlines: MURDER ON THE UPPER EASTSIDE! RESPECTED DOCTOR KILLED! Kadee noticed the front page caption as she was hurrying by a newsstand on the way to school that morning. But it wasn't until later when the cops showed up at her apartment to question her that she realized what happened.

There is a type of humiliation that can occur that is so subtle in the beginning of a relationship, you don't even recognize it as such. They are small comments geared toward slowly chipping away at your self-worth, eventually making you feel so small and insignificant that by the time you realize the comments are demoralizing, you actually believe them. It was in this deject-ed frame of mind that she became a prime suspect in a murder investigation.

Kadee had had homicidal fantasies before; she had thought about killing him. "It's normal to fantasize," her psychiatrist, Dr. Tracy would say. Her words echoed in Kadee's mind as the two detectives questioned her. Their demeanor was severe; and their harsh, unwavering tone unnerved her as she found herself fum-bling for her words. The headline: FORENSIC PSYCHOLOGY STUDENT GUILTY OF MURDER flashed through her mind. The awareness of the irony was mixed with dread, her lips curl-ing as she tried impossibly to get the words out and to explain her whereabouts just three days prior on the 19th of September, nearly a year since she met him. There is a difference between thinking—even ruminative, rage-filled compulsive thinking—and acting on those thoughts. And she was not guilty of the latter.

Or was she? Somewhere in the midst of all the chaos and tur-moil, her perception of events had become blurred. Her memory of events were wiped away. Her responsibility for the crime, un-certain. And she needed to find her way back to the truth.

CHAPTER 1

Kadee spotted Vanessa, who was seated at a small table in the back of their favorite West Village restaurant. It was a little hole-in-the-wall type of place where the food was delicious, but it was always packed. The occupants at the neighboring table could easily hear your conversation. Sometimes during holiday weekends, they would go there and sit for hours sipping mimosas, the city seemingly evacuated. During the rest of the year, with the city bustling, they only met there when there was nothing too confidential to discuss. That afternoon turned out to be an exception.

With such a radiant fall afternoon, they were squeezed in like sardines between two larger tables. One table was filled with a group of twenty-something men who looked as though they had been out all night. One of them gave Kadee a conspicuous look, his eyes piercing through her clothing as he smiled. Kadee pursed her lips together, the corners revealing only the slightest upward movement, and gave him a quick glance. It was the type of exchange she would have relished in her twenties, possibly even taking his look as an invitation to stop and talk.

Kadee was one of those women who was the object of envy. She was born gorgeous, possessing the type of beauty that was so perfect it seemed as if she were painted by the gentle, careful strokes of the most talented artist. At 5 foot 9 inches, with long thin extremities, small rounded hips, large green eyes, and dark brown hair that draped over her shoulders effortlessly, she was the type of women who would stop traffic. Men and women alike would stop whatever they were doing to catch a glimpse of her, to take in her beauty, awe-stricken.

It always seemed to Kadee that other people imagined her life to be easy. Her girlfriends definitely did. They thought that because she was born beautiful, her life was painless, as if she had a free pass from all of the difficulties that her contemporaries had to endure. When she was younger, Kadee noticed that she was treated differently because of her beauty; without even trying, she got thing other girls didn't. But as she matured and life disclosed more complicated challenges than who was taking who to the high school prom, Kadee found herself feeling lonely and experiencing difficulty navigating the obstacles that adult intimacy and romance disclosed.

Kadee blamed her gifted appearance for her circumstances. She was thirty-five years old. And she was alone. Her guardedness against men had evolved slowly during her twenties when she thought men only wanted her for how she looked. No one, she felt, would take the time to see her, to discover who she really was, her whole personhood. Because of this, Kadee had only had one significant relationship, and that was back in college. She thought she was destined to spend her life alone, a single woman. She was grateful for her girlfriends, especially Vanessa, who adored her unconditionally.

Kadee leaned over and gave Vanessa a hug before she sat down, draping her mid-length flowing skirt over her long legs as she crossed them. She was excited to tell Vanessa about Noah, about their chance meeting earlier that morning, but she noticed a look of distress in Vanessa's eyes. Her pupils were dilated despite the abundant light. Her gaze, penetrating and serious.

"Are you OK, Ness?"

"I broke it off with Neil last night. He's devastated." She released a gasp of air as she sunk back into her chair. "I'm so glad you're here," she whispered, glancing over at the twenty-something table as if she was afraid they would hear her.

"You look devastated, too, Ness. What happened? I thought things were getting better. Last time we spoke...last week when we spoke, you said you were feeling better about him. What happened?"

"I don't know. I just...I just," she choked back tears. "I just don't love him. I wanted to love him. I mean feel in love with him. On paper he's perfect for me, but I don't feel any sort of passion. He's like a friend. There's no romance, and at thirty-six years old...if I waited this long...that's just..." she lowered her voice to a whisper again. "It's not enough. You know? It's just not enough..." She trailed off, her gaze distant.

Vanessa looked at Kadee again. Kadee could see the moistness behind her dark brown eyes as she tried to hold back her tears, "I just can't compromise. You know it's always the same story with me."

Kadee moved her chair next to Vanessa, trying not to cause too much of a disruption. She didn't want to draw attention toward them. Kadee then leaned over and hugged her tight.

Vanessa's parents were divorced when she was only ten years old. Her mother's recollection was that she married her father because she thought she should. At twenty-six years old, her mother thought it was time to settle down and raise a family. She loved Vanessa's father, but wasn't in love with him, so she decided to file for divorce right after Vanessa's tenth birthday.

Vanessa had vivid memories of her parents fighting about it. Then there were the looks and back and forth glances between her parents during that time. Those looks that could kill were worse than the fights. Vanessa could see the pain, but no one was talking about it. It was like they were putting on a front for her, trying to protect her from some harsh reality of adult life, but Vanessa could feel the pain. And because they didn't really discuss it, she still carried it with her.

Vanessa was so afraid of making the same mistake, to marry someone because it was time, or convenient, or because he fit into some sort of larger life plan. Ness wanted to marry the real thing. She wanted the type of love that they make movies and write love songs about.

"I just can't compromise," she would repeat after the end of nearly all of her intimate relationships. Her adult life was a long list of serial disappointments when it came to men. With each new budding relationship, she started hopeful, only to experience the same disillusionment every time. Her hopes shattered, depression soon followed.

Kadee always thought that Vanessa was idealistic, that what she wanted, expected to find, was an illusion. That it was a love created to sell books, movies and songs. That it made the false promise of happily ever after. This type of love made little girls dress up like princesses waiting hopefully for their prince to come once they had grown into young women. Kadee believed this to be what she called "a delusion of love."

Then she met Noah.

Vanessa pulled Kadee's chair a little closer, took a sip of her coffee, and asked, "So what's new with you?"

The women had known each other for more than fifteen years, having been roommates through most of college. Kadee knew that as soon as she told Vanessa about Noah, she'd be planning their wedding. One of Vanessa's most endearing qualities was her perpetual optimism. She was hopeful to fault. It was what always pulled her out of her disappointments and allowed her to try again.

They were opposite in that way. Kadee was cynical, strong-willed and always had her guard up with men. She liked to flirt and toy with their affection, using her beauty to allure them, but she could never quite get the whole intimacy thing down. It wasn't for lack of effort; she dated constantly, always hoping that one day, given the right set of circumstances, she would find someone who would see her for who she was and who she liked enough in return to spend her life with.

Kadee looked up at Vanessa and squeezed her forearm, "Are you sure you're done talking about Neil?"

"Yeah, yeah." She was flipping her hands back and forth in the air. "There's really not much else to say. And I'm sick of listening to myself."

Kadee wrinkled her nose.

"I know, Kade…I know…it's awful careening toward fucking forty and being single. I thought I was a spinster at thirty. Sorry, I didn't mean…I didn't mean that you were a spinster too, I'm just being dramatic. … um… anyway, you don't seem to care so much if you ever meet 'the one.'"

"Nice save." Kadee smirked at Vanessa. "I care. I do. I just don't think it's wise to invest your future in something or someone when the chances of meeting 'the one' are precarious."

"I wish I had your attitude. You're always so in control of your life. Always are, always were."

"And sometimes I wish I had yours. Seriously, you'll be fine." Kadee hesitated.

Vanessa glared at her. "What?"

"I really wish you would see that therapist I gave you the referral for. I think it would help you."

"You're right. You're right," she looked away for a moment, flipping back her curly hair.

She knew Vanessa wouldn't call. There was a part of Vanessa that didn't want to change. Deep down she was afraid that if she saw a therapist, her illusions of romantic love would be destroyed—and with that her idealism and hopefulness. Kadee couldn't blame her. She always felt so hardened compared to Vanessa. There was something so warm and vulnerable about her. It was really appealing. Vanessa was really appealing.

Vanessa had dark brown eyes. They were almost black. She had black hair with beautiful spiral curls that hung down to the middle of her back, a blessing from her Mexican mother's side of the family. Her skin was olive and her cheeks full, revealing a dimple on the left side, which brightened up her face whenever she smiled.

Vanessa was curvy. Not overweight, but not lanky like Kadee. As much as Kadee got attention for her appearance, her dark hair and green eyes, a striking contrast against her pale skin, Vanessa's Rubenesque figure and exotic features drew the attention of men. Vanessa never seemed to appreciate her appeal, though. She was a modest woman, even awkward at times. She always wore clothes that were just a little too big in an attempt to cover her assets.

Kadee squeezed Vanessa's arm. She could feel a smile forming on her face, as she began to tell her Noah story. "I met a guy in the coffee shop by my apartment this morning."

She proceeded to give Vanessa the details of her chance encounter with Noah that morning. It was strange for Kadee when she thought back on that afternoon with Vanessa when she was feeling excited and hopeful about Noah. The space and time where our lives take place in the present becomes the past so quickly. Sometimes when you look back you wonder what you could have ever been thinking, what detail you might have missed, what you could have done differently that might have changed the outcome, creating an entirely different future. Kadee used to think of these sorts of questions philosophically, but when the consequences are lethal, the answers become urgent.

If one moment, one task, had just been different, she might not have met Noah that morning. There were a series of circumstances that took her out of her morning routine and landed her at the coffee shop on line right in front of him. First was the phone call she received from her friend Hailey at around 8 a.m. that woke her from her slumber. As she reached clumsily for her cell phone, she knocked a glass right off her nightstand, leaving orange juice mixed with broken glass splattered all over her bedroom floor.

Kadee was a graduate student and had set her alarm for 9:30 a.m., as she had been up late the night before working on her research paper; she planned to sleep a little later than usual. But the ring jolted her, and when she saw Hailey's name flashing across the phone screen, she figured it must be important if she was calling so early. So she picked up. Hailey's speech was pressured as she spoke, her words shaking.

Hailey had been having an affair, and in the early morning her husband had read her text messages, which revealed her indiscretions. While Kadee didn't condone Hailey's decisions, she couldn't believe she was sloppy enough not to have erased the texts between her lover and her. Hailey attended to details. Her appearance always impeccable, she left nothing undone. As a psychology graduate student, Kadee couldn't help but wonder if Hailey had wanted him to know. She wasn't happy in her marriage; maybe she hoped if he found out, something would change. Maybe she hoped he'd leave her. Kadee couldn't be sure because Hailey wasn't always honest.

Kadee secretly thought that Hailey didn't want to leave him because of money. Hailey's husband, Dean, was a big Wall Street banker, and Hailey had become accustomed to a lavish lifestyle. That morning, Hailey was too distressed for any confrontation, so Kadee just listened, trying to offer the support she needed. As they spoke, she cleaned the orange juice-saturated wood floor, her knee-high rain boots protecting her feet from the glass shards. They were still talking as she went into her cabinet to get her morning fix: strong coffee.

Kadee must have been distracted because she dropped the coffee. The small specks of brown were all over the floor, nestling into the creases of the kitchen tiles. It was close to an hour before their conversation ended. Kadee was in a morning-without-coffee withdrawal, so as soon as they said their goodbyes, she threw on jeans and a long sweater, not stopping to even put eyeliner on, and raced out the door to the coffee shop around the corner. And that's why she met Noah. In the beginning, she was thanking Hailey for the phone call that led to their fateful meeting. Eventually, Hailey grew disgusted with Kadee's difficulties with him. After his murder, Hailey stopped calling. Once Kadee's name was made public, Hailey turned her back on Kadee altogether.

The line at the coffee shop was long, and Kadee was feeling impatient when Noah casually initiated a conversation with her. For the first few moments, she thought little of their meeting, or of him. These sorts of exchanges happen regularly in New York City. People always seem to think New Yorkers are rude and discourteous. This is not accurate. New Yorkers tend to be quick-lipped and straight forward, but they can be very friendly and an interesting chat with a stranger is not uncommon.

After a few minutes of casual talk, Noah offered to pay for her coffee. Kadee tried to politely decline, but he insisted, so she let him. They then carried on their talk for more than an hour, both of them getting a second cup of coffee as they nonchalantly found themselves seated at one of the tables. Noah was tall and lanky, nothing like the men Kadee was typically attracted to, most of whom had a more athletic bulky build. As a taller woman, Kadee always liked a bigger man; one whose body would feel strong as his arms were wrapped around her.

Kadee wouldn't have given Noah a second look if he hadn't started talking to her. Within only a few moments, she became mesmerized by their conversation. Not necessarily the content, what he was saying almost didn't matter. It was the way he talked, or maybe more accurately the way he listened.

Six months later when Kadee would look back on that morning, she would feel empty as she realized that it was all a game for Noah. That nothing he said or did was real. Everyone is endowed with unique strengths, and one of Noah's greatest gifts was the art of manipulation. It was as if he knew her intimately before he even knew her at all. Perhaps he read her body language, the look in her eyes, her style of dress, something that gave him all the information he needed to immediately disarm her so that she was melting on his every word.

Then there was his whole manner of being. His movements slow and gentle, and his temperament calm and even, he seemed so sensitive. Kadee felt like she wanted to lie down with him, sipping wine next to a warm fire, and tell him her every thought. He had dark penetrating brown eyes, too. They danced as she spoke; sparks of white twinkling, making it feel like he was hanging on her every word.

Kadee remembered her aunt telling her that a wise woman falls in love with a man that makes her feel like she is the only woman he sees. "When you see that look in his eyes, you know you've got him, and he is there to stay," she would say. Kadee never quite understood her words until she recognized that exact look in Noah's eyes. Kadee would never forget that look, either, forever imprinted in her memory, not as a look of endearment, but rather the working eyes of a predator.

She wanted to sit there all day with Noah, possibly even have him back to her apartment. Maybe this was the first red flag; for sure it was. She had felt attracted to men upon an initial meeting before, sometimes imagining what the sex would be like, but her urge for Noah was more intense than she was accustomed to. *What's this about?* She asked herself as they were talking. *He's not even my type. What does that mean anyway? It never works out with those guys. Maybe I have been going with the wrong men. Whatever. He seems interesting, stop thinking and just go with it.* It felt so good that she decided to stop questioning it, at least temporarily.

Kadee had to leave anyway, which she thought was a good thing. She had her downtown lunch date with Vanessa. She had originally thought her lunch date rescued her from tearing Noah's clothes from his body and he hers. What a classic New York moment: having the guy you met at the coffee shop and had only known for an hour, over for some Saturday afternoon sex. In the end, it turns out none of the rules mattered. Whether she was with him that first hour or that first weekend, it did not matter. The outcome would have been the same.

While Noah was talking, his mouth curling out words that had the rhythm of a Robert Frost poem, she was imagining what it would be like to take him home. She was fantasizing about calling Vanessa to cancel so she could be with him. The way he looked into her eyes made her feel really sexy. He seemed genuinely interested in getting to know her, asking questions about her life and interests, nodding and smiling as he watched her talk. She enjoyed that a lot.

The date with Vanessa was her excuse, but she believed it was thinking of the wisdom of Hailey Beckhem that stopped her before she decided to invite him home for an afternoon rendezvous. Hailey liked rules; it gave her a sense of control over her life. She was always talking about recipes of love, baiting the guy, reeling him in, getting the ring. For her, love had stages, and she had regulations for each stage. Her first and perhaps most important instruction was never —"under any circumstances" — were you to sleep with a guy on the first date.

"Three dates, at least, maybe four," she would insist was the correct formula. Kadee didn't always follow Hailey's instructions, which caused frequent disagreements between the two women. Hailey would raise her voice, she could become really nasty sometimes, and say, "You're thirty-five years old, Kadee

Carlisle. It's time to think about finding a husband and settling down already."

Kadee wasn't rigid like Hailey; she didn't think relationships were so black-and-white, but grayer, more nebulous, more mysterious. But her desire for Noah was unusually strong; it confused her a little. She had always felt in charge of her choices—that is, before Noah. But when she excused herself to go into the bathroom, to throw cold water on her face and take a moment to think, she had the vague sense that it might be better to wait. There was something about this guy that was different. Kadee liked to dissect all of her feelings intellectually. It was a way for her to feel in control. She wanted a little time to think about her desire before she jumped into bed with him. The possibility of a spontaneous sexual encounter did excite her, though. She was getting really sick of her guardedness. But her natural proclivities took over in those few bathroom moments before she decided that she should leave and meet Vanessa.

At that time, Kadee still owned her free will. Hailey's words echoed: "You have to leave them wanting more." Of course, that didn't help Hailey much with her husband. He wanted her, he loved her, but after all the rules and regulations, the big diamond on her finger and the fancy New York penthouse, she didn't want him.

In the end, it didn't help Kadee, either. Noah had his own set of rules that Kadee would soon be subject to, eventually her own free will escaping her, leaving her prisoner with Noah as her keeper.

"Well, it was really lovely meeting you, Noah," she said, as she was getting up, trying her hardest to seem casual while hoping he would ask for her number. But his eyes were penetrating as he looked at her, making her feel unusually clumsy. He touched her hand and stood up next to her, moving in a little closer. Not too close, but just close enough that she could smell him. He had a fresh scent, like he had just taken a shower. For a moment her body tingled, almost like an electric current crossed the small space between them, fusing them together. "It was such a pleasure, Kadee with a D," he smiled wide with boyish charm.

People always confused Kadee for Katie and her nickname Kade for Kate. She hated that. Noah made sure not to make *that* mistake. *He really listens. I like that,* she thought.

"May I call you? I would love to continue our conversation over dinner." He was so nonchalant, and Kadee wondered if he was feeling anything similar to what she was. She thought maybe the intensity of their connection was only in her imagination. What Kadee figured out later was that that was exactly what he wanted her to think.

"Sure, sure...that would be great," she said as she was looking for a pen in her bag as a way to avoid eye contact. She was afraid he would see her desire.

"Here," he gracefully pulled out his cell phone. "I'll put it in here."

"Right, of course," she blushed. She felt uncharacteristically awkward, and she was pretty sure he could tell.

Noah put her phone number into his cell phone, kissed her on the cheek and said simply, "I will call you."

"I look forward to it," she smiled and left.

While in the taxi on her way downtown to meet Vanessa, she couldn't stop thinking about him. She didn't know much about him really. He also lived on the Upper East Side, only a few avenues away from her. But the few avenues that separated them suggested that they most likely had different financial circumstances. His apartment was on 76th between Madison and Park Avenues. Of course she hadn't seen his apartment yet, but she knew he lived in a brownstone; and that area was one of the wealthiest places in the world. Kadee was further east also on 76th street, only a five-minute walk, and a lovely area, but for the most part not as exclusive.

He also shared that he was a medical doctor, an internist in a joint practice. She wasn't sure how old he was, but based on his looks and the status of his career, she assumed he was somewhere between his mid to late thirties. Later she would find out that he was a little older, having just turned forty. She liked that. Other than that, she didn't know much about his interests, what he did in his spare time, or his family. He spoke mostly about work, his experience of medical training, the lack of sleep, the stress and pressure, and food. He enjoyed food and trying new restaurants. That much she knew.

They had only been together a little over an hour, but she was usually good at asking the sorts of questions that help you know someone. She realized that she hadn't done that with Noah. She was so attracted to him, yet found him elusive. And she was so distracted by fantasies of an unplanned sexual escapade, it was hard for her to even remember the details of their dialogue. She should have known he was dangerous. She should have known when her reactions were so incongruent with her usual temperament.

But...

Kadee had a *but* for everything. She was always contemplating all the different possibilities, almost like her brain enjoyed the back and forth of a cerebral tug of war. *But* Kadee had been hearing for years that she was closed off, detached, unavailable. She started to think maybe she wasn't any of those things, maybe she just hadn't met the right person. The truth was that Kadee's confusion started right from the beginning and only worsened as the relationship grew.

When she finished her Noah story, Vanessa was smiling wide. Her dimple was lighting up her face, as she blurted out, "See, Kadee, real love is possible. That's how I want to feel." Unlike some women in her situation, Vanessa wasn't jealous; rather, she experienced the story as a sign of hope and possibility.

Kadee's approach to love and relationships had always been conservative, perhaps to a fault. Her one serious relationship during her undergraduate years was with Alex Suarez. The curly-haired boy she had met in her abnormal psychology class. He pursued her relentlessly until she finally agreed to go out with him. She liked him a lot. She might have even loved him, but he was not demonstrative with his feelings. Kadee didn't like that so much, so she remained guarded. In the end after two years, he broke it off abruptly, with no explanation. After that, there were a few shorter term relationships, lasting only a month or two, but no one that she felt too emotionally invested in. Kadee knew she was guarded. Sometimes she wondered if she was even capable of feeling romantic love. Sure she felt lonely sometimes. When she would look at couples walking down the street, holding hands or caressing, kissing in bars and restaurants, she felt a sense of longing. It was a sharp sensation in her stomach that would pierce quickly, begging for attention, but she would push it aside. She didn't like to feel victim to circumstances.

There was just something about Noah Donovan. Was it his charm? *What does that even mean anyway: charm?* She asked herself. *Maybe he's spewing a secret pheromone concoction, one that isn't out on the market yet. Those sparks of white twinkling as he listened intensely to my every word really got me aroused. To have someone really listen like that, well, most people have to pay a therapist for that level of attention. Or maybe it's just me. Either way, there is something about the way that man looked at me when I was talking that is different than anything I have ever experienced. Although knowing me, I'll change my mind about him after a couple of dates. So typical, Kadee. Let yourself feel intensity for some stranger only to conclude he's not for you after a few dinners. Regardless, he did make my morning more interesting. I just love that about this city, you never know who you'll meet when you go out.*

Kadee grew up in Edgewater, New Jersey, a small suburb right across the Hudson River from Manhattan. She had a relatively normal childhood, whatever that means; no one makes it through childhood completely unscathed. Her parents loved her. That in and of itself is one major developmental hurdle: feeling loved. And that she did.

But she was a bit of a rebellious type. Nothing terrible. She never did drugs or got arrested or anything like that. But she did color her hair dark blue her freshman year in high school, then she added a nose ring a week later. Her parents were not tolerant of her need for self-expression. They made her remove the nose ring and color her hair back. She wanted a tattoo, too. Her friends all got them. But her parents said she would be thrown out of the house if she got one. She didn't want to be a homeless high school student or have her parents be mad at her, so she didn't get one. She also had an affinity for '80's horror movies, and one day during her senior year in high school, she decorated her room with posters from different movies from that genre. She called them collector's items. Her mother came in, took one look and insisted they be removed.

The next week her mother bought her a gift: posters of different flowers. There were all kinds of different arrangements of flowers on six different posters. Liza, Kadee's mom, hung them up. Kadee walked in her room and immediately felt like she was smacked in the face. She hated lots of bright colors in her room, and it looked like a crayon box had exploded all over her walls. She preferred an edgy, dark atmosphere. But there was no arguing with Liza Carlisle. And she thought she was doing something nice for Kadee. "They are a present, for Christ's sake," Kadee said to herself. "You know she'll flip out if you say you don't want them."

Kadee began her therapy with Dr. Tracy toward the end of March, after about five months with Noah, when things between them started to feel totally unmanageable. She had gotten the referral from one of her classmates at John Jay College. She knew she needed help. Her concept of her own reality once clear and steadfast was becoming increasingly precarious. Dr. Tracy was trying to help Kadee understand how she went from feeling in control and self-possessed to feeling trapped by desire and emotional dependence.

After about five months with Noah, Kadee noticed that her mood was affected by how much attention Noah was giving her. She was naturally passionate, edgy and sometimes moody, but she had never felt that her day could be so affected by whether or not someone called her. She recognized that if Noah called her early, the day went better. If he didn't call until afternoon or, even worse, he didn't return her phone call for hours, she would feel rattled, sometimes snapping at other people for no reason.

And she waited for him to call. She hated that. She never wanted to feel so out of control in a relationship with a man. She had been attached to Alex and he could be a real jerk sometimes, but she had not felt like this with him.

She even started cancelling plans with Vanessa last minute if he called asking to see her. It almost felt like her body craved him, like she suffered physical pain which could only be relieved by the touch of his hands or the kiss of his lips. She knew that this type of attachment toward someone else was unhealthy. No one should have enough power to control the quality of your days, everyday.

Kadee had described herself as independent, yet she could not disengage from Noah; instead, she was overly enmeshed with him. The incongruence seemed important to Dr. Tracy as she tried to pick through Kadee's psyche. She was becoming increasingly distressed, and Dr. Tracy was concerned for her.

Dr. Tracy's hypothesis was that Kadee's outward strength, the persona she showed to the world, was sometimes used as a way to mask her weaknesses. She explained that it takes real courage to show human vulnerabilities and weakness. "And we all have them," she said a few times. She knew Kadee was strong, but she also thought that she was afraid to show her softer more sensitive self to other people, especially to a man after what had happened with Alex.

One day, Kadee became irritated with her. This was happening more frequently as Kadee's functioning deteriorated. Kadee stood up. She was waving her arms around, as she raised her voice, demanding some kind of interpretation.

"I am sick of your psychobabble already. I want to know what you think. I want you to tell me the truth! What's wrong with me? How can someone go from being strong and independent to…to…*this*? I want to understand why I feel like this! I can't take it anymore! I want to feel — to *be* — the way I used to. And I need you to help me."

Dr. Tracy was taken aback. She had never seen Kadee so angry, so on the verge of losing control. She was on edge and her impulses seemed barely containable. Dr. Tracy decided to share her thoughts. "I believe your strength is a type of armor. You have been using it for years to protect yourself from being hurt. It's failing with Noah as you have allowed yourself to be vulnerable with him. This may sound like a bunch of psychobabble, but the truth is that we are all filled with contradictions; personality is fluid not black and white. And, well…we are all both strong *and* weak. That's what it means to be human. We all have flaws, weaknesses. The real strength is when we can admit these to ourselves and become able to show them to others. I think this is the essence of your struggle here. You are exposing yourself to a man, one that you love. I know it's scary, but this could be a good thing if you can tolerate it." Dr. Tracy had a gentle voice; it always calmed Kadee down

Kadee sat down, bowed her head and nodded. "I see what you mean." She raised her voice slightly, "*But* do you understand what I am feeling…is not normal? Scary? Sure. I get that. After what happened with Alex, it has been hard for me to be open, but I feel like I'm falling apart over here. It just cannot be normal to live with this amount of insecurity. And if this is what love is…I DO NOT fucking want it!"

"I think you're afraid to really open yourself up to a man, Kadee. Somewhere buried deep down, I think you're afraid to really let a man see you. You say that's what you want, but at the same time as you want that, I think you are afraid of it. Noah has broken through your armor, and I think that terrifies you." Dr. Tracy paused, giving Kadee a minute to contemplate their discussion. Then, "What do you think about what I just said?"

Kadee nodded her head up and down, indicating her answer was yes. She added, "I *am* terrified, *but* still something seems wrong. Though I do see what you're saying." She sat back in her chair, a stream of tears dripping silently down her cheeks.

As time went on, Dr. Tracy would begin to realize that there was more to the story than simply Kadee struggling to tolerate her own vulnerabilities. It is common to feel anxious when exposing intimate layers of yourself to someone new, especially a romantic partner. However, as Dr. Tracy would learn, Kadee's distress was more complicated than that.

Dr. Tracy's description resonated. But instead of using the information to help her understand why she was unraveling,

Kadee listened, stashed it somewhere in her subconscious, and continued on with Noah. Pleasure and pain had become inseparable at this point. Kadee just wanted to feel something intense, something that would remind her that there was a world out there larger than her. She had never felt such pain as she had with Noah, but she had never had such pleasure, either. Kadee wasn't ready to let go of the latter, so she stayed, becoming only a shadow of her former self.

Kadee stopped seeing Dr. Tracy for a few weeks after that session. She called and said she couldn't afford her anymore. That wasn't the truth; and Kadee was sure her doctor knew it. She would only miss three weeks of therapy when an upsetting event would send her right back.

It happened one night at a strip club, when Noah begged her to dance naked in front of him. In the privacy of their apartments, she would dance naked for him, slowly peeling off her panties, as he always requested; that was his favorite part. But this only happened when they were in the privacy of their apartments, but that night he wanted a public show.

"I want other men to see you and know that only I have you," he said, putting his arm around her and pulling her close. "Here let's have another drink first; it will loosen you up," he waved the topless bartender over. Most strip clubs in New York City are topless, bottoms stay on, but Noah had found this club that was totally nude. Apparently he knew the owner; he may have been one of his patients.

While drinking her vodka cranberry, she was trying to think through how she was feeling. She didn't like what Noah wanted, but in an odd sort of way, it also turned her on. Noah started to put his hand down the front of her pants. His front finger was massaging her clitoris.

"What are you doing?" she whispered in his ear. She thought people could see; that made her uncomfortable.

"I want you to be moist down there when you get on stage. This way I know you are wet for me when you pull your panties off. Come on, DeeDee," he kissed her softly on the cheek. DeeDee was Noah's new nickname for Kadee, a term of endearment as he liked to call it.

She wanted to stop him. Later she would say that he wouldn't let her stop him. But she could have left, run out, never seen him again. Truthfully, by this point, Kadee was afraid if she didn't do it, he would leave her. That fear made it feel like he wouldn't let her stop him. This was when she began to lose her grip, and the truth blurred.

The other confusing piece was that on some level what he wanted her to do was exciting and arousing. As he continued massaging her, she was so wet, even her slacks were moist with fluid. When he said that it would bring them closer, she decided to believe him. She gave him what he wanted. She gave him his dance. But the next morning when he was cold and distant, she felt confused.

He had lied. One some level she knew that, but she was so attached to the man he was in the beginning that she just couldn't accept the truth. That's when she called Dr. Tracy back and resumed her therapy sessions. The therapy didn't seem to be helping much, but it was comforting to have a place to talk.

She tried so hard to remember the woman that she was in the beginning of their relationship. She wanted that woman back, the one who never for a second would have given in to Noah Donovan, the one who would have told Noah Donovan a big NO when he asked for that dance. She tried to remind herself of her strength, her independent spirit, but her self-esteem was so damaged by this point that woman she was in the beginning felt very far away.

Then again, the Noah Donovan in the beginning of their relationship was nothing like the one he was now, either. She could not understand how she let this happen to her. But it did happen, and this was her life now. The deeper she fell into Noah's world, the more terrified she became of her own urges. But she just couldn't stop.

CHAPTER 2

After her West Village lunch with Vanessa, the one where Kadee spilled her fascination about her first meeting with Noah, Kadee went back home with the goal of finishing her research paper. She was in the second year of her doctorate in forensic psychology at John Jay College. Her plan had been to complete her degree and pursue a career as a psychologist in the legal system. She had been contemplating work as a consultant within either the New York City Police Department or the court system. She was also interested in researching criminality.

Kadee always liked darkness, maybe because it seemed to hold more truth than light. As a young girl, Kadee would sit in her room doing homework on her computer with the lights out. She liked reading in the dark, too, using only a flashlight. Liza Carlisle would come in and turn the lights on. "That's not good for your eyes, Kadee," she would say. As soon as she walked away, Kadee would turn them off again. It went like that through most of her adolescence.

There was also a period somewhere between ten and eleven years old, when she overheard her parents talking about a serial killer in Milwaukee; he was loose, running around killing other men and eating parts of their bodies. Kadee would sneak into the living room after her parents went to bed to watch the story on the news. After Jeffrey Dahmer was taken into custody, Kadee started watching the news every day after school while her parents were at work.

When her mother discovered her secret interest in the Dahmer case, she was concerned. "Kadee, you shouldn't be watching this. It's not for kids, she said. Her tone was calm, but stern, and her body looked rigid.

"But mom, I…"

"Kadee there are no buts about this. You have to listen to me. This isn't the sort of thing that kids should be watching or reading about; it will give you nightmares. I'm just trying to protect you. Please do not do it again. Understand?"

"But mom…"

She scrunched her nose, her nostrils had the slightest flair, but her tone was even, "Kadee," she cleared her throat, "Kadee, dear, there are no buts here. Now tell me you understand…you are too young for this sort of thing. Do you understand?"

Kadee bowed her head, stared at the floor and nodded, "Yes." There was just no arguing with Liza Carlisle.

This may have ended her attention to the Dahmer case, but it did not stop her interest in criminality. In some ways, the forbiddance only made her more fascinated.

Her current fascination was the study of catathymia. She was doing research exploring the relationship between catathymia and stalking. Catathymia is a psychological process used to understand interpersonally charged murders where there is a buildup or incubation period prior to the ultimately explosive murderous act. Following the murder, the perpetrators describe an enormous sense of relief. Stalking behaviors are common during the tense buildup phase, as the perpetrator usually has the torturous combination of a need to be close to the victim along with a corresponding rage. She was using the research to explore if stalking could be used as a predictor of a catathymic homicide.

The further she got into the forensic files, studying the different profiles of catathymic and other types of stalkers and murders, she became consumed with two larger questions: What leads someone to commit murder? And how does love turn into murderous rage? Some of the psychological histories lacked any convincing evidence explaining what led the perpetrators down their lethal path.

She was knee deep in her research when her phone started ringing. She looked at the screen: an unfamiliar New York number. She hoped it was Noah. She had imagined him texting instead of calling; that's what most guys did for first contacts. But Noah was not like other guys.

She cleared her throat and flipped her hair back and forth. She was trying to shake off her dark serious side in order to sound light and bubbly. Kadee didn't think a good first phone conversation topic was "What do you suppose leads someone down the dark, spine-chilling path of murder?"

She took a deep breath. "Hello."

"Hello, Kadee? Hi, Kadee, this is Noah," his deep, gentle voice had such a soothing tone.

"Hey, Noah." She was trying to sound casual, but her stomach did a cartwheel, "So nice to hear from you."

"I know it's last minute, but I was wondering if you are free for dinner tonight? I'd love to take you to that new French restaurant I was telling you about."

Kadee felt her lips form a smile; she noticed her palms were sweating as she wiped them on her jeans. She wanted to say yes immediately, but she was anxious. It was Hailey's rules repeating in her head: "Never accept a date on the same night he asks. You have to act unavailable." And then she also had committed her Saturday night to finishing her research paper. Kadee didn't like breaking her commitments to herself. Ever.

"Sure, Noah. Sounds great. I'd like that," she found herself saying without conscious intention.

"Excellent, Kadee with a D."

They discussed the details. They would meet at the restaurant at 8 p.m. He had offered to pick Kadee up and escort her to their dinner. *What a gentleman,* Kadee thought, but she was afraid that she would be inviting him up and they would be having sex instead of dinner. She decided it was safer to meet him there. Not that sex before dinner or instead of dinner was necessarily a bad thing. After they hung up, she thought of calling him back and having him pick her up. It's not like she never had sex on a first date before.

But she decided she would look totally neurotic if she called him back and changed the plan. She didn't want to expose her affinity for cerebral gymnastic before they even had a first dinner.

Kadee looked at the time: 4:02 p.m. She began pacing. She moved across her linoleum floor onto the wood part and then back again, her cadence fast as her mind raced. She felt a mix of excitement and apprehension, her palms still sweating as she wiped them along her jeans again. She hated how easily her palms sweated. Sometimes she wondered if she had enlarged sweat glands on the inside of her hands. And why was she so nervous anyway? *He's just a guy, for Christ's sake*, she told herself. She *had* broken her commitment to finish her paper, and there was no way she was going to be able to work on it before their date. Maybe that's why her hands were all clammy — not because of Noah Donovan, but because of the guilt over not staying home to work on her paper. She *was* a little disappointed in herself, but then she said aloud, "It's the weekend, Kadee. You'll work on it tomorrow." Getting ready for a first date is always distracting.

She brushed off any thoughts about her emotions and instead took control over her angst by focusing on the concrete preparations. If she let herself stew in her emotions, she would probably miss the date all together. Kadee was good at taking simple tasks and making them complicated. "*Focus*," she admonished her own psyche. She needed a bikini wax. That was her first thought. Even though she wasn't planning to give herself so easily, she liked to be prepared just in case. And hadn't she made *that* mistake before. Going on a date, her bush unruly, wild like the jungle, thinking, "I'm not giving it up tonight," only to find herself naked a few hours later. NO, she was not going to let *that* happen again. She would get *those* hairs tamed this time.

She went to her closet as she wondered what to wear. He had said the restaurant was pretty casual. She wanted to look her best, but not like she had spent the four hours between their phone call and their date preparing. She decided that jeans and a sexy blouse was a good choice. She rushed out, leaving her research sprawled out all over the floor and went to have her bikini line and legs waxed.

After her shower, she was in the mirror brushing her long dark hair. She was imagining what the dinner would be like, the things they might talk about. She hoped that he was as interesting as she thought he was. She became bored so easily. Even if this wasn't going to turn into some grand love affair, she was looking forward to some good conversation and a nice dinner. She had taken the night off from her schoolwork afterall. Her mind shifted as she pictured him pulling her close for a first kiss. His lips would be soft and his touch gentle. She was in a daze when she looked at the time and realized she only had a half hour before she had to leave. She finished getting ready; her eye makeup alone would take ten minutes. She hurried, barely making it to the restaurant by 8 p.m.

He was waiting in front for her. His eyes penetrated, as he reached in for a soft kiss on the cheek. "You look stunning, Kadee."

She felt herself blush as she looked up and said, "Thank you."

"You have the most amazing eyes. I've never seen anyone with such deep green eyes before. Beautiful." He took her hand, holding his look for a moment, then they followed the hostess to their table.

The dinner went well. They shared a bottle of wine—expensive wine, Kadee noticed—which relaxed her. She was enjoying their conversation. Noah seemed genuinely interested in getting to know her. He asked questions about her work and school, her family, her interests. But he also asked how she felt about those things. He seemed sensitive and caring. He really listened and heard what she was saying. She liked that. He did comment on her beauty, as he took her hand across the table and gently held it, weaving his fingers through hers. But he also wanted to know her more intimately. She felt that immediately, and it was intoxicating.

Kadee wasn't sure if it was the wine or Noah's manner that disabled her usual reticence. As he was walking her home, she endured an agonizing inner dialogue of whether or not she should invite him in. She must have gone through at least ten of her "buts," back and forth, back and forth. She felt pretty certain if she invited him in, they would be having sex within minutes, the keys still hanging in the lock as they were stripping each other naked. She wanted him, *but* was concerned she might fall in love with him as soon as they were intimate. This scared her. *Is that even really possible?* she thought. Kadee didn't believe in love at first sight. *But* Noah Donovan was making a good argument for the possibility that it existed. *Or maybe*, she continued her confidential dialogue, *I'm just confusing intense sexual chemistry for love. People make that mistake all the time. And look at those long fingers, my God.*

I shouldn't invite him in.

But she invited him in anyway; the words abandoned her lips before she made her own decision. "Would you like to come up for another drink? I have a nice bottle of red."

He turned to face her, holding both of her hands in his and stared into her eyes. She could feel the intensity between them as he continued to hold eye contact.

"Not tonight, Kadee, but thank you," he leaned in and kissed her softly on the lips. He stood back again, holding his gaze, and penetrating her with his eyes. It felt like he was metal resisting a magnet. Or maybe, Kadee wondered as she was walking up her stairs, maybe he wasn't feeling the same passion that she was.

Kadee went upstairs, changed into her nightclothes and got into bed. She curled up with her pillow, she developed a small knot in her stomach as she remembered his last words, "I had a nice time with you, Kadee with a D." He winked and said, "I'll call you."

As she stared at her ceiling waiting for her sleep to come on, she wondered why she had a knot in her stomach. It felt like a small marble or something like that, and it was rolling around. Their exchange was odd. He seemed to want to come up. She wouldn't have asked him if she thought he wasn't interested. And she was intuitive. So what was it that made Noah Donovan say, "Not tonight, Kadee, but thank you?" *Eureka, Kadee, maybe he's not that into you. But...he totally seemed to be. But...he didn't come up. Well, whatever...I'm never going to figure the guy out after one date, just like I haven't solved the world peace quandary, either. They will both have to wait for the morning...*She finally dozed off.

The next morning, Hailey, despite how she had damaged her own marriage, had the gall to give Kadee one of her digs. "What were you thinking? You don't invite a guy up to your apartment on a first date! In fact, you should never be the one to initiate. You have to let them make the first move. Always! They have to be the one to do it or it never works. This is dating 101, Kadee."

"I thought that's what he wanted. I can't really explain it. There is just something between us. And it's intense. Or at least that's what I thought. You had to see the way he was looking at me…the way…the way he talked to me. You know I don't normally react this way to guys. I'm telling you, I felt it. I did." Kadee swallowed. "Or at least I thought I did."

"Even if that's what he wanted, you still have to wait for him to ask. And sorry to say this, but if that's what he wanted, he would have come up. Right?"

"I guess you're right. Listen, it's no big deal. I'm not upset about it. It was just strange, and you know me always tossing around all the different possibilities. Whatever…And speaking of which, I have to go. I need to get my damn paper done. I shouldn't even have gone out last night. It's due tomorrow."

"It'll be OK, Kadee," she softened her tone.

"I'm fine Hail. *It's* fine."

But it wasn't.

Kadee could not stand Hailey sometimes. She loved her, but often didn't like her very much. In addition to her pretentiousness, Hailey could be quite unsympathetic, particularly when it came to matters of the heart. Hailey was unhappy in her own marriage, having an affair, and yet pontificating her personal brand of dating and relationship advice. Kadee had wished Vanessa was home; she would have called her instead for a compassionate ear. But Vanessa had her Sunday morning writing seminar for the next six weeks and wouldn't be available to talk until the afternoon. So Kadee opted for Hailey, which was a mistake; she should have known better.

Vanessa and Kadee had met during their first college semester at New York University; they hit it off immediately. At the time, both of them were planning to major in psychology and were taking an introductory course. One day after a class lecture discussing Freud, particularly his theory of the id, ego and super-ego and the Oedipus complex, Vanessa grew aggravated.

"I just can't believe that all boys are in love with their mother and want to kill their father! I don't buy it. Freud was on coke, right? I think he may have been under the influence when he came up with this one." And just like that, Vanessa changed her major to English.

After completing her degree, she was employed part-time for a small magazine while working on her MFA in creative writing at Hunter College. Since earning her degree, she had maintained a relatively lucrative career as a freelance writer. She had some wealthy regulars and she enjoyed the flexible schedule, but in her free time she was working on her own writing. Vanessa wanted to be a published novelist; she was in the midst of writing her first romance novel.

Kadee tried to work on her paper; she *had* to work on her paper. She made a pot of coffee and sat down at her computer, but she was having a hard time concentrating. Thoughts about Noah and those last few moments in front of her apartment were intruding upon her usual flow. She just couldn't figure out if the magnetism between them was all in her mind; his last words swarmed around her head, exhausting her brain, as she tried to make sense of it, of him. His voice may have said "not tonight," but those lips—oh, those pillowy lips—they said "I really want to." But did he, or was it just her desire playing tricks on her?

She just hated how easily her mind became preoccupied with the incongruences in other people's behaviors. Sure that's part of what led to her fascination with passionate homicides. Could there be anything more paradoxical than someone killing someone they supposedly love? She was planning to make a career out of figuring *that* out. Picking through murderous psyches was one thing, but she knew better than to do that mental dissection on someone from her personal life that she barely knew. She was never going to figure out what motivated Noah Donovan, because she didn't know him. She didn't have file upon file of research and case material, affording her a privileged look into his inner world. Was she really so grandiose as to think that after one dinner she could profile Noah? That was a big NO.

She did this type of analysis on nearly every man she went on a date with, even the one's she had no interest in. Sometimes she wished she could take a sabbatical from her own personality. *"Trying to figure out a person that you don't know is like foreplay with no consummation,"* she said to herself. *Why do you always do this, Kadee?*

To a certain degree, Kadee's examination of the minds of the men that she came into contact with was a way to keep emotional distance. By scrutinizing their psychological pieces intellectually, it kept her from being vulnerable; almost like she was the scientist and they were her experiment. She had a sense that she was doing this, but she wasn't sure exactly how to stop doing it. As safe as it kept her, it also left her lonely, and she was getting tired of feeling that way. There was something about Noah that Kadee found particularly enigmatic, which was part of his allure when they first met, almost like he was a puzzle to be solved. And then there was the sexual attraction. It was the proverbial perfect storm. Unfortunately, what Kadee found to be a delicious mystique encapsulated in an appealing package was really a mask covering someone deeply tormented and riddled with conflict.

After close to an hour of thinking it through, she decided she had to let it go. Maybe he just wasn't interested. She didn't like the idea of his rejecting her; perhaps he wasn't attracted or feeling the same connection as she felt. Love and chemistry were for the most part intangible. Since they were beyond rationale thought, she knew she wasn't going to be able to make sense of it. Ultimately, she pushed the thoughts aside and continued her paper—at least temporarily.

But she just couldn't stop checking her phone; she wanted to stop, tried to stop, but the pull would not let her go. It was a strange experience for her to be doing the obsessive phone-checking thing. Vanessa talked about it, and she had heard stories about it from other friends. One date with a guy and suddenly the phone becomes like an appendage endowed with some super power to predict your future. Kadee always being the independent cynical one saw it as a dysfunctional emotional dependence, first on the phone and second on the man.

But here she was, she who used to think that she was one of the most sane woman to ever walk the streets of Manhattan, here she was doing the obsessive phone-checking thing. And why? *He's just a guy*, she reminded herself. But, she was still hoping he would contact her.

She was interested in him. And he seemed interested, too. The inconsistency between her intuition and his action intrigued her, making her attraction feel more intense. She did have a fascination for the dark mysteries of the human psyche after all, and as she would eventually find out, Noah was filled with dark secrets.

Maybe I'm just sick of being lonely, and this man swept in at the right time, she thought. She opened her notes on the Drew Peterson case. There was nothing like a good psychopathic wife killer to distract her.

The day turned to evening and still no call from Noah. Kadee thought to call Vanessa, but she was exhausted and hadn't finished her paper. She was also admittedly a little embarrassed that she was so captivated by him after one day; she didn't even know him. *He's just a guy,* she reminded herself. He was just some guy she met at a coffee shop and had one dinner with. Sure, she had fantasized about what it would feel like to be intimate with him. But nothing actually happened. It didn't make sense. Of course, Vanessa wouldn't judge her. But saying aloud that the whole thing was even bothering her felt like she was giving up her dignity. And Kadee had a lot of pride.

She ordered Chinese takeout and shut off her phone. She was annoyed with herself for continuing to look at the screen hoping to see his number or perhaps a sweet text message. She shut it off. Before bed, she set her old alarm clock, keeping the phone off. She turned on *A Nightmare on Elm Street.* Freddy Krueger still had a few people left to kill when Kadee fell asleep with the movie still running.

In the morning when she turned her phone on, there was a short text from Noah.

Had a great time last night. Dinner Tuesday? Noah

Kadee looked at the phone with a detached fascination as she thought, *"So I was right about his interest. He was probably doing that wait twenty-four hours rule thing. Maybe he got a pamphlet from Hailey."* She felt her shoulders drop, as she recognized that she was experiencing a sense of relief. She could have accepted that he wasn't interested; it would have bothered her a little, but she could accept it. It happens. What was plaguing her had more to do with her sense of what was real. She felt strongly that there was a mutual connection. Contemplating the possibility that that was not true made her question her own thinking and intuition. All the doubt washed away when she saw his text. She couldn't have known it at the time, but this feeling was temporary; it was a quiet before the storm, so to speak.

Kadee was free Tuesday night. In the late afternoon, after her classes, she sent Noah a text back.

I had a great time, too. Tuesday night's good. I'm free after 6.

An hour later, he called. They spoke for more than an hour, casual chit-chat, but he did remember to ask Kadee about her paper. She liked that. The plan was to meet at a small hole-in-the-wall Italian restaurant that was in their neighborhood at 7 p.m.

When they hung up, Kadee was wondering why she had become so bent out of shape on Sunday. He seemed genuinely interested. She reminded herself to stop analyzing him and the situation, telling herself, as always, that it wasn't of sound mind to get so tangled up in the web of her own thoughts. He probably just didn't want to jump right into bed. It's always strange when the guy is the one that wants to wait, but there is something old-fashioned and really romantic about it. After that idea came to her, she told herself that she had used up all of her allotted rumination time for the week and that she was not to go over it anymore. And that was it, for the time being at least.

Tuesday night after dinner, Noah invited Kadee up to his apartment. He lived in a brownstone; his apartment occupied the entire first floor of the two-story building. As they walked up the long flight of stairs in the front of the building into the outer hallway, Kadee was taking in her surroundings. She loved the architecture in New York, particularly older buildings such as Noah's; there was so much diversity, so much history, each structure had its own character, which also made it feel like each building had its own back-story.

Kadee wouldn't see much of Noah's apartment until afterward. He immediately reached over, gently pulling her in close as soon as he closed the front door. He was running his fingers along her face as he kissed her softly, tenderly. He locked the door, and their embrace became more passionate, an urgency that grew as he pressed his body against hers. She felt a tingling sensation deep in her vagina as her physical desire was mounting. He slowly raised her skirt with the sides of his arms and pulled her panties right off. She opened her legs to step out of them, as he was caressing her face, saying, "You are so beautiful, Kadee; you are so beautiful."

His touch was so tender and loving, Kadee melted in his arms. She wanted to feel his naked body next to hers. She tore the rest of her clothes off as he carefully moved his fingers across her breasts, as if he was relishing every inch of her. He guided her into the bedroom as he removed his shirt and pressed his body against hers. Soon they were naked, Noah on top, both breathless as he raised his lower body and entered her.

His upper body lay right on top of hers, almost like they had merged, their skin fusing together never to separate. He thrust himself inside of her over and over. They rolled over, still connected, so that Kadee was on top where he could see her better. He kept saying how good she felt, how beautiful she was, and asking how she liked it. He wanted to please her. And he did. Kadee came three times; by the end she was so exhausted, she rested her head back on the pillow, dizzy, until she stopped panting. As Noah exhaled, a satisfied smile crossed his face. He curled up behind her, his fingers slowly traveling up and down her arm, gently caressing her as they both fell asleep.

In the morning, Noah got up and made Kadee coffee and toast with peanut butter: her favorite. They sipped coffee for a short while, until the tension built up and they were ravishing each other again. Noah had to leave by 10 a.m. for a patient, and Kadee was meeting Hailey at their Wednesday morning yoga class.

Her body was exhausted, but she knew Hailey would be upset if she cancelled, so she put her clothes on from the night before and prepared to leave. Noah kept pulling her back to kiss her, running his hands along her face, down her shoulders and around to her back. "I had such a nice time, Kadee with a D. When can we do this again? Are you free Friday night?"

Kadee felt wobbly. She didn't know if it was the hours of sex or her feelings toward Noah; probably both, she thought. She smiled, her eyes glowing, "Yes, I'd like that. Friday night is great."

Kadee ran home to change. She only had thirty minutes before she was meeting Hailey. She was dizzy with excitement, but also apprehensive about telling Hailey the details. She didn't know why exactly. She had her theories, but Hailey was sometimes nasty toward her whenever something good was going on in her life. Truth be told, over the last year or so, since Hailey disclosed her marital dissatisfaction, she had become more hardened. Hailey had always been harsh and insensitive ever since they met in college, but Kadee thought she was much worse now.

Vanessa thought Hailey was jealous.

"Jealous…of what? She has everything she said she wanted. A husband who adores her, a huge apartment, the big ring. Hailey is a socialite, for Christ's sake. That's what she always wanted. What she said she wanted all through college. And now she has it."

"But she's not happy, Kade. You know she's not happy. Let's be realistic. She's having an affair, and not a one night sex thing. She's carrying on a second relationship. That means something. You're the psychology student. Isn't this text book something or other?"

"You know me. I don't think anything is text book; things are usually more complicated than they seem. She never really tells us how she feels. She likes to pretend things are fine, even when it's obvious there're not. So it's hard to know what she's thinking. But she's always been harsh, even before the affair. And by the way, did she tell you who she's having the affair with?"

"No. Did she tell you? You're closer with her than I am."

"No. I know he has money—she did say that—but she said she didn't want to say who. Something about his reputation. Blah…blah…blah…I can't stand that elitist bullshit sometimes. It really irks me. She wasn't always like that. She used to make me laugh all the time. She used to be fun. Not so much anymore."

"But friends during good times and bad, right?" The threesome had made that pact in college, back when life seemed simpler.

"Right, Ness. Right."

But Kadee wasn't convinced that she could keep the charade up much longer. Eventually, she would have to call Hailey out on her attitude. Kadee was not the type of woman who allowed herself to be someone's punching bag. But Hailey had secrets that could make her nasty, at times, one of which would eventually change everything.

CHAPTER 3

After yoga class, Hailey and Kadee went for pancakes. It was a ritual they shared for years. This week, Hailey was more irritated than usual as she listened to Kadee tell her about her evening with Noah. Hailey had been envious of Kadee ever since they met in their first semester at NYU. She kept her feelings private; she tried to, anyway. But hearing about the passionate evening with the wealthy doctor was unnerving her more than usual. She couldn't stop the unconscious urge to tap the tips of her fingers on the table in the diner, agitation oozing from her pores.

It was so unfair, she thought. Kadee has everything and now this, a doctor, wild sex, another date, the promise of a future with him. Kadee was everything Hailey wasn't, and because of this, Hailey always wanted what Kadee had. Hailey was an attractive woman. She had curly blonde locks that bounced as they skimmed her shoulders, clear blue eyes and perfect shiny white teeth that would light up her whole face when she would smile; although she wasn't so smiley lately.

When she was younger she had awful acne, a long wide nose and a plump body. She was teased all through grade school and high school; those were terrible years for her. The summer before her freshman year in college, she convinced her parents to let her have a rhinoplasty to reduce her nose and skin grafts for the acne scars. And she went on a strict diet. By the time she met Kadee, she looked totally different; unfortunately despite her outer transformation, she didn't feel very different at all.

Kadee was like a nightmare for Hailey. She was tall and lanky with radiant skin and eyes that were such a unique shade of green, you just couldn't help but look at her. She wasn't sure how exactly they had become close when she carried such resentment toward her. Maybe she thought she would become beautiful by association; that by being close with Kadee she would automatically feel attractive, too.

But what Kadee had that Hailey was missing wasn't something skin grafts, plastic surgery or a diet could help. Kadee had pride and she understood real value, things that no amount of financial resources could buy. Hailey grew up with some money and she married even more, but she didn't know the value of anything. She spent outrageous amounts of money on material items thinking it would assuage her, make her feel worthy, and give her life meaning. But none of these things alleviated her unrest; if anything she was left feeling worse. She didn't understand why. Whatever it was that she didn't have, Kadee had it, and this infuriated her.

After the murder, Hailey turned her back on Kadee. Too concerned with her own reputation, she decided it was best that she not associate with Kadee. Even when Kadee called, asking for her help, Hailey resisted her friend's request. She spoke to her once, only once, then that was that. Her reputation was more important than being a supportive friend. Besides, she didn't think Kadee would do that for her. She was wrong, of course. Hailey's perception of the world was colored by her own bitter contempt; she experienced others as malevolent like her, but this wasn't the truth. Kadee would have done anything to help her friend if she was the prime suspect in a murder investigation.

Hailey's most recent attempt to make herself feel better was to carry on multiple liaisons with men. Men had replaced her material objects of desire with bodies of desire. Of course, there was some excitement involved. She enjoyed enticing them; it made her feel attractive, wanted, especially if they were married men. It made her feel particularly triumphant when she could captivate and capture the attention of someone who belonged to someone else.

It started with one man; it was a clandestine lunchtime sexual delicacy with a guy she met at one of Dean's business galas. They would meet for sex once a week during his lunch hour. After a few months, Hailey became restless and bored, so she moved onto someone else. It became a quest for personal validation with men. With each new man, she would feel attractive, even loveable. But once the initial excitement diminished, she would feel bad again. She would then use her artful allure to capture a new one.

When Dean discovered the text exchange between her most recent victim and her, she finessed him, saying it was a mistake, she was sorry, she loved him. Dean adored Hailey; they had been married for more than ten years. He blamed himself; he wasn't able to give Hailey a child. An accident when he was a boy left him sterile. Hailey said she didn't want children anyway, that his condition was not a problem for her. Dean began to think maybe it was.

Dean was committed to working things out with Hailey; and she told him that she wanted the same. His one request was that they see a therapist to discuss their difficulties. Hailey, afraid to lose him, agreed. Their first appointment with Dr. Tracy was that evening. She was going to talk to Kadee about it during breakfast. But after hearing her enthusiasm about the wealthy doctor, she decided not to share, not while Kadee was feeling so good. She was too consumed with envy, so the conversation took a different direction.

"What were you thinking, Kadee? You went back to his apartment! It was only a second date, right?" She was tapping her fingers harder.

Feeling attacked, Kadee leaned back into the seat cushion as far away from Hailey's shrill criticism as she could get. "It just happened; it felt right, so I went with it. I'm not like you. I can't plan for sex, it just sort of flies for me. You know this about me."

"You know it's never going to work out, right? You know that, right?" her voice sharp and cutting. "I just don't want you to get your hopes up." The thought that things might work out between Kadee and Noah left Hailey seething. Afraid Kadee might see her envy, she took a deep breath, ate a few bites of her pancakes and calmed her voice. "I'm just looking out for you, Kade. I don't want to see you get hurt. These wealthy doctor types go out with other wealthy doctor types. I don't want him to use you and then throw you out for some wealthy blue blood. You know?"

"I'm going to be a doctor, too, you know. And besides, I don't buy that 'type' shit. Everyone is different. And I believe Noah is genuinely interested. And not just for sex."

"You're getting a Ph.D., which is great, but it's not the same as an M.D., and you know it. Besides, your parents are teachers. Come on, Kadee...you know what I mean."

Kadee was insulted, and she wasn't going to mask her feelings with her usual contained composure. "Yeah Hailey...I know exactly what you mean." She crossed her arms and stared at Hailey, furious.

"I'm sorry, Kade. I shouldn't have said that." Hailey's duplicity was masterful. "I just know that world and how it works. Just— be careful, OK?"

Kadee uncrossed her arms. "Let's talk about something else. We never agree on things like this. You're very black-and-white, while I see things as...well, more complicated than that."

"Sure, Kade. We can drop it." But the argument left an untidy space between them. They both finished their pancakes without saying a word.

After they paid the bill and were standing outside, they hugged and Hailey apologized again. Kadee said she accepted. But things between them would become increasingly tense. Hailey did say that she hoped to meet 'Dr. Noah' sometime soon and that the four of them should have dinner once Kadee knew him a little better. Kadee agreed.

Hailey had planned to stop by the pharmacy on her way home. Instead, she rushed home to look up Noah on her computer.

CHAPTER 4

Kadee was livid after her time with Hailey. She found Hailey's attitude about money and status offensive, and she couldn't believe the audacity she displayed devaluing her Ph.D., saying that somehow an M.D. was superior. Hailey had neither, so who was she to criticize. She thought Vanessa was right; Hailey was unhappy, so she wanted to make those around her unhappy, too. She wasn't going to let Hailey squash her enthusiasm or confidence. But the conversation left her anxious. For the first time in her life, she felt her guard was down with a man. She was stripped of her armor and felt the risk of love's uncertainty.

But you never grow and change if you don't take a chance, she said to herself. *At some point, Kadee Carlisle, you are going to have to let your guard down, or you really may spend the rest of your life alone. Besides, Hailey is just being a bitch. You can't let her get to you.*

Kadee had the sense that she could love Noah, and part of her wanted to love him; she was getting so sick of living in her safe cerebral world. Instead of her usual cautiousness, she had dived right in, head first. It even seemed that Noah met her at the bottom of the pool, having jumped right in himself, taking the dive into the nebulous waters of romance, desire, passion and love.

Kadee knew that loving someone meant taking a chance. She experienced the risk of chance first hand as a young girl when her father violated her mother's trust with a betrayal. When Kadee was just eleven years old, her father had an affair. She didn't know the details; her parents tried to protect her brother and her by not sharing the specifics. But the silence only made it worse. Provided with only an infinitesimal amount of information from her parents, Kadee was left alone to fill in the blanks.

Kadee tried to prod for information. For many months she would overhear her parents fighting about Ramona—this other woman. Her mother would cry alone in the bathroom, trying to muffle the noise without success. There a few months when her father was staying at her paternal grandmother's, too. But her parents explained that all relationships have peaks and valleys and that they were just in a valley. "All marriages have rough patches, sweetie," her mother would say. But Kadee was old enough and precocious enough to know that her father had been carrying on a relationship with another woman, Ramona; and she knew that what he was doing was wrong and that it hurt her mother.

After months of hearing her parents fighting, one day it just stopped. And they never argued about it again, at least not that she could hear. Sometime around Kadee's eighteenth birthday, her mother told her that her father had had an affair. It was brief, another teacher at his school, and that he didn't love this other woman. They had worked it out. She forgave him.

But the scars remained, and when Kadee would talk about boys with her mother, she was overprotective. She made comments, seemingly innocuous caring maternal statements, but they made Kadee feel like it was important to have her guard up with men. She should not trust them so easily. If she ever did fall in love, she could wind up crying into a towel alone on the bathroom floor for months. That's what Kadee heard her mother saying from actions rather than words. Between the spaces of silence surrounding the ugly truth of her father's indiscretions, that's what Kadee heard.

As it turned out, taking a chance with Noah would leave blood smears on a bathroom floor in addition to the tears. But in the beginning, being with Noah felt more extraordinary than she ever could have imagined; in the beginning being with Noah was like a dream. Everything felt different, better, almost unreal. It was the dead of winter, and Kadee had never felt more alive.

On the surface, Noah seemed invested in getting to know Kadee. He asked questions about her thoughts and feelings. She loved that about him. He was someone who really heard what she said. It was so refreshing to feel his total investment in knowing her. And he seemed to dangle on her every word making her feel that he accepted her unconditionally. It just made her want to expose her whole self to him. She never in her wildest dreams would have imagined that she could let herself be so vulnerable with someone, especially a man. To think of all those men she lay next to naked, never giving a piece of herself. But with Noah, she could be fully dressed and totally exposed. It was the most intoxicating experience she had ever had and she found herself wanting more and more.

They spent much of the winter months lounging in his bed, cuddling, his long arms enveloping her body, talking. He would hold Kadee so close, and with such care, it never occurred to her that it was all a façade. Kadee felt safe with him, believed she was safe. She shared intimacies that she never had said aloud before. She spent hours naked with him while he studied every inch of her. And the whole time, Noah was storing her confidences as ammunition.

Kadee did notice a few oddities during those months. They spent all of their time alone. He would talk about friends, but Kadee hadn't met any of them. And when she asked Noah to have dinner with Vanessa and her, he said he wanted to know her more before he met her friends. Kadee thought it strange, but brushed it off; everyone has eccentricities.

Even more puzzling was Noah's relationship with his mother. She would call every Saturday morning at 9:30. Noah would stop whatever he was doing to take the call; sometimes they would speak for almost an hour. It irritated Kadee, especially if they were in the middle of morning sex; he would cut it short, right before she climaxed and leave her alone and panting, wanting more of him, to take his mother's call. When she asked him about it, he was evasive. His eyes shifty as he avoided eye contact, he would say, "I can't explain it. She needs me. Sorry, but I have to take her calls."

After a few months of this behavior, Kadee grew annoyed. If he *knew* his mother was going to call and he was going to pick up, why on earth would he initiate sex so close to that 9:30 phone call. It almost was like Noah timed the sex to be interrupted by the call as Kadee was approaching climax. Kadee wasn't sure if he was playing mind games with her or if he was simply oblivious. When Kadee would try to put off the sex in anticipation of his mother's phone call, Noah would pout, or go down on her, or kiss her—God, he was a good kisser—while fingering her, or ask "Don't you love me?" Anything to get the sex going.

Kadee had asked Noah if his mother knew about her. He said she did and that his mother was asking to meet her. Kadee wanted to meet her, too, but Noah wasn't ready yet. One Saturday morning in early February, Noah was inside of her, their eyes penetrating each other's as they were about to come together. The phone rang. Kadee's eyes pleaded him not to take the call. He didn't. Finally. Unbelievably. Kadee was ecstatic.

An hour later there was a knock on his door, and they could hear the key turning in the lock.

Kadee's heart raced. She broke out in a sweat, perspiration slicking her body as she rushed to put clothes on. Kadee assumed it was either his mother, or an intruder. Turns out the two were indistinguishable.

Noah stayed calm, but Kadee was palpitating. She put her hand on her heart and pressed down, trying to get it to stop pounding. It felt like it might crack through her breast bone and burst out of her chest. "It's mother. Stay here," his eyes vacant, and voice expressionless. He threw pajama bottoms and a T-shirt on, left the bedroom, closing the door behind him. Kadee, still pressing her chest, was taking long deep breaths. She was trying to calm herself while listening to their conversation. *How could he be so nonchalant?* she wondered. *We could have been naked on the couch in the living room.*

She couldn't really make out what they were saying. She heard muffled words, with an occasional rise in intonation from his mother. She heard the words "she" and "thirty-five," a few times, and assumed they were talking about her. At one point she heard two clear sentences from his mother. "You must listen to mother. Mother loves you." Kadee began perspiring again, and she started pacing across the wide bedroom floor.

Eventually she heard the door close. Noah came back into the bedroom. His thick brown hair was tousled and his eyes still had a vacant look. "What was that about?" Kadee blurted out.

"Nothing. I don't want to talk about it." He stared at the wall, two saucers of emptiness, never meeting her eyes. He then went in the shower and stayed in there for more than an hour.

Kadee's attention was on high alert after this incident with Noah's mother. It made the peculiarity of his relationship with his mother difficult to ignore. And the fact that he wouldn't discuss it made it seem all the more pertinent.

Kadee had grown up in a home where bad thoughts and feelings were pushed aside, ignored; there was this pretense that everything was OK when it wasn't. The situation between Noah and his mother left her with the same uncertainty she experienced as a child. She sensed something was wrong, but because it was being denied, she doubted her own feelings. If she had really listened to her intuition, she would have known the truth; there would have been no doubt. But she wasn't ready to hear the voice that nagged in her mind saying that something was amiss in the psychological dynamics of Noah's mother-son relationship, so she rationalized the situation.

That was easy enough. Noah was an only child. His father had passed away suddenly from a heart attack when Noah was only ten years old. Noah felt a sense of obligation toward his mother, particularly because she had supported him financially all through medical school, even purchasing his luxury condo on the Upper Eastside of Manhattan. This made rational sense to Kadee.

But there was a disturbance in their mother-son relations that was far more subtle, yet more problematic. Noah's mother treated him like a partner; she placed him in his father's role. Noah assumed it was his obligation. Now as a man, he still felt obliged, which enabled his mother to intrude on nearly every aspect of his life. His romantic life was no exception, and her intrusion was more than Kadee could have ever imagined.

CHAPTER 5

When Hailey arrived home after her yoga and pancakes date with Kadee, she couldn't get to her computer fast enough. She was tapping her fingers on her desk as she waited for her Google search to find Dr. Noah Donovan. A few links popped up, the most enticing was the link to his Facebook page. Although his page had a number of privacy settings turned on, she could still see some of his pictures with their associated comments. Hailey thought her eyes deceived her as she leaned forward with a gasp. She knew the name sounded vaguely familiar. To get a better look, she made the picture of Noah smiling wide in his scrubs as large as she could.

And there he was: Noah Donovan, the lanky awkward boy from her tenth-grade class. It had been a long time, but she was sure it was him. She sat back in her big lounging desk chair. *Wow, he looks good,* she thought. She leaned forward, squinting at the picture again, her nose practically touching the computer screen. She took a deep breath, folded her arms and again leaned back into her chair. *This must be my lucky day,* she nibbled on her lower lip. She felt certain; indeed, that was the boy she once knew from school. She also saw that they had a handful of mutual friends, which confirmed any doubt that it was him.

Hailey wasn't even sure why she was looking up Noah. The impulse felt irresistible. Perhaps she wanted to convince herself that it would not work out between Kadee and the doctor. Or maybe she just felt like intruding on Kadee's privacy because she felt entitled to. Regardless, her discovery left her quite satisfied as she wondered what exactly she could do with this information. Later that same day a serendipitous occurrence left Hailey utterly flabbergasted.

Hailey took a shower and decided to take a nap. As she pulled her comforter around her, she thought back to tenth grade. Noah was not particularly popular in high school. He was awkward and not athletic, but she did remember him receiving academic achievement awards. She didn't really know him well, but they did have an English class together, and she vaguely remembered a few trivial conversations with him. She also remembered hearing that his father had passed away when he was a young boy. At the time, his mother was an attractive woman, young looking. Hailey recalled her attending a few of their class events alone.

She thought he had dated a short skinny girl named Amy. She only remembered this because she was always envious of Amy's svelte frame. Hailey had struggled so much with her weight during her youth; she always resented the skinny girls.

Part of her wanted to tell Kadee, but then she wondered what she would say. She could not tell her she rushed home to peruse the Internet in search of some information about Noah. Also, there was not much to tell—at least not yet. All she really knew at this point was that Noah and she had had a class together in tenth grade and that he was a smart kid. She was fantasizing various options for a casual encounter with Noah where she could perhaps use their past to seduce him into a cocktail, then maybe a romp back at his luxury apartment. Hailey could feel a smile cross her face as she began to doze off. The thought of getting something Kadee possessed comforted her. She would never do anything like that—probably—but the image soothed her as she dozed off.

Hailey was annoyed as she arrived at Dr. Tracy's office for her first couple's therapy session with Dean later that day. She had seen a therapist once before. It was the summer before she started college. Her parents had encouraged her to go, recognizing that she seemed depressed. The therapist was a young woman in her early to mid-thirties. She was thin with flawless porcelain skin. Her appearance distressed Hailey, reminding her of all of her own imperfections.

The therapist must have been astute because she tried to get Hailey to talk about her low self-esteem. Hailey remembered the experience as humiliating. She didn't want to open up to a stranger about how much she despised her appearance; it made her feel too vulnerable. After just three sessions, she refused to go back. She never thought she would find herself in a therapist's office again. She was not looking forward to a repeat of that experience. She kept her deep insecurities private. She didn't want some stranger peeling away the layers of her veneer, exposing the truth of her feelings: She felt ugly, worthless and rotten. And she certainly did not want Dean to see that side of her. He thought she was a goddess, and Hailey wanted to keep it that way.

She had arrived almost fifteen minutes early. She was sitting in the waiting room, distracted by her own annoyance while carelessly flipping through a magazine. Dean had sent her a text message saying that he was on his way. Hailey had her right leg crossed over her left, her thigh and lower leg dangling out of her knee-length skirt. She was shaking her right foot back and forth as she sat impatiently.

The room was silent with the exception of the rustling magazine pages turning when Hailey heard the muffled sound of voices behind Dr. Tracy's office door. Seconds later, the door opened and a tall attractive man walked out. Hailey saw him out of her periphery as she noticed him glance her way. Hailey looked up, pursed her lips, and nodded her head, politely acknowledging him. He smiled wide, nodded back and slowly walked out. Hailey's stomach dropped; her body responding before her mind registered what she saw, leaving her feeling like she just dropped down the dive side of a roller coaster arch. The tall attractive man was Noah Donovan.

Hailey sat in disbelief as she wondered what Noah was doing there. She assumed he was in therapy with Dr. Tracy, but why and had he mentioned this to Kadee. *Did Kadee know why he was seeking treatment?* she wondered to herself. She was still trying to process the coincidence when her husband opened the door and came strolling into the waiting room.

"Hi, honey," he leaned down and kissed her on the cheek when he noticed her dumbfounded expression. "What is it, Hail? Are you OK? You look pale."

"Oh?" she acted nonchalant. She sighed, arched her back in a stretch and said, "I'm fine. Just tired," she then cocked her head to the side, softened her eyes and adjusted the hem on her skirt. Hailey knew just how to manipulate Dean.

She could have told Dean what happened. She could have told Kadee, too, which would have been the right thing to do, but Hailey decided to keep the information a secret. Eventually, the truth would be disclosed, shocking everyone. Hailey would make sure she appeared equally shocked.

Hailey and Dean stayed in couple's therapy with Dr. Tracy until she took a leave of absence right after the murder. Every week, Hailey made sure she arrived at least fifteen minutes early. Feeling excited, she would wait in anticipation to see if Noah had his session before them. For the first couple of months he would come out of Dr. Tracy's office a few minutes before her session. The two would give smiling glances of acknowledgement and he would leave. One week it almost seemed that Noah paused for a second longer, perhaps with a moment of recognition. Hailey's stomach dropped like she was diving on that roller coaster again, wondering what on earth she would do if he recognized her from tenth grade. But then he reached for his umbrella and walked out. Hailey took a sugar-free lollipop out of her bag, opened it, and started sucking hard, as she tried to reassure herself that she looked totally different. There was no way he could ever recognize her.

As time passed, she saw Noah less and less frequently. At first she assumed he had stopped his therapy. But then one day as she was flipping through a magazine waiting for Dean and her session,

Noah came walking out of the office again. She would see him there a few more times, but his attendance became sporadic.

In the meantime, despite the unresolved tension, Hailey and Kadee still met most weeks for yoga and pancakes and spoke on the phone often. Kadee had begun to reveal some of her reservations about Noah. Hailey suspected that Kadee wasn't being totally honest, that things were worse than she was describing. Then one day, Kadee broke down crying as she described feeling that she couldn't trust Noah, that his words and actions didn't match, that she felt he was pulling her close and then pushing her away.

Seeing Kadee's vulnerability, perhaps for the first time, Hailey felt some empathy toward her. She was actually able to commiserate. In spite of her newfound compassion, she still did not reveal anything about Noah and Dr. Tracy. Instead, she advised Kadee to get out of the relationship.

In her very best effort at a compassionate tone, she said, "Listen, Kade, there's something wrong. I don't want to sound mean, but I told you from the beginning to be careful with a guy like this. You really need to break it off. Things will only get worse, you know. And I can tell you right now, he isn't good for you. Quite honestly, I have never heard you sound so weak before. I know that probably sounds really nasty right now, but I am only trying to help, and like I said, he isn't good for you. He bought you those earrings, right? Trust me. Just take those and whatever else he's bought you and cut your losses."

Kadee touched the earrings with her fingers, nodding yes, then wiped the tears from her eyes with a tissue and blew her nose. "I feel like I can't separate from him. I know something's wrong... I know you're right, but as soon as I try to pull away, he calls, says just the right thing. Then even though I know deep down it's not good for me, I go back. It's like I don't even remember who I was before I met him. Part of me can't stand him, and part of me feels totally in love with him. I feel like a trapped fucking loser, and I don't know how to get out. I *have* become weak. And I hate myself for it." She looked down. Looking into Hailey's eyes was almost too much to bear.

Hailey didn't know what to say. Just as she was mustering up all of her resources for an empathetic response, Kadee looked up, tears still hanging in the corner of her eyes and said, "I'm going back into therapy. I've got to figure this out. I just feel really… I…I feel really unstable."

Hailey nodded, and then asked, "Have you made an appointment yet?"

Kadee took a deep breath; she wiped her eyes dry. "Yes," she sniffled. "Her name is Yvonne Tracy. I have an appointment tomorrow."

Hailey swallowed hard, trying to eat her words before they came out. She couldn't believe what she was hearing; she wasn't sure how to respond, what to tell. She had kept her "Noah secret" for so long, maybe too long, and now she didn't know how she would explain her disloyalty. She hadn't exactly lied to Kadee, it was a dishonorable omission. The type of thing she never thought would be known. It was the same mistake she made over and over with Dean, when her betrayals would reveal themselves.

Kadee was observant, and there nothing like a puzzle to snap her out of her emotional cloud momentarily. "What is it, Hail?"

It wasn't guilt Hailey felt—she rarely could take responsibility for her actions—it was shame. She felt exposed, as if Kadee had x-ray vision that could see through to her insides revealing how bad of a person she really was. If she had felt guilty, she may have told Kadee about Noah and Dr. Tracy. If Kadee didn't know he was in therapy, perhaps it would help her in some way to know he was. Instead, Hailey gave a partial truth; she wanted to keep the whole truth hidden.

"Oh...nothing, Kade," she looked away, her leg bouncing up and down under the table.

Kadee's eyes narrowed, penetrating Hailey's thin façade. "Hailey? What is it? Do you know something?" She leaned forward.

"No, nothing really." She took a sip of her coffee and breathed slowly to calm herself. "It's just that Yvonne Tracy is the therapist Dean and I are seeing for couple's therapy." She shifted in her seat. "You just caught me off guard."

Kadee chuckled. "What a small world. You always refer to her as 'the therapist,' so I had no idea, huh."

"Now that I think about it, Vanessa, who recommended Dr. Tracy to me, did say that you had referred Vanessa to her. So, I guess the world's not that small. Just full of coincidences." *Quite a few,* Hailey though as she pondered Noah's connection to Dr. Tracy.

Kadee sat back in her chair and thought for a moment. "You like her, right? You never say much about her, but you're still going?"

"I like her OK as far as therapists go. Dean likes her and I am going for him, for us, you know because I agreed to go for our marriage."

Although Kadee knew Hailey was still carrying on indiscretions, she nodded and said, "Good." She knew it wasn't the time for a confrontation. But she did wonder if Hailey would ever be able to discontinue her extra-marital affairs or if she even really wanted to.

"A friend at school gave me the referral months ago when Vanessa was looking for a therapist," Kadee said. "She said she was very good and that she helped her get out of a toxic relationship. Dr. Tracy really helped her and...well, she's married now to a lovely man."

"Her office is right around the corner from you, too."

"It's very convenient," her eyes began to well up again, but she controlled the tears. "I just hope it helps. I have never felt like this before...like I can't stop thinking about him. I just don't understand what happened, or why he acts distant, then says everything between us is fine. He is always telling me he loves me. I go around and around in my head with this. It just doesn't make any sense. I keep trying to figure it out, but no matter how I look at it, the pieces just don't fit." She pulled her knees up to her chest. "If it made sense, then maybe I could leave. Like if I knew something tangible...something that would kick me in the ass, screaming he's a fucking liar and manipulator. Why I think I need that is beyond me. Anyway, I hope the therapy will give me the kick that I need. Hopefully."

Hailey knew that pain, the anguish, the torture of loving someone too much. She had experienced it with a boy during her senior year in high school. They had dated for three months, then when he broke it off, Hailey was consumed with thoughts of him. She followed him home a few times. She called him all the time, trying to keep their connection going. He was still friendly toward her, which just made it even more torturous. She kept thinking maybe they would get back together, that he would change his mind. But he never did. And by the end of the school year, he had a new girlfriend. Hailey became depressed, and her parents sent her for therapy.

When the therapy didn't work to mend Hailey's broken sense of self, she opted for her physical transformation. On the surface, this appeared to lift Hailey's spirits and give her more confidence. But because the wounds beneath were never repaired, her self-worth was tenuous at best. She was in constant need of outside affirmation of her value. It was truly awful, but because she wouldn't admit it, no one could really help her, not Kadee, not Dean, not her many men, not even Dr. Tracy.

That would change. Sometimes life can provide openings for emotional growth. There was going to be an opportunity for Hailey to confront her demons in her near future. It would be a defining moment, one she never could have anticipated. Perhaps it would be one of the most important moments of her life. But in the meantime, her self-hate and envy continued to pervade her.

It would have soothed Kadee to hear Hailey's tortured love experience. It would have left her feeling less alone in her pain, helped her feel validated, understood. When feeling so on edge, it is always comforting to know that other people have had the same emotions, the same experience. Unfortunately, Hailey would never share her vulnerabilities or the fact that she felt rejected—ever. So she tried to soothe Kadee using a reassuring platitude. "It's gonna be OK, Kadee," she said. "Everything will be OK."

On her way home, Hailey was thinking about the uncanny synchronicity of Kadee seeing Dr. Tracy and what the possible outcome might be. She knew there was a chance that she would run into Noah there. *Maybe that would be a good thing*, she thought. Though part of her felt a disturbing satisfaction that Kadee was suffering, another part of Hailey did feel bad for her.

She assumed Noah's inconsistent behavior had to do with their different social stations, that Noah wouldn't become serious with someone of Kadee's background. But she also wondered if perhaps there was more to it. Maybe it was more complicated. He was seeing a therapist, after all. Maybe he had some real commitment issues. Maybe he was married. Or maybe he was a playboy. She thought about it for a few moments, then decided it was her first choice, that Noah couldn't take Kadee seriously. That truth satiated her envy, so she went with that explanation.

Hailey should have told Kadee that Noah also was seeing Dr. Tracy. Not telling left Kadee in the precarious situation of possibly bumping into him unexpectedly. But integrity was not one of Hailey's redeeming qualities. Besides, she would have to explain that for all these months, she learned who Noah was after she had raced home to research him. She'd have to explain why she never told Kadee that she knew who Noah was. After all, even Noah didn't know she recognized him. No. She decided as she approached her home to once again keep the information a secret. The truth would soon reveal itself without Hailey having to do a thing.

CHAPTER 6

Despite her reservations, Kadee let her guard down. Perhaps, more accurately, it just came down without her notice. It was not a conscious decision, but rather more like a reflex. She was gradually feeling more and more vulnerable in the relationship when, one day, she realized she was totally disarmed. Noah held her heart in his hands and, by the middle of winter, Kadee was totally in love. As is often the case, once Kadee was gripped by the power of her feelings for Noah, she lost her judgment, then eventually her control.

Right before the murder, Kadee had written in her journal: *Is there a thin line between love and hate? Or is it that once reality becomes blurred and boundaries confusing, love and hate merge?*

It was toward the beginning of spring when Kadee found herself consumed with thoughts about Noah. They had become very close through the winter months, spending most of their free time together. They went to fancy restaurants, museums, and even a week-long ski trip in Salt Lake City. It seemed as though they couldn't get enough of each other. Behind closed doors, they were two animals ravishing each other. Filled with lust and passion, they were having constant sex. And when the weather started to turn, things changed.

It was subtle at first, and the beginning of the end was hard to pinpoint. Sometime around mid-March, Kadee noticed Noah pulling back. At first he'd convinced her that it had to do with his work. Noah said his practice was getting busier, so when he had less time, Kadee assumed it had to do with work. He also discussed a research project he was engaged with that was taking up some of his evening time.

There was something else, though, and it was more insidious. Noah began to share some sexual fantasies with Kadee. This was normal, she thought. He felt closer to her, so he was sharing deeper intimacies. Everyone has fantasies and some seem more twisted than others. But as they began to engage in some of the fantasies, as Kadee indulged him, he became increasingly distant.

Kadee started to feel that he was emotional disengaged. But when she mentioned her feelings to Noah, he denied it, saying it was all in her mind, saying he loved her. The contradiction between his actions and his words was turning Kadee around, disorienting her as though she had been spinning around and around, like children do, then suddenly stopping while the world continued spinning. She could not find her bearings.

Kadee and Noah had never had the official "we are exclusive" conversation. Vanessa had admonished Kadee, mentioning a few times that she shouldn't assume he was committed unless they had discussed it. Kadee felt that the amount of time they spent together and his telling her he loved her, that he never felt this way before, was enough. But when she began to sense this change, she found herself wanting to discuss where the relationship stood. She wanted to believe that his confirmation that they were monogamous would mean something.

One Sunday morning in late March, with reticence, she asked him. His living room windows were open; a nice breeze was flowing through the curtains while the two were eating breakfast. The sunlight streaming through the room cast an angelic glow upon Noah. When Kadee looked up from her peanut butter toast and saw him, her love for him overwhelmed her. She had been going back and forth in her mind if she should bring up their relationship. She was admittedly a bit anxious about it. And she was getting really sick of her own angst. She felt so vulnerable, and she couldn't stand it, but ultimately, she needed to hear him say that they were exclusive. *Most woman need that*, she tried to reassure herself. She hoped that the conversation, hearing the words directly from him, without having to extrapolate, might take away her nagging insecurities.

It is an awful feeling to be so in love, to want to be with someone so completely, yet plagued by uncertainty. Kadee had the distressing sense that Noah could leave her and their relationship without flinching. She played with a string at the bottom of her nightgown, curling the fraying edge tightly around her finger until the tip of her pointer turned white.

"Noah…," she breathed in and looked up. Their eyes met. Her legs felt a tad weak but she continued. "Umm…This might seem silly. I feel silly, but…umm…"

"What is it, DeeDee?" His voice was gentle as he leaned slightly toward her.

"I…well, I…find myself in unfamiliar territory. I find myself, umm…wondering if we are in an exclusive relationship. We have never really talked about it." She tilted her head and could feel her heart pounding.

His eyes had a devilish twinkle as he listened to her, "No, we haven't had that conversation, have we? Well…," his voice even and matter-of-fact, "what do you want, Kadee?"

His lack of reassurance left her heart beating faster. *He didn't answer the question*, she thought. She wound the string tighter until her finger began to throb. She mustered her courage, hoping her voice wasn't shaking, and said, "I guess, I assumed we were exclusive. I haven't been with anyone else, nor do I want to be. I'm hoping you feel the same." She got it out without cracking her voice. *He is not making this easy*, she thought.

He took her free hand in his, looking her up and down and with his same even tone, "Of course, Kadee. I love you. I thought that was obvious. I am sorry if it wasn't. I love you." He took her hand and guided her until they were both standing up, then took her in his arms and embraced her tightly. She freed her pointer from the string, the pulsating throb easing as the blood rushed back to her fingertip.

This feels good. But…

Kadee took a deep breath as she melted into his arms. *But…* she felt uneasy. It was hard for her to pinpoint, but she knew he had not really answered her question. Something between his words and actions just didn't make sense. She found it disquieting.

As they hugged, she could feel his erection press against her thigh. He slowly pulled her nightgown up and moved his hand between her legs where he found she wasn't wearing any underwear. His fingers massaged her clitoris, making her wet. Then before she knew what was happening, they were back in his bedroom, naked, and he brusquely entered her. And with that, Kadee's uneasiness washed away.

But... following their conversation, Kadee became increasingly anxious. She realized Noah's answer was evasive, leaving her even more insecure about their exclusivity. Because of her deep attachment to him, she vacillated between intuitive feelings of doubt and rationalizing that it was all in her mind. She tried to tell herself that everything was OK. It was a lie she told herself, a lie that she tried to make the truth. She noticed that she felt better when she was with Noah, but between the spaces of their time together she had moments of genuine despair.

A few weeks later, Noah surprised her, temporarily assuaging her misgivings. He wanted to take her on a vacation. He had a conference in Fort Lauderdale, and he asked her to join him. They would stay for a long weekend and be able to have some time at the beach. Kadee said yes immediately, even though she would be missing her Friday classes. She figured she could make up the work and spend time studying while Noah was attending a few of the conference presentations.

As they booked the trip together, Kadee was thinking about how irrational her worries were. Of course, he felt the same way she did. She was feeling insecure because she had never been so vulnerable with a man. *Of course, that's it,* she said to herself. *Stop being such a fucking neurotic mess. You are a strong, desirable woman, and he should feel lucky to be with you.* She looked in her bedroom mirror and kept repeating it: *You are a strong, desirable woman, and he should feel lucky to be with you.*

And, she reminded herself, *he is just a guy.*

But... while away, a few weeks later, she again had a sense that something wasn't right.

The first couple of days of the Florida trip were relaxing. Noah spent part of the day at the conference while Kadee did yoga, studied, and lounged on the beach. Noah joined her later in the afternoon, and they sat on the beach relaxing. The rhythmic sound of the waves lapping along the shore, the palms trees blowing softly in the breeze and the cloudless blue sky all made for a tropical nirvana. It was a delightful respite from the hustle of their lives in the city. They watched the sun set along the horizon from a big blanket, their nearly naked bodies wrapped around each other. It was a romantic setting, and Kadee felt contented.

Unfortunately, that feeling did not last.

The third night of the trip, Noah announced that he wanted to take Kadee to a strip club. At first she was uncomfortable with the idea, but Noah explained that it was something he wanted to share with her. "It will be very arousing, DeeDee. I promise. You trust me, don't you?" he nudged.

"Yes...yes, of course I do," she shifted her eye contact momentarily. It was only a partial truth. "It's just, you know, a strip club. I'm not a huge fan," she lied.

Kadee was a bit hesitant, but she didn't want Noah to think she didn't trust him. At this point, she wasn't sure about her trust, but he hadn't actually shown himself to be untrustworthy. He hadn't violated her trust to the best of her knowledge; it was more of a feeling she had, a hunch. So she wanted to give him the benefit of the doubt. Truthfully, Kadee didn't have any moral problem with the whole strip club thing. Her cautiousness had to do with not understanding Noah's intentions. She had a nagging feeling that he was perhaps putting her in a precarious situation where he could ogle other women right in front of her.

He was being persistent. "Come on, Deedee. It'll be fun. I promise." He kissed the nape of her neck, weakening her resolve.

Kadee rested her head on his shoulder as he slowly began rubbing her back. She wanted to make him happy, so she rationalized to herself that it was no big deal. She liked to imagine herself as someone who enjoyed trying new things. And with that thought, she agreed.

The strip club was filled with beautiful, mostly naked women. Many of them had enormous, perfectly rounded breasts. The couple sat down and ordered drinks from a topless bartender. Their seats at the bar left them inches away from the women performing on stage. One woman with straight blonde hair that reached down to her waist had her legs wrapped around a pole as she slowly slid down. She was wearing nothing but huge platform boots. There were two other women dancing on stage. One came over and spread her legs right in front of them. Noah gave her a five dollar bill. She stretched her neck, leaned in and whispered "Thank you, baby," into Noah's ear.

Kadee didn't find the strip club arousing, but Noah made it clear that he did. He took Kadee's hand and placed it on his crouch so she could feel his bulge grow. *I'm definitely not feeling turned-on,* she thought. The longer they stayed, the more uncomfortable Kadee became. Noah was clearly enjoying the other women standing before him, spreading their legs, bending over and flirting with him. He was handing them one bill after another. At one point he put a twenty in his mouth, leaned in and stuck it into the garter belt of a particularly shapely woman. Kadee's stomach curdled. They had not been there an hour, but she was ready to leave. Noah asked that they stay just a bit longer. Kadee felt trapped even as she agreed.

The Noah in the strip club seemed unfamiliar. He had always seemed so gentle, so respectful, so loving. After witnessing his behavior in the strip club, Kadee felt turned around. He seemed more like a predator stalking the women and going in for the kill with money as his weapon. The more money he threw at them, the weaker his prey became, the more attention he received, and the more skin the strippers exposed to him. One woman bent over on her knees; she spread her butt cheeks apart to show Noah her anus. Noah was so engrossed in the experience he was practically ignoring Kadee, and when she did try to get his attention, he brushed her off, leaving her feeling betrayed. It felt as though he was cheating on her.

Finally after more than two hours, Kadee insisted that they leave. When Noah tried to convince her to stay for one more drink, Kadee said she would take a taxi alone and he could stay if he wanted to. Noah finally conceded, but he was noticeably irritated, spitting out a "Fine," his intonation stern as he slammed his drink on the bar. He didn't say a word the entire ride back to the hotel.

Once in their hotel room, his demeanor changed. He lay down on the bed and asked Kadee to undress for him. He wanted her to dance naked for him while he watched, fully clothed, from the bed. This is something Noah asked for often, and Kadee always indulged. She also found the scenario arousing. But the previous times it had felt intimate, special. This time his request felt exploitative, as if he was using her. Something just wasn't right, she really felt that.

"Come on, DeeDee. You know those woman don't really turn me on, not the way you do. You are the only one I really want to see dance. I shouldn't have asked you to go there...It was a mistake. And I'm sorry."

Kadee didn't respond. She didn't know what to say, her answer to the dance was a big NO, but she didn't know if she could hold steadfast to her position if he continued asking. She didn't want to get into a back-and-forth about it, eventually giving in and doing what he wanted, so she chose to say nothing.

Noah must have sensed her reservations because he pulled her gently down on the bed next to him, wrapped his whole body around her, holding her tight, saying, "I love you so much." And just like that, Kadee wasn't sure what she was feeling once again. This uncertainty continued to become more frequent—and progressively worse.

When they returned from their Florida trip, Noah didn't call Kadee for three days. This was abnormal. Kadee knew then that something was terribly amiss. Well, she already sensed it, but it was the first time that she allowed her mind to register what her intuition already knew. Noah wasn't being honest. She was being manipulated, and yet she loved him and felt stuck in the relationship. *I'm totally fucked,* she thought, *I don't see this ending well.*

Since their first night together, the two had had contact every day, some days they would text back and forth throughout the day. Kadee called Noah twice and sent two texts; when she didn't hear back from him, she became panicked. She kept going over the details of their Florida trip wondering if, aside from the strip club incident, she had done something to turn him off or make him angry. His lack of response left her alone to fantasize scenarios in which he would break it off with her. She just couldn't make sense of it; she was blaming herself.

Deep down she knew it wasn't all her fault. But blaming herself was better than feeling helpless and out of control. Sometimes people blame themselves when they are in difficult circumstances that don't make any sense. That's what Kadee was doing. But it only made her damaged self-esteem worse.

After the third day of not hearing from him, as she paced around her small apartment she contemplated showing up at his apartment unannounced. She wanted to know what happened, what he was thinking. The not knowing was awful, and she just couldn't distract herself. Thoughts of going to see him intruded upon her like an unwanted guest as she tried to engage herself in her school work without much success. There was also the trepidation that something had happened to him. What if he was incapacitated in some way and couldn't contact her?

It was late that night when Noah finally sent Kadee a text.

Sorry DeeDee. Been crazy at work. Exhausted. Dinner tomorrow night?

Kadee noticed her hands shaking as she held her phone to read his message. Relief washed over her momentarily, but after she responded with *Yes. Sounds good,* she felt her jaw clenching. She was angry. Relieved and angry. It was an unsavory mix. Even though it was late, she poured herself a glass of wine hoping it

75

would relax her enough to stop ruminating and fall asleep. Even if he had been busy, he could have sent a quick message. She wanted to believe what his message said, but deep down she was aware that it was not the truth.

As she swooshed the remainder of her wine around the bottom of her glass, she decided she was going to ask him for the truth at dinner the next night. The thought of confronting him about his mini disappearing act quieted her angst, and Kadee finally fell asleep, emotionally exhausted.

CHAPTER 7

Kadee was anxious about her dinner with Noah. And she was sick of feeling distressed. It was exhausting. She wanted to feel excited to see him, the way she used to feel in the beginning of their relationship before a date. Before their trip to Fort Lauderdale. Before he started acting strange. But her sense that something wasn't right, her growing resentment, and insecurity all left her feeling like she had a pit of snakes in her stomach and they were slinking around, knotting themselves into a tight ball.

She had started seeing Dr. Tracy. She knew from talking it through with her that Noah was hiding something and that her apprehension was justified. She still hoped that whatever *it* was could be worked out between them. This was perhaps naïve of Kadee, but love often blinds people to reality. Kadee's perception was blurred by her feelings.

Dr. Tracy was the calming influence Kadee needed, whether or not Kadee would allow Dr. Tracy to do her job was yet to be determined. She was a petite, attractive woman in her late thirties. She had a long crooked nose that made her beauty unconventional, but it suited her face. She had dark thick hair that skimmed her shoulders, clear pale skin and blue eyes that were partially concealed by wire rimmed glasses. She dressed conservatively in pants and a blouse or blazer. Her intonation had the slightest twang to it; Kadee wondered if she was originally from the south.

Initially, Kadee was concerned that Dr. Tracy might be too conservative and perhaps not the right therapist for her. She appeared to be the type of woman who followed all the right paths, never making an error in judgment; someone who would never get tangled up in a toxic relationship or lose control over her impulses. But, of course, Kadee knew about transference and assumed that her perception of Dr. Tracy revealed more about her own feelings about herself than about who Dr. Tracy actually was. Besides, Dr. Tracy's calm demeanor and soft voice soothed Kadee's agitation during their sessions. So she decided after a couple of sessions to continue seeing her.

Dr. Tracy was in support of Kadee having the discussion with Noah. She did caution that the outcome was nebulous, that he could end the relationship, or further deny anything was wrong. She wanted Kadee to be prepared for whatever the consequence. There was something about the way Dr. Tracy spoke to her that left her feeling strong when she left the session, but the feeling didn't last long. It was like a temporary fix, dissipating soon after Kadee left her office.

Kadee arrived at the restaurant a few minutes early. It was a little Italian place near their apartments that she and Noah liked to frequent. Noah was already there and at a table. She had not seen him since their tense weekend in Fort Lauderdale. Her palms felt a little sweaty, so she wiped them across the legs of her pants. He waved her over and stood to kiss her on the cheek before she sat down. On the cheek. Not on the lips. Kadee wondered if this meant something.

The dinner started in a pleasant way. Noah was warm and engaged. It was so enjoyable that Kadee wasn't sure if she should bring anything up. Despite what she felt, in his presence she began to question herself again. Maybe he *was* just busy with work, maybe she just felt vulnerable, maybe she had become one of those women who needed too much attention, someone who would never be satisfied. Oh, she did not like that. She never wanted to see herself as someone who needed too much. Ever.

As the dinner went on, Noah reached across the table and took Kadee's hand, weaving his long fingers into hers. Kadee felt her whole body tingle, she decided right then to wait to confront him. After dinner, Noah began to walk Kadee toward her apartment. Kadee was confused; she had assumed she would be staying at his place like she always did. When she asked him about it, he said he had a very early morning, and he needed to get a good night sleep.

"That never bothered you before," the words screeched out of Kadee's mouth. Her heart was racing, but she tried very hard to look calm.

"Deedee, this is a really early morning meeting with the research team. I need to be fresh and rested to present my proposal." The words rolled off his tongue without a hint of disappointment or really any kind of emotion.

But when Kadee pressed him, insisting that something had changed, he became irritated. He had never spoken to her with such an edge of annoyance before. "I don't need this, Kadee. What's gotten into you? This isn't like you. You're acting really needy. You know I don't like that."

Kadee's stomach was tight; she felt like she had been punched. *I don't like that*, she said to herself. She never wanted to seem needy, or *be* needy. Ever. "You're blaming this on me? You're the one who's been acting different."

"I've just been busy."

"You've been distant. It's more than busy, isn't it?"

"Nope. Just busy. Really." His tone was curt, which left Kadee feeling even more anxious and agitated. She tried to stay composed.

"OK. But if there is something, if something has changed for you, I want you to tell me. You would, right?"

"Absolutely. Nothing has changed."

Kadee looked up at him, staring straight into his eyes, looking for some information in his gaze, the slightest hint that might betray a secret, but there was nothing. His eyes revealed nothing.

The rest of the short walk was silent. It was that loud sort of silence where the absence is painful, when there's so much to say, but nothing is said. Kadee had such strong stomach cramps, those snakes still knotting in her abdomen, that she had to slow her pace down. She had never experienced such profound loneliness. Her body ached from desire and longing as she walked beside her greatest love all the while feeling like they were total strangers.

After he kissed her lips and said goodnight, he assured her that he would call her tomorrow. She wanted to continue discussing their relationship, but she felt shut down, that she couldn't bring it up again. If she did, he would say she was being needy. She felt afraid of his response, so she said nothing, trying to act casual and in control of her emotions and herself. She kissed him back. It was an estranged kiss as his lips felt foreign. She responded simply, "OK."

As soon as he walked away, disappearing into the anonymity of the city streets, Kadee's stomach was churning, feeling like the snakes were now feasting off her intestines. She shuffled into her apartment and immediately started doing dishes to occupy herself, but it did not help. Her mind worked in overdrive as she thought through every detail of their conversation. She was scrubbing her frying pan ferociously. When the sponge ripped, she broke out in tears.

She looked at the clock: 11:06 p.m. She wanted to call Vanessa, but thought it was too late. She needed to talk it through; she needed reassurance, to be soothed. She kept thinking of what Noah said: "You're being needy." Kadee was angry at herself. It was not just that she was being needy, she felt needy—and she did not like that feeling one bit. Her need for him felt so desperate that she thought a part of her would die without him.

She sent Vanessa a short text: *Are you up? Call me.*

Kadee sat alone crying, waiting. When fifteen long minutes went by and Vanessa had not called, she went out. She didn't know where she was going at first. She was walking quickly, but aimlessly toward Noah's apartment. She wanted to go over there and be with him. Just lay with him in bed, his body wrapped around hers. She could feel his warmth just thinking about it. Then her thoughts shifted abruptly as an image of her going to his apartment and punching him flashed through her mind. She recognized her anger and pushed it aside. She pulled her thin sweatshirt closed, trying to comfort herself, and turned the corner. She was headed toward the 24-hour convenience store.

Although she had quit smoking more than two years earlier, she didn't know what else to do, so she went to the store and bought a pack of Marlboros. When she arrived home, she ripped open the pack, pulled out a cigarette, lit it up and took a long drag. She held it in, then slowly exhaled as she turned on her computer. *Now that feels good.* The smell was gross, but the inhaling actually calmed her.

She began with a Google search on Noah, trying to gather whatever information she could to help her understand what he might be thinking. She hated herself for looking, but she felt frantic. She had to do something; she wanted to find something that would help her know what he wasn't telling her.

She spent the next couple of hours smoking and scouring innocuous web links. She found nothing of import about Noah, so she finally turned to his Facebook page. He rarely posted updates, but she looked through all of his pictures and read all of the comments, every single one, trying to figure him out. There wasn't really anything on there, but she couldn't stop staring at his pictures with a mixture of desire and anger—and torment.

She stubbed out her final cigarette of the evening. Disgusted by the smell and herself, she got into bed. Staring at the white empty ceiling, she tried to soothe herself to sleep, but his last comment that he would call her kept replaying in her mind. And she kept telling herself that he would. Eventually she dozed off into a restless sleep.

That night she had an awful dream; it was a nightmare, actually. She was in her parents' house, the house she grew up in. Her family was in the periphery. She couldn't see their faces, but she knew they were there. At first she could hear laughing, but then there was silence: The family dog, Brownie, the dog she had as a child, rushed into the room to cuddle with Kadee. She was sitting on the couch in the TV room. She opened her arms to embrace him. As he approached her, she noticed a trail of blood behind him. As he got closer, she saw that his front leg was missing, and there was blood coming out of the empty space. She woke up choking for air. She felt like she couldn't catch her breath.

She sat up startled; her eyes were puffy. She felt so drained, she took a few deep breaths before lying back down. A moment later, she sat up again before quickly lying down. She could find no comfort, so she got up to make coffee and an early breakfast. As she waited for the coffee to brew and nibbled on her peanut butter toast, she decided she had to pull herself together. She had a lot to look forward to in her life. She had to ease up, go with the flow, just see what happens with Noah. No matter what, she would be OK. She didn't *need* him, she wanted to be with him, but she didn't *need* him.

She mustered up strength using positive self-talk, but the dream left her with a nagging ominous feeling. She couldn't get the image of the blood and dismemberment of Brownie out of her mind. She wrote down the dream, trying to literally rid herself of the images. She planned to bring it to therapy. For the rest of the day, she continued to push aside thoughts about the dream, reminding herself to save it for session.

In her therapy session that week, Dr. Tracy helped Kadee recognize what she already knew subconsciously. The dismembered dog represented Kadee in the dream. She felt that when Noah walked away, he took part of her with him. Kadee felt part of her had been ripped out. She was injured, bleeding, and not whole without him.

Kadee wondered if the dream also represented some violent impulses she might have. What if Brownie was Noah and Kadee had torn off a part of him, leaving him injured and bleeding.

"Hmm…" Dr. Tracy was scribbling notes. "Interesting, Kadee." She looked up, adjusted her glasses and continued. "Seems you're recognizing some aggression toward Noah. That's good. I'm glad you're becoming more aware of your anger."

Dr. Tracy didn't always take notes, but during that session she was writing feverishly. Of course neither of the women could have known at the time just how incriminating those notes could be. It never occurred to either of them that the session notes would be subpoenaed, overriding doctor-patient confidentiality. It wasn't the type of thing that typically happened.

Kadee was sipping her coffee. She put the television on. She was too tired to get any school work done before class, so she just tried to distract herself hoping to relax a bit. Her first class was at 12:30. At around 10 a.m., Vanessa called.

"Hi, Kade, I didn't get your text 'til this morning? Everything OK?"

Kadee fought back tears as she filled Vanessa in on the events of the last few days with Noah.

"Oh no, I'm sorry. I hate hearing you like this. You of all people; you've always been so strong. And he sounds like an ass. He's probably commitment phobic. Manhattan's full of 'em. You know, they come on strong, making you feel like you're the most special woman in the world, the only one for them. Then when it gets a little more serious, they pull away and blame it on you."

"Sounds like you might be right."

"The best thing you can do—and I know how hard it is—but the best thing you can do for yourself is end it."

"He'll probably end it first. Unless…maybe…if I can pull myself together, be that independent woman he first fell in love with, then maybe things will go back to the way they were. Right?"

"I'm not so sure. I don't think this is your fault or something you did. It really sounds like he's the one with the problem. You know I've been there more than once. I know how hard it is."

Kadee sniffled. "I love him. I've never felt this way before. I'm afraid I'll never feel this way again."

"Listen to what you've been saying. You may love him, but he's causing you pain, too. Love shouldn't be painful, not the kind of pain you're describing anyway. He should be building you up, not breaking you down. Right? Isn't that what you'd tell me?"

"Yes. Yes. You're right, Ness. You're so right. It's just so hard. I keep thinking it's my fault and maybe, you know, maybe I can fix it." She was feeling a little stronger. "But you're right. Deep down I know he isn't good for me. Leave it to me to fall in love at thirty-five with a total lying commitment phobe…or whatever's wrong with him. I feel like a fucking idiot. And then he told me that I'm being needy. Me, Ms. Independent…too needy. Ugh! What's wrong with him!"

"One: It's not your fault. Two: You're not too needy, so screw him! And three: You're perfect. Come on, I'm the one who's obsessed with the image of ideal love. You've always been the rational, logical one."

"True. It's just… I don't know what's happened to me. How this has happened to me. I don't like myself like this. I love him. I guess that's what happened."

"I know what you mean, Kadee. It will get better. It really will. You're gonna be OK. Remember, he's just a guy. This time last year, you didn't even know he existed."

"I know. I know! It's crazy!"

"Let's say we get together over the weekend. We can have a girl's day."

"Sounds perfect. Thanks, Ness."

They continued to talk for a little longer. When they hung up, Kadee felt a lot better. She wasn't sure she would end things with Noah, even though she thought Vanessa was probably right, but she would try to be calmer, more logical about his behavior. And she wanted to give the relationship a little more time.

Noah called Kadee later that day. It was Friday. He said he was tired from work, but he asked her if she wanted to meet for dinner the following night. Kadee felt relieved, and immediately said yes. They spoke on the phone for about a half hour. He asked about her day and seemed engaged and interested in the conversation. When they hung up, Kadee again wondered if her concern was all in her mind or perhaps she sounded stronger, less needy, which put Noah more at ease.

Noah seemed more attentive over the next few weeks. Although Kadee sensed some distance from him on a few occasions, she started to think he was just moody. It takes a long time to really know someone, maybe this was just who he was: someone who needed emotional distance occasionally. Kadee could live with that, and just like that she convinced herself she could trust him.

Kadee believed their relationship was progressing, needed to believe their relationship was progressing. One Sunday morning, she asked Noah if he wanted to have dinner with Vanessa and her. She thought it was strange that they still hadn't met each other's friends. Noah looked up from his cereal, his eyes hardened, as he said it was too soon.

Kadee had an immediate reaction. She was exacerbated, and she told him as much. They had been together for seven months. What was he waiting for? A year? Two? "Don't you think it's odd that we spend all of our time alone? I haven't met any of your friends, or you mine! Are you ashamed of me?"

"Stop pushing me, Kadee," he gripped the end of his spoon, putting it down purposefully while raising his voice. There was that edge in his tone again. She didn't like when he sounded irritated by her questions. They were in a relationship. She had a right to ask what was going on.

"Pushing you!? I never ask for anything!"

"You're being needy again." He breathed in, calming his voice. "You're being needy, Kadee. I hate when you're needy. You know I hate that."

Tears began to form at the crests of her eyes.

"I like things the way they are right now. Can't we just take it slow?" His voice turned gentle, but his eyes could have been shooting flames.

Kadee was sobbing. She tried to stop the tears, but they streamed down her face despite her resistance. She grabbed her napkin and cupped her face in her hands, her shoulders slouched. She hated letting him see her so broken down, but she couldn't stop the floodgates.

"You're a mess, Kadee. Pull yourself together."

She didn't look up.

"Why are you crying? Kadee, you're behaving like a petulant child. Pull yourself together," he hissed.

She didn't look up.

"You're making things worse crying like a spoiled brat who's not getting her way. You're boxing me in."

She was still sobbing. She grabbed another napkin and brought it to her face without looking up.

There were no words between them for a few minutes. The sound of Kadee crying was the only noise filling the space between them.

Kadee debated leaving. She couldn't believe how nasty he was being. The things he was saying and his tone were unduly harsh. She felt beaten. And part of her hated him right then, she hated him because she loved him. It was a twisted feeling and her head felt split in two. *But* she couldn't get up. She actually tried, but it was like her brain and limbs stopped communicating. *I'm scared*, she thought.

She was afraid if she got up and left, she would never see him again. She wanted to get up, but her body felt cemented to the chair. She sat paralyzed by fear. *Get up and go, Kadee. Just go...*But she just couldn't.

After a couple of minutes, Noah went into the bedroom and closed the door. Kadee could hear him talking, but the words were muffled. She blew her nose and wiped her eyes as she strained to hear what he was saying. The words were inaudible, but she did hear him laugh a couple of times. This cut her. Here she was, devastated, left to cry alone while he laughed it up, probably about her and what he thought was her needy behavior.

She kept telling herself to get up and leave, but she just couldn't. Within a few minutes, Noah came out, calmed, and said, "I'm going out. I think we need a break today."

"What? Where are you going?"

"Out with Theo."

"Where?"

"I'm not sure yet, but I need to take a shower. I'm meeting him at his place in an hour." He was standing outside of the bedroom door. She could tell he was waiting for her to leave. His demeanor was cold. He was distant, but she didn't want to leave things the way they were.

"Can we talk about what happened first?"

"Nothing happened, Kadee. I just need a little space today. I'll call you later," he walked toward her, bent over and kissed her on the lips. "OK?"

No. It wasn't OK, but Kadee had risked enough of her pride. She opened her heart to him—and he stabbed it.

"Sure," she said, as she got up to change and gather her stuff together.

Kadee tried to hold her head high, composed, as Noah walked her to the door, kissed her cheek and said, "I'll talk to you later."

"Okay. Whatever." She wanted to punch him right in his face.

The walk back to her apartment was awful. Her body felt shaky, almost like she might fall. Her feelings started as sadness, but quickly moved to rage as she turned the corner to buy another pack of cigarettes before she went home. His words were downright malicious. How could he talk to her like that? How could she let him? She got home, changed and lit up. She took a long drag in, then exhaled as she sat back in her lounge chair.

She knew asking him to have dinner with Vanessa wasn't being demanding or needy. This is what people in a relationship do, they do things together. They meet up with friends. But she did *feel* needy; even if she wasn't *being* needy, she felt it, and that made the situation between them confusing. Who knows? Maybe feeling needy *was* being needy.

But regardless, the way he spoke to her was unwarranted *and* unacceptable. He had never used such cruel language before. It felt as though an imposter had come from out of nowhere and temporarily inhabited her boyfriend's body.

Or maybe her neediness was making him pull away. He always told her he disliked needy women. He told her that on one of their first dates. His last girlfriend was needy. He had told her that that was what had destroyed their relationship. He was attracted to Kadee's independence. Maybe she needed to be more independent.

Later that day when she met Vanessa, she told Kadee that the notion was ridiculous. "Something is really wrong with him, Kade. I can't believe he blamed you!"

They were having a pedicure. Vanessa insisted they indulge in some self-care after hearing what happened on the phone. Kadee felt she compromised her pride that morning. She felt humiliated.

Vanessa was worried about Kadee; she had never seen her lose control over her emotions before. She made it her personal project that day to help her friend get out of the situation she was in.

"I think he's going to break it off." Kadee was biting her cuticles. It was another bad habit that she had started up again.

"Hon, I know this is so hard. But I really hope if he doesn't break it off, that you do. This is really unhealthy. You're smoking again, biting your nails, having trouble sleeping, this isn't good."

"Right. But when things are good, they are wonderful, and he's loving and kind and considerate. I'm just telling you the bad stuff."

Vanessa contemplated for a moment. "Don't you remember Marcus, the guy I dated a few years ago? The screenwriter? That relationship tortured me for four months."

"Of course, I remember Marcus. He was such an asshole. He made you so freaking miserable."

"I know. He was a total jerk. But it was the same sort of situation, if you remember? 'When he was good, he was very, very good; but when he was bad, he was horrid.'" Kadee smiled at the play on the Henry Wadsworth Longfellow quote. "There was a little girl" was a favorite poem of theirs, one of the first bonding experiences between Kadee and Vanessa, who could never pass up an apropos literary reference.

Kadee was feeling stronger. "Yes. Right."

"Every woman has at least one Marcus in her lifetime. Noah is yours."

At that moment, Kadee could not love Vanessa more. She gave her a warm hug right before they sat down at an outside café. They decided to put an end to the Noah talk for the remainder of the night. Kadee was still distracted by thoughts of him, but for the couple of hours they were at the outside café, she really tried to push the thoughts aside.

Kadee was feeling better after her time with Vanessa, but then on her way home, something terrible happened.

Walking back to her apartment from the subway, just as she was passing Dr. Tracy's office, she spotted Noah across the street at a little Mexican place. He was sitting outside. Although she could only see the back of her head, she could tell he was with a woman. The faceless woman had dark hair pulled back in a high bun and they were seated right next to each other. The moment felt surreal as Kadee stopped walking, stared at them, trying to register what was happening. She felt like everything was in slow motion.

What is he doing? That's definitely not Theo. She was puzzled as her mind raced through the options of what was happening. She did not want to believe he actually had the audacity to take another woman on a date. She especially didn't want to think he would be so careless as to be on a date only a few blocks from her apartment. She decided right then that it had to be his mother. For sure. Noah had made a plan with her once he knew he wasn't going to be with Kadee that evening.

But she wasn't sure how to handle the situation. She did want to meet his mother. Should she go over to them? She stared at the back of the woman's head, uncertain what the right thing to do was. She thought that it might be time that she met Noah's mother, Annabelle Donovan. She couldn't just ignore them. He was her boyfriend, after all. Of course, he would be glad to see her. She did have the thought that it might be slightly awkward to meet his mother spontaneously. *But...*then she reminded herself that Mrs. Donovan knew they were dating and that Noah did tell her that his mother was interested in meeting her.

She was wavering on a seesaw of uncertainty, when, without forethought or insight, she suddenly found herself crossing the narrow street headed toward their table. Her voice echoed in her mind with, *Yes, it is time that I meet the mysterious and omnipotent Annabelle Donovan.* Her walk became more determined. Everything started moving fast. She approached their table and Noah looked up, his eyes wide with surprise.

The woman with the high bun twisted her head around, her dark brown eyes staring right at Kadee. She gave a half smile. She was stunning with high cheek bones, deep set eyes and full lips painted with red lipstick. She had a thin scarf elegantly wrapped around her shoulders. And she looked to be somewhere in her forties, early fifties at the most. *Too young to be his mother,* she thought. *Then who is she?* Kadee looked at Noah, then at the woman, then back.

"Umm…Kadee…umm…what are you doing here?" he stood up to face her.

"I live here. What are you doing here?   She looked at the woman and smiled.

The woman pursed her lips, releasing a slight chuckle.

Kadee didn't think it was funny. Neither did Noah. He looked really uncomfortable; he put his hand on Kadee's back and attempted to guide her away from the table toward the street.

Kadee was not entertained. "Stop it." She stood firmly in her place, wanting to know who the woman was. "I just want the truth." She addressed the woman again, politely saying, "Hi, I'm Kadee."

"Come on, Deedee…just calm down. Let's talk over here for a minute," he pushed gently on her back toward the street.

Kadee didn't budge. It felt like he was shoving her. He was making it worse. She was becoming exasperated. "Stop pushing me."

She looked at the woman again and blurted out, "Did you know that he is my boyfriend? Did you know that?"

The woman opened her mouth to respond, but before she could get the words out, Noah put his hand on the woman's shoulder and said, "Friend."

Kadee looked at Noah's hand touching the woman. She had had it. She was furious. His lack of acknowledgement of their relationship felt completely disrespectful. After all of these months of telling her how much he loves her, she could not believe his utter dismissal of their relationship. *Friend? What nerve!* She was losing control. She raised her voice, "Friend? Friend? You're freaking kidding me, right?!"

He placed his hand on Kadee's back again, trying to maneuver her away from the table.

That was it. She had never felt so discarded as she did in that moment; it was like she meant nothing to him. Kadee became overwhelmed by her emotions. She felt a surge of adrenaline; she was furious. Her body shaking, she grabbed Noah's drink off the table and threw it in his face. He was drenched, transparent fluid dripping from his forehead down his chin and onto the top of his shirt.

Kadee stared in disbelief at what she had done, humiliated by her loss of control. She had never acted so impulsively before. She was horrified. How could she allow herself to get to this point? She burst out crying right in front of them. The tears of shame and rage streaming down her face as she turned and ran away from the whole ugly scene. She ran the few blocks home without stopping and arrived at her apartment panting and disoriented.

Noah was about to go after her, but the woman took Noah's hand, gently pulling him to sit back down. "Let her go, dear," she said. "Let her go. You can call her tomorrow."

He sat down. "OK, Mother."

CHAPTER 8

After dinner with his mother, Noah went home, showered, and tried to call Kadee. Although he was furious about the scene she made at the restaurant, he thought he should at least explain that the woman he was with was his mother. His mother had asked how Kadee could possibly not recognize her. Her pictures were all around his apartment. She made sure of that. How could she not know?

Noah made up a pathetic excuse to his mother, blaming Kadee, saying she was oblivious. But the truth was that Noah would hide his mother's pictures under his bed whenever Kadee would come over. He would replace the pictures of his mother with pictures of her when she was there; then he would switch back to his mother's photos when his mother visited. He didn't understand why he felt compelled to hide the pictures. His mother was beautiful, and she looked like she was in her forties. At least she looked forty-something after that second facelift. But for some reason, letting Kadee see the pictures made him feel uncomfortable and exposed.

Another peculiarity his mother's presence roused was his need to wash himself obsessively. After seeing his mother, he would need to shower, wash his hands and face, and/or change depending upon where he was and how much time he had. He didn't understand the compulsion. He only observed it and was ashamed of it.

Kadee's phone kept going to voicemail. He tried three times. He didn't leave a message. He didn't know what to say really. He was never going to get more serious with her. He would never marry her. He could tell she wanted the relationship to progress and he kept putting the brakes on. It was causing problems between them, but he wasn't ready to let her go yet. He felt confused about her, about his feelings. But he knew two things: He wasn't ready to let her go, and he was never going to give her what she wanted.

When he first met Kadee, he was so taken by her beauty. He couldn't believe she was interested in him. She was the kind of girl all the guys would be after in high school and college. She was the kind of girl that would never be interested in him, except maybe for help with schoolwork.

Having sex with her that first night, watching her as he was inside of her, her panting, wanting more, was the most arousing experience he had ever had. Feeling the command of his virility, seeing the power he had over her gave him a sense of control and confidence he never had before.

This was addicting.

She was addicting.

The more he had, the more he wanted — more sex and more control. The more he had the better he felt. He wasn't ready to let go of that.

Over lunch, Theo asked him what the problem was, why he didn't take her seriously. "She sounds perfect, man. What's up?"

"I'm not sure. It doesn't feel right. I don't know why. The sex, though. It's fucking awesome. Her ass…her ass…man, it's fucking perfect."

Theo laughed. He had been married for five years, and though Theo did enjoy living vicariously through Noah's myriad exploits, he did wonder if Noah would ever settle down. He seemed to go from one unsuccessful relationship to the next. Maybe he just liked the chase, or maybe it was something more serious.

"Are you ever going to settle down?"

"Sure, someday, I guess," he didn't sound too concerned. "When the right woman says yes, I guess."

Noah wasn't sure what "the right woman" meant exactly. He had an idea, but he was uncertain. What he did know was that Kadee was not the right woman, and that he probably should tell her the truth. But he didn't.

Kadee wasn't the type of girl he imagined settling down with, the type of girl his mother would have introduced him to. Mother always talked about women as being seductive, using their sexuality to manipulate men. Mother was trying to protect him from this type of woman. As attracted as he was to Kadee, and he was very attracted, his sexual desire for her scared him.

She was just the type of woman his mother had warned him about. He twisted his own desire and blamed it on her. Of course, he didn't understand this. He just kept her at a safe distance while continuing to have sex with her. Many men and women spend a good portion of their adult lives behaving like this, careening from sexual partner to sexual partner, then emerging from each mostly unscathed. But for Noah, it turned out to be the gravest error of his life.

When Noah first told his mother about Kadee, that her parents were teachers, where she was from, her immediate reaction was, "She's not for you, dear. A woman like that will just use you. A woman like that will want to marry you and take all of *our* money. You must listen to mother. Mother is trying to protect you."

No doubt Noah's mother understood this intimately, having married Noah's wealthy father for his money.

He tried Kadee's phone again. No answer. He assumed she was home and avoiding his calls. He didn't like that, so he decided not to call again. He went online, responded to a few emails, looked at some pornography, then finally at around 1a.m., he went to sleep.

In the middle of the night he heard his phone ringing, he rolled over to see who was calling, but before he could grab his phone, he noticed a dark mass hovering over him. Without his contacts in, he could not tell if it was just the play of light and shadow or something more. He rubbed his eyes and tried to focus. The dark shadow seemed to whisk across the room. He sat up startled, feeling a presence. He put on his eyeglasses, but he didn't see anything unusual.

Floorboards creaked in the hallway, then in the living room. With his uneasiness growing, he quietly slipped out of bed and tip-toed down the hall, glancing into each room as he went along, but saw no one. Relieved, he went into the kitchen to get some water. When he returned to his bedroom, he looked at the recent calls on his phone. The call had come from a blocked number, and there was no message. He wondered if it had been Kadee. He still felt unnerved, but chocked it up to a weird dream. He got back in bed, but it took him a while before he could fall back to sleep.

In the morning, he looked around the apartment to make sure everything was in place. He was sure the shadow was a dream, a strange dream, but a dream nonetheless. He still felt chilled by the event, though, and he couldn't help but wonder if Kadee had somehow broken in. He always kept a spare key under the mat. He never told Kadee about it, only his mother knew, but a key under the mat was not exactly original. It would not take a genius to figure it out. Maybe she wanted to see if he was sleeping with the woman she saw him with. Maybe she thought she would catch him in the act, but seeing he was alone, she left.

He knew it was a far-fetched scenario. He couldn't imagine Kadee committing a felonious break-in, but he did entertain the possibility. Perhaps he should have taken himself more seriously.

That day at work Noah was distracted by thoughts of Kadee. He was surprised that she hadn't called or texted. Not hearing from her made him uncomfortable, as though he was losing the control. He noticed himself checking his phone repeatedly between his patients.

When he got home after work, he went on Match.com. He was perusing the various women he might be interested in. Despite the fact that he led Kadee to believe they were in an exclusive relationship, he was still dating other women. There was one in particularly that he was interested in. He rationalized his actions, telling himself that he never promised her exclusivity. He never made any long-term commitments.

His Internet search left him feeling unfulfilled. His thoughts kept going back to Kadee and her lack of contact.

He called her. This time when she didn't answer, he left a message.

Hi, Deedee. We should talk about last night. That was my mother that I was with. Umm...I want...well...just call me so we can talk about it... OK...umm...bye.

About an hour later, the phone rang. Noah jumped up to answer, assuming it was Kadee. But when he looked at the incoming number, he saw it was his mother. "Again?" he said aloud with irritation. They had already spoken three times that day. He huffed before answering. "Yes, mother."

She wanted to introduce him to a new woman, the daughter of a doctor in her building. Noah wasn't interested, but as always his mother was relentless. She again admonished him about Kadee, saying she was clearly in love with him and that since he was never going to marry her, he should break it off. He shouldn't waste his time, or hers.

He looked at his mother's picture sitting on his nightstand and rolled his eyes, as she was going on and on about why he needed to break it off with Kadee.

He felt trapped by his mother. There was no room for him to assert any independence when it came to her. And she would not drop the Kadee issue. He could not get a word in. He finally conceded. He had no choice but to. He agreed she was right and that he would break it off. He agreed to meet the new woman. He would have agreed to almost anything at that point, knowing it was the only way to get his mother off the phone.

When they hung up, he put her picture face down. He felt so smothered by her, disgust seeping through the pores of his skin. But he also had a twisted sense of guilt; he felt guilty for his loathing. It was something he had difficulty explaining, but it always left him riddled with internal conflict. Yvonne had helped him understand it a little better one day during one of their lunchtime rendezvous. Sometimes Yvonne seemed more like his therapist than his friend.

He took a long hot shower, attempting to rid himself of his mother's emotional intrusion and the shame and guilt which accompanied it. Later that night while flipping through a medical journal, Kadee returned his call. They talked about what happened, resolved their differences and reconciled. Although it was almost 10 p.m., he invited Kadee over to spend the night with him.

Of course, his promise to his mother complicated his relationship with Kadee even more. Now he had to keep her a secret. And it was not easy to keep secrets from his mother.

CHAPTER 9

After Kadee ran away from Noah and his dinner companion, she stormed back to her apartment and immediately began pacing. Her thoughts and heart were racing. She wanted to call Vanessa, but she could not even think straight, nevermind being able to formulate words for a conversation. So she kept pacing, back and forth, back and forth across her small apartment, faster and faster.

She was aghast that Noah was out with another woman and humiliated that he referred to Kadee as just a friend. She had suspected something. She had thought it was possible that he was seeing other women. But when confronted with the possibility of this truth, she did not want to accept it. She lit a cigarette and continued to pace.

She was on the verge of ripping her hair out; she wanted to rip something, break something. She thought about taking her kitchen knife, going back up to the restaurant and stabbing him. Of course, she told herself she could never do something like that, but the image of it felt relieving.

She sat down and pushed her hand down hard on her heart to try to get it to stop beating so fast. She put her cigarette out and quickly lit up another one. Her world felt so small. Before Noah, she had a life, a full life, one where she had interests and passions, a sense of meaning. Now her world had shrunk, a tunnel where the only thing driving her interest and passion was him. She wanted to stop, rewind, and go back to her former life, her former self, but she felt like she couldn't. She didn't know how. Her life existed in this new awful place, her own private hell.

Unable to calm herself, she grabbed an open bottle of wine, took a few big gulps and went out. She found herself headed toward Noah's apartment. When she got there, she decided to sit outside on a stoop across the street. She wasn't sure why she was there or what she expected to happen, but sitting there waiting for him made her feel more in control. Sitting there made her feel like she was doing something.

She waited.

When an hour passed and he hadn't arrived home, she debated going upstairs. She would go upstairs and use the key under his mat to get into his apartment. He didn't know she knew about the key, but she overheard him talking to his mother about it one day. While he was taking one of his marathon showers a few weeks ago, she checked and there it was.

She could sit and wait for him—or them. If he brought the woman home, surely she would leave if Kadee was there when they walked in. As she was going through the various scenarios, she noticed Noah walking toward the front of his building. She put the hood of her short sleeve sweater up, trying to be inconspicuous. She rested her elbows on her knees, keeping her head mostly down. But her eyes never left Noah. Her heart was thumping so rapidly she thought it would beat right out of her chest. She was perspiring all over.

He was alone.

Kadee watched as he walked leisurely into his building. Kadee's heart slowed to a normal pace. She felt totally exhausted. She again thought about the key and showing up unexpectedly, but she already felt so demoralized. Though part of her indulged in the fantasy, she knew it would likely make her feel worse.

She walked back home, mumbling to herself to get it together. She felt like she was really losing control. She was trying to talk herself out of it, out of him. When she got home, she had a little more wine. She berated herself for her actions. She had class in the morning and was going to feel like crap. How could she allow him to take her dignity and cause her to disregard the things that were important to her?

She took out one of her meditation books, skimmed through a chapter about letting go. She felt a little better, but when she looked at her phone, she saw Noah's number — three missed calls, no message. She felt sick to her stomach. What could he possibly say? She read through the chapter again, determined to get a hold of herself. The words gradually began to soothe her. Finally feeling drowsy, she got into bed and fell asleep.

Kadee's sleep was restless. It was the kind of sleep where the body is exhausted, but the mind is troubled. She was tossing all around her bed, pushing the comforter off, pulling it back on, positioning her pillow, trying impossibly to find comfort. She wasn't sure if it was the wine or her distress, but she was having strange dreams, too. The images were broken into small parts, none of which made much sense to her rational mind, except the part about Betty Broderick.

Kadee was writing a paper about Betty Broderick for her criminal personality class. On November 5, 1989, Betty Broderick killed her ex-husband Dan and his new wife, Linda, while they were sleeping. She had used her daughter's key to get into her ex-husband's house. There had been a long buildup of rage manifesting in Betty's serious harassment of Dan. One dramatic incident included her driving through the front of his house in an out-of-control rage. Kadee was exploring if the explicit buildup phase in the killings suggested a catathymic homicide. In interviews, Betty described relief after the murders, also suggesting catathymia.

Kadee had been working on the paper throughout the week, so it made sense that it would enter her mind during sleep. Our unconscious often discloses images from our daily lives. But the context her mind constructed scared her, leaving her feeling like she was a participant in her own horror movie. The flashes of the images that Kadee could recall had Betty Broderick retrieving the key from under Noah's mat. Then there was Noah in bed with Linda, the woman didn't look like Linda, but it was her. Betty was standing over the bed watching them sleep.

Kadee roused in a haze, recalling the disturbing visions, but she rolled over in a moment and fell back asleep. She continued the dream. There was a knife; it was from her own kitchen. And Betty Broderick was holding it.

Kadee woke up startled. She sat up in bed, feeling strangled, choking, her cotton top plastered to her sweat-slicked back. She put her bedroom light on and paced around to slow her breathing.

She changed her shirt. The nightmare felt so real, but the most alarming part was that Kadee felt rage toward Noah. She wasn't sure what aspect of the dream led her to this feeling, she just knew what she felt—and it was powerful.

For a second, she wondered: Is this how Betty Broderick felt? Am I the "Betty" in the dream? The thoughts terrified her. She quickly pushed them aside, took out her meditation book, and forced herself to read. She woke up to her alarm with the light on and her book on the floor, which felt strange because she felt like she never went back to sleep.

That week in session, Dr. Tracy prescribed Valium. It was a temporary solution to Kadee's problem sleeping. As is often the case with drugs, it solved one problem, but caused another.

Throughout the day, Kadee's brain felt jumbled. Images of Betty, the knife, her knife, were mixed with images of Noah and the nameless woman. She spent the day with her stomach in knots, feeling that collection of worms again, and her emotions twisted between sadness and rage. She went through the motions of her day. She attended yoga, then her classes, but she was in a foggy storm, like she was stuck inside a cloud that was about to explode with torrential rain. She felt disconnected from her activities and instead consumed with the tangled thoughts in her head. Distracted by her thinly veiled rage, she snapped fiercely at a man on the subway when he innocently bumped into her.

She could not leave the subway fast enough. She knew she had to get her emotions under control, and there was no way she would be able to do that in such a tense New York spot. She would have to reconnect with her life to feel stable again. And one way to do that would be to do a mundane task from her daily life. So, she went to the grocery store, deciding that maybe cooking a nice healthy dinner and watching a good movie would help her regain her balance. She knew she needed to work on her paper, but she thought a night off from Betty might be a good thing.

While meandering up and down the aisles of the grocery store, still feeling detached from her surroundings and absorbed by her thoughts, she heard someone call her name. It jolted her as the voice interrupted her thoughts. It was a familiar man's voice. She turned around to see her ex-boyfriend, Alex Suarez. She was not in the mood, but she could not ignore him.

Alex Suarez lived nearby, and occasionally they would run into each other. She didn't particularly enjoy seeing him, but she was always polite. He was not a bad guy, just not great at expressing his emotions. It used to frustrate Kadee. She never really knew what he was thinking. One day during their senior year, he just broke it off for good without any real explanation. Kadee had asked, but he did not offer much of an explanation. After the final breakup with Alex, Kadee became even more guarded when it came to romance.

Whenever she saw him, she anticipated some conversation about the ending of their relationship. Maybe over the years he gained some emotional insight and would be able to acknowledge what had happened between them. But every time, it was the same. *He* was the same. They would engage in casual conversation. It was not unpleasant, just unsatisfying. Feeling as distressed as she did, she was really in no mood for their typical courteous but trivial chitchat.

This meeting turned out to be different. Apparently Alex had gone through his own trauma. He met a woman, fell in love. They married after only about two months together, and then were divorced only a few months after the marriage. Ironic, since he was a divorce attorney.

As it turns out, his wife had been cheating on him with his business partner's wife, and she decided she preferred her mistress to Alex. She immediately filed for a divorce. They hadn't even been married for three months at the time. This had happened only a few months earlier. Alex was admittedly still heartbroken.

While they stood talking in the pasta and sauce aisle, Kadee sensed vulnerability from Alex that she had never felt before. It was appealing, making their conversation more enjoyable. He must have learned something from his personal tragedy because he actually apologized to Kadee for the abrupt ending of their relationship, saying it was a mistake, that he was immature. He then asked if they could grab dinner one night soon.

Kadee looked at Alex, really looked at him, took him in as she wondered if she could ever be attracted to him again. Noah had such charm. Alex just didn't exude that same magnetism, that same magic that left Kadee's body tingling all over.

Maybe that was a good thing.

Kadee said yes to the dinner, deciding that whether she was interested in Alex romantically or not, it would be good to go out with another man. If nothing else, perhaps they would be able to be friends. They exchanged phone numbers. And they exchanged a friendly kiss on the cheek. No spark, Kadee thought. But then again, she realized no man had a chance while her heart still belonged to Noah. The exchange did snap her out of her emotional haze a bit. Her world looked clearer as she walked back to her apartment with a little bounce to her step.

When she got home, she poured a half glass of wine, put some music on and began preparing her dinner. She ruminated over her conversation with Alex. It felt good to be able to think about something other than Noah and the nameless woman, Betty and her knife, and Kadee's torment about all of it. She felt lighter. There was something about Alex's apology that gave her a sense of hope about her future. *Maybe things do work out in the end,* she thought. Vanessa believed that. Maybe Vanessa was right.

She had just finished cooking when she saw that Noah had called. This time he had left a message. Her mood immediately shifted. She felt sick. What could he say? There was nothing he could say. She resisted the temptation to listen. But after dinner she could not stop staring at her phone while contemplating deleting his message. In spite of her rage, she still loved him. With that thought in mind, she listened.

She heard the message, but the words didn't quite register. She listened again. She sat back, sipped her wine. She listened a third time.

She burst out in tears. She cried tears mixed with so much emotion that at first she wasn't even sure why she was crying. There was some momentary relief knowing that the nameless woman was Noah's mother, but as she continued bawling she knew underneath that there was still something wrong. She knew there was something about the relationship with Noah that just wasn't good for her. If it had been a date, maybe she would be forced to move on.

Perhaps she wasn't crying tears of relief. Perhaps the true relief would have been finding out he was with someone else. She would have been forced to let go. But learning that it was all innocent left her exactly where she was before: stuck. She was mixed up with sadness and rage, yet she didn't have the emotional fortitude to leave. For a moment, she recognized that her tears were really screams of dread.

She cried for a long time; eventually, she exhausted all of her tears. She went into the bathroom and washed her face. When she looked in the mirror, her eyes bloated, her face splotched with red, she barely recognized herself. She looked aged and tired; her vitality was gone. She played with her hair, moving it all around trying to find her former self in her own gaze. Eventually she took her long, dark hair and pulled it all the way back into a severe pony tail. She put on eye makeup, her favorite shadow, to accent her green eyes. She blew her nose, then returned to her small living room. She sat down, mustered some strength and called him back.

They talked, his gentle, even voice enveloped her, and for a few moments she felt love again. While they spoke, she felt the uncomplicated feelings of love she had in the beginning, before they became knotted with rage and sadness. They resolved their differences. It was that twisted sort of reconciliation where she felt good in the moment, but afterward, deep down she knew this was only temporarily. Eventually, it would get much worse.

Chapter 10

Yvonne Tracy was tiding up her office before her next appointment. Noah had just left her office after one of their lunches. She was making sure she eliminated any evidence of their sexual liaison. She primped the pillows, folded up the blanket and made sure to stuff the used condom and wrapper in her bag. Using the small mirror from her compact, she was reapplying her makeup. Her hair looked wild, so she pulled it back in a ponytail. She had mixed feelings about using her office as a stand-in motel room, but her lust for Noah was growing, and she was having a hard time saying no.

Yvonne and Noah had met during her first year of medical school at Columbia University. She felt immediately drawn to him, but he seemed to just want to be friends, so Yvonne kept her infatuation secret. One night during her second year at Columbia, they were out for drinks with some friends. Everyone else had gone home, but the two of them stayed, continuing with their cocktails and conversation.

The more they drank, the closer they sat, and the more of each other's bodies they were touching. Soon they were kissing, the kind that was so impassioned, they were no longer aware of their surroundings. Time stood still as their lips merged, their desire for each other mounting. The tension became irresistible. Soon they were back at her apartment ripping each other's clothes off.

At the time, Yvonne was just twenty-five years old and had had only one previous sexual partner. Noah was a year older than her and seemed more sexually experienced, but she wasn't sure. She had fooled around with other guys, but she really believed sexual intercourse was reserved for committed relationships. So when the two were in his bed kissing in their underwear and Noah went to take her panties off, she stopped him. She took his hand, moved it to her back. He took her bra off instead. She let him. As he started sucking on her breasts, her nipples hard with arousal, he again moved his hand downward.

He began massaging her clitoris. Yvonne grew so aroused, her passion over took her, compromising her judgment. When he tried to take her panties off again, she let him. As she lay there naked, he moved down, his face was between her legs as his tongue entered her. Her vagina was pulsating as her back arched with pleasure. The tension was building. Her breathing changed. She was panting and about to climax when he pulled his tongue out, took his underwear off and quickly entered her.

Within seconds, Yvonne climaxed, screaming with pleasure as her body released all the built-up tension. She was still trembling with pleasure as Noah quickly followed, pulling out so he could come all over her stomach. The two lay panting, naked on the bed. There were no words between them, just the sound of their breath for the next few minutes.

She reached for him, taking his arms and wrapping them around her body. He scooped his body behind hers and enveloped her with his long arms. Yvonne was blissful. Whatever feelings she had kept in abeyance for the past year came to the surface as she lay with him, her whole body quivering with delight. She loved him.

Just as she was getting comfortable and assumed they were going to spend the night wrapped around each other, Noah got up and put his clothes on in a hurry.

Yvonne looked at him askance. She pulled the sheet over her naked body and sat up in bed. "Is everything all right? Did I do something wrong"

"No, nothing…nothing…I just like to sleep in my own bed." His tone was off-handed, indifferent.

Yvonne had never experienced this detached side of Noah. It felt awful.

She felt awful.

She felt dismissed and vulnerable. She watched as he finished getting dressed. She wanted to say something, but the words wouldn't come to her. She didn't understand what he was doing, why he was leaving, but she felt too vulnerable to ask. So she just watched him. She could feel a dull headache coming on. She was massaging her temples and squinting her eyes, trying to relieve the pressure.

After that night, things were awkward between them for a few weeks. Yvonne thought he might offer an apology or explanation. He didn't. He remained distant. It was strange because for the year they had been friends, Noah always seemed so open. It was part of what she liked about him so much: his sincerity.

The two spoke or saw each other only a few times over the next few weeks. Yvonne assumed his distance meant that he thought what happened was a mistake, that he wasn't interested in her. She was mortified.

She never intended to have sex with someone who was not interested in a relationship. She felt she had compromised her principles. It left her with a sour feeling. When they slowly began talking again, Yvonne kept her guard up. Over time, she forgave him for his behavior, but she certainly wasn't planning on doing *it* again.

Yvonne was strong that way. Despite the fact that she still held some residual romantic feelings for Noah, she wasn't going to keep herself open for rejection or mistreatment. She wanted to be with someone who was crazy about her, someone committed, someone who would make her feelings a priority. During the remainder of their years at medical school, Noah tried to put his charms on a few times and bed her. Yvonne stayed firm to her boundaries, halting him before he could even kiss her on the lips. Honestly, it turned her off. She wanted a strong, self-assured man, someone who knew what he wanted. Noah was not that.

They did remain friends. In many ways, Yvonne was Noah's confidante. He shared things with her he didn't tell anyone else. Over the years, an intimacy developed between them, an understanding. Yvonne always liked that. She enjoyed knowing that she was one of the only people who knew him. When Yvonne was married five years later, Noah was at her wedding. And when she divorced eight years after that, Noah consoled her while she was mending her broken heart.

It had been thirteen years since that infamous drunken night. The image of it faded over the years. During her healing process, while she was most vulnerable, Yvonne trusted Noah as a source of comfort. A deeper closeness evolved between them during this time, a closeness that soon was consummated. This time it was different. This time it was Yvonne who wasn't ready to move forward toward commitment, at least not yet. She was no longer the young inexperienced girl in medical school pining after Noah. She was a strong, confident woman in charge of her life.

Besides, she knew Noah, really knew him. Maybe too well. At least she thought she did. The odd relationship between Noah and his mother, Annabel Donovan, Belle, as she preferred to be called, was troubling to say the least. She tried not to judge Noah. She was a psychiatrist, after all. But she knew if she were ever to get more serious with Noah, she would have to deal with Belle and her intrusiveness. Belle was domineering and Noah was not good at setting boundaries. Yvonne wasn't sure she could live with that, with them, or if she wanted to.

Interacting with Belle Donovan was like managing an unruly adolescent. She wanted what she wanted when she wanted it, and there was no room for sensible negotiation. Honestly, Yvonne didn't know how Noah dealt with his mother sometimes. Whenever Yvonne went out with them, she would feel totally overwhelmed and would always leave exhausted.

Yvonne met Belle during her first year in medical school when Belle threw a huge party for Noah's birthday. At the time, in her late forties, Belle was gorgeous. She took immaculate care of herself and over the years, after hours spent each week with her trainer as well as a few nips and tucks, she pretty much looked the same. She truly looked like she was still forty-something. She was quite lean and her skin was flawless; there was not a wrinkle to be found. She wore expensive clothing that was always elegant but youthful, giving the appearance of someone much younger.

Belle exuded grace, too. She was able to carry a whole room, charming those around her with her mellifluous voice, upright posture, and refined manners. Yvonne was captivated by her that first night; the way she mingled with everyone at the party with such poise, never seeming ruffled and always polite, always saying just the right thing. With her long, proud neck, she almost seemed as though she were dancing through the crowd.

But there was another side to Belle, one that Yvonne didn't meet until about six months later when Noah invited her to join them for dinner. Yvonne was excited to have dinner with Belle, to get to know her better. She wasn't anything like her own parents or any of her other friends' parents. Initially, Yvonne thought she would look up to Belle, possibly aspire to be like her when she was older. That changed quickly when the real Belle Donovan emerged at dinner.

Belle was well-mannered, but underneath her honey-glazed voice and flowing movements was a ruthless woman. Yvonne noticed the contrast immediately when Belle pulled Noah's hand to sit next to her. She pulled his chair close and put her arm on his leg. When he tried to create a little physical distance between them, she smiled gently and pulled him closer. Yvonne was so young at the time, she couldn't really understand the complexity of Belle and her actions, but she knew something was off.

Belle also referred to herself in the third person; it was off-putting. She would say things like, "Noah's mother knows him best," and "Noah and his mother are very close; no one is closer to Noah than his mother." Noah would squirm when she spoke that way, but either she didn't notice or she didn't care. She was marking her territory and no one, not even Noah, was going to stop Belle Donovan.

Over the years, Yvonne would occasionally spend time with Noah and Belle. As she got older, particularly during and following her psychiatry residency and psychotherapy training, she realized the depth of Belle's inappropriateness. She treated Noah as a partner, instead of a son. She seemed to be implicitly telling Yvonne, "Don't even think about it; no one is ever going to replace mother!"

One night with a single disturbing gesture, Belle Donovan took things up a notch. They had just finished dinner and were taking a leisurely walk through Central Park. Maybe Noah and Yvonne were walking too close for Belle's comfort. Yvonne couldn't be sure what inspired her, but Belle suddenly stopped walking. She turned toward Noah, caressing his face, staring into his eyes; she kissed him slowly on the cheek, too slowly, her lips lingering right by his ear. The moment gave Yvonne chills.

That night, for the first time ever, she questioned Noah. She swallowed hard, "You're mother isn't interested in remarrying? She's always going to all of these socials, she never meets anyone?" She approached the topic inadvertently, knowing it was sensitive.

He seemed oblivious. "She says she's not interested. I don't understand it, either."

Yvonne pried a little further. "She hasn't been with anyone since your father?"

"There have been a few men...they were...umm...short term, I guess you could say. She used to tell me it was because... umm...you know, because she was a single parent and she needed to take care of me. Doesn't make much sense now, I guess. I'm grown. Sometimes I think she thinks I'm still a kid."

Yvonne felt sad for him. "Well, you'll always be her little boy. Right?" she smiled and shrugged her shoulders, trying to lighten the moment.

"Yeah, right...I guess." His words trailed off.

"What are you thinking right now?"

"Oh, nothing, really," he bowed his head for a moment. "I just feel guilty sometimes. Like she sacrificed her whole life for me, and now that I'm grown she doesn't know what to do. I don't know."

Yvonne looked into Noah's eyes and saw such sadness. She wanted to say more, but he changed the subject. She let him.

During her marriage, Yvonne didn't see much of Belle. She didn't see Noah all that often, either. Her life was different, of course, as a married woman. But they did maintain regular contact via phone and meet for an occasional dinner. Yvonne always counseled him on his women troubles. Try as he might, Noah just couldn't seem to stay in a relationship for more than a few months. He couldn't seem to find "that girl," that right woman to spend his life with. On occasion, he would joke that he let the right girl get away years ago, Yvonne being that right girl.

Yvonne thought that perhaps Noah wanted her while she was married because she was no longer available. But following her divorce, as they grew closer, she did sense authentic feelings of love from him. She was too vulnerable to consider the possibility of opening herself up to him, but she did enjoy his attention. As she healed, she started to feel drawn toward him. As her desire grew, she found herself thinking about him more and more. The longing to be physically intimate also grew.

They began meeting at her office a few days a week just to talk. Both his office and apartment were close to her office, so it was convenient to meet there. Yvonne was also trying to keep their relationship platonic; she believed being in her office set a boundary that might not exist at one of their apartments. She thought it was a safer atmosphere.

But sometimes a deep yearning builds between two people, and there's no way to stop it. When desire burns so deep, gnawing at the stomach, the craving becomes painful with the need to satisfy immediate and urgent.

They started out as two friends spending time. But as time went on, they sat closer. He would put his hand on her leg or arm while they were talking; she could feel his affection, really feel his genuine interest. She eventually felt the urge to kiss him, yet she resisted. She denied her feelings, pushed them out of her mind. She created some distance, telling him she was busy with patients and didn't have as much time between her sessions to see him. Their visits became a little less frequent. But that didn't stop her from thinking about him. And oh, how she tried.

It was Yvonne's thirty-ninth birthday when Noah picked her up at her office with a bottle of champagne. He was taking her to dinner. Yvonne had had her hair done and bought a new outfit for the evening. She told herself that she was treating herself to her own birthday present. Deep down she knew that wasn't the whole truth. She wanted to look good for him. Deep down she was hoping something was going to happen between them.

They were drinking and drinking. Yvonne was still nervous, so she drank more. When Noah walked her home, she invited him in. Within seconds, they were kissing. They kissed for a long time, slow, gentle kisses filled with care. He was letting Yvonne lead, and when she pulled him toward her bedroom, he whispered, "Are you sure?"

She nodded, "Yes."

They stripped naked. They laid on top of the comforter, kissing, their bodies touching, enjoying each other for a long while. He whispered, "I love you, Yvonne." She got on top of him, positioning herself. He slowly penetrated her. Breathy sounds of pleasure filled the room as they thrust their bodies back and forth until they both released. That night, Noah stayed; they slept wrapped around each other.

In the morning, Yvonne was the one who was distant, or at least she felt a little distant. She enjoyed the evening, and she definitely had strong feelings for Noah, but Yvonne was also a very rational person. She wasn't the type of woman who followed her emotions if they went against her logical understanding of things. And honestly, she wasn't sure she wanted to be in a serious relationship with him, or if he was safe to have a relationship with.

Life can be a sad, ironic ride. Yvonne wanted to be with Noah so much during medical school, but he wasn't interested. And now the roles were reversed. He wanted to be with her, or at least she was pretty sure that's what he wanted. Now she didn't know what she wanted. She assumed they would continue having sex and she knew they would be friends, but beyond that she just didn't know.

Yvonne really tried to resist her feelings. She would only see Noah about once a week, and they weren't always intimate. She told him that she wasn't sure what she wanted. Beyond friendship and occasional sex, she didn't know if she imagined anything long term. She told him she was still dealing with residual feelings related to her divorce. Her second statement was a lie. It was one of those lies that she thought was justified to protect his feelings. The truth was that she was protecting herself, not him. Deep down, she wondered if Noah was capable of sustaining an intimate relationship. He would have to be emotionally separate from Belle for that. She wasn't so sure that was possible.

Belle must have sensed a closeness growing between Yvonne and Noah because she began to criticize Yvonne whenever she saw her. One night during dinner, Belle interrupted the meal in a shocking manner.

In her saccharine tone, she asked, "Dear, you might think about having that bump on your nose removed. My friend and I were just discussing it. You would be such an attractive woman if you had a different nose." She put her hand on Noah's head and rubbed his hair.

Yvonne was speechless. She had no idea how to respond to such an obnoxious statement. She looked at Belle and then Noah and then back. She had hoped Noah would say something to his mother about the inappropriateness of her comment, but he just shifted in his chair. As uncomfortable as the silence was, it was apparent he would feel more uncomfortable challenging his mother.

In her best attempt at a restrained retort, Yvonne said, "Thank you, Belle, but I like my nose just the way it is."

There was a moment of silence; Belle looked through Yvonne as if she didn't hear what she said, continued to rub Noah's hair, then changed the subject.

Another time she mentioned that Yvonne needed to lose a few pounds, offering her trainer for a few sessions. Yvonne was short, but quite thin, a size-four thin. Belle reached over and rubbed her hand over Yvonne's stomach. "Just a few, dear... Not much, just a few. You know you're thirty-nine, almost forty. You're not getting any younger."

Yvonne removed Belle's hand from her body. "I like myself just fine, Belle," she said firmly, the side of her lip curling.

"Mother, please!" Finally, Yvonne thought. A word from Noah.

Belle patted her hand on Noah's leg. "Mother is just trying to help, dear. If she ever intends to find a new man, she needs to keep her figure."

"She's fine, Mother."

"OK dear. OK." She rubbed his leg up and down and changed the subject.

Yvonne suspected that Noah had a compulsive need to wash himself as a result of his mother's behavior. He would wash himself obsessively after he would see or talk to her. Yvonne didn't blame him. She often felt like she had to wash off Belle, too.

They had been sleeping together sporadically for the four months since Yvonne's birthday dinner. That day in her office, right before he left, Noah asked Yvonne to marry him. He said it in a joking manner, but Yvonne thought he was using humor to conceal the vulnerability his true desire elicited. He had mentioned a few times that he wanted to marry Yvonne, but this time it wasn't just the statement, "I want to marry you." It was *the* question: "Will you marry me?" And he seemed to be waiting for a response.

Yvonne smiled at him; she felt close to him, but something made her deflect. "Come on, Noah," she chuckled, trying to keep the same joking tone as him, but she felt flushed. She tossed one of the small pillows from her couch toward him.

He stood tall, his dark brown eyes penetrating.

She faced him, staring back into his eyes.

There was such intensity between them. It was then that Yvonne realized the seriousness of the question. She put her hands to her cheeks and could feel the heat emanating from them.

She moved toward him, resting her body against his, and gave him a long hug. When she gently pulled apart from him, she said, "I'm sorry, Noah, but I have a session at 4:00. You have to go."

He nodded, then kissed her. He stood looking into her eyes again. His gaze was severe and penetrating.

Yvonne could see his longing. He almost looked desperate for her. As he turned to leave, Yvonne kissed him one more time and said, "See you soon."

He responded in kind. "See you soon."

Yvonne watched him until he walked through the waiting room and out the door. She heard the sound of his feet going down the stairs as he left.

Yvonne didn't know what to think when he left. Her face was so hot. She went in the bathroom and threw water on it. She loathed how easy she was to read. Whenever she got uncomfortable, her face would redden. She knew Noah noticed. He always liked to tease her about it.

She pushed her thoughts aside. It was a technique she had become very good at. It was something most therapists learn to master — the ability to push aside your own personal issues to attend to your patient's needs. Of course, Yvonne could never have imagined the interweaving of lives that was going on or how circumstances might compromise her objectivity.

Life is unpredictable. And sometimes situations can be so unbelievable that they can make even the most stable person unravel. The first of these events started during her next session when Hailey arrived without Dean and told Yvonne she was pregnant.

CHAPTER 11

Just as Yvonne was trying to figure out what she wanted from her relationship with Noah, Kadee was living in a constant state of anxiety. During the few weeks following the drink-throwing incident, Noah seemed more attentive toward Kadee. Unfortunately, Kadee couldn't rid herself of the feeling that Noah wasn't being totally honest. She had the sense that he could break it off at any moment, but she still couldn't figure out if it was her intuition sounding an alarm or if it was her insecurities playing tricks on her mind. It was an awful feeling; one that was foreign to Kadee. She had always been able to trust her intuition. This was no longer the case.

Vanessa had tried to remind Kadee of who she was before Noah. Kadee heard everything she said. She really did. A few times she had planned to break it off, only to change her mind once she was with him. *What is it about him?* She would ask herself over and over as her mind flip-flopped back and forth between wanting to stay and knowing she should leave. *He's just a guy and probably not even a good one.*

But for the most part when they were together, he made her feel so loved and listened to. Then when he would act distant and indifferent, it confused her, like she was always waiting, knowing that the warm, sensitive Noah would reemerge if she was patient. She knew that was not a healthy pattern, but it did not matter. Noah was a master at pulling Kadee back to him as soon as he felt she might leave.

In the meantime they were having constant sex. A few times between his patient appointments, Noah stopped by Kadee's for sex. He came over, they quickly had intercourse, and he left immediately. Kadee didn't like that at all, but she couldn't say no.

Her resentment was building.

One afternoon, Kadee reached a breaking point. It was a late summer Sunday mid-afternoon. They were relaxing in Noah's bed just after sex. Noah's phone started ringing. He reached over to the nightstand, looked at the number, and said he had to take the call. He went in the other room and closed the bedroom door. Kadee tiptoed to the door, put her ear in the crack, and tried to listen. *I feel like a crazy person,* she thought. *Maybe I am.*

She sort of assumed it was his mother, but it wasn't her usual time to call, so Kadee wasn't quite sure what conclusion to jump to. She couldn't hear everything, but she was pretty sure he made plans for dinner. A dinner Kadee was certain she would be excluded from again. After nearly a year of dating, another opportunity to meet his friends or family would pass.

In a matter of just a few moments, Kadee went from that post-sex natural high to feeling disgusted with herself for playing the role of a mistress. How could it be possible to feel like some mistress hidden away behind closed doors when she was the girlfriend of someone who assured her they were exclusive. *That is what Noah had said, wasn't it?* Kadee thought. She dug back into her memory. No, Noah had not said the actual words "we're exclusive," but he agreed to it when she asked. Or did he? Kadee was so turned around, she could not be sure of herself anymore. She went in her bag and took half a Valium. She was only supposed to use them for sleeping, but they were the only thing that relieved her growing distress. She was taking them more and more frequently.

When he came back into the bedroom, he was distant.

Kadee asked who was on the phone.

He looked away as he answered, "My mother."

Kadee's doubt was confirmed, so she pressed him. "But it wasn't your mother's time to call. That's very unlike her."

"I said it was my mother, Kadee. Jeez." He threw his arms up in the air. "Let up already. You're being too needy. Wa-a-ay too needy. I hate when you start this shit."

Kadee glared at him. Her rage simmered silently beneath. There were no words for a few moments as Noah sifted through random papers on his desk. He finally faced Kadee. "I have to go out for a minute. My mother needs my help with something."

"I'll come with you."

"No, no…wait here… if you want. I won't be gone long."

She decided to wait. Noah had never left her alone in his apartment before.

Kadee had never violated someone's privacy. In fact, she had condemned Hailey numerous times for going through her various lovers' things. But she felt disconnected from her own will.

Her emotions driving her, she was mixed with a toxic combination of rage and desperation. She had no control.

As she began opening his desk drawers and going through his belongings, she was mumbling to herself aloud. "If he would just talk to me, I wouldn't have to go through his things. Right? Right. I have to do this because he doesn't tell me what's going on. He says one thing but then he acts opposite that. He says he loves me, but then excludes me from all aspects of his personal life. Only people who are hiding something do that. Right? Right."

She wasn't even being careful to keep things in their place, to cover up what she was doing. She just didn't care anymore. "I don't give a rat's ass what he thinks about this…not one rat's ass…not one FUCKING rat's FUCKING ass." She was tossing the papers on the floor after she looked at them.

Her desk search wasn't resulting in anything of much interest. He had a lot of handwritten scribbled notes about various medical-related topics. She didn't know if it was not finding any evidence that he had a secret life or the Valium kicking in, but she started to feel a little calmer.

Calmer, that is, until she spied the plastic container under the desk. It was shoved all the way back against the wall. She never would have noticed it if she hadn't been crawling under there like a crazy woman. "Well, who's crazy now? Huh?"

It had been a few weeks earlier when Dr. Tracy prescribed Valium. Kadee was having such a hard time sleeping. The Valium was helping, but she also began taking it to relax during the day. She knew it was the easy way out, a temporary fix for her larger Noah problem, but for the time being she was using it to get through the difficult times.

Sharing her feelings with Dr. Tracy was uncomfortable, particularly her aggressive fantasies. Dr. Tracy assured her that fantasies were a type of defense mechanism and that having them did not mean Kadee was going to do anything. She said they were a way Kadee was managing her growing rage. Kadee wasn't so sure. She knew all about defense mechanisms, but the fantasies felt so real, and the thoughts were persistent and intrusive. Kadee feared one day she might just lose control and hurt him.

Sometimes, Kadee wondered if Dr. Tracy truly understood her level of distress. She always seemed so calm. Kadee imagined that she would never be the type of person to lose control. She made sure to stress that this relationship was causing her to react in ways that she never would have imagined possible. She told her about the thrown drink, sitting in front of Noah's apartment, the key under his mat, the knife and Betty Broderick holding it.

Dr. Tracy never told Kadee directly to end the relationship, but the direction of her questions suggested that she thought she should.

Every week when Kadee went into session with Noah still in her life, she felt like a therapeutic failure. She believed that Dr. Tracy thought she was weak-willed and one day might just end the treatment saying she was beyond help. Of course on some level, Kadee knew this was a ridiculous scenario. But fearing abandonment from Noah now extended to Dr. Tracy. In fact, the abandonment fears became so terrifying, they began to permeate all aspects of her life.

The experience of terror was hard for Kadee to explain when Dr. Tracy probed for more information. It was such an intense feeling, the type of emotion that is felt at the very core of the self. Kadee believed that if Noah left her, she would fragment into pieces. She would crack apart, her body crumbling to bits, as the chunks of her broken self hit the ground, disintegrating, until she no longer existed. Holding on was the only way Kadee would stay alive. She would die without him. She really felt that. Rationally, she understood that this could not be true, but emotionally, nothing ever felt so certain.

Dr. Tracy made an interpretation. She said that perhaps that is what Kadee's mother felt while she lay crying on the bathroom floor following her father's indiscretion. Kadee, having absorbed her mother's emotions, now experienced them as her own. Kadee thought the theory made sense, but it didn't help her. Her fear of losing him endured, as well as her rage and the fantasies of acting on them. Sometimes she felt that the only way that she would ever be free of him, her feelings, the relationship, was if he was dead. It was a scary thought, but one that felt true.

As her fears evolved, Kadee began anticipating being left by even those she trusted. If she called Vanessa and Vanessa didn't call right back, she became anxious, thinking Vanessa was mad or otherwise didn't want to talk to her. She even had this disturbing thought when it came to her own mother. She felt terror, that type of abandonment terror that makes people do outrageous acts in an attempt to preserve a relationship.

One session, Kadee blurted out in desperation, "Help me... please...please...help me...I don't know how much longer I can go on like this."

Dr. Tracy seemed unruffled and in her calm tone said, "I will, Kadee. I will."

"You don't think I'm beyond help?" She wiped away the tears flowing from the corners of her eyes.

"No, no, of course not. But I am concerned about you. I won't tell you to leave him, but I am concerned that if you stay with Aaron you will continue to feel this way…and, well, and maybe even worse, Kadee."

"Why won't you tell me to leave? I want you to tell me to leave."

"It has to be your decision, Kadee. What do you think would happen if I told you to leave?"

"I don't know," she was biting her cuticles.

"Do you think it would help you leave?"

"I don't know. Probably not," she looked down, studying her finger bleeding from the cuticle. "But, I want to leave. I want to want to leave…You know…I… umm…want help leaving…well, part of me does anyway. Maybe I want you to help the other part to want to leave, too. You know…so I can… leave him."

"Yes. I do know. I really do."

She was still looking down. Looking into Dr. Tracy's eyes was too much to bear. "Sometimes I try to pretend he's dead. You know, to help me move on. If he was dead, I'd have to move on. I'd have no choice. But then he calls and invites me over. It's very hard when he calls…so hard. I really wish he would stop calling."

"Well, it may be that Aaron is also having trouble letting go. He may never stop calling. I wonder if there is a way we can look at this, so that you might not take his calls, at least for a while."

"Yeah, maybe. I wish…" she raised her voice and slowly looked up. "I wish he would fucking tell me the truth or leave me alone!"

"I understand. You feel trapped."

Kadee cupped her face in her hands. She was crying as she bobbed her head up and down in agreement. "Yes," she whispered.

Over the last couple of weeks, Kadee could see how hard Dr. Tracy was working with her. She felt a growing trust in their relationships, which is probably why the fear Dr. Tracy would terminate therapy was also growing. But something else bothered Kadee. She had lied to Dr. Tracy. It wasn't a direct lie. It was more of a twisting of the truth, a concealing of the truth.

When Kadee entered Dr. Tracy's office the day of her first session, she looked at the wall with her degrees. This is something she always did whenever she met with a new doctor. When she looked at Dr. Tracy's degrees and saw that she graduated from Columbia University a year after Noah, she thought she probably knew him.

Kadee's older brother Jake had gone to medical school for a year before dropping out to pursue his Ph.D. in biology. He had talked about the small classes in medical school and how everyone knew each other. So when Kadee saw Yvonne Tracy's degrees, she felt pretty certain that she must have known Noah. She was so ashamed. She didn't want the doctor to have a face for the name; if Dr. Tracy personally knew who she was in this toxic relationship with, it was going to make being open about the depth of her distress even harder. With Noah's name being uncommon, she decided, rather impulsively, to give him a pseudonym — Aaron— during that first session. In retrospect, she hated that she did that, but it just fell out of her mouth before she could stop it, and then she committed to it. Besides, she sort of assumed that she wouldn't stay with Dr. Tracy because of the possible familiarity between Noah and her. But then Kadee felt so soothed by her presence, she decided to stay; so did Noah's alias.

As she grew closer to and felt more comfortable with Dr. Tracy and her rage toward Noah continued to seethe, she found herself wanted to tell Dr. Tracy the truth about Noah's identity. Noah never mentioned an Yvonne before, so she assumed they weren't close friends. It wasn't like she wanted to "tell" on Noah, purposefully disclosing his identity with ill intent. It was more about wanting to share full disclosure with Dr. Tracy; having finally developed a closeness and trust with Dr. Tracy, she wasn't concerned about his anonymity anymore.

She planned to tell her in the next session. It wasn't a big deal, she told herself. Dr. Tracy would understand why she changed Noah's name. She wouldn't see it as malevolent. It would deepen their relationship. But after Kadee found the container under Noah's desk, things began to escalate. Kadee spiraled deeper into obsession, making the discussion about Noah's pseudonym seem insignificant.

Kadee reached her arm all the way under the desk and pulled the plastic container out. It was slightly smaller than the drawer of a filing cabinet. The contents juggled around as she retrieved it. She opened her legs in a half straddle, placed the container between them and popped off the lid.

The first thing she pulled out was a framed picture of Noah's mother. *No big deal,* she thought. She placed it off to the side. She continued. There were a few more framed pictures, two of his mother, one of his mother and him and then one that she assumed was Noah's father and mother on their wedding day. She inspected the pictures, rubbing her fingers across the front. "Interesting," she whispered aloud.

She placed them to the side and reached her hand in again. There was another picture of his mother, laminated with no frame. And in red letters on the lower part, it read, *"Love Mother."* Kadee's stomach dropped. There was big black X across her face. She stared at it. The moment felt dreamlike, almost like it wasn't real. It was the type of thing she never would have believed if she hadn't seen it herself. She pressed her eyes closed hard, then looked again. Noah's mother was smiling through the black marker.

Kadee rubbed her hands along her arms. She had chills. She debated throwing the pictures back in the container and shoving it into its rightful hiding place under the desk, pretending she never saw it, ignoring the disturbance she was just exposed to. But she couldn't stop. Her mind was racing. She had so many thoughts simultaneously, it felt like her mind was on fast forward, and the content was jumbled. All she knew was that there was more in the container and she felt compelled to look.

There were three pairs of women's underwear. One pair, a black lacy thong, she recognized as belonging to her, then two others that were unfamiliar. Her stomach felt like she had eaten a pound of spoiled meat. She was so tired of her stomach doing those nauseating loop-the-loops. Feeling frenzied, she dumped the remaining contents on the ground. There were a bunch of memory sticks. She picked one up and examined it.

She looked at her phone. Noah had been gone close to an hour. He could be home any minute. She didn't care. She jumped up, pulled her laptop out of her bookbag and booted it up. She popped the first memory stick in. She was perspiring; she wiped under both of her arms with her hand. Her foot was shaking with impatience as she waited. As the image came onto the screen, she saw Noah's bed. In less than a minute, she saw Noah and some blonde woman kissing as he was taking her shirt off.

She watched as Noah and the blonde woman continued. Eventually they were both naked on top of his bed having sex. Kadee could see everything. Their naked bodies, Noah entering her, them thrusting, she saw everything. "What the fuck?"she asked herself. It was hard to process what she was seeing.

This time the loop-the-loop invited the contents of her stomach up into her throat. She tried to swallow it down, but it wouldn't go. She went in the bathroom and threw up. She felt dizzy. She knocked into the wall as she walked back into the bedroom to continue. Her eyes were watering from vomiting. She had that horrible sour post-vomit taste in her mouth, but she didn't care. She took another half a Valium. She sat back down and popped another memory stick in.

She was so disturbed; she knew she shouldn't watch more, that it was only going to further upset her. But Kadee's curious nature would not let it go. Her need to know overcame her rational mind, superseding even her need for self-protection. Part of her was totally disgusted, but there was also a part of her that became suddenly empowered, like this confirmation of his disloyalty justified her right to keep looking. For a moment she reminded herself that she was a researcher and that this could be considered research. "If he's not going to tell me, then I have no other choice but to keep looking."

The second memory stick had a similar story. It was Noah on his bed with a woman. This time the woman had long curly blonde hair and huge breasts. Kadee watched with disgust as the two undressed each other and lay naked on his bed kissing until finally they were having intercourse. Kadee was seething. She wanted to cry, but the tears wouldn't come. She felt disconnected. She continued.

As the next video started, Kadee saw herself dancing a strip-tease in Noah's room as he lay on the bed watching. She watched in disbelief as she saw herself on the computer screen. She knew it was her. She had on the purple bra and underwear set that Noah had bought her. She knew it was her, but the image felt foreign, like she didn't know the person on the screen. He had filmed her without her permission. She felt a ball of tears forming in her throat, she swallowed it. She felt strangled. She had believed he wasn't being totally honest with her, but she never expected anything so sick and disgusting.

As their sexual life played out on her computer screen, she leaned over to her bag, grabbed a cigarette and lit up. Noah hated cigarettes. He would kill her for smoking in his apartment, but she didn't care. She took the smoke in deep, then slowly exhaled, using smoking to calm herself. It helped a little at first. She got up, cracked the window and then sat back down. She was puffing away as she watched herself with Noah until the clip was finished. For a moment, she imagined that she was just watching some porn movie with a woman who had actually consented and was employed as an actor for the film.

She took the stick out, stood up, and threw it in her bag. It felt like steam was releasing in large puffs from her nose and ears. She was seething and planning to confront him. The cigarette was hanging out of her mouth, while she grabbed the recording of Noah and the large-breasted blonde woman and smashed the stick on his desk. Ashes were falling onto the wood floor, but she barely noticed. The stick wasn't breaking. She kept banging it, and banging it, over and over; she couldn't stop. When it still wasn't mangled to her satisfaction, she threw her cigarette out the window, took the heel of her shoe and pounded it on the floor until finally the memory stick shattered into pieces.

She burst out in tears. "That's it!" she was yelling aloud through her tears, some were flying into the air. "That's so it! I am done with him. What kind of sick twisted bastard does something like this? He's like a freaking serial killer, collecting women and keeping trophies. What a freaking sick twisted freaking bastard!"

She was still sitting on the floor with the laptop and memory sticks when Noah came into the bedroom. Kadee was so agitated, she hadn't heard him come in. When he came up behind her and she heard his voice, she jumped up, startled.

"What the fuck is this shit, Noah?" she was holding up a memory stick and screaming right in his face.

He looked confused. His eyes skimmed the entire room, taking in the mess on the floor and on his desk. He looked at the container, then at Kadee, then back. He backed away from her.

His neck was so far back it almost looked like it wasn't attached to his body.

"You tell me! What the fuck is this shit? You went through my things!" his voice was raised, but he seemed in control; his body tight. "And what is this?" he pointed to the container and the memory sticks.

"It's your stuff! Why don't you tell me what *this* is?" she picked up another memory stick and held it up to his face.

"I have no idea what *that* is, Kadee!"

"You're such a fucking liar. I watched a few. What are they? Trophies of your conquests? And what about these?" she held up one of the unfamiliar pair of panties.

He looked confused — angry, but confused, too. "They're your underwear! What are you talking about? You're the one who trashed my desk, invaded my space. This is nuts. *You* are nuts."

"And you're a liar. Tell me the truth. Tell me the fucking truth already. You owe me that much for my porn movie."

"What the hell are you talking about? A porn movie?"

"See, you're such a fucking liar! You know exactly what I'm talking about," she held up the memory stick again, glared at him and threw it against his head.

"OK, that's it, Kadee. I think you should leave. I want you to leave."

Kadee's shoulders dropped, seeming defeated. "You're throwing me out?"

"I'm asking you to leave."

Her eyes welled up. "Right. You're throwing me out."

"No, I'm asking you to leave."

"Same thing."

"Call it whatever you want, Kadee, but I want you to go."

"So you're breaking up with me?"

"I didn't say that. I don't know. I just want you to leave. Right now. We can talk about this later or tomorrow."

She didn't believe him. "You're breaking up with me. Just say it."

"We can talk later."

"Just say it!" she yelled, tears streaming down her face.

"Fine," he crossed his arms across his chest.

"Fine, what? Say it!"

"Fine. I'm breaking up with you!"

She picked up all of the contents in the container, the memory sticks, the panties and even the pictures, threw them in her bag, then grabbed a book from his desk and threw it at him. She sobbed as she gathered her belongings. *That's it. Finally. We're done. It's finally ended.* He walked her to the door and opened it. They stared into each other's eyes for a moment. When she turned to leave, he said, "I'll see you."

"God, I hope not." She ambled half-dazed out the door, through the narrow hallway, and out of his sight. That was the last time Kadee would remember ever being inside Noah's apartment.

Chapter 12

It was official; Hailey was pregnant. After missing her period for a second month, she took a home pregnancy test. The first one indicated that she was indeed pregnant. She couldn't believe her misfortune. She took another one; same results. She scheduled a confidential appointment with her doctor. Of course, she had to hide this information from Dean. The result of that appointment was that Hailey was four weeks pregnant.

She had been taking the pill behind Dean's back for years, but after he found out about the affair, he looked through her things and found the pills. She had promised to change, to be faithful. As a gesture of her fidelity, Hailey stopped the pill. But she didn't stop having sex with other men. She almost always used condoms, almost always. But sometimes swept away in the heat of the moment, she didn't. And thus she found herself in her current situation.

She knew the baby wasn't Dean's; he couldn't have children. It was Richard's, her latest side dish. They had been careless and had unprotected sex one night. It must have happened then. She wondered if it even mattered, she was going to have to have an abortion. But that side of Hailey that was never satisfied with what she had, always wanting more, had her contemplating what she might get out of having the baby.

Richard was a celebrity, an actor on a television series and a rising star. Images of herself dressed impeccably in an Oscar de la Renta gown, her photos being taken on the red carpet as she made a witty comment on camera, flashed through her mind. She smiled at the thought. That would be a dream come true for Hailey. She had wanted to be an actor as a child, but never felt thin enough or pretty enough. She had performed in a few school plays, but never pursued her dream. She really wasn't interested in the art of acting. Hailey wanted the fame, to be known and loved by everyone. Community Theater or even larger theater venues wouldn't get her that. She had visions of being a famous movie star.

Having Richard's child just might be her ticket into that world, but there were two major hurdles: Dean and Richard's wife. Richard had made it clear from the outset that there was no way he would ever leave his wife. He liked Hailey and enjoyed their clandestine meetings, but it would never be more. He also stressed the importance of discretion. He was a celebrity, after all, and he did not want, under any circumstances anyone to know. He had a lot to lose if there was any public exposure.

Hailey had assured Richard that she understood and that she also had too much to lose. That was only a partial truth. Hailey did enjoy the idea of seducing Richard away from his wife. He was a handsome, wealthy, powerful man. If she could steal him, maybe she would finally feel fulfilled. Of course, that wasn't possible; no man could ever fill the deep void that sucked at the core of Hailey's being. It was a vortex that took all that she had and made it seem like nothing, leaving her always feeling empty and always wanting more.

Hailey worked part time as a buyer for Calvin Klein. She had met Richard one afternoon while consulting at their downtown retail store. When he came in, she recognized him immediately. He was more handsome in person than on television. He had such presence. Standing tall at more than six feet, with dark hair and crisp blue eyes, and just a little scruff of facial hair, he struck a formidable pose. In her artfully demure demeanor, she went over, introduced herself and offered her assistance.

For someone who thought so little of herself, Hailey was able to finesse men with such assurance. She seemed confident, but subtle at the same time. She knew just how to talk to them, always asking just the right questions, nodding, giggling, and smiling as she looked at them with her big pleading eyes and perfect teeth. Soon Richard was engaged in a conversation with Hailey. They spoke for more than an hour; by the time he left, he was asking for her phone number. Hailey was ecstatic.

They met the following week at his apartment in the West Village. He often stayed there during the week while he was busy on set. His wife and son remained at their large house in suburban New Jersey. It was the perfect setup. They had been seeing each other for close to four months. Sometimes they saw each other as much as once or twice a week. She liked Richard, but more importantly he liked and wanted her. She really needed that validation. He always told her how beautiful she was. For someone surrounded by gorgeous female celebrities, this meant everything to Hailey.

She didn't intend to get pregnant, although now that she was, she did think about having his baby. They were usually careful; as Richard always was clear that he never intended to leave his family. It happened one night after they had been drinking. They were just about to have sex when they both realized neither one had a condom. But they couldn't stop. Richard tried to pull out before he came and Hailey took the morning after pill. Unfortunately, neither worked.

Hailey wasn't sure if she should tell Richard or not. Although she wanted his wife's life, she also wasn't sure she could leave Dean. They had met in college, and in the best way she could, Hailey did love him. She wasn't capable of that deep bonding love that really holds people together through a marriage. But Dean treated her like a goddess. He built her up, and for that she loved him; she needed him.

It was another one of those sad ironies where it was only through Dean loving her so much that she was even able to exude confidence. She needed him in order to carry on these liaisons with other men. Before Dean, she almost never dated. It was him loving her that precipitated her other relations. Dean did not excite Hailey, though, and this was a problem for her. She didn't recognize the comfort of a loving stable relationship as love. She went outside of the relationship to try and find what she already had.

As soon as Hailey entered Dr. Tracy's office, she started crying. It was unusual for her to show emotion; she really had a hard time being vulnerable. But after Richard insisted that she have an abortion, he then broke it off. Hailey was devastated. Rejection is always hard, but for Hailey it was nearly shattering. It was as if Richard pulled out the IV for her self-esteem, leaving her without nutrients. Thankfully she had Dean for emotional sustenance; without him, who knows what she might do.

Dr. Tracy knew about the affair Hailey was having prior to Richard. Dean and she were working with Dr. Tracy to rebuild the trust in their marriage. But like Dean, Dr. Tracy had no idea that Hailey was with someone new. Hailey was feeling really bad. She was too ashamed to talk to Kadee or Vanessa about what happened, so she decided to see Dr. Tracy alone. During that first session, she disclosed the whole Richard story, then asked Dr. Tracy what she should do.

Hailey left the session frustrated. Dr. Tracy would not dish out advice and instead suggested that she come in for more individual sessions. Deep down, Hailey knew she would probably benefit from talking through some of the things on her mind, but hearing it aloud from a mental health professional made her feel like there was something wrong with her. She did not like that feeling. But she did agree to come in for another individual session.

When she left Dr. Tracy's office, she indulged in another one of her shameful secrets. She went on a food binge. Hailey kept tight control over her eating, trying to maintain a perfect figure. She ate very small meals, rarely snacked and exercised constantly. Sometimes when she was feeling particularly distressed, she consumed large amounts of food quickly. It was another way she tried to fill her inner void. Maybe if she ate enough, she would finally feel filled up. Of course, this only made her feel worse. Following these food benders, she would go home, lock the bathroom door, lie near the toilet, and make herself throw up over and over until she rid herself of everything in her body. The problem was that she could never rid herself of all her ugly, polluted feelings.

It had been months since she engaged in this behavior, but feeling discarded by Richard left her feeling so empty, she could not resist the urge. She did it again the next day. She went to the grocery store and bought donuts, sugary cereal, cookies, cinnamon bread and an apple pie — all foods she normally didn't allow herself to eat.

She went home and within a half hour ate everything she bought. And following her modus operandi, she hid herself in the bathroom, stuck her finger down her throat, and threw up over and over. She curled up on the floor in the bathroom for about fifteen minutes, then she got up, washed her face, brushed her teeth, and went to the gym for two hours. She arrived home in time to shower, change and prepare dinner. When Dean walked in the door, she put on her charms as if nothing happened.

She spent the next few weeks working with Dr. Tracy on her feelings about aborting her baby. There was a part of her that still thought Richard would come to his senses and want her to have his baby. But what would she do if he actually did want her to have it? She was good at secrets, but you can't hide a pregnancy, birth and baby from your husband. She was in Dr. Tracy's office, sounding almost deluded as she went through the scenario of how she would leave Dean. She created a fantasy, which she almost believed, where Richard left his wife to be with her. She could not bear the thought that he didn't want her.

When he didn't call her or respond to the few text messages she had sent him, she had no choice but to acknowledge that it was over. So she made up a truth. She decided that he didn't want to risk his reputation. It wasn't that he was committed to his wife, or that he loved her more; it was a practical career-based decision. Hailey had convinced herself of that; she needed to believe that was the truth. It was that sort of lie that feels so real that it becomes the truth. Hailey was so relieved by her own self-deception, she was finally able to make an appointment for an abortion. And not a moment too soon, as time was quickly ticking away on her first trimester.

She finally told Kadee about the pregnancy. She didn't want to go for the abortion alone; she planned on asking Kadee to go with her. She hadn't been talking to Kadee as often as usual partially because she didn't want to admit what happened. She felt weak. She didn't want Kadee to see all of her inadequacies. She was also so sick of hearing about Noah Donovan. Every time she talked to Kadee, she would go on and on about the problems she was having with Noah Donovan. Hailey couldn't take it anymore.

Just a few days earlier, the two had a tiff when Hailey became irritated enough to lose control. "Kadee, Kadee, Kadee...I'm so sick of hearing about Noah. You need to get a hold of yourself. You sound certifiably insane. Let it go already! It's over."

It was Kadee's vulnerability that Hailey couldn't take. So afraid of her own human weaknesses, Hailey couldn't listen to Kadee expose herself. Kadee's willingness to be so open about her feelings threatened to fracture the thin veneer that was holding Hailey together. Of course, Hailey didn't understand this about herself. All she knew was Kadee was driving her nuts with the Noah Donovan drama, and she was losing patience.

"Hailey, please don't yell at me. I can't take it. I'm at my breaking point. I feel like I'm losing it."

"I'm sorry, but you sound so weak. Pull it together. It's time to move on and be done with him."

Of course, Hailey didn't share how upset she was over Richard or how she had broken her own rules by reaching out to him after he ended it. She simply relayed the facts. She had been having an affair with a celebrity, she got pregnant and the relationship ended. She wanted Kadee to come with her when she had her abortion.

Kadee, not yet fully without her faculties, switched gears immediately after hearing Hailey's story. "I'm sorry, Hail. Are you doing OK?"

"I'm fine, really I am. He was just so in love with me. He loved me more than I loved him. But he was afraid if we had the baby, it would affect his career."

"You wanted to have the baby? What about Dean?"

"Well, no, not really, I don't know. Obviously we couldn't have the baby, so there wasn't much to think about. Listen, I don't really want to talk about it. I just want to know if you will come with me to have this thing removed. I just want to get it over with."

"Of course I'll go with you."

"Great. Thanks a mil. And listen, if that Noah Donovan won't leave you alone, if he's doing the "one foot in, one foot out" thing, you should stop returning his calls and never see him again." She chuckled. "And if all else fails, you could take that key from under his mat, break into his apartment and kill the bastard. That's what I would do," she snickered. Hailey was only half joking.

She thought about telling Kadee that Noah was in treatment with Dr. Tracy, but decided not to. The part of her that envied Kadee enjoyed knowing something that she didn't. It gave her a feeling of power. She figured she would probably tell her at some point, but not yet.

The next day while waiting for her session, she saw Noah Donovan as he was leaving Dr. Tracy's office. She thought about seducing him. Maybe she could get him to love her. She found the idea very satisfying. The idea that he didn't love Kadee but would love her was arousing. It certainly would fill the emptiness she felt following the whole Richard situation.

It never occurred to her that perhaps the problem was Noah, not Kadee. She believed that Noah couldn't take Kadee seriously. Kadee wasn't the type of girl he should marry because of her middle class background. It was another one of Hailey's made-up truths. Whether or not that was the reality didn't matter; for her, those were the facts. And with that thought, she leaned back in her chair, exposed more of her sculpted legs and batted her eyelashes as she said, "Noah Donovan? Noah Donovan, is that you?"

He looked at her, confused. He did not recognize her. "Yes?" He slowly walked toward her.

She stood up, moved closer to him, arching her back while smiling. She was batting her eyelashes ferociously. "It's Hailey... Hailey Beckham, oh, sorry, I mean Whitman, its Hailey Whitman from JFK High School."

It took him a moment as he studied her. His eyes widened as he nodded, "Right…right. I never would have recognized you. You look totally different. Fantastic. How are you? How have you been?"

She took a sugar-free lollipop out of her bag, opened it, and began sucking on it slowly, purposefully. She felt turned on. Seduction always turned Hailey on. Her nipples became hard; she hoped he noticed. "Oh, I have been great, fabulous, actually. How about you? You look great, too." She took a long slow suck, then began circling the lollipop with her tongue.

He noticed the show she was putting on for him, and he was in no mood. He backed away slightly, creating more space between them. Hailey did not like that, not at all. He was supposed be interested. She was supposed to be irresistible. She moved in a little closer, closing some of the space between them.

This time he backed up further, clearly uncomfortable, even Hailey could not deny this. His eyes shifted around as he said, "I'm doing great…just great. I've got to run, but it was nice bumping into you." He turned and disappeared out the door, leaving Hailey completely deflated and furious.

On another day, Hailey probably could have rationalized away Noah's abrupt dismissal of her invitation. But she already felt so small and insignificant as she stood in the waiting room alone, pregnant with Richard's baby. Every rejection she ever encountered coalesced in that moment. The room was spinning round and round, the walls closing in on her. She was overcome with a rage she had never felt before. She bit her lollipop, swallowing the two big pieces whole. "I could kill that man. If Kadee doesn't kill him, I just might."

The door to Dr. Tracy's office opened. She peered into the waiting room. "Hi, Hailey, are you ready?"

Hailey looked up, flipped her blonde locks off her shoulders and smiled back, "Yes, yes I am." She walked gracefully into Dr. Tracy's office, saying, "Hi, Dr. Tracy, how are you? It's a lovely day, isn't it?" It was as if the rejection that enraged her only moments ago never happened.

It was later that evening when Dean went back to the office for a teleconference with Japan that Hailey sat home alone stewing in the juices of her rage. She had scoffed down a whole pizza and a box of oatmeal raisin cookies. She had just gouged out a bite of a chocolate donut, preparing to continue her consumption until she finished the entire box, when it occurred to her to show up at Noah Donovan's apartment. The idea came to her and suddenly the emptiness that gnawed in the pit of her stomach was temporarily sated.

Of course, he wanted her. She probably just caught him off guard in the waiting room. He had just left his therapist's office after all. Naturally, he would be distracted. The notion that he would be involved with Kadee, and not be interested in her, had left her seething. She was riddled with contempt, and she thought she just might eat until she imploded from the inside. But once the idea that she was going over to his apartment entered her mind, and she realized she might have another chance to seduce him, she felt a sense of purpose and with that immediate relief from her emptiness.

She dashed to the bathroom and stuck her finger down her throat, inducing mass amounts of vomit. She had to get rid of that uncomfortable bloated feeling. She threw up repeatedly, getting up each time to look in the mirror, inspecting her lower abdomen waiting for it to flatten out from her food elimination process. It would not fully flatten out, but she *was* pregnant. She sucked her stomach in and reminded herself to keep holding it that way.

She washed her face, brushed her teeth, then spent close to an hour getting dressed, applying makeup, and fixing her hair. She was wearing a push-up bra with a fitted low-cut shirt. If she had one thing that Kadee didn't, it was her perfectly rounded C-cup breasts. The men always commented on how much they enjoyed them. She knew Noah Donovan wouldn't be able to resist once he got a look at her A+ cleavage.

For a moment, she wondered what she would say once she got to his place. But she decided that he would be delighted to see her. She would bring a nice bottle of red wine. Kadee had mentioned that he liked Cabernet. She decided to bring an expensive bottle, one Dean and she had purchased on their most recent trip to Napa Valley. Dean wasn't a big red wine drinker, so he wouldn't notice that it was gone. Hailey would show up on Noah's doorstep with the wine and say that it had been so nice to see him earlier in the day and that she just wanted to catch up with him, that she knew they lived in the same neighborhood, had mutual friends, etcetera, etcetera...

She told herself it would all be fine and that once she conquered Noah Donovan, she would feel much better about herself. Of course, this wasn't true, but she needed to believe that it was, so she betrayed herself with a lie.

Unfortunately, despite her newfound confidence, things did not go as planned. She arrived at Noah's, walked up the long flight of stairs to the front of his brownstone. She knew his apartment was on the first floor. His light was on, so she assumed he was home. She tried to peer in the window, but the blinds were almost closed, so she couldn't see in. She did hear muted voices, one was a man's, assumingly Noah, and the other a woman's voice. It didn't sound like Kadee, but she couldn't be sure.

She had the slightest flash of warmth, almost like she was about to perspire, as she took the key from under the mat, opened the front door and entered the hallway. It was an old building with thin walls, the hallway was long and narrow.

When she got to his apartment door, she heard moaning. She stood with her ear to the door. She could make out a woman panting cries of sexual pleasure. She knew she should leave. Clearly she would have to come back another time when he was alone. But was that Kadee making all that noise? She wondered. She could not be sure, and she wanted to know. She thought about waiting to see if it was, but she might have to wait all night for that. Kadee, or whoever he was with, was probably spending the night. If it was not Kadee, as awful as it was for her to admit to herself, she would be pleased. It was just difficult for her to believe that Noah wanted someone like Kadee while he might have rejected her.

Then she reminded herself that he hadn't *really* been disinterested in her. No, it definitely was not *that*. He had been distracted because of the context under which they met. She caught him off guard, that's all. And with that, she turned, walked out, placed the key back under the mat and made up her mind that she would try again later in the week. As she began her short walk back home, she decided that it would be a good plan to go back on a day when she knew for sure that he wasn't with Kadee.

Chapter 13

Kadee was in Dr. Tracy's office early Monday morning crying. She would have thought that she had cried out every tear that she had by now, but there they were again running down her cheeks. She was trying to get the words out between sobs. She was upset about what she found in the container. Even more distressing was that she believed the relationship was over and that somehow the demise was her fault. Dr. Tracy was challenging those thoughts, but Kadee really felt responsible.

"Please tell me more, Kadee. I want to understand how this could be all your fault," she probed in her usual calm tone.

"Well...well...," she was trying to stop the tears so she could speak clearly. She blew her nose. "Well...I...umm...I was being too needy. He hates that. He told me he hated that over and over. And I...well...umm...you know...you know, I just couldn't stop." She blew her nose again. "I shouldn't have gone through his stuff. It's my fault that I found those things under his desk. I had no right to go through his things, you know. I never did anything like that before. I'm so ashamed. I'm just so ashamed." She cupped her face in her hands and sobbed quietly.

The tissue box was empty. Dr. Tracy handed Kadee a new box. "I understand, Kadee. This is a very difficult situation for you. I can see that, and I'm sorry."

Kadee nodded, "Thank you." She took a bunch of tissues out of the box and wiped her face. "It was a mistake to go through his things. I knew that while I was doing it, but I couldn't stop myself. I scared myself in a way."

"Feeling out of control is scary."

"If I hadn't been so needy, we would still be together. Maybe that was the whole problem. It was me, my fault. I was just too needy. He told me I was suffocating a few times. No one has ever said that to me before, you know. I was always so...you know, independent before him. It's like I don't even know myself any-more. That's the scariest part. I don't even remember how to be who I was. And it's getting worse."

"That's a terrible feeling, Kadee. I'd like to hear more. I'm not as sure as you that this is entirely your fault. Don't you think it's possible his behavior had something to do it?"

"You think so?" her eyes were wide as she sniffled.

Dr. Tracy tried as best she could to hide her disbelief. Was Kadee serious? Aaron's behavior is what drove Kadee to go snooping in the first place. "Yes, Kadee, I do."

"I was so out of it yesterday that I think I blacked out or something. It was weird. I don't know how to explain it."

"Please say more."

"I...umm...I umm...I'm not sure. I just know that there are parts of the nighttime that I don't remember. I called Vanessa and told her what happened. I know that because she called me this morning to see how I was. But I don't really remember talking to her. I sort of remember having a dream that I talked to her. It must have really happened, but I thought it was a dream. It totally freaked me out this morning. And then I…umm…oh, no…" she took a new tissue and cupped her face again.

Dr. Tracy leaned forward, seeming concerned. "What is it?"

"I had a dream that I called him last night, too. I called him a few times, but he wasn't there. He didn't answer, and I was panicked in the dream. I wanted to go back to his apartment. I thought of going back over there to talk, I think. I'm not sure. Then I walked over there in the dream, but I never made it to his place. It was like I didn't know how to get there. I was lost or something. I don't know. What if I…what if it was real?"

She reached in her bag, pulled out her phone, looked through her call history and burst out in tears again.

"What is it, Kadee?" Dr. Tracy leaned toward Kadee.

"I did call him. I called him five times last night. Oh, no. I'm scared. I really don't remember what happened."

What Kadee neglected to tell Dr. Tracy was that she drank a bottle and a half of wine and took at least four Valium when she got home from Noah's the previous afternoon. She was more agitated than she had ever been before. She didn't know how else to calm down. She started drinking, and once she was drunk and her judgment was impaired, she started popping the Valium. She only knew that she took so many because when she woke up in the morning, she noticed that there were some missing from the bottle. She remembered taking one, but after that she had absolutely no recollection.

At the end of session, Dr. Tracy recommended that Kadee attend a group for people recovering from toxic relationships. She gave her the psychologist's card and insisted that she call. She wanted her to supplement their sessions with this group. She felt Kadee was in crisis and needed the added support. Kadee agreed to call.

Kadee was too depressed and too hung over to go to her classes after session. She was angry with herself for missing classes, but she really didn't feel well. She went home, pealed her clothes off, put the air conditioning on, and got into bed. She was tossing and turning, ruminating over and over everything that had happened the day before.

She got up to take a Valium and remembered that she hadn't taken the contents of the container out of her bag. She planned to watch the rest of the memory stick videos, but she was going to wait for Vanessa. Vanessa agreed to watch them with her, to give her support. When she went to retrieve them from her bag, they were gone. She stuck both of her hands into the bottom of her bag and began shifting everything around looking for them. They weren't there.

She dumped the entire bag upside down; the contents now sprawled out on her living room floor. She went through every single thing that was there. There were no memory sticks. She looked around her apartment. She even went through her garbage thinking maybe while she was out of it, she had tossed them. They weren't there. They were nowhere.

She tried her hardest to think through the evening, to try and remember, but she couldn't recall anything having to do with the memory sticks. Not remembering was frightening. She got back in bed, pulled the comforter all the way over her body including her head, and assumed the fetal position. She felt the hard edge of one of the picture frames under her pillow. She lifted it up and there was Noah's mother with that big disturbing X across her face staring back at her. She threw the pillow off the bed and there they were, every single disturbing item she had discovered the day before. She got up, stuck them all in a manila envelope and shoved it in her filing cabinet so they would be out of her sight until she was emotionally ready to revisit what she had learned.

How could she ever have allowed herself to become attached to a man who would keep a collection of his conquests, a man who would put an X over his own mother's face? How could she have missed the truth about Noah Donovan? She flipped her pillow over and tried to sleep herself into oblivion.

Her phone rang. She must have been half asleep because she incorporated it into her dream. A phone was ringing and ringing in her dream. She was trying to answer, but couldn't. At first it was her cell ringing; the phone wouldn't pick up when she pressed the answer button. But then the dream images shifted. There was another phone ringing. It was an old land line that was attached to a wall in her kitchen. She went into the kitchen and over to the phone, but she couldn't pick it up. It was like the receiver was glued on or something.

She took a hammer from under the sink and smashed the phone. The pieces scattered across her floor. Mixed in with the pieces of phone on her floor were cut up pieces of paper. When she bent down to look closer, she saw they were cut up pieces of the picture of Noah and his mother.

She was trying to put the pieces back to together in her dream, but she couldn't figure out how they fit. It was like pieces were missing, leaving her unable to finish the task. Her buzzer was ringing. She was annoyed. She decided not to answer; she wanted to fit the pieces of the picture back together. Her buzzer rang again. This time waking her up as she realized her buzzer was really ringing. Someone was at her front door.

She got up, tip-toed over to the door and looked out the peep hole. It was Noah.

"Kadee, Kadee, I know you're there. Please open the door. We should talk." He seemed calm. His voice wasn't raised, but she still felt alarmed by his presence.

She hesitated, saying nothing, still staring at him through the tiny hole in the door.

"I know you're there. I can hear you. Please…please open up."

She didn't know what to do. Part of her wanted him, part of her hated him.

"Please, Deedee. I'm sorry."

She turned around, checking the floor where the smashed phone and pieces of the picture were in her dream. There was nothing there. She patted down her hair and wiped her face. She opened the door. He walked right in, agitated.

"Where did those pictures of mother come from? Where did you get them?"

"There're yours. I found them under your desk where you were hiding them along with the other things."

"There're not mine. Did you cross off mother's face? I need to know where you got them." He was pacing.

"I found them under your desk. Listen, I shouldn't have been under there. I shouldn't have gone through your things. It was wrong of me. But those videos—"

"There're not mine!" he raised his voice.

"Well, whose are they then? They were under your desk. They aren't mine." She raised her voice to match his.

"And you're right. You shouldn't have gone through my things."

"I apologize. I was out of line. I wish you would have just been honest with me. I didn't know what was going on with you, with us. It was driving me crazy. Did you know that? You're driving me crazy!"

"You're driving me crazy!"

He stopped pacing and stood facing her. They stared at each other for a moment. No words, uncomfortable stillness; the space between them was thick with conflict.

He grabbed her, pulled her close and began kissing her fiercely. They started kissing harder. The kissing was aggressive, lacking any tenderness, bordering on violent. He pushed her up against the wall, took the neck of her long T-shirt and ripped it down the middle, leaving her only in her panties. He grabbed the sides of the panties and tore hard until they ripped. The two pieces fell to the floor, and she was naked.

He stuck his finger all the way in her vagina and began massaging it.

She moved to unbutton his pants.

He took her hand and stopped her. "Not yet," he whispered. He pushed her down onto the couch and stood back. He was staring at her, his eyes piercing her naked body.

She wanted him. Despite all that he had done to her, despite knowing all the videos he had recorded in secret, despite all the lies he told, she still wanted him. She grabbed his hand to pull him down, but he didn't move.

He stood staring at her naked body, her exposed flesh, her vulnerable state.

She started to feel uncomfortable. She reached for the thin blanket that was hanging over the side of the couch.

He stopped her. He grabbed the blanket and threw it at the other end of the couch. Holding her arms up above her head with one hand, he removed his pants with the other. He positioned himself on top, entered her, and began thrusting up and down, quick, deep thrusts over and over until he pulled out and released all over her neck. He grabbed the blanket, wiped himself off, then dropped it on the floor. He pulled up his pants and fastened the button.

Kadee tried to pull him down, but he wouldn't budge. "I have to go."

"What? She was wiping her neck off with the remnants of her T-shirt, feeling as used as the ripped tee."

"Sorry. I have patients. I'll call you later."

"Wait, Noah, please...please." She reached for him again. She was tearing up.

"Don't be needy. I have to go." He shook her hand off his arm and walked toward the door.

Kadee was horrified. She pulled the soiled blanket over her body, walked up behind him and pushed him out the door, yelling, "You fucking bastard, don't call me later. Don't call me ever.

I fucking hate you. Do you hear me? I fucking hate you, you sick, twisted asshole."

She watched him as he walked through the hallway and down the stairs. She felt humiliated. She hated herself for allowing him to use her like that — and she hated him even more. But that part of her that was caught up in the awful dynamic of their love-hate relationship still wanted him and wanted him to want her. She slammed her door, took a Valium, then sat on her floor crying.

That night, Noah sent her a text message: *It was great to see you today. Sorry I had to rush off. I'll stop by with coffee in the morning.*

Kadee didn't remember reading the text message. She didn't even know he sent it until she saw the exchange early the next morning. She saw she had responded: *OK, bring me a croissant, too. See you then.* She didn't remember any of the exchange.

That week became increasingly blurry.

Chapter 14

Yvonne's phone was ringing. When she looked at the number, she saw it was Belle Donovan calling. It had been a long week with patients; she wasn't particularly in the mood to deal with Belle and her craziness, but she knew a conversation with her was inevitable. She picked up to get it over with, but Belle wasn't going to let her off the hook with just a quick conversation.

"Yvonne, dear, it's Belle Donovan. How are you, dear? Well, I'm sure." Belle was practically having the conversation with herself.

"Hi, Belle, I'm—"

"Are you free for dinner tomorrow night? If not, make yourself free, dear." Her tone was sweet — overly sweet — and laced with bitterness. "We should talk. Noah's mother wants to talk to you."

"Umm...Belle tomorrow night isn't—"

"I've already made a reservation, dear. I expect you to join me. If you have other plans, change them." Her intonation became harsh, exposing the real Belle Donovan momentarily. Yvonne knew then that there was no negotiating.

Before Yvonne could respond or even acknowledge what Belle said, she proceeded to give Yvonne the time and location. In her most sugary tone, she added, "And Yvonne, dear, it will be lovely to see you."

Yvonne didn't let Belle ruffle her. It took a lot to upset Yvonne, but the thought of their dinner was unsettling. She could not stand Belle's tone. She could feel her underlying hostility and it really antagonized her. Of course, on some level that's what Belle wanted. She wanted to provoke her. It was her way of trying to maintain the power in her relationships.

It was just the day before that Noah spoke frankly with his mother about Yvonne. He was going to marry her. The two were going shopping for engagement rings. They planned to tie the knot in a small intimate ceremony soon thereafter. Yvonne didn't want another big wedding, and Noah wanted to do whatever made her happy.

Belle, however, wanted Noah to do what made Belle happy, which was not to marry Yvonne. "She's not right for you, dear. She's not pretty enough, or young enough. Don't you want to give mother a grandchild? She's almost forty. You would have to have a baby right away. That is if she can even give you one, dear. You must listen to mother. A woman of her age probably doesn't have any good eggs left anyway."

It was just a few days after Noah had first proposed the marriage question to Yvonne in her office that he asked her again.

She didn't answer. A few days after that, he asked her again. This time she did answer. She answered with a yes.

Yvonne had her reservations. But after listening to a few of her patients struggling in bad relationships, hearing what was out there, she decided that Noah was a good man. She decided that she was being overly cautious and possibly depriving herself of something wonderful, something special. Noah loved her, even though she wasn't making it easy for him. She was going to let him love her, and she was going to open her heart again. She was going to love him back.

She had been vacillating back and forth after Noah had first asked her. Even though it wasn't a formal proposal — he didn't get down on one knee with a ring or anything like that —she believed that he meant it. Once he put it out there, once it existed in the space between them as a real possibility, she couldn't stop thinking about it — or him.

The sessions with Kadee had a great impact on her, too. Her account of her relationship with Aaron made Yvonne realize that she was being overly careful with Noah. Noah was good to her; he was stable and consistent. He would never do to her what Aaron was doing to Kadee. She could trust him. She did trust him. Of course, there was the whole Belle Donovan dilemma and Noah's investment in that relationship. But she felt they could work through it together. She really believed that.

Yvonne was not the type of woman to fall into something without thinking it through. When she put all the pieces together, being with Noah seemed like a good decision; a choice that would bring her happiness and contentment.

How could she have missed the truth? That question would soon be plaguing her. She was a trained mental health professional. She had seen a lot and heard a lot. How could she have possibly failed to see what was really happening? Sometimes the truth isn't obvious; sometimes it exists in the silence, in the emptiness between the spaces, but we're too afraid to hear it.

Yvonne knew about the importance of looking between the words for the truth. This is something she learned through her work: to notice nuances, to listen not just for what was said, but for the latent content under what was communicated. But she was also a trusting person; she neglected, perhaps to a fault, to anticipate duplicity from people in her personal life, unless it was blaringly obvious, as with Belle. She trusted Noah, and because of that it never occurred to her that he was being deceptive. That is until the truth revealed itself. Even then, she would have a hard time believing what she knew. Instead, it would leave her questioning her own reality.

Yvonne didn't have an idyllic childhood. When she was fourteen years old, her older brother, James, killed himself. He had struggled with depression all through his adolescence. Her father, a psychiatrist, sent him to all the best doctors in their affluent South Carolina community.

Just when he seemed to be doing better, Yvonne went into his room one night to tell him dinner was ready. She found him hanging from a ceiling beam in his room. She screamed in horror. It was one of those loud shrilling screams that arise from the pit of the stomach, a scream of absolute terror. Her parents came rushing upstairs, pulled him down. Her mother sat on top of him, screaming, panicked, trying to resuscitate him, over and over until the paramedics came and had to peal her off. He was already gone. He was only eighteen years old.

Yvonne's mother went into a depression following her brother's suicide. Yvonne tried to help her mother. She would go into her room and try to talk to her. She would try to get her to go out for a walk, but her mother just curled up in bed, staring at the wall for the good part of a year.

Yvonne was sent for therapy. The visual images of James hanging intruded upon her daily life, and there was no remittance. She was traumatized. She had moments where she actually felt like she was reliving the horror of the experience.

Yvonne's father held the family together during this time. He supported his wife through the tragedy and made sure she went to talk to someone. It was a very difficult time for her, for all of them, but they managed to get through it. Of course the scars never went away — and never would. It was not the type of thing anyone would ever totally recover from. But working together as a family and talking about their pain gave them some resiliency. Life would never be the same for them, ever, but they managed to hold each other together and continue living.

It was the honesty within her family that Yvonne remembered as being the most helpful. They never pretended everything was OK. There was no pretense. It was a life-shattering experience. The best they could do was to talk about it openly and support each other through it.

It was a tragedy that shaped Yvonne's life. As she worked through her trauma, trying to understand what happened to James, what he must have been feeling, how the depression ate him up, she became interested in helping others. It was a way she was able to give meaning to the worst experience she ever had. If she could go on to help others, then it would make some sense of her brother's death. It would give meaning to the experience. It would also keep her connected to him. When she entered college, she immediately chose pre-med as her major.

It was also part of what attracted her to Noah. He had also experienced a shattering loss when he was an adolescent. And he, too, was shaped by it. It wasn't easy to discuss what happened with her peers. The magnitude of that type of loss, especially at such a young age, was hard for friends to really understand.

It was different with Noah. Yvonne sensed that as soon as she told him. When she talked about James with Noah, she felt like he really knew how she felt. She didn't have to say much at all, he just knew. This made Yvonne feel close to him. It also built a trust that was premature and unwarranted. She felt like they knew each other, their awful losses connecting them, even though she didn't actually know him at all.

The night Noah proposed and the moment Yvonne said yes was another one of those life changing moments. One moment, one decision and suddenly her whole world was different. In this instance, Yvonne thought her world was altered for the better. Who wouldn't? She had said yes to spending her life with someone she loved and wholeheartedly believed loved her. It was one of those awful truths about life. While it was happening, it was one of the happiest moments of Yvonne's life. But when she would look back on it, it wasn't at all what it had seemed. It was a grave error, one that would shatter the illusion of her reality, making her doubt everything she believed.

After that night back in medical school when Noah was dismissive of her feelings for him, her mother told her that when it comes to love, timing is everything. Noah wasn't ready for someone or something so serious. Until he was ready for a committed relationship, there wasn't anything she could do. It was one of those totally unromantic, rational statements her mother would communicate to her. Loving someone wasn't about hearts and flowers swarming around nebulously; in part, love was a decision.

Yvonne was in the midst of deciding if she would commit herself to loving Noah. She felt love. She was contemplating if she would take it to that next step, where she would really open her heart to him, entrusting him as her new life partner. She had remained uncertain. That is until her session with Kadee.

When she was training to be a psychotherapist, she had learned ways to maintain objectivity. It wasn't just about neutrality, it was also about preserving a level of emotional independence from her patients' struggles. Without a certain amount of distance from their problems, she would be vulnerable to a constant state of fatigue. Their problems would become her problems, leaving her constantly exhausted and unable to live her own life freely.

It was something she had struggled with during her mother's depression. She felt the heaviness in her home, and it was hard for her to live the life of a teenager. She was very serious, and sometimes even depressed. Her therapy had helped her understand what she was feeling. It helped her separate her own feelings from those of her mother. Because of this experience, she understood the importance of emotional distance, really understood it. She also knew it was a clinical vulnerability for her. She was mindful of this.

It wasn't that she took Kadee's difficulties home with her. It was that she was greatly affected by her narrative. She had listened to many tales from other patients struggling in negative relationships. She heard story after story from people staying in situations that were bad for them and, for one reason or another, feeling they could not leave. But Kadee's story resonated.

Kadee was beautiful. She possessed the type of beauty that was impossible to ignore. The type of beauty that would stop people on the street, leaving them wondering who she was, making them think her life was somehow easy because she was endowed with such physical perfection. Of course, Yvonne already knew the world didn't work that way. No matter what one had, what one was gifted with, everyone had life struggles. She knew this. Yet, Kadee being in an obsessive relationship with a man who was so clearly unworthy, fascinated her. It helped remind her that the demise of her own marriage was not her fault. That no matter what a person had to offer in a relationship, sometimes the other participant just can't see it, or won't see it.

Yvonne knew the pain of not knowing, realizing something was amiss, yet not being able to put her finger on it. She could hear Kadee struggling with this emotional contradiction. And she knew her pain intimately. Her ex-husband Dustin had a fetish for a younger woman. After eight years of marriage, Yvonne began to sense something was wrong. Dustin was a heart surgeon, so late nights were not unusual. But suddenly he was staying late all the time. Sometimes he wouldn't come home at all, saying he slept in the call room because he was so exhausted and had to be back in surgery early the next morning.

When she became curious with Dustin about this new habit, he insisted that everything was fine. He was just busy with work. She didn't believe him. She kept asking. Eventually he became irritated with her constant inquires and would say she was hounding him. He had so much pressure at work. Yvonne was supposed to be a source of support, not an added stressor. This made her feel awful, but still she knew deep down he wasn't being honest.

She was too ashamed to talk to anyone about her feelings. She felt that somehow it was a personal failure. That if her marriage wasn't going well, it must be something she did. When he was no longer interested in sex, she began a fitness program, working with a trainer four days a week. She had gained a little weight over the years; she thought if she looked better maybe he would want her again. She had her long hair cut into a trendy shoulder length bob, and started dressing sexier. Having always had a more conservative style, she began wearing tighter shirts and shorter skirts. But nothing changed.

One evening, the strain of knowing and not knowing got the best of her. Although it was totally out of character, she couldn't take the ambiguity anymore. She needed confirmation of her suspicions. She went to the hospital under the pretense that she wanted to bring him a nice dinner. She put together an elaborate basket of food, made her way through the hospital entrance, up the elevator, and through the doors to his office.

He wasn't there. She waited. The time passing felt endless as she tried to distract herself. It was only about fifteen minutes later when the office door opened. There stood Dustin with a twenty-something woman wearing a white lab coat that had *resident* printed on it. The two giggled as they walked in. They immediately saw Yvonne. They looked at each other, communicating with their eyes. The resident said hello, then awkwardly scurried off. Yvonne asked what was going on. Dustin insisted he was working, he was training the young woman. Yvonne should not have come.

Yvonne wanted to scream at him, make a scene, and demand the truth. She wanted to hear him say what she already knew. But she didn't want him to have the satisfaction of seeing her break down or think she was crazy. So she left his office without saying another word.

Afterward, the late nights increased in frequency. She could not take it. One night while he was in the shower, she went into his phone, figured out his password, and searched his text messages. There they were hundreds of texts between him and Madelyn, all filled with erotic content.

One read: *I'll see you at your place at 8. I can't wait to tie you up and lick your pussy. You'll like it. D*

The response read: *I can't wait, dirty boy. I'll be spread out waiting for you. with hearts, M*

Yvonne was disgusted and furious. She stormed into the bathroom and opened the stall door. Dustin was naked, humming to himself, water cascading down his body. She shoved the phone in his face. He shut the water off. He fumbled for words. While Yvonne waited for a response, Dustin nearly tripped trying to reach for a towel to cover himself.

"Yvonne, I'm so sorry. I didn't mean for this to happen. I really didn't."

Her stomach dropped, but she didn't show him any vulnerability. She wanted to cry and ask him how he could do this to her, to them. But instead she watched him squirm. "You're a coward, Dustin. Just say what you have to, then you can leave. I'm sure Madelyn will be spread out waiting for you." She tilted her head and pursed her lips.

She hoped he would say he was sorry, that he didn't love Madelyn, and that he wanted to work things out with her. She wouldn't stay with him, but she still wanted to hear those things.

Instead, he said, "You're right, I am a coward." He gathered up a few things, threw them in a small suitcase, and said, "We should get a divorce." Not "I want," but "we should get." Like he was granting her some long-desired favor.

Yvonne nodded yes. What else could she do? She was working so hard to hold back tears that she could not speak. As soon as he left, she broke down sobbing. Later, through conversations with Dustin, as they were settling their divorce, he broke down and told her a truth. He was actually crying, saying he felt so guilty for what he did. He had been sleeping with Madelyn for a few months. He thought it was a mid-life crisis. It had started right after his fiftieth birthday. He was sorry and he wanted his Yvonne back. Yvonne didn't believe him, and she was most definitely not going to stay with him. He kept trying. She kept turning him down until one day she refused to take his calls anymore. Her lawyer took care of the settlement, and that was the end.

It was the end, but not *the* end. It took Yvonne a long time to recover from the pain. She often wondered if she did something, or perhaps didn't do something that led him to stray. Yvonne did get some relief when she finally knew the truth. It was such a painful reality, but it was better to know than not to know. She was able to move on, and work toward a new future without him.

She heard some of the same troubles in Kadee's narrative. She really felt for her. She believed Aaron was being deceitful, but she wasn't sure exactly what he was up to. She also knew from clinical experience that she wasn't going to be able to help Kadee leave until she was ready.

Perhaps most compelling was Kadee's ability to express her emotions. Yvonne was always so well contained. She worked very hard to be proper, never wanting to behave in a way that might appear inappropriate. She was very conscious of this. It was part of why she thought Dustin lost interest in her, going for the younger more adventurous Madelyn. Yvonne was sexually conservative. She didn't like losing control, would not let herself lose control.

Yvonne admired Kadee's ability to express herself without regard for consequence. If she had something to say to Aaron, she said it. If she wanted to experiment sexually, she did it. Yvonne was intrigued by this. Truth be told, she was also a bit envious of this. Part of her wished she could be that free. Part of her wished she could maintain that level of emotional honesty. Sometimes she really despised her own cautiousness.

Yvonne's clinical thoughts about Kadee, merged with her personal thoughts, making her lose some of her objectivity. It was this very collusion that caused Yvonne to miss some subtle indications of what was happening. As much as Kadee wanted to know the truth about her relationship, perhaps Yvonne did not want to know what was going on in her own.

Aaron seemed like a nightmare to Yvonne. There was something creepy about him. The memory stick sex shows were disturbing, too. It just made Noah and his integrity that much more appealing. Belle Donovan was a small annoyance compared to some of the problems between Kadee and Aaron. At almost forty years old, Yvonne did not like the idea of spending her life alone.

After the session when Kadee disclosed what she had found in the container, Yvonne convinced herself that being with Noah for the rest of her life was the right decision. She remembered feeling so happy the night she said yes. She recalled feeling totally contented as she curled up in bed with him, discussing their wedding plans and future. She had never felt so close to someone, not even Dustin.

It was the next evening at her infamous dinner with Belle Donovan that Yvonne's life took a dramatic turn.

CHAPTER 15

In the meantime, Kadee's life was unraveling quickly. She was having more and more blackout periods; she stopped going to classes and was sleeping all the time. She had no clue that just a couple of days after she found the disturbing contents in the container under Noah's desk, he had become engaged to another woman. And that the woman was her therapist. He was still calling and texting her incessantly that week. He continued to come to her apartment unannounced and have sex with her. The sex became increasingly forced, seeming almost violent.

A few times she didn't even remember him coming over. She would only know that he had been there because of the text exchanges on her phone that she would read afterward. Of course, she could have stopped drinking bottles of wine and popping the Valium like candy, but she didn't. Her distress increased. So did her need to self-medicate.

Perhaps not the best choice of entertainment while she was in the middle of a total breakdown, she decided to watch the entire Jodi Arias trial online. A few weeks earlier, a criminal profiler had come to her school as a guest lecturer to present on the Arias' case. Kadee had followed the case over the long seven-year period — from the time of the murder through the trial into the sentencing— but she had never watched the trial footage. She believed it was a catathymic homicide, her area of interest. What she found most interesting was the relationship between Arias and her ex-boyfriend, victim Travis Alexander.

On June 4, 2008, Jodi Arias killed her ex-boyfriend Travis Alexander. It was a heinous crime, obviously filled with rage. She stabbed him in his shower twenty-seven times, slit his throat, nearly decapitating him, and shot him in the head. She denied any involvement in the crime initially. She even went on national television and denied it. The evidence against her was overwhelming, particularly the photographs that were retrieved from a memory stick from the victim's camera. They showed Arias and Alexander in naked sexual poses right before the murder, and then a few shots of the crime as it was happening. The evidence in the camera was both shocking and ironic: Arias was a photographer.

Still she maintained her innocence. That is until right before her trial when she declared that she indeed was the perpetrator, but that the murder was committed in self-defense. She alleged that Alexander was physically and emotionally abusive. She slaughtered him when he came after her, angry because she dropped his new camera, and she feared for her life. The prosecution did a good job of proving that the crime was pre-meditated. There was evidence that she had been planning his demise for at least a couple of weeks before it happened. After five long months of a nationally publicized salacious trial, she was convicted of first degree, pre-meditated murder.

There was a lot of evidence of the volatile nature of their relationship shown through their digital communication. There were text messages, instant messages and even a long phone sex conversation between Arias and Alexander that were used as evidence. It was all available online as public information. Kadee read and watched everything and anything she could find, trying to piece together the unraveling of Jodi Arias.

There was no concrete evidence of physical abuse. There was just Arias' word, which didn't mean much because she had lied so convincingly before. But there was evidence of emotional abuse that went back and forth: they had been abusing each other psychologically.

It seemed to Kadee that there was a catathymic buildup phase, but it was unclear for how long. Unlike Betty Broderick, who clearly had been building up to her explosive moment for months, it seemed that Arias' buildup was shorter, or at least less obvious. The speculation was that the planning began following an instant message exchange that took place only a few weeks before the murder, where Alexander told Arias, "You are the worst thing that's ever happened to me."

Arias held steadfast to her self-defense story while also alleging that she suffered a fog; she did not remember the details of what happened. She remembered grabbing his gun and the first shot, but after that, she claimed she had no clear recollection. Figuring out the circumstances and Arias emotional state surrounding the planning and execution of her crime was like putting pieces of a puzzle together.

Kadee believed that the crime of pre-meditated murder always involved an element of entitlement. In the mind of this type of perpetrator, there was a certainty that they had the privilege of doing what they did. It was Kadee's belief that no one ever had that right. Yet in catathymic homicides, she thought that the executor also felt like they had no other choice. The internal tension becomes so unbearable, there is no sign of relief unless the other person dies. It was a chilling thought, but one that Kadee concluded to be the truth, extrapolating from all of her research.

Kadee believed Arias to be guilty and that she needed to be held accountable for her actions. She had to go to prison for the rest of her natural life. But she also thought that spending the rest of her life in prison was no match for what she did. There really is no punishment that accounts for purposefully taking someone else's life.

However, her relationship with Noah did give her a certain perspective that she had not had before. She understood how Arias felt, at least she thought she did. Kadee knew the feeling of being psychologically abused, yet remaining attached to her abuser, feeling totally trapped and unable to leave. Of course, Kadee would never kill him; she may have thought about his death as a way out of her emotional agony, but she was missing that entitlement. She had no right to do it; she knew that for sure, at least she thought she did.

But that week was a blur. Everything was merging together: the Arias trial, her blackouts, Noah's sex visits, her dreams, memories, even Betty Broderick and her knife. It was all percolating, accumulating in the pit of her stomach. She knew between the spaces of Noah's visits that she should not let him in, never mind continue to have sex with him. There was no question that he was using her at this point. No question. But the deluded part of her, the part that could not handle the truth, kept thinking if she continued to sleep with him, give him what he wanted, he would want her, too.

Vanessa came over toward the end of the week to try to get Kadee into the shower and out of her apartment. It was mid-September and the air had that slight coolness that was always welcomed after the dense humidity of July and August. Kadee was a mess. So was her apartment. The dishes were piled high in the sink, empty food containers were lying all around the kitchen, papers were strewn across the living room floor, and Kadee looked like she had been run through a drier. Her hair was sticking up all over her head. It clearly hadn't been combed in days. Even more upsetting were the dozens of empty wine bottles spread throughout the apartment.

Vanessa cleared up some of the mess while she pleaded with Kadee to take a shower. She wanted them to go out for a massage or to eat, maybe both. She even mentioned simply getting a coffee as a possibility. She just wanted Kadee to feel engaged with the world again. She was afraid for Kadee; she really wanted to help her, but Kadee was out of it. She was rambling on and on about Noah, the Jodi Arias trial, just babbling. Vanessa could tell she had been drinking: Kadee was slurring her words and her eyes were glazed over. Vanessa didn't know about the Valium, and Kadee didn't tell her.

Kadee refused to leave the apartment, but Vanessa did get her to agree to take a bath and order a pizza. Vanessa went into the bathroom to prepare Kadee's bath for her. When she bent down on one knee to lean over and start the water, she noticed three small red smears on the white-tiled floor. She looked closer. It was bright red. She rubbed her finger over it; she was pretty sure it was blood. She called Kadee in and asked her about it. Vanessa was afraid that Kadee, being in the compromised condition she was, had cut herself.

Kadee stared down at the stains and said she had no idea where they came from; she was sure it was nothing. She took some toilet paper, stuck it under the running bath water and wiped it clean. Vanessa was still concerned. She asked Kadee if she had her period, mentioning that it could be menstrual blood, but Kadee told her it was not.

She checked Kadee's wrists and arms. She never would have thought Kadee would hurt herself, but now she was worried she could. Since there was no sign of any cutting, Vanessa let it go, but she made a mental note. She was worried about Kadee. She had never seen her like this before.

While Kadee was in the bath, Vanessa went to organize some of the papers scattered on the floor. There was a book on stalking, articles on stalking and catathymia, as well as tons of print outs relating to the Betty Broderick and Jodi Arias trials. There were some communications between Arias and Alexander that had notes in the margins. Vanessa obviously knew that Kadee was studying forensic psychology and that the materials probably had to do with her research, but given her state of mind, Vanessa found it concerning.

She stood right outside the bathroom door. "Kadee, now might not be the best time to be diving headfirst into all this research. Maybe it would help you to read or watch something lighter. Maybe a comedy. You know, something that might put you in a better mood."

Kadee was still slurring, but she seemed a little clearer than before, "You know I loovvve that stuff, Nessss. It's my passion."

"I'm just worried about you. Maybe we could watch something funny while we're eating the pizza?"

"OK."

"Where's the menu? I can order it now. Do you want the usual?"

Before Kadee responded, the door buzzer rang. It rang one long buzz, then it immediately rang again and again.

"Do you want to me to get that?"

"Yeah… yeah get it."

Before Vanessa could get it, there was a series of knocks on the door. "Kadee, it's me. Let me in." It was Noah.

Vanessa rolled her eyes. "Kade, it's Mr. Wonderful."

"Hello…Kadee?" he knocked again.

"It's Noah?" Kadee began to get out of the tub. She reached for a towel and was quickly drying herself off. She peeked out of the bathroom. "Let him in."

"Really?"

"Kadee…come on, let me in." His pleading was layered with a touch of annoyance.

Kadee, now out of the bathroom, threw shorts and a T-shirt on, shoved past Vanessa and reached for the doorknob. "I'm sorry, Ness." She opened it.

Vanessa backed away from the door. "I want to go on record by saying this has disaster written all over it." Defeated, she plopped down on the living room chair.

Kadee opened the door wide and Noah came rushing in. "DeeDee…" He was very intense. He went to reach for her, but stopped when he noticed Vanessa on the chair. His whole demeanor changed. He glided across the floor, smiled at Vanessa, gently reaching for her hand and said, "You must be Vanessa."

She had her arms folded across her chest. She hesitated, but took his hand, glared at him and said, "Yes, I am. I'd like to say it's a good guess, but—"

"Well, it's a pleasure to finally meet you."

"Yes. Finally. After eleven months. And why is that?"

He moved to Kadee, put his arm around her back and said, "DeeDee talks about you all the time. I feel like I know you."

"Me, too. To think we could have actually known each other all this time." She pushed her lips together hard, doing nothing to conceal her distain.

"We should all have dinner sometime," he said, ignoring her obvious aversion.

"Really? You think that's likely?"

"Ness, please. Don't start."

With his arm still around Kadee, he asked, "Do you mind if DeeDee and I speak in private for a moment?" He did not wait for an answer from Vanessa. Or Kadee. He took her hand and led her into the bedroom. He shut the door behind them.

Vanessa was left speechless, her mouth agape as much at his nerve as for Kadee's spineless reaction to him showing up.

Once alone, Noah embraced her, gently kissing her neck.

"Deedee, baby. Do you think we could be alone?" He kissed her cheek, then moved toward her lips. "Maybe ask Vanessa to leave?"

"I don't know, Noah. She came all the way over here." Kadee threw her head back in ecstasy as Noah kissed her neck. "Why don't you stay? You can have pizza with us. Get to know Vanessa."

"It's obvious she doesn't like me. I could feel her eyes burning a hole in my head." He rubbed her back slowly, kissing her all over. "I just want to be with you. You want to be with me, don't you?"

"Will you stay tonight?" she looked up at him. She felt desperate. She needed him. She hated needing him, hated it, but she couldn't stop her feelings. He had taken everything from her, without him she felt like nothing.

"Yes. I'll stay tonight. Just ask her to leave. OK? So we can be alone?"

Kadee agreed. She knew he was manipulating her, and that she should kick him out immediately instead of asking Vanessa to leave. That would be the right decision; the one that was in her best interest. But she just couldn't. Her need for him was magnetic. She couldn't resist him.

She went into the living room. She whispered to Vanessa as much because she was ashamed of what she was about to ask of her as because she did not want Noah to hear her giving in to his demands. "Vanessa, please don't be mad at me. Noah wants to spend time alone with me, but he doesn't feel comfortable with you out here because you don't like him."

"Are you serious? Do you even remember the state you were in half an hour ago? Because of him?"

"Ness, really, I appreciate you coming over. You're the best friend ever. But I'm fine now. I want to be with him."

Vanessa shouted to make sure Noah could hear. "Kadee, you have to be crazy to think I'm leaving you here alone with that psycho."

"Vanessa, please," Kadee begged as she tried her best to hush Vanessa. "Don't make me beg."

"What are you doing to yourself? I know you know this isn't right."

"Shhh…I don't want him to hear. Please, I'll call you in the morning. I'm sorry."

Vanessa was losing her cool. She hated him. She hated what he was doing to Kadee. And she was helpless against his control over Kadee. And she was angry with Kadee for choosing Noah over her, her best friend who only had her best interests at heart. "I don't know what to do for you, Kadee. I'm finding it really difficult to care when it's obvious that you don't." She shouted again so she was sure Noah would hear every word she said. "He's a worthless piece of shit. And a psychopath. A shitty, pathetic psychopath. And I'm going to make sure he pays for what he's doing to you!"

Kadee hugged Vanessa. "I'm sorry."

Vanessa shrugged off the hug. She felt used. Kadee reached for her again, but Vanessa hurried to the front door. Before she left, Vanessa yelled, "This isn't going to last forever, Mr. Wonderful. Eventually, she's going to see you for the piece of shit you are. I will make sure of that!"

When Kadee opened the door for Vanessa, two of her neighbors walking by asked if they were OK. Kadee nodded yes. She was so embarrassed. She went to hug Vanessa, but she dashed down the hallway before Kadee could say another word.

Kadee closed the door, on the verge of tears for disappointing Vanessa and on a joyous high that Noah was waiting for her.

Vanessa stormed off down the hall. She was so pissed at Kadee. After all she had done, all she was trying to do to help extricate Noah from Kadee's life, Kadee took him back with open arms in half a heartbeat.

Vanessa knew Kadee had it bad for this guy, knew that she was a mess, but she had no idea how bad the hold he had over Kadee truly was. Vanessa had to do something about it. Kadee was not strong enough to do it herself.

When Vanessa left Kadee's apartment building, she marched across the street and parked herself in the Starbucks with her eyes glued to the apartment entrance. Kadee said that Noah promised he was going to stay the night. Unlike Kadee, however, Vanessa was thinking clearly. She knew Noah had no intention of staying the night. She'd be surprised if he stayed the hour. So she was going to wait for him.

Kadee could not do what was required in this situation, so Vanessa was going to take matters into her own hands. After tonight, one way or another, Noah was going to be gone from Kadee's life — for good.

When Kadee went back into the bedroom, Noah was naked, holding a huge hot pink vibrator. He wanted her to stick the vibrator in her vagina while he watched. Kadee wasn't particularly turned on by the idea, but she did it anyway. She took her clothes off and spread her legs wide, like he asked her. He wanted to see it going in and out, in and out. She was moaning and arching her back, pretending she was more turned on than she actually was.

He showed her his erection. "You make me crazy."

He pulled the vibrator out of her, turned her over on her stomach and penetrated her from behind. He was thrusting really hard. At first she liked it, but then it began to hurt and not in a pleasurable way. She tried to get him to ease up, but he didn't listen. He kept going and going, eventually releasing all over her back.

"That was great!"

"Umm huh." She took his arms and put them around her. He moved in wrapping his body around her. They laid there for about a half hour in silence. She felt so comfortable spooning, his body wrapped around her, but she knew it was a temporary quiet. As soon as he was ready to leave — because she knew he would leave despite his promise to stay the night — she would feel distressed again.

Still, she hoped she was wrong for once. She prayed he was going to spend the night with her. He promised he would, and she believed him. She so wanted it to be true.

"Do you want to order Italian for dinner?"

"I can't stay. I just remembered I have a dinner meeting for work."

"But you said you would stay. You promised."

"I know, but—"

"So, you lied. You lied so I would ask Vanessa to leave and you could fuck me. That's what happened, isn't it?"

"No. I mean, yes, I did want Vanessa to leave so we could be together. I also have a meeting, but I plan to come back afterward. You didn't ask me if I would be having dinner with you. You asked me if I would stay the night."

"I asked you if you would stay tonight. And you said yes."

"Right. And I will. I'll come back after the meeting."

"I thought tonight meant dinner, too."

"Come on, Kadee, please," he got up from the bed. "Stop it. I have a dinner meeting," he was becoming irritated. She could hear it in his voice. "I'll come back later. That is if you want me to." He sounded sarcastic.

She could still smell his semen on her as she watched him getting dressed to leave. She wanted to punch him, stab him. She wanted to hurt him. She wanted him to feel what she was feeling, the rejection, abandonment, the emptiness. She wanted to know that she mattered to him, that he felt something, that she was more than a sex toy.

"You're such a dick sometimes."

"And a piece of shit and a psychopath too, right? I think psychopath is my favorite," he chuckled.

His comment just made her more furious. "Is this a joke to you? Am I a joke to you?"

"Of course not. I just don't appreciate being called a dick because I have a dinner meeting."

"You don't take me seriously. You never did. Did you?"

"Kadee, stop it! I can't get into one of these arguments right now. You're driving me nuts again. Back off. I'll be back in a couple hours."

"Fine. Whatever. You're the one in charge, right?" She was steaming, but overwhelmed with a longing for him, too. He kissed her on the cheek, an empty, perfunctory kiss.

And, as it turned out, it was also their last kiss. She slammed the door behind him. Noah would not come back that night. In fact, he would never come over again.

Chapter 16

Yvonne was not looking forward to her dinner with Belle Donovan. She had wanted Noah to join them, but he said that his mother insisted that they have dinner alone. There would be no compromise. Belle wins again. Noah had warned Yvonne that his mother was having trouble accepting the news of their engagement. "I think we just caught her off guard. She probably just needs a little time."

Yvonne wasn't so sure, but she was trying to be optimistic. She prepped herself for the dinner by sitting in front of her bedroom mirror repeating, "I love your son. I love your son. I want to spend my life making him happy." She was not going to let Belle interfere with their happiness. She had been through way too much in her life. Belle was just an obstacle to be navigated. Of course, she knew she needed to be navigated with finesse.

She dressed casually, but elegantly, wearing a black knee length straight skirt with a dark blue button-down blouse. She threw a thin sweater of the same shade of blue over her shoulders. She was trying to be the woman Belle would want for Noah, so she put a lot of thought into her presentation. Of course, on some level she knew Belle didn't think any woman was good enough for her son, but she intended to try her best.

Yvonne arrived at the restaurant ten minutes early. Belle was already there seated at a table, sipping a glass of wine. She had a thin red scarf placed carefully over her shoulders. She almost always wore a scarf. It was a staple for Belle. Yvonne chuckled to herself as she pretended that Belle needed the scarf to keep her head screwed on straight. She waved toward Yvonne. Yvonne smiled, bolstered her spirits in the face of Belle's inevitable resistance and headed toward the table. Belle immediately called the waiter over and ordered Yvonne a glass of red wine.

The two exchanged some trivial chitchat, which was making Yvonne anxious. She sipped her wine faster than usual. She ordered another. She wanted to get the difficult part of the conversation over with. Finally Belle dove in. She explained that she had concerns about Yvonne and her son. She thought Yvonne was too old for him; he wanted children; she might be too old to have any.

Then there was the way Yvonne presented herself to the world. Noah needed to be with a proud, refined woman. She thought Yvonne's posture wasn't straight, she had a little bit of a belly and she found her to be awkward in large crowds of people. Yvonne was offended, but she knew it was to be expected. Belle did not know how to behave in any other way. She nodded politely without becoming defensive.

When Belle didn't get a reaction from Yvonne, she upped her game with a more provocative subject. She went into her bag and pulled out an envelope. Yvonne wondered what was in it. Belle placed it on the table, but said nothing. "Shall we order?"

"Of course."

Yvonne looked at the waiter. "I'll have the bow tie pasta with meat ragu and—"

"We'll both have the grilled chicken with steamed vegetables," Belle told the waiter. "Yvonne, dear, this is what I mean. Noah likes very slim women." She took her hand and rubbed it across her own flat stomach. "You always order pasta. You should never eat pasta."

"Of course, you're right, Belle." Yvonne smiled at Belle and turned to the waiter. "But, if you bring me anything other than what I ordered, I will send it back to the kitchen. Thanks so much." She turned back to Belle. "I love your son, Belle. We love each other."

"Dear, this isn't about love."

"Isn't it? Your son doesn't want me to change for him. I'm certain he doesn't want me to change for you."

She took her hand and rubbed the top of Yvonne's hand. "Dear, aren't you sweet and innocent. Mother always tells Noah what a sweet girl you are." She took her hand off of Yvonne's, her eyes becoming two daggers, "You have a lot to learn." She smiled, cocking her head, "Dear."

Yvonne was disturbed and disgusted. She excused herself and went into the bathroom. She called Noah. He didn't answer. She tried again. No answer. She texted him: *You're mother is crazy. Please come.*

She felt so alone as she went back to the table. Here she was being attacked by Belle Donovan, for Noah, and he was nowhere to be found. He really should have stood up to his mother, insisting he join them and be there to protect her from the wrath of Belle. He really should have. Of course, she couldn't have known that at that very moment he had just mounted Kadee and was inside of her, thrusting into her from behind, in and out, over and over. She couldn't have known that.

She mustered her courage. "Belle, Noah and I love each other. We are going to get married. I know he really wants your blessing. We both do."

"You think you know my son? Don't you, dear?"

"Well, yes…yes, I do. Of course, I do."

Her tone became increasingly menacing. "No, dear. You don't know him at all. Only I know him. The only person who really knows my son is his mother."

"Belle, I really want us to get along, to be family, but I am not going to allow you to intimidate me." It was a strong statement, but expressed calmly.

She laughed, just a little. It was a sinister laugh, and it gave Yvonne goosebumps. Belle was difficult, even infantile at times, but Yvonne had never seen her so menacing. There was a part of Yvonne that began to feel afraid, and she was not sure why. Belle wasn't a physical threat. She just seemed cunning, cold, like she would risk anything to get rid of Yvonne. She was a woman filled with entitlement and with nothing to lose. Yvonne took her sweater off her shoulders and put it on. She felt chilled.

She peeked at her phone. There was still no word from Noah, not one peep. *Where is his?* she thought. She began to feel irritated. That was nothing compared to what was to come.

"If you're waiting for my son, he won't be joining us. I told him not to come. I thought we should discuss this alone."

"He mentioned that." She sighed. "Belle, I would really like us to work this out somehow."

"Are you sure, dear. Maybe you don't have all the information." She cleared her throat. "There might be some things you need to consider before you decide to walk down the aisle with my son."

"What things? What are you talking about Belle?"

She pushed the envelope that had been sitting on the table over to Yvonne's plate. "Here, you might be interested in these."

At the very moment that Yvonne opened the envelope, Noah pulled his penis out from inside of Kadee and ejaculated all over her back. While Yvonne took the contents out, he was naked with Kadee as they both lay panting. While Yvonne's heart was beating so fast she could feel it in her throat, he lay relaxed embracing Kadee.

Yvonne pulled out about a dozen pictures from the envelope. She could feel Belle's eyes poking her like sharp daggers while she waited for her response. Yvonne could hear her own heart beating. It was one of those moments that seemed unreal. She felt disconnected from what was transpiring as she looked at the photos. They were all shots of Noah and Kadee. It was Noah and Kadee leaving his apartment, Noah and Kadee at an outdoor café, Noah and Kadee hailing a taxi, kissing, holding hands. The photographs were a visual chronicle of Noah and Kadee in what appeared to be a relationship.

She looked hard at what she saw, but it didn't register for a moment. It was so unexpected, she couldn't quite grasp what she was seeing. Then it hit her. All the information coalesced. Her cheeks flushed, were burning up. Yvonne was not a crier, but she felt tears burning in the corners of her eyes. She was about to excuse herself and run into the bathroom. She didn't want to break down in front of Belle, and she could feel a knot of tears forming in her throat. The image of her crying in the bathroom flashed through her mind when Belle threw salt on her emerging wound.

"This is Noah and his girlfriend, Kadee," her voice sweet and hostile simultaneously. "You do know about her. Well, I shouldn't be so presumptuous. How silly of me. I'm just assuming." She began sifting through the photos. She pointed to one where Noah was leaving Kadee's apartment and said, "Now this one, this one was taken just a few days ago."

Yvonne mustered all of her strength, but she couldn't take it. She got up and grabbed her bag. She could barely contain the quivering in her voice. "Excuse me." She rushed to the bathroom as fast as she could without appearing to be rushing.

Once behind closed doors, Yvonne immediately burst into tears. It was an awful revelation and a complicated one. Kadee was her patient. Of course Belle probably did not know that. Or did she? And what was the real truth. Was Noah seeing Kadee? Was Kadee's Aaron, Noah? And if so, why didn't she use his real name? It felt like a conspiracy. Were they all in on this together in some twisted plot? And what could possibly be the intention?

"Compartmentalize, Yvonne, compartmentalize," she said aloud to herself as she threw water over her burning eyes and face. Her goal in that moment was to set aside her questions and go back to the table and face Belle Donovan. She began humming a Mozart symphony, moving her fingers in the air, as if she was playing a piano to calm herself down. She texted Noah: *I don't know where you are, but you need to come now! Something has happened.*

She looked in the mirror, composed herself, touched up her makeup, and returned to the table. When she sat down, she was not the same woman; instead of feeling weepy and fragile, she was angry, determined, focused. She had spent years pussyfooting around Belle Donovan; she was done.

Belle immediately put her hand on Yvonne's and asked, "Are you OK, dear? Mother was worried. She was just trying to help."

She tossed Belle's hand off of her own. "Belle, listen, I do know about Noah and Kadee. He told me everything. So you can stop this charade."

"Really?" the words rolled off her tongue.

"Yes, really."

"Well, I'm surprised that a woman like you would want to marry a man when he already has a girlfriend on the side. This does not bode well for your future."

"Let me worry about my future, Belle."

"If you marry my son, I will be your future."

Yvonne hated Belle, really hated her. "You don't care about your son. All you care about is yourself. I know who you are, Belle. I know who you are."

Yvonne turned to the waiter and ordered her own drink, a chocolate martini, filled with gluttonous calories. Just as Belle was about to open her mouth again, Noah walked over to the table, kissed his mother, then Yvonne, and sat. He ordered a glass of wine.

There was a murky tension at the table. It was the type of atmosphere that was so painfully quiet, it was deafening. Noah looked at his mother, then Yvonne, then back. Belle placed her hand on his leg. As the women glared at each other, no words passed through the thickened space between them.

"What is it?" Noah asked. He seemed concerned. "Mother?"

Belle readjusted her scarf and rubbed her hand along Noah's thigh. "Yvonne and I were just discussing some things," she overenunciated her last word. "Things" was still hanging in the air, taunting him.

He squinted. Yvonne tossed the photos in front of him. He looked through the pictures. His eyes scanned the images while he kept his head down. He ran his fingers through the tangles in his hair; finally he looked up, staring at Yvonne and asked, "What are these?"

She veiled her anger. Her voice flat and overly contained. "You're mother brought these for me. She wanted me to see… she wanted me to know," she paused, "she wanted to make sure I knew about this woman, about you and Kadee."

He swallowed, his eyes still narrowed, his brow a V. He was thinking.

"But I told her that I already knew about her, that you had told me about her ages ago." She looked at Belle. "We don't keep secrets from each other."

He looked at Yvonne, running his fingers through his hair again, clearly uncomfortable. "Right…of course." He looked toward Belle, "Mother, where did these come from? Where did you get these?"

"Well, I took them, dear. Mother took them."

"You took them. I'm confused Mother." He raised his voice slightly, "You followed me?"

"Of course not, dear. What dignity would there be in that. I paid someone to follow you and to take those pictures. I'm a woman of means, not some two-bit gutter trash skulking after her cheating man." She tilted her head and rubbed his thigh again. She was completely unruffled.

Noah removed her hand from his thigh. "You had me followed?" He looked at Yvonne and said, "Yvonne, would you mind giving us a minute?"

"Not a chance. I'm not going to miss one moment of this."

"Mother, why would you have me followed... and photographed?"

"She stalked you. Isn't that what this is, Belle?" Yvonne cocked her head as she spoke.

Things were backfiring for Belle. What she thought would tear apart Yvonne and Noah seemed to be binding them together. She coughed on purpose and adjusted her scarf again. She tried a different approach. "Noah, dear..." she coughed again. "You know if you marry Yvonne, I will cut you off financially."

"But mother, you had me followed! Why would you do that? Why?"

"Dear..."

"Mother! Answer my question!" he raised his voice again.

"Please don't raise your voice to your mother."

"We're leaving." Noah grabbed Yvonne's hand as he stood up from the table.

She looked at Belle. Part of her almost felt sorry for her. The woman was clearly damaged. Malevolent, but damaged. "Good night, Belle."

"Didn't you hear what I said?" Belle pulled at Noah's forearm. "If you marry Yvonne, there will be no more money."

"I heard you mother." He leaned down and kissed her on the cheek. "We can talk about this later."

"No we won't, dear." Belle was becoming increasingly agitated. She was desperate. "If you leave now, there will be nothing to talk about. If you leave now, there will be no more money!"

"I'm a successful doctor, mother. I don't need your money. I'll talk to you later." He took Yvonne's hand and the two exited the restaurant leaving Belle Donovan alone and abandoned at the table.

Three days later, Noah would be found dead in his bathroom.

Chapter 17

It was a bright Wednesday afternoon in September. It was a perfect late-summer day. There was not a cloud in sight. The sun emanated warmth while the air held just a touch of coolness. It was the type of weather Kadee would normally have enjoyed, but the darkness of her mood made the light almost too much to bear. She had not heard from Noah in three days. She had checked her phone repeatedly wondering if they had had contact that she didn't remember while she was still spiraling in her Valium and alcohol stupor. But there was nothing.

She had managed to peel herself out of bed and go to her classes that morning. She had a research seminar on Tuesdays and Wednesdays. She felt it was too important to miss, so she pushed herself. The subway was packed. Everyone had returned to Manhattan following that end-of-summer period when it was au courant to escape to more pleasant environs, making the city feel abandoned. She was in no mood for the crowded, noisy energy; and the radiant sun was just making her feel worse. She couldn't get home fast enough. She wanted to shut all of her curtains and remain in the darkness of her apartment, feeling the pain of Noah's desertion.

She had reached out to him a few times. She re-read her texts to him. She reached out with: *Where are you? Come over? I miss you. Where are you?*

When she received no response, her rage settling in, she wrote: *Forget you. You're such a dick. Don't ever contact me again.*

She didn't remember sending the last one: *If you don't respond tonight, then don't ever call me again! Ever again! You are an awful excuse for a man!*

She was running low on her Valium. She had reached out to Dr. Tracy for a refill the day before, but she hadn't responded, either. That was unusual, and it left Kadee feeling even more alone. She had just gotten home, changed and was about to call Dr. Tracy again. She was feeling desperate. She needed the drugs to get her through this Noah-free time. But her buzzer rang. Her stomach dropped as she was mixed with excitement and apprehension. She assumed it was Noah. Was he there to apologize? To end if for good? To tease and taunt her with more sex and empty promises? She went in the bathroom, fixed her hair in a rush, then buzzed him in.

She opened the door. Instead of Noah, it was two police officers. Her heart sank, disappointed, relieved, angry. Noah had turned her so upside down, she did not know how to react anymore. The two officers introduced themselves as Detectives Poole and Gibbs. She was upset and confused. *This can't be good*, she thought as she zipped up her sweater and opened the door wide to let them in. They sat on the couch and Kadee on a chair. She was biting her nails ferociously.

The visit was surreal. Kadee felt like she was a guest suspect on a *Law and Order* episode. But of course, this wasn't television, this was her life. They informed her of Noah's demise. They could not reveal the details as it was being considered a homicide. There was an investigation going on. They were there to ask her some questions.

Detective Poole was doing most of the talking. He was a tall man, with a muscular stature. He had a shiny bald head, small dark eyes with a piercing gaze, and a red nose. He seemed intense, and Kadee found him intimidating. Detective Gibbs was also muscular. He was shorter than Poole, with broad shoulders, dark eyes and chocolate skin. He seemed less harsh than Poole; his eyes had a more compassionate looked to them.

After Kadee heard the words "Noah," "homicide" and "investigation," her hearing became temporarily compromised. She heard mumbling and a ringing noise. Although she did know Poole was talking loud, she felt like she couldn't hear him. She was reading his lips.

Although the details were confidential, he did reveal that Noah was found on the floor of his bathroom and that he had been stabbed to death. Kadee asked Poole to repeat what he said.

"Dr. Donovan was found dead on the floor of his bathroom. We believe the cause of death was a stab to his heart. The body was discovered with the knife still in his chest, but there appears to be at least three other injures."

Kadee finally understood what he was telling her. Noah was dead. Dead! He was never going to come by again. No more calls. No more texts. No more sex and empty promises. No more kisses. And just like a moment before, she didn't know how to react. Disappointed? Angry? Relieved? All of them at once. Then in an instant, she slid off her chair onto the floor, and began sobbing uncontrollably.

"I'm sorry, ma'am," he sounded genuinely empathetic. "We just want to ask you a few questions. Would that be OK?"

She nodded yes. She was still crying, but she was trying hard to hold it together. She wanted to help them. They explained that they had gone through Noah's cell phone and had read some of their recent text exchanges. They knew Noah was in some kind of relationship with her. They wanted details.

Kadee told them everything she could think of. She didn't think she had anything to hide. She started with the wonderful beginning, their encounter at the coffee shop, their evolving love, the winter months. She then told them about the increasing distance between them, her distress around it and her growing resentments.

She knew the last part did not sound good for her, but she also realized that they had read their texts; eventually they would figure out that things had not been good between them for a while. He then asked if she knew of anyone who would want to hurt Noah. That was a complicated question for Kadee, as she herself had contemplated hurting him a few times. Maybe there were others. The memory sticks and foreign panties flashed through her mind. She didn't mention them. Instead between the tears, she responded, "No, no, not that I know of. But our relationship was kind of strange. I didn't really know any of his friends."

"What about work colleagues?" Poole asked.

"No, no, I didn't know anyone he worked with, either."

Poole had a curious look on his face. It made Kadee uncomfortable. Then he asked the most disconcerting question. "Where were you yesterday afternoon?"

She stopped breathing for a moment. "Is that… is that," she looked down, tears dripping down her cheeks. She wiped her eyes, looked up and continued, "Is that when he died?"

"We believe so, yes, ma'am."

"Well…umm…umm…I had class at 9 a.m. and was there until 11."

"And then what?"

"Well, then I umm…I umm…" She stopped for a moment and then asked, "Am I a suspect, sir?"

"Right now we are just trying to gather information, ma'am." He was not reassuring.

"Well, I umm…umm…I just, I just came home after that." She lied.

"Can anyone confirm that? Did you call anyone? Did anyone see you?"

"Well, no. I don't know. I don't think so. I have to think about that."

"OK, ma'am, I'd advise you to think hard about that." His demeanor was stern. Kadee was scared. "This is an ongoing investigation. We will find out who did this, and they will be punished. Do you understand?"

She looked down at her fingers. She then looked up, "Yes sir. Yes, of course, I understand."

They got up to leave, Gibbs said, "We'll be in touch." He handed her his card.

Right before they left, she asked, "Do I need a lawyer? I mean, I didn't kill him, but should I be worried?"

Poole wondered why she would ask that question. It would not be the normal gut reaction of someone who just lost a loved one. He wanted to say something like "I don't know, do you?" Instead, he said, "Not yet. Have a good day, ma'am. Sorry for your loss."

After they left, Kadee's head was swarming with an array of complex feelings that were all sort of jumbled together. But one thing was clear, part of her felt relieved. She hated to admit it to herself; it was an awful thing to feel, but it was the truth. Kadee felt like a weight was lifted off of her. With Noah gone, she actually felt liberated.

There was some shock, too; she had not quite absorbed the news just yet. It was difficult to wrap her head around. She kept repeating Poole's words to herself: "Dr. Donovan was found dead on the floor of his bathroom. We believe the cause of death was a stab to his heart." She wanted to cry, but the tears wouldn't come. Sure she felt sad, and scared. He was murdered after all, which was frightening. But as she sorted through all her emotions, if she was really honest, totally honest, the most prominent feeling in that first hour was relief.

For the first time in months, Kadee wasn't waiting, anticipating Noah's call or visit. She wasn't trapped in her own head wondering if he would come around and love her totally, being fully honest and intimate. There were no more questions about why he was acting weird, or if there was something she did or didn't do to make him not want her. He was gone; she could finally grieve, let go and move on.

She opened her windows, letting the light breeze into her apartment, as she stood there inhaling the air. She slowly breathed in and out, feeling the gentle wind envelope her as she relished her first few moments of freedom. She began cleaning. Her apartment was disgusting. For the last couple of weeks she had really let things go. She felt a new beginning, and with that the impetus to straighten up her life.

She put some music on, did her dishes, went to the laundry room, washed her sheets and clothes, organized the accumulation of mail, paid some bills, scrubbed her entire floor on her hands and knees. The whole time she was cleaning, she wasn't thinking at all about what happened. She felt strange in a way. Her mind had been so consumed with Noah, it was an odd experience to not be thinking about him, particularly since he had been murdered and the detectives clearly were interested in her.

It was when she went out to the grocery store that things shifted. She was on the cashier line waiting to check out, her basket full, when she noticed the headline of the newspaper. She picked up the paper and read: DOCTOR STABBED TO DEATH IN UPPER EASTSIDE APARTMENT. She stared at the words, a piercing sensation ran up her back and she shivered. She threw the paper in her basket and proceeded to check out.

When she went home, she quickly put her groceries away, made herself a tuna fish sandwich, sat down at her kitchen table and began reading the story. Noah was found on the floor of his bathroom with a knife penetrating his chest into his heart. It was a bloody scene. There didn't seem to be any clean up, he was found in a pool of his own caked blood. His body was with the medical examiner, but it appeared that he had at least three other stab wounds, one to his shoulder and two to his back. While reading, Kadee had a detached feeling, almost like it was a case she was analyzing for research.

A work colleague had phoned the police station informing them that Dr. Donovan had not shown up for his patients nor had he called anyone from his practice to notify them of his absence. When they tried to reach him and were unsuccessful, they all became quite concerned. It was not like Dr. Donovan to be irresponsible when it came to his work. The police went to investigate. They knocked and there was no answer. So they broke the door down and found Noah on the floor of his bathroom. He was on his back, lifeless in his own blood, with a knife sticking straight out of him. There was no evidence of a break-in and the circumstances were highly suspicious. It could be nothing but a homicide.

His apartment was taped off as a crime scene. There was going to be a full investigation. Detective Poole was quoted saying, "There is no doubt that this was a homicide. It was a very bloody scene. We will find out who did this and bring the person to justice." Kadee felt tears hanging in the corners of her eyes. When she thought about him really being gone, his life purposefully cut short, she did feel sadness.

Sadness for him. Relief for herself.

After she re-read the story in the paper a second and a third time, she started to think about a fact that she had been pushing aside since the detectives came to her apartment. She didn't remember where she was the day before. She was having periods where she lost chunks of time, which she attributed to her regular cocktail of alcohol and Valium. During the time when the murder allegedly took place, Kadee had no recollection of where she was. The acknowledgement of that truth terrified her. She lit a cigarette and sat on her lounge chair rocking back and forth trying to soothe herself. She found no comfort as she rocked back and forth and back and forth, staring straight ahead, wondering if she had killed him.

Making things even more alarming was the vague recollection of a nightmare she had had the evening before. She hadn't remembered it, until she read the article about Noah, which must have triggered her memory. She was walking down a narrow corridor. It didn't look like the hallway leading to Noah's apartment, but she had the sense that it was. She was wearing a flowing white nightgown that had a train, like a wedding dress. The scene shifted and she was standing over Noah's bed watching him sleep with a knife in her hand. Then she saw blood. It was trickling down her fingers over the knife and onto the side of her gown.

There was more, but the images weren't clear. There was a single image of her in her own apartment with blood on her feet. She couldn't see herself, only her feet. She recognized the white toenail polish, and there were drops of crimson. There was another image of her sweatshirt covered with blood smears on what appeared to be the seat of a car, a taxi perhaps. She wasn't sure.

She went in her closet looking for her sweatshirt. It was nowhere. She lit another cigarette, continued to rock back and forth and back and forth, feeling terror.

She noticed the card Detective Gibbs had given her. She picked it up, while contemplating calling and telling them the truth. Maybe they could help her. But the possibility that she had murdered someone, someone she supposedly loved, was too terrifying. She couldn't bear the thought. Instead, she opted for denial. She tried to convince herself that she couldn't have done something so heinous, that the detectives would find the real killer. The best thing she could do was to do nothing. So, she continued to sit on her chair rocking back and forth and back and forth, petrified.

When her phone rang a little while later, she was afraid to look at who it was. She kept thinking Poole was going to call or come over and inform her that she was going to be arrested. Maybe there was something in Noah's apartment linking her to the murder. She knew they were searching his place looking for evidence. If she did do it, she no doubt would have been sloppy. She wasn't a trained criminal. If she did do it, she would have left a trail of information leading back to her. Having no memory, the experience of losing her recollection of time and space was terrifying.

She looked at the number on her phone. It was her mother. She let it go to voicemail. She didn't have the courage to tell her parents what had happened. They would be disappointed in her; she also didn't want to alarm them prematurely.

A few minutes later her phone rang again. She covered her eyes with her hands, and looked at the number through her spread fingers. It was Vanessa.

She had thought about calling Vanessa earlier, but she was scared to tell her that she didn't remember where she was, that she had no alibi. She didn't want to involve her, but she really needed to tell someone. Dr. Tracy still had not responded to her calls and she needed to talk. She needed to speak aloud about her fears, having someone she trusted bear witness, so she wouldn't feel so alone. She picked up.

"Kade, are you OK? I heard what happened. It's all over the news!"

Hearing Vanessa's voice soothed her. She pulled her knees up to her chest, bowed her head and began crying. "Ness, oh my gosh, oh my gosh."

"I'm so sorry, hon. How are you holding up?"

Kadee started rocking back and forth again as she relayed the details of how she found out, her visit with Poole and Gibbs, the article in the newspaper. She told her that she was mixed with grief and relief, that she felt free of his grip, but also sad that he was gone. "He's dead. I just…it's so horrible. I can't even imagine. The whole thing is unbelievable. Just…unbelievable."

She was still rocking back and forth. She took a deep breath in, blew her nose and told Vanessa the truth. "Ness…this may sounds nuts, but I don't remember where I was when he was killed. The detectives asked me where I was…where I was yesterday afternoon and I…I…I can't remember. I can't remember anything. I must have blacked out. I don't know where I was when he was killed!"

She heard a clang on the line, like Vanessa dropped something. "Are you there, Ness?"

"Yes, Kadee, I'm here. Sorry I dropped a fork on the floor."

"Did you hear what I said?"

"I did. It's going to be OK. We'll retrace your steps. Figure out where you were. OK. We'll figure it out."

"But what if I…what if I…you know…?"

"What? Killed him? No way, Kadee. There is no way that you could have killed him."

"How can you be so sure? I was so angry at him, so angry. I did think about killing him. I thought about it a few times, many times. Of course, I didn't mean it. I didn't think I would actually do it. But what if I dissociated, what if I couldn't take it anymore, and my mind just split off and I lost control?"

"Come on. We're talking about you. That's not possible. I just don't believe it."

"It is. Ness. It happens. I've read forensic cases where that is exactly what happens. This is so scary. I just can't remember."

"You're too strong-willed for that to happen to you."

"No...no, I'm not. Maybe a year ago, but not these last six months. He broke me down. I lost my strength, my own will. You know what I was going through. I was nuts. Everyone has a breaking point. Maybe I reached mine."

"I understand what you're saying, I really do. But I can't believe that's what happened. I definitely don't think that's what happened. We'll figure it out. I promise." She paused for a moment. "Did the detectives say they had a suspect?"

"No. But I know I'm on their radar. They read our texts and who knows what they will think. It was pretty volatile between us the last few months."

"Well, let's say it wasn't you. Any idea who it could be?"

"I have no fucking clue. I wish I did. I would feel a lot better if I did."

"Don't you worry. We'll figure it out."

After they hung up, Kadee flushed all of her Valium down the toilet. As much as she felt that she needed them, she also believed that they were responsible for her blackouts. She would manage her anxiety without them. She would have to. She didn't want to lose any more time. She wanted to be awake and conscious if she had to defend herself. The other truth was that with Noah gone, she didn't need them as much. The possibility that she killed him and could go to prison for the rest of her life was actually less distressing than feeling trapped in a relationship with Noah. "What a fucking awful thought," she said aloud to herself.

She poured herself a glass of wine and put the television on. She was trying to distract herself, but then she couldn't resist. She put on the local news and waited for the story. It was only a brief clip, and there wasn't really any new information. They were still investigating the crime scene. There would be details reported as the story unfolded. When she again heard that there was no evidence of a break in, she thought about the key under his mat. She thought the detectives should know about that. But if she told them, it could make her seem culpable. She decided to wait. Most likely they would find it on their own, during the apartment search.

She had just flipped the channel when her phone rang again. It was Dr. Tracy. "Finally," she thought. She was beginning to wonder if she somehow found out what happened, decided Kadee was a murderer and was too afraid to meet with her. But of course, that was ridiculous. Dr. Tracy didn't even know Noah's real name. She planned to tell her everything at their next appointment.

"Hello, Kadee," her composed tone was immediately calming. But the conversation turned out to be enigmatic, leaving Kadee puzzled and uneasy.

Dr. Tracy informed Kadee that due to unusual circumstances, she would be taking a leave of absence. She had a colleague that she was referring Kadee to. She thought the two would work well together. Kadee started biting her cuticles.

Kadee couldn't believe the unfortunate timing. This was no time for her to be switching therapists, but there was nothing she could do. She asked Dr. Tracy if she was OK. She responded, "Yes, I'm fine. Thank you."

Kadee wanted to ask her to divulge her personal information and explain what circumstances would cause her to take a leave of absence, but she knew that was not appropriate. It would make Dr. Tracy uncomfortable. Then she thought about blurting out the details of her own situation. Maybe if she knew what was happening, she would make a concession and continue seeing Kadee. Instead, she just asked when she would be coming back.

Dr. Tracy responded with, "I don't know. But I apologize for my abrupt departure. You'll like Dr. Ramirez, and best of luck to you."

As if her day could be more unreal. Her boyfriend, or lover, or whatever, was killed, and she might be the killer. Then her therapist, on the very same day, terminates suddenly by phone, saying merely "Sorry for my abrupt departure." It sounded encrypted. What could have happened? But that wasn't the end of it.

Things would become increasingly surreal when, two days later, Poole and Gibbs showed up at her apartment with sections of Noah's journal and a search warrant.

CHAPTER 18

It was a bloody crime scene. Detective Poole, a veteran officer with the force for almost twenty years, had witnessed a lot of ugly scenes, but this one was particularly gruesome. Blood had splattered all over the bathroom, across the walls, the sink and caked into the creases of the white tile floor. The victim was blanketed in blood. It surrounded the entrance wounds; his entire chest was covered, and it was also smeared on his face. Poole suspected the face smear was done posthumous.

The large butcher knife, the murder weapon, protruded straight out of the victim's chest. Poole believed it to be a purposeful statement by the perpetrator, whom he was convinced was of an intimate relation. The Crime Scene Investigation Unit had been working close to twenty four hours searching for evidence. They dusted for fingerprints and put any items of suspect in sealed plastic bags. They took samples of blood, inspected the body, and were engaged in a thorough search of Dr. Donovan's belongings.

Poole was overseeing the entire team. His job, along with Gibbs and a few other detectives, was to figure out the truth: Who killed Noah Donovan and why? He already had a hunch that getting to the truth in the case of Noah Donovan was going to be complicated. There was a lot of compelling information revealing intricacies of Dr. Donovan's life, which appeared to be complex. But they hadn't found any direct evidence yet; everything he had was circumstantial, at best.

There was no forced entry. There were no fingerprints on any of the doorknobs or the weapon, none at all. Poole assumed the killer wore gloves and may have even wiped the surfaces afterward. The butcher knife appeared to belong to the victim. There was an empty sleeve in his knife holder that matched the size of the knife in his chest. He hoped they might find some of the perpetrator's DNA on the victim's body or mixed in with the blood. So far, there was nothing.

While the forensic scientists were still searching for evidence, Poole and Gibbs directed their attention toward understanding Noah Donovan. They wanted to know who he was, who the important people in his life were, and how he spent his time. Basically they wanted to know who would want him dead. They were questioning many people, but their greatest suspicion was with Kadee Carlisle.

In the midst of the difficult task of piecing together Noah Donovan's life, Poole had to deal with Belle Donovan. Of course, she managed to make everything he did significantly more difficult. He did feel compassion. She was a grieving mother. He had two children of his own. He couldn't even imagine what she must have been going through. But she wanted to be in charge, she wouldn't stop calling him. She had scheduled a press conference, even though Poole had admonished her that it could have a negative impact on the investigation. It was as if she didn't hear him or didn't care. He couldn't be sure. Even with his twenty years of experience with the New York City Police Department, he had never experienced anyone quite as difficult as Belle Donovan.

Poole and Gibbs first met Belle Donovan when they went to her apartment to inform her that her son was dead. It was a tender duty and one that was always unpleasant. When they exposed the details, they were as delicate as possible. Belle first stared in disbelief. Poole had to repeat himself, "I'm sorry, ma'am, but we are here to inform you that your son, Noah, has been found dead."

Her eyes opened wide, practically popping out, as she uttered, "No, no, no." She dropped to the nearest chair, sobbing. The detectives sat with her until she calmed down. They needed to ask her a few questions. They wanted her help in figuring out who did this. She sat forward in her chair, adjusted her scarf, and said she was going to make it her personal mission to find out what happened, that whoever did this to *her* would pay heavily.

Poole found something off-putting about Mrs. Donovan. Her voice had a sweet quality, overly sweet, but he detected an edge of hostility. When he requested her fingerprints and a DNA sample, which they were gathering from those close to the victim as part of the investigation, he thought she was going to burn off his nose with the flames of fire in her eyes. He thought they might have to get a subpoena for them, but then Gibbs stepped in and in his more empathetic style, he was able to convince her that it was to help her son, to separate her DNA from the evidence of unknown suspects. Miraculously he got her to cooperate.

Her manner made Poole a little suspicious, but she had an alibi; she was having lunch with her son's fiancée, Yvonne Tracy. Besides, Poole had a hard time believing a mother would murder her own son. Of course, he had been a detective long enough to know that anything was possible. He would have to check her alibi. But in the beginning, he didn't suspect her.

From the crime scene, the team also surmised that the murder was committed by someone Noah Donovan was in an intimate sexual relationship with. That would turn out to be quite complicated. Initially, they were looking at either Yvonne Tracy or Kadee Carlisle as the person responsible for Noah's death. They were both romantically involved with Noah Donovan. From some of the entries in his journal, it seemed they both could have had a motive: betrayal.

When they met with Dr. Yvonne Tracy, she confirmed Belle's alibi, saying they were indeed together that afternoon. She was a bit weepy. She kept fighting off the tears that were hanging from the corners of her eyes. Of course, that was to be expected. Noah and she had just become engaged. Despite her tears, she was quite composed for someone who had just learned her fiancé had been murdered. Poole assumed it had to do with her occupation. Psychiatrists are trained to be calm even under extreme circumstances.

For the time being, her alibi assuaged Poole as he and the team turned their attention toward Kadee Carlisle. Poole had interesting insights into the secrets that people keep. He knew that everyone had skeletons. Part of his job was to strip people of their covers, making them uncomfortable, while exposing the truth. So when he asked Yvonne if she knew Kadee, he had expected squirming.

They had discovered Noah's journal hidden under his mattress. From reading some of the entries, they knew Noah was carrying on two separate relationships, with two separate women. When he uncovered that information, Poole turned to Gibbs and said, "Shit, this guy was carrying on with two women. Poor guy must've missed the class on femme fatale. But at least we may have found our motive."

Yvonne told Poole and Gibbs that she did know about Kadee. She was Noah's ex-girlfriend, an "in the meantime girlfriend," clarifying that Noah was just spending time with her until Yvonne came around. He didn't love Kadee. He was never going to marry her. He loved Yvonne; they loved each other.

Poole was mesmerized by Yvonne Tracy's soothing voice; words rolled off her tongue so gracefully. He imagined that she was great at her job. He felt an attraction toward her. It happens, he was only human. He would never act on it, of course. He always maintained his professionalism. So he pushed the thought aside and continued questioning her.

Poole asked Yvonne if she was aware that Noah was still involved with Kadee at the time of the murder. He mentioned their text exchanges. Yvonne said that she did. "We told each other everything. There were no secrets between us," she dabbed at the corners of her eyes.

She went on to explain that Kadee was having troubling letting go of Noah, of accepting the truth that he didn't want to marry her. Yvonne put her hands up to her face; her cheeks were bright red. She scooped some water from a glass on the table and splashed her face.

"Are you OK to continue?" Poole thought she looked faint. This could not be an easy conversation for her.

"Oh, yes, thank you. I'm OK. This is just very hard," she was twisting a tissue around in her hands.

"I know, doctor."

She stared at the tissue in her hand, sniffled, dabbed her nose, then continued. "He was trying to let her down easy. I think he was afraid she was going to kill herself. He did care about her, you know. He did. Noah was a very compassionate person and a wonderful doctor," she wiped her eyes again.

"Interesting," Poole scribbled in his notebook. He pondered something for a moment taking a beat longer than comfortable for Yvonne — and Poole noticed it. "Tell me, doctor. Did you ever have the occasion to meet Kadee?" He watched Yvonne as she shifted on her couch. Bingo! He hit a nerve. "It's important that you tell us the truth. Do you understand?"

Yvonne looked away, nodding her head. "Yes," she said softly. "This is complicated, detectives. I'm not trying to hide anything. It's just complicated."

"I understand. Take your time," he had his note pad ready. His curiosity was piqued. Of course, Poole and Gibbs were used to surprises. But Yvonne's revelation was totally unexpected.

"Can this be… off the record?

Poole and Gibbs looked at each other. In their shorthand exchange, they told each other that whatever she was about to say was going to be juicy. Poole responded first. "Yes, but please

know that your confidence will be breached if it in any way com-
promises out investigation. But we will not disclose anything you
are about to tell us without discussing it with your first."

She nodded and took a deep breath. "Kadee Carlisle was my patient. I shouldn't even be telling you. It violates her confidentiality."

Poole informed her that it was best that she did. They would
have found out during their investigation. It was better that she
told the truth right from the beginning. He then asked for more
details. It seemed like a unique variation on a ménage a trios. For
a second, Poole felt a little aroused. The awareness of that made
him uncomfortable. He stood up, adjusted his pants, then sat,
working hard to concentrate on the investigation, pushing his
elicit thoughts aside.

Yvonne Tracy went on to describe each of their exclusive
relationships, while also exposing the blurry areas where they
both occurred contemporaneously. She told them of her long relationship history with Noah, her evolving romantic feelings, his
proposal, their engagement. She also divulged that Kadee came
into therapy to discuss her relationship with Noah, but for some
reason, she had not revealed his real name. Instead, she used the
name Aaron. Yvonne still had no idea why.

Poole and Gibbs were leaning forward, listening intensely,
and trying to keep the facts straight. She then explained that
Noah disclosed his relations with Kadee following their engagement. He was in the process of ending it with Kadee, but she was
making it very difficult.

Poole looked at Gibbs, an unspoken note of curiosity passed
between them. Poole turned to Yvonne. "So you had no idea that

the man Kadee Carlisle was talking to you about in her therapy was Dr. Donovan?"

Yvonne winced, "Correct."

"I'm sorry, doctor, no disrespect, but that's a little hard to believe. Didn't you recognize details about this man, the man who you were sleeping with, who you would marry—didn't you recognize things about him when Ms. Carlisle divulged her stories about him?"

"She was describing a totally different person. Because Noah wasn't serious about her, he acted very differently toward her than he did with me. Besides, she was...well, obsessed," she paused, took a deep breath, "I shouldn't really be talking about this without Kadee's permission or a warrant for my files. But I can say this: In general, people's perceptions are subjective. What Kadee reported to me was very different than Noah's side of the story."

"So you're saying she was making things up in therapy."

"No, I'm saying people report things based on their own perception of the events."

"So they twist the facts?"

"No, they tell the truth as they believe it. Kadee may have believed Noah loved her, that was her perception, her truth, but it may have been very different than how Noah saw the truth, or how he actually felt."

"So Ms. Carlisle told you things about their relationship that made Dr. Donovan seem very different than he actually was. Can you give us an example?"

"As I said, detective, I've already revealed more than I should have. Even with the circumstances, I still feel a professional responsibility. You need to obtain written consent from Kadee or you need a warrant. Otherwise I'm not comfortable saying more."

"I understand, Ma'am. We will get that paperwork. I am curious, though…" Poole paused contemplating his words. "What did you do when you discovered that your patient Kadee Carlisle was involved with your fiancé? You said that you knew about them. I'm trying to understand how you would be able to continue working with her without compromising your ethics?"

Yvonne put her hands to her cheeks and gazed downward. "This is not easy. I guess it all happened very quickly. The chain of events is a little blurry in my mind. Noah proposed, then once I said yes, he told me the truth. Naturally, I was disconcerted. I couldn't reveal that Kadee was my patient, so we discussed his relationship with her, and I pretended that I did not know her. I was upset that he had been sleeping with someone else. But when he explained that he had ended it, and that he was just trying to make sure she didn't kill herself…well, I had to forgive him. I knew he didn't love her. And I knew of her obsession. After that, I called Kadee and terminated our treatment. It was not an easy decision. But I couldn't treat her. My objectivity was totally compromised…and…I felt it was in her best interest to end the therapy. I didn't tell her what happened…" she looked down and covered her mouth with her hand. In a whisper, as if it was a moment of painful recognition. "I'm sure she knows the details now. I feel terrible about the whole thing, really. It could not have been easy for her to learn the truth."

"Thank you, doctor. Would you mind if I ask you one more thing? It's nothing to do with what Ms. Carlisle shared with you as her patient. I'd just like your opinion on something."

"Sure, detective."

"Do you think Kadee Carlisle killed your fiancé?"

Yvonne's face flushed again. She took a deep breath in and then a long exhale. "That's a complicated question, detective. The best I can say is it's possible, but I really don't know. I just don't know." Her eyes began tearing up again. "This is all so horrible. It's like a living nightmare. I don't know what to think."

"We've taken enough of your time. We will be back once we have a warrant. Thank for your time, doctor. We're very sorry for your loss."

Poole and Gibbs exited Yvonne's apartment building. There was no denying that Poole found Yvonne alluring. "That's one classy lady," he said nonchalantly to Gibbs, who nodded his head in agreement.

Gibbs looked at Poole. "Yeah, one classy lady with one crazy story. What a tangled web. I always say these classy types have the most secrets." Gibbs was half chuckling, but his statement was serious.

"Everyone has some secrets."

"True, but some have more than others. I think there's more to this story." Gibbs paused for a moment. "You think she did it? Her manner was a little off. She almost seemed too calm. She could be our perp."

"She's probably in shock. It's too soon to tell, but my money is on Kadee Carlisle. You heard Dr. Tracy. She was obsessed with the victim. And some of Donovan's journal entries about her are pretty damaging. He was afraid of her."

Just as they were about to get into the car, Officer Brenner from the Crime Scene Unit called to say that they found a spy cam video recorder hidden between two books on a shelf, which faced the victim's bed. It was turned off. There didn't seem to be anything recorded on it, but when they dusted it, it was loaded with fingerprints. They were sending it to the forensic lab for further analysis along with Noah Donovan's computer, which seemed to have some suspicious activity on it.

"See, what I mean," Gibbs said. "There's more to this story."

Of course, even with their combined years of experience on the force, they would find surprises at every turn in this investigation. Noah's computer would reveal even more secrets, leaving Poole and Gibbs flabbergasted.

CHAPTER 19

Kadee wasn't shocked when Poole and Gibbs came buzzing at her door early Friday morning. Although she was not looking forward to their visit, she sort of expected it. Poole showed her a search warrant. She looked at it and let them in, offering them coffee. Gibbs accepted; Poole, who had an air of intensity about him, declined. Kadee could tell he wanted to get straight to business. She was pouring Gibbs his coffee when Poole said, "We're gonna have a look around."

She nodded, "Go ahead." Kadee had read and watched enough crime drama to know that he was trying to disarm her, hoping if he made her comfortable enough, she would slip up. Of course, Kadee wouldn't even know if she slipped up. Guilty or not, without any memory of the events, she had no idea what her role was.

As terrified as she was, part of her wanted to know what happened as much as they did. In between their visits, she had thought a lot about what it would mean if she did kill Noah. If she knew she did it, would she turn herself in? She liked to think she would. She prided herself on integrity, but the price was big, basically the rest of her life. She had interned at various correctional facilities. She knew the dreadful conditions in which she would have to survive her remaining years, if in fact she was a murderer.

Then there was the whole internal responsibility factor. If she did kill Noah, she wasn't sure she could live with the guilt. Sure, he tortured her; sure, part of her wished he would die. But kill him? Actually take it upon herself to end his life? She didn't think there was any excuse for that. If she was guilty of murder, she would be living with unbearable guilt for the remainder of her days. Perhaps prison would be a relief; at least she would feel she was being punished for what she did.

She was sipping her coffee, without enjoying it, without even tasting it. She just wanted to be doing something while she was observing them perusing her apartment, anxious for what they might find. The image of her missing bloody sweat shirt from her dream flashed through her mind. Gibbs pointed to her books and journal articles on stalking and catathymia that were sitting on her kitchen table. He then picked up some material on Betty Broderick and asked what Kadee was doing.

She explained that she was a doctoral candidate at John Jay College.

Gibbs nodded, "I have some friends who studied criminal justice there."

"My field is forensic psychology," she shrugged her shoulders. "It's strange to be on this end of things. Usually I'm the one behind the research. I like it better there."

He nodded and continued looking around. It was taking them a long time. Her apartment was small. She started wondering what they were really doing there. They must be thinking something. They must have found something that made them want to talk to her again. She knew she had rights, so she finally asked, "Are you looking for anything in particular? Have there been any leads in the case?" She bit a whole chunk of a cuticle off.

Poole took a seat and motioned for Kadee to sit down across from him. "We spoke with Dr. Yvonne Tracy."

"OK," Kadee cocked her head to the side, looking confused. She wondered how he knew Dr. Tracy.

"Do you know Yvonne Tracy, Ms. Carlisle?"

"Well… yes, I do. She was my therapist. I don't understand. Why would you speak with her? How would you even know she was my therapist?"

"Ma'am, did you know that Yvonne Tracy was engaged to Noah Donovan?"

Kadee felt totally confused. It took her a minute to digest what Poole had just disclosed. "Excuse me sir, what? Can you repeat that?"

"Did you know that Yvonne Tracy was engaged to Noah Donovan?"

She could feel a lump forming in her throat, it was sitting stuck, and it prickled, like a Brillo pad was wedged in there. She was trying to swallow it down. "No…no, Detective Poole," she looked down. "I did not know that." A couple of tears rolled over her cheeks. Her head was spinning with images of her pouring her heart out in Dr. Tracy's office.

"Well, did you know that Dr. Donovan kept a journal?" His tone sounded accusatory, like he knew she did something. She broke out into a sweat.

"No...no, Detective Poole, I didn't know that. Noah was very private." Kadee thought for a moment. "Excuse me. Can we just rewind for a second? You're telling me that Dr. Tracy and Noah were having an affair?"

Poole looked at her as he pulled a few sheets of paper from a folder. "No, Ms. Carlisle. Not an affair. *They* were engaged. Apparently, *you* were the affair."

"So for the last year that we were dating, he—" Kadee choked back more tears. "He was in a committed relationship? With the woman who would become my psychiatrist?"

Gibbs took a sip of the coffee. "In a nutshell."

An ominous cloud loomed over Kadee. She suddenly realized how the way the events unfolded were now pointing all guilty fingers at her. She was growing increasingly scared, like any minute Pool was going to throw hand cuffs on her, read her the Miranda rights, drive her down to the station and book her.

He sifted through the papers. She could see that some of the text was highlighted. "Here are a few excerpts from his journal that I found interesting." He read it with a monotone that made Noah, despite what he did, come off as less creepy, but Kadee more creepy. *"I think Kadee is stalking me. She went through some of my things. Maybe I should break it off. Maybe she's crazy. Theo said I should break it off with her. He's probably right. It's just the sex is so good. I've never had sex like that before. She'll do anything I want. Man, I love fucking her."*

Kadee was holding back tears. Having access to Noah's inner dialogue was painful, but she was also terrified that there was something in his journal that revealed her culpability. She wanted to say that she wasn't stalking him, but of course there was that night she sat outside of his apartment. From her research, she knew that would be considered stalking. She was watching him without his knowledge; it was intrusive. Her stomach knotted as she wondered how he could have known she was there and if there was more. Maybe she had stalked him during one of her blackouts and forgotten.

Poole continued. "Here's another: *Kadee is definitely stalking me. I felt her in my apartment last night. I'm sure of it. And I think she hacked my email, too. I'm breaking it off. This is scary. But I'm gonna miss fucking her.*"

Poole looked at Kadee and continued. "Here is the very next one. *I broke it off with Kadee. I feel bad. She was crying. But then I went to her apartment and fucked her again. It's like I can't stop fucking her. I will stop. I'm writing this to hold myself accountable. I will stop fucking her. If I don't she might kill me. She already threatened me. I'm tormented. I will stop fucking her. I will stop fucking her.*"

Kadee asked Poole to stop. It was too painful. Noah was lying to his journal. That's not what happened. She pulled her knees up to her chest as Poole said, "Just a couple more. You don't have much of a choice here. We're dealing with a murder."

He pulled out another paper. "Dr. Donovan didn't date his entries. But here are some lines from his last few. *I proposed to Yvonne. She said yes. I should be happy, but I'm still fucking Kadee. I have to stop. I made her bleed yesterday. I fucked her up the ass in the bath. I stuck it all the way up her ass. There was blood on the floor after. She saw it and said she was going to kill me. I have to stop. She's dangerous.*"

He looked up, his eyes were two slits. Kadee knew he was trying to gauge her reaction. She was perspiring all over, her shirt was damp and her stomach was doing flips. She was sure he could tell.

He read one more: "*I'm marrying Yvonne. I'm going to make her my wife. Yvonne will be my wife. I have fucked Kadee for the last time. Today was the last time. I really mean it. I hope she doesn't kill me. It's crazy to even think she would kill me. But Mother always told me that women can be evil, that the only woman I can trust is her. Maybe Mother is right. Maybe Kadee is crazy. I'm a man and I'm scared. I'm scared. I will stop fucking her. It's going to be OK. Good night.*"

"So, Ms. Carlisle, as you can see from Noah Donovan's journal, he was afraid of you. He thought you might kill him."

Kadee felt like she was ready to crack. She always wanted to know what Noah was thinking, but hearing his thoughts made her think she was deluded. She thought he loved her. She knew things weren't going well, that the relationship was nearing the end, but she couldn't believe he was afraid of her. But then again, maybe his fears were justified. Her thoughts were flipping back and forth; she needed a minute to think. Poole wasn't going to afford her that luxury.

"Ms. Carlisle? Ms. Carlisle? Did you hear me? Noah Donovan was afraid of you. He thought you might kill him."

"I heard you."

"Did you do it? Did you kill Noah Donovan?"

She wanted to say that she didn't know the answer, to tell them the truth, but she was pretty sure that would be enough for them to bring her down to the station and charge her with murder. She wanted some time to think. So she lied. "No, no Detective Poole. No. I didn't kill him." The tightness in her throat was making it hard to swallow.

"Ms. Carlisle, I think you did kill Dr. Donovan." He tossed the paper with the final journal entry toward her. "That's what Noah Donovan is telling me."

"I understand. I know this doesn't look good, but a bad relationship doesn't make someone a murderer," she was crying.

Poole wasn't sympathetic. His search for the truth far surpassed any compassion. "Ms. Carlisle, the crime lab is looking into some suspicious email activity on Dr. Donovan's computer. I'm guessing we will find evidence of your stalking on there. We will be subpoenaing IP addresses. It really is best for you to tell the truth now. I'm trying to help you. If you tell the truth now, things will go better for you. Do you understand, Ms. Carlisle?"

"Yes, I understand." She needed some time. She knew she would eventually have to tell them she had absolutely no idea if she did it or not. She couldn't confess, because she didn't know. But she wanted a little time to process everything she heard that morning. "Before we go any further with this, I'd like to speak to an attorney."

Poole sighed, clearly annoyed. He wanted a confession. "It's your right. It won't change the outcome, though. We will still get to the truth."

"Of course, detective."

Poole was about to say something when Gibbs, who was still searching around the apartment, said, "Poole, check this out."

Poole stood up. Gibbs had Kadee's daily planner. She had been looking for it to see if she had anything scheduled on the day of Noah's murder, but she couldn't find it. Gibbs found it wedged between her desk and the wall. Her heart was racing; she could feel the palpitations in her throat. Maybe she had an alibi.

Gibbs pointed to September 19th. In black ink was one word: **Terminate**. Kadee stood up to look, when she saw the word, her legs became wobbly. She had to immediately sit back down.

"What?" she said the word out loud. It was meant to be a private thought, but it just came out of her mouth.

"Ms. Carlisle?" Poole actually seemed angry.

It may have been an act to intimidate her, she couldn't be sure, but either way she was frightened. Would she actually be stupid enough to write the word terminate on her calendar marking off the day she planned to kill Noah. She knew that was totally crazy, but then again, she was totally crazed at the time. She was unraveling rapidly and loaded up with drugs and alcohol. She started at the word in disbelief, "I want to call my lawyer."

She knew Poole was drooling at the thought of arresting her. Her mind was racing, matching her rapid heartbeat, when Poole got up and said, "Excuse me." He stepped out into the hallway.

When he came back in, he took his handcuffs out, saying, "Kadee Carlisle, you are under arrest for the murder of Noah Donovan. You have the right to remain silent..." He continued reading Kadee her rights, but she stopped hearing him. Her world became silent as Poole and Gibbs escorted her out of her apartment, down the hallway past her fellow tenants, out the door past her neighbors, and into the back of the police car.

The ride to the police station felt long, as Kadee looked longingly out the window wondering if this would be the last time she would ever see her neighborhood. The things she took for granted, the sun on her face as she strolled down the New York City streets, admiring the architecture, having dinner with Vanessa, browsing a bookstore, even her subway rides might all be gone. They would be memories of her former life if, in fact, she was guilty.

The word **terminate** in her planner was nagging at her. What was she thinking? Why would she write that? It just didn't make any sense. Somewhere in the middle of the ride she made a decision; she was going to tell the detectives that she didn't remember what happened. It was plaguing her; she wanted to know, needed to know. She believed that her best chance of knowing the truth started with telling the truth. She planned to tell them as soon as she consulted with her attorney. She wanted to tell them before she was formally charged, but she thought it was wise to seek legal counsel first.

When they arrived at the station, they took Kadee's personal items and brought her into an interrogation room. She was going to be booked, but Poole wanted to try once more to persuade her into a confession, but she insisted that she consult with her attorney. He moved her into a small consult room and gave her a phone. She called Alex. Although he was primarily a divorce attorney, she thought he might be able to help her. At the very least, he would be able to recommend someone.

Kadee was relieved when she reached Alex. She divulged some of what had happened. Tears streamed down her face as she told him the truth: She did not know if she killed Noah Donovan. He was shocked by her story. That was to be expected. It was not the sort of thing you expect to hear from someone you know. It was the type of thing that happens to other people, or something that you see on television. It is not something that happens to people in your own life.

He reassured her that everything was going to be fine. Of course, she knew he was placating her. There was no way he could know that everything was going to be fine. But she accepted his words, trying her best to feel reassured. At least he was on his way to the station. As it turns out, he had been practicing criminal law for the last few years. He offered to be her attorney, and she accepted.

His last words before he hung up were, "I'll be there in about fifteen minutes. And Kadee, don't say anything to anyone. Not one word. I'll be there as fast as I can."

She sat alone in the small room. There was nothing in there except four chairs, a table, a clock, and the phone they had let her use to call Alex. It was so empty. She had no distractions, her own ruminative thoughts consumed her. She was pulling at the ends of her long hair as she sat feeling helpless. There were doors opening and closing outside the room, inside the room echoed with only the ticking of the clock. She tried to call Vanessa. No answer. She wasn't ready to talk to her parents yet, but she wanted to talk to someone. She called Hailey. The phone rang and rang; finally she answered.

Kadee had tried to call Hailey a couple of times since the murder, but hadn't reached her. Hailey hadn't called back, either. She wondered if Hailey was avoiding her. Even though Hailey wasn't the most reliable friend, Kadee had a hard time believing that she would turn her back on her during such extreme circumstances. She knew Hailey was sick of hearing about Noah, but this was different, she was under arrest for murder. She needed all the support she could get.

Hailey was not sympathetic. It was an awkward conversation, with spaces of silence where there should have been words of comfort. When Hailey did speak, her words sounded forced, like she was verbally constipated and her tone was judgmental.

She told Kadee that it was her own fault for loading up on the Valium. She had brought the circumstances upon herself, first for staying with Noah, then for being too weak to handle him without self-medicating.

Sitting in the empty stillness of the small room, the clock tick-tocking, reminding her that the rest of her time might be spent in small dilapidated quarters, she could not believe Hailey's cold reaction. Her eyes were swollen, two pockets of puff, from all the tears. Hailey was making her feel worse. She was shocked at Hailey. Kadee was ready to hang up, defeated, but Hailey had two more things to say.

Kadee had abandoned her in her time of need. Being too loaded up on drugs to function, she had left Hailey alone to get her abortion. Kadee felt awful, but at the same time she couldn't believe Hailey was making this about her. It wasn't Hailey that was the unsupportive, unreliable friend, it was Kadee. Of course, that's what Hailey always did. Kadee shouldn't have been surprised. Hailey was just being herself.

The last thing Hailey said was downright merciless. "I'm sorry, Kadee, but I can't talk to you anymore until this is over. It's already all over the news. Once the media finds out you're being charged, your name will be all over the place. I can't be associated with that. I just can't risk my reputation." Then without even saying goodbye, she hung up.

Kadee folded her arms on the table, put her head down and sobbed. About twenty long minutes passed when Poole opened the door and let Alex in. Kadee got up, rushed over and hugged him as tight as she could. His presence was soothing.

Poole interrupted the moment. Kadee thought his nose looked extra red under the fluorescent light. "We need to book you, so make this a fast visit."

Kadee decided she didn't like Poole. He was treating her as if she was already convicted.

Alex advised Kadee not to tell the truth, at least not yet. He listened to the whole long awful story, the relationship, the blackouts, the murder, the evidence against her, the lack of alibi. All the evidence was circumstantial. The journal entries in particular were damaging, and the lack of alibi was a problem, but he really believed Kadee was innocent. He wanted her to wait to tell the police that she didn't know where she was the day of the murder.

Once she was officially charged with first degree murder, the state still had to prove they had enough evidence to arraign her. He wanted a little time to do some research and see if he could get to the truth before she was formally charged. If she was, she would enter a plea of "not guilty," and Alex would continue his investigation to prove her innocence.

The booking was humiliating. They stripped Kadee naked, searched her, went through all of her things, took her fingerprints, her photo, gave her a few thin sheets and a small flat pillow, put her in a tiny cell, slammed it closed and locked it behind her. They took everything from her. She felt totally helpless. As she lay on the hard thin mattress they called a bed, she began thinking it all through. Even though she was taken out of her apartment against her will, stripped of her own clothes, required to wear others, unable to choose her own food, read her own books, call her friends and family, even though she had no choice over most of her choices, she felt freer than she had in a long time.

She was in control of her thoughts. She was in control of her actions and reactions. She felt an inner fortitude she had not had since the beginning of her relationship with Noah. She had power, even in the face of these extraordinary circumstances. She had the power to be who she was. With that thought, Kadee decided to adjust her attitude. She would stop being the weepy defenseless girl she had become; instead she would be the strong, free-willed woman that she had been most of her life. And that woman was not a murderer.

Vanessa was right, Kadee was strong. The possibility that she allowed Noah to get her to the point of sacrificing her own life just to have him dead was small. It was possible, of course, anything was possible, but it was unlikely. And just like that, Kadee decided her purpose was to figure out what happened with the hope of proving her innocence.

Her first mission was to figure out if she had an alibi. As she lay on the bed, staring up at the chipped ceiling, she began piecing together the missing parts of her life. The word **terminate** kept running through her mind as she tried over and over to think about her associations to the word. She was talking to herself out loud. There was a slight echo in her cell. "Terminate, terminate, what did I mean…did I mean kill, no, that's not it. Execute, hmmm…no, that's not right, either. End, hmm…end… maybe…or if not end, then eliminate, huh…eliminate," suddenly it clicked. "Holy shit…eliminate. That's it!"

She took a couple deep breaths to calm herself as it dawned on her that she might have an alibi after all.

Chapter 20

Poole and Gibbs were in the station going over some of the details of the case. Poole had no doubt that Kadee Carlisle had murdered Noah Donovan. The journal entries not only showed motive, it was strong evidence that she was stalking him and had threatened to kill him. She had no alibi, and the word **terminate** strongly suggested premeditation. He didn't just believe Kadee was the murderer, he thought she was a cold-blooded psychopath.

Gibbs wasn't so sure. The two had been partners for nearly nine years. He knew Poole had a tendency to develop blind spots once he honed in on a possible perpetrator. Gibbs agreed that there was a good chance Kadee Carlisle was the killer, but he wasn't convinced.

As much as Poole could have tunnel vision, Gibbs was unsystematic, often pursuing a few potential leads simultaneously, not just looking at evidence, but following his intuition. It's probably the reason they worked so well as partners. Each balanced the other's weakness.

Gibbs was considering other suspects. Being the more sympathetic of the duo, Gibbs placed a lot of emphasis on not having someone wrongfully convicted. He first considered Yvonne Tracy. He had a strange feeling about her. She seemed overly calm. He knew everyone reacted differently in these types of situations, but he had never seen a family member of a victim seem quite so composed before. She also had a motive. Her fiancé had a girlfriend. Sure she said she knew about it and appeared to accept it, but Gibbs had been a detective long enough to know that this sort of triangle often throws people over the edge.

And then her story that she just forgave Noah Donovan because he was being compassionate, wanting to make sure Kadee Carlisle didn't kill herself. Was she lying to them or did she really believe that was the truth? There was nothing in Donovan's journal entries suggesting that he was concerned that Carlisle might be suicidal. In fact, the tone of his words suggested that he was more worried about himself than her.

Curt Gibbs' thoughts shifted to his twin sister, Veronica. They were very close. She was like a princess to him, and he was always protective of her. He believed that women should always be treated with the utmost respect, and never, ever be taken for granted.

A few years ago, Veronica had been in a relationship with a man named Mobee. They had dated for about six months, and then for some reason, Mobee just broke it off. But he continued calling Veronica. He would tell her that he wanted to get back together or some variation of that untruth, so that she would continue engaging in sexual relations with him. It was clear that his emotional commitment was over and Veronica kept trying to end things, even though she still loved him. It was a very difficult situation. The man would not stop calling her. It was breaking her down. Veronica had always been so confident, so full of life, and she became meek and hopeless. She was crying all the time. She kept pleading with Mobee to leave her alone, but he just would not stop reaching out to her.

One day Curt Gibbs took it upon himself to make sure that this Mobee-man, never called Veronica again. He went over to his house and, in his stoic but strong manner, he told Mobee that it was in his best interest to leave his sister alone. He didn't overtly threaten the man; he didn't have to. Gibbs' presence always exuded an exquisite style of courage that made people know he meant business without having to toss bravado around. His meeting with Mobee made the implicit statement that Mobee just might wind up eating his own tongue if he didn't leave Veronica alone. After Gibbs' visit, the man never called Veronica again. And after a few months, she was able to move on, meeting a man who appreciated her.

He knew that remaining impartial was imperative, always doing his best not to let his own bias color the direction of his investigation. But in the privacy of his own mind, he felt that Noah Donovan's callous behavior toward the women he was involved with brought on his own demise. Of course, being someone who believed in justice, Gibbs didn't think Donovan should have been murdered, nor did he believe that there should be any pardon for the perpetrator. But he could understand how both the doctor and Carlisle could want him dead.

He shook away those thoughts and went back to thinking about the conversation with Yvonne Tracy. *Where does her truth rest?* he wondered to himself. Did she know Donovan was manipulating her with the "Carlisle is suicidal" story? *And could he have been any less original in his lie?* It left Gibbs with a sour taste in his mouth. *And she's trained to pick up on nuances, how could she believe his story? Sure, her love could have blinded her. It's much easier to see the truth when your objectivity isn't compromised by feelings. Regardless, whichever version of the Noah Donovan story she chose to believe, one thing seemed undeniable: she had a motive.* Gibbs did a little research, but nothing of any relevance came up. There was also no evidence that suggested she committed the murder, other than her potential motive. It was a strong impetus for a murder and one that he had seen over and over in his work, but without an iota of information linking her to the crime, it seemed that it was only a good theory. He kept her in the back of his mind and moved on, directing his attention toward Belle Donovan.

It was hard to imagine any motive Belle Donovan could have had. Noah Donovan was her son. The thought that she would kill her own child was unsettling. She was an arrogant, self-centered woman who would not take any advice, making her a real nuisance during the investigation. But that wasn't a crime; it was a personality problem. Poole who often used psychological jargon had called her "one of those narcissistic types."

The more Gibbs directed his energy toward other suspects, the more Poole grew annoyed with him. He thought Gibbs was wasting his time and should be putting all of his efforts into preparing the case against Kadee Carlisle. He was determined to gather enough evidence for the district attorney to get the court to formally charge her.

They were in the middle of one of their disagreements when a call came in from the forensic lab. The fingerprints on the video recorder were not Kadee Carlisle's or Noah Donovan's. They were running them through the data base to see if they could find a match. Though it was strange, it did not deter Poole from his focus on Kadee. As far as Poole was concerned, the video recorder did not necessarily have anything to do with the crime. Gibbs disagreed. He was determined to investigate it further.

The forensic technician also brought the detectives attention to some email exchanges between Noah Donovan and Belle Donovan. They had forwarded them to the detectives in a document. More of Gibbs' nonsense, which set off Poole's ire again.

There was something about Kadee Carlisle that Poole did not trust. He felt she was holding back information, that she was not telling the whole truth. He saw her as one of those manipulative women who used sex to allure and control men. He thought she seduced Noah Donovan, gripping him with her sexual prowess. Then when he didn't give her what she wanted, she stalked and killed him in a rage.

Gibbs thought Poole might be losing his objectivity, that his interpretation of the events was somewhat personal. Poole's ex-wife, Felicia, looked a bit like Kadee Carlisle. She was also tall, thin, had long dark hair, and a striking beauty. From his conversations with Poole when he was going through his divorce, Gibbs surmised that Felicia had total control over Poole, that she used her beauty and sex to manipulate him. After fifteen years of marriage, she got bored one day, decided she wanted a divorce, took his children and his money, and left. Gibbs knew it was a sensitive topic, so he didn't mention his arm-chair analysis. But he did make sure they looked at all of the information, not just the evidence that implicated Kadee Carlisle.

They printed out the document with the email exchanges between the victim and his mother and began to read. Poole huffed and puffed the entire time. The exchanges began at midnight on September 16th, three days before Noah Donovan was killed. The first one was from the victim.

From Noah to Belle: *Mother, I've been naughty, I know. I shouldn't have left you at the restaurant. I'm sorry. Will you please forgive me?*

From Belle to Noah: *You have not listened to Mother. Haven't I taught you anything? Women are evil. They can't be trusted. They will only hurt you. You must believe Mother. I wouldn't do anything to hurt you. You are my baby boy. All I ever wanted to do was protect you. But if you don't leave her, you will be sorry. Love, Mother*

From Noah to Belle: *Oh, Mother, I'm sorry. I'm sorry. I love you. You will always be the number-one woman in my life. I just want what other men have — a wife, children, someone to make a family with. I know you're trying to protect me, and I trust you. But Yvonne is different. She would never hurt me. She really wouldn't, Mother. Please give her a chance.*

From Belle to Noah: *She's evil, son. I knew that from the very first day I met her. She doesn't care about you, not the way Mother does. She will reel you in, take all of your money, your sperm for babies, if she can even have any at her age, which is highly unlikely, then she will leave you. She's also fat. She doesn't take care of her appearance for you. Selfish, selfish, selfish woman, she is. They all are. You are leaving Mother, who took care of you your whole life, for another woman!!! There's no excuse for that.*

From Noah to Belle: *Mother, please! I would NEVER EVER leave you. Don't you know that? Please can we meet and talk about this. Or at least pick up your phone so we can talk. I can't believe you won't pick up your phone.*

From Belle to Noah: *I'm not playing games here. If you trust me, you will leave her. Or you will be sorry. You must listen to Mother. Are you going to listen to Mother or that evil witch of a woman?*

From Noah to Belle: *Mother, PLEASE! I want to listen. I promise if you pick up or meet me, I will listen. I promise, Mother. PLEASE! Please can we talk or meet?*

The last one read at 5:49 in the evening on September 17th, just two days before he was killed. Gibbs and Poole looked at each other, both shaking their heads. It was a disturbing exchange to say the least. Poole stood up, adjusted his belt and motioned to Gibbs to walk over to the coffee station. He was speechless.

They both poured coffee, then walked back over to Poole's desk. Gibbs squinted, "I told you there was more to this story. That's some sick shit. You just never know what really goes on with people."

Poole nodded, "There's no denying Belle Donovan is a sick woman. I told you, a narcissist type, remember I said that the first day we met her. I know the type. And man, those emails are sick…makes my stomach turn. The things she said are sick," he paused, sipping his coffee. "But that doesn't mean she killed him. Besides, the woman has an alibi. Kadee Carlisle does not."

Gibbs rubbed his hand over his forehead. "I still believe it's possible that she could be our killer. We should at least go question her more." He paused for a moment. He was thinking. "Her alibi is that she was with Yvonne Tracy. Interesting how they were together after Donovan's death, sounds like she didn't want anything to do with Yvonne Tracy when he was alive. We need to question her. Something's not right."

Poole knew he was right, although he did not like the idea of having to talk to her. "I'm still leaning with the Carlisle woman, but I agree we have to check Belle Donovan out." He sighed, and adjusted his belt, "I'm not looking forward to dealing with that woman. Noah Donovan never had a chance with a mother like that. Imagine the things she said to him when he was a kid. Crap, women like that should not be allowed to have kids."

Gibbs nodded in agreement.

Poole stood up, adjusting his belt. "Let's go and get this shit over with."

Just as they opened the office door to leave, another detective shouted, "Poole, Gibbs, you need to see this."

They walked toward the small kitchen area where there was a television. Three other detectives were standing watching the screen. One pointed toward the monitor, "Check her out."

On the set was Belle Donovan holding her press conference. She was seated on a large white sofa, wearing all white, except for a sky blue scarf that was draped across her shoulders and around her neck. She was going on and on about what she was going through as a result of her son's murder, saying that her own life was over now that he was gone. "The murderer killed two people on September 19th, first my son, Noah Donovan, and then his mother," she said in her most honeyed tone. "There can be no justice for what's been done to *me*."

A press person asked, "Do you think Kadee Carlisle did it?"

"There is not a doubt in my mind," she adjusted her scarf. "I just hope the police and district attorney's office do their job.

People can be so incomp…ahem," she coughed, "ahem, well, let's just say that Noah Donovan's mother hopes Kadee Carlisle is sent to prison for the rest of her life. She has ended the life of not just one person, but two." She took a tissue and dabbed at the corners of her eyes, clearly being careful not to mess up her makeup.

There was a rumble from the press as they all tried to ask questions at once, but Belle Donovan abruptly ended the conference by walking off the dais. The news station switched to a commercial.

"Wow, just wow," said Detective Sheehan who was standing right next to Poole. "That woman has some set of balls on her."

Poole looked stunned, his red nose redder. "She's behaving as though we should have been able to stop the murder before it happened. Is this woman for real?"

"No doubt," said Gibbs. He was shaking his head in disbelief. "That woman is certifiable."

"She kill her son, Poole?" Sheehan asked.

"Nah…I don't think she's our killer. She's crazy, but I don't think she's *that* crazy. But me and Gibbs are going to check her out anyway."

The two began their journey through the heavy city traffic. They decided to stop at Hot and Crusty for a bagel sandwich before they went to Belle Donovan's penthouse. It was a good thing they did; they wouldn't have much time to eat later. Their day was about to become much more complicated.

Chapter 21

Just as Poole and Gibbs finished up their lunch and headed to Belle Donovan's, Alex arrived at the jail for a meeting with Kadee. She had been anticipating his visit all morning. She could not wait to tell him that she thought she had an alibi. At the very least, she knew what the word **terminate** meant, and it did not mean "terminate" Noah Donovan. That, in and of itself, was a weight off her mind.

Alex usually had a cheerful demeanor. When he came into the small consult room, he looked somber. His eyes had that serious look that people get right before they deliver bad news. Kadee's mood shifted from hopeful to afraid. "What is it, Alex? What?" Her eyes were wide.

"Nothing Kadee…well, not nothing, but it's not a big deal," he paused and looked at her, his eyes wincing.

"It's OK." He looked so pained. Kadee's immediate reaction was to soothe him, but her stomach was doing somersaults. "It's OK, Alex. Just tell me."

"Noah's mother, Belle Donovan, did you ever meet her?"

"No, no, I thought I mentioned that. I never met anyone in Noah's life. Well..." She averted her eyes. "Except for Dr. Tracy," she looked up again. "Why?"

"Belle Donovan held a press conference today. She's an audacious woman." Alex hestitated.

"Don't leave me hanging. What did she say?" she raised her voice.

"It's not what she said. If anything, she made herself look bad. I can't believe what a self-absorbed narcissist that woman is."

"You said that...what is it?"

"The press conference drew a lot of media attention to the case. It's on every TV station and website, Kadee. Your name is all over the news as a suspect in custody."

She cupped her face with her hands and was shaking her head back and forth, "Oh, no...no."

"You know how unforgiving the media can be when they're gripped by a juicy story. They're reporting the story almost as if you've already been convicted."

"Can you hand me those tissues?" Kadee was wiping away the tears with the back of her hand. She cried for a couple of minutes while Alex repeated that everything was going to be OK.

What else could he say? Kadee knew how irresponsible some reporters could be, more concerned with ratings than actually providing the public with objective facts. There was nothing she could do. It was one of the things she had no control over given her current circumstances. She had to let it go and focus on what she did have control over, which included figuring out if she was where she thought she was on the day of the murder.

Thankfully, she had called her parents and informed them of what had happened. It would have been worse for them if the first bit of information they had was the sensationalized facts reported by the media. They were going to support her through this and help in every way they could. They were already in the process of trying to organize their financial resources for bail, if, in fact, she was indicted and the judge gave a bail option at the arraignment. Alex was not optimistic; with the charge of first degree murder, bail was unlikely, but it was possible. Her parents were getting the money together, trying their best to be hopeful.

Kadee shifted gears, pushing Belle Donovan and the media aside to focus on her defense. She told Alex what she remembered about **terminate**. On September 19th she was supposed to go with Hailey to "terminate" her pregnancy. She had written it encrypted, almost as a joke to herself, because Hailey had made such a big fuss about making sure it was confidential.

Given her association with the Manhattan elite, her marital status, and Richard's fame, the abortion needed to be top secret. It was scheduled to be at a small clinic somewhere in New Jersey. She was going to rent a car that she'd pay for in cash, and she was using a pseudonym. She wouldn't even tell Kadee her alias.

Kadee had joked, "Are you going to keep me blindfolded the whole ride over, too?" Hailey did not think the comment was funny at all.

Kadee couldn't be certain that she actually went. Try as she might, she was unable to retrieve the memory. But she was supposed to go. It was an important commitment, and it was unlike her to back out of things. Of course, she wasn't herself at the time. She was a crazy woman using massive amounts of drugs to dull her pain. But if she knew Hailey at all, and she thought she did, Hailey would have made sure that Kadee didn't abandon her in her time of need. She would have made sure Kadee went with her.

Even though Hailey had been angry the day before, remarking that Kadee had been unavailable to her on the day of her abortion, Kadee felt certain that Hailey was lying. It was more consistent with Hailey's character to hide the truth in an effort to protect her reputation than to allow Kadee to back out of a commitment to her. No, Hailey would have made sure she did not leave her alone in her time of need. That's who Hailey was.

Alex seemed suddenly more hopeful than when he entered the room moments earlier. He knew what this meant for the case. If her alibi was confirmed, Kadee would be vindicated. They would have to let her go. He asked for Hailey's phone number. Kadee gave it to him, but she also told him about their conversation. Kadee wasn't so sure Hailey would tell the truth. She would be more concerned with her privacy, that her abortion be kept secret and that there was no smudge to her reputation. Hailey was no idiot. With the extensive salacious media coverage, if she revealed the truth that Kadee did, in fact, go with her, it would be on the evening news, in the paper, buzzing all over the city. Everyone would know her secret.

He called anyway. Hailey picked up. The two shared a few moments of casual chitchat. Hailey hadn't seen Alex since Kadee and he broke up years earlier. Then he cut straight to the point. He told her that he was Kadee's attorney, reminding her of the seriousness of the charges Kadee was potentially facing. He explained the word terminate was discovered in Kadee's calendar, that she remembered Hailey's appointment, that she thought there was a good chance she was with Hailey at the time of the murder. He ended his speech, pleading with Hailey to tell the truth. His last sentence was a dramatic finale, "You can save her life, Hailey. You can save her life. All you have to do is tell the truth."

Hailey responded in four sentences. "That's some story, Alex, but I have no idea what you're talking about. I didn't have an abortion. Kadee must still be out of it. Please **do not** call me again." She slammed the receiver.

Alex was shocked. It had been a long time since he and Hailey had spoken, but from what he remembered about her, he was positive Hailey was lying about the abortion. He would have liked to believe that Hailey would not leave Kadee rotting in prison for the rest of her life rather than risk some temporary public disgrace, but he knew Hailey was selfish enough to do just that.

Kadee wasn't shocked. She was disappointed and saddened, but she knew how important pretense was for Hailey. It was all-defining. Yet there must be another way to prove her alibi now that they knew what it was.

Alex was determined. He rubbed his hand through his curly dark hair and squinted. He had another idea. It was a long shot, but he thought it was worth pursuing. He didn't care about Hailey's reputation. His concern was saving Kadee.

He called his office; spoke with his research assistant, giving her all the information he had. She was to gain access to the videos of cars going through the tolls on the New Jersey highways, as well as the bridge and tunnel crossings from New Jersey back into Manhattan on September 19th. If they could find a shot of

Hailey traveling, in her paid-in-cash rental, perhaps Alex could use it as leverage to get her to come forward with the truth. In his mind, she was going to be exposed either way. Either she could tell the truth or he would be calling her as a witness and she would be committing perjury. Her reputation wouldn't do her much good if she was doing time in prison for lying under oath.

And if they got lucky, they would find a video of the car with a clear image of Kadee in it, too. A photograph of Kadee elsewhere at the time of the murder would be enough to save her. And they would not need Hailey for this scenario, either.

If Hailey had come forward as soon as Kadee was arrested, there was not a doubt in Alex's mind that Kadee would have been released from custody before she was formally indicted. Unfortunately, Hailey was not cooperating. But one thing was for sure, he was convinced that Kadee was innocent. Now he just had to find a way to prove it.

He left the small consult room. He could still hear the clock ticking in his head as he walked out of the building and into the hustle of the city streets. The noise was a welcome relief. The echo in that small empty room was deafening. He shook his head a few times, trying to rid himself of the ticking.

As Alex approached the subway on the trip back to his office, Poole and Gibbs were sitting with Belle Donovan on her perfectly white sofa in her luxury apartment engaged in an unbearable dialogue made more impossible by Belle's obdurate behavior. They had started by questioning her about the email exchanges that occurred right before her son's murder. Poole read them to her and asked what had happened between them. The content was contentious, and they could see that Belle grew more irritated with each line read to her. When he was done, she glared at the detectives, her cheeks flushed with rage. Poole pressed the topic. He wanted to know what had led up to their conversation.

Belle spoke calmly, in her usual sugary tone, but she was clearly perturbed. "My son is murdered and you're bothering me with this nonsense. Shouldn't you be questioning that Kadee Carlisle, that murderess? She's the one who did this to me."

Poole shifted on the couch. "Mrs. Donovan, we're sorry to have to bother you with this. We're just trying to piece together the last days of your son's life."

Gibbs chimed in, trying to assuage her. "We really need your help."

She told them that Noah and she had disagreed about his engagement to Yvonne. Belle explained that she wasn't good enough for her son; she was trying to stop him from making the biggest mistake of his life.

Gibbs asked, "You were with Yvonne Tracy the day of the murder?"

"Yes, Detective Gibbs, I was. What does that have to do with anything?" She raised her voice slightly, making her hostility apparent.

"Well, it sounded like you didn't like her very much, that you thought she was 'evil.' That's what you wrote to your son, Mrs. Donovan."

"She's fine. I didn't like her for my son. I never said I didn't like her. Who I like and who I liked for my son are two different things. Clearly, you don't understand, so let me clarify. Noah needed my help for everything. He was a poor decision maker. As his mother, I had to make sure he didn't marry the wrong woman. Yvonne Tracy was not the right woman, so I told him she was evil, to get him away from her. Are we clear, detectives?" She coughed, purposefully, "Are we done now? This discussion is ridiculous. It has nothing to do with Kadee Carlisle killing us."

Poole did not like her tone. He felt provoked. He wanted to raise his voice. Instead, he took a deep breath and tried to respond unemotionally. "We are in the process of collecting the evidence against Kadee Carlisle. It's just important that we have the whole story."

"I understand, detective, but I am going to make sure you do your job, which is to go after that woman and make sure she goes to prison for the rest of her life. That woman, that Kadee Carlisle…she is one big whore. I know that for a fact."

Poole's interest was piqued. He definitely thought Kadee Carlisle was a temptress. But a whore? "Mrs. Donovan, what do you mean you know for a fact?"

She hesitated; she was about to say something, but stopped. She adjusted her scarf. It appeared that she was thinking about his question. "Well, let's just say I know things, detectives. A mother knows her son."

At first Poole thought she was using the word "whore" carelessly, but now it sounded like she actually knew something, something about Kadee Carlisle. He persisted. "It's important that you tell us the truth, ma'am. If you know something about Kadee Carlisle, it's important that you tell us. Do you suspect that Ms. Carlisle is a prostitute?"

"Some things are supposed to remain private. Clearly, your own mother did not raise you with any manners." She patted her scarf and stood up saying, "I think we're done here."

Poole ignored her comment. He knew the type. He wasn't going to take it personally, but he would not allow her to impede the investigation, either. And he wanted her to answer the question. His tone was biting when he responded. "Ma'am, you must answer our questions. Do you understand that? You have two choices: You can answer our questions here, or we can do it down at the station. Your choice, but I highly recommend doing it here. It's not too comfortable in our dark, empty interrogation room. And may I remind you that this is to find out who did…"

She cut him off; her tone was sharp. "I said I think we're done here, detectives. That means I want you to leave. Or I can call my attorney, if you'd prefer." She cocked her head to the side and smiled.

"Call your attorney, Mrs. Donovan. You can tell him or her that I look forward to our meeting down at the station within the next couple of days."

Just as Poole and Gibbs were walking through Belle Donovan's living room into the dining area to make their way to the front door, Poole's phone rang. It was Julie Brown from the forensic lab. The fingerprints on the spy cam video recorder were Belle Donovan's. There was more. They traced the camera back to an account under Belle Donovan's name. She owned the camera and it was hooked up to the IP address on her home computer. She was video recording her son.

Poole was privy to the private lives of people; he had heard many bizarre stories, but this information was shocking. Belle

Donovan was recording her son in the privacy of his bedroom. It took a minute for the information to sink in. He probably should have waited for further investigation to ask her about it. It didn't mean she killed him; it only indicated that she was invading his privacy. But he couldn't resist the urge, so the question just spilled out.

He stopped walking, turned and faced Belle. "Mrs. Donovan, there was a video recorder found in your son's bedroom. Do you know anything about that?"

She gave him an evil glare. "What are you talking about, detective? I thought I asked you to leave."

Gibbs looked confused, but stopped walking and stood next to Poole as he continued, "Mrs. Donovan, there was a video recorder found in your son's bedroom, which I know you know about. Your fingerprints are all over it, and it's registered under your name and attached to your home computer. It's important that you tell the truth, ma'am. Do you understand?"

Belle looked at Poole, holding his eye contact with a defiant stare. "Detective Poole, what does this have to do with my son's murder?"

Poole closed the space between him and Belle. He was trying to intimidate her, unnerve her into answering his question. "I'd advise you to answer my question honestly. It's better if you cooperate. We will get to the bottom of this one way or another. You cannot record people without their consent. It's a felony. I assure you that I will be able to obtain a search warrant, and I will look through your computer myself. If you tell the truth now, the court may show you some leniency. Do you understand?"

If Belle was ruffled, she didn't show it. She moved in even closer, the two were practically nose to nose. Poole held his position steadfast. He didn't budge. Gibbs' eyes were wide with surprise; he could feel the intensity of the moment as he observed the two in a face off.

"Listen, Detective Poole, it's really none of your business. I haven't done anything wrong. My son was killed...killed... slaughtered by that evil slut," she was speaking softly, but her tone was cutting and filled with vengeance.

For a moment, Gibbs was afraid of her; he checked for his gun, placing his hand on it for reassurance. He could feel her rage. He was sure she was ready to lose it.

Poole didn't move; he was waiting for an answer. He could tell she was losing her cool, but he didn't care. He knew she was on the verge of divulging information.

"I'll answer your foolish question. After that, I expect you to take your large, overly unscrupulous derriere and your assistant," she gestured to Gibbs, "and vacate my apartment."

Poole nodded.

"My son, Noah, needed my help, but he wasn't always open with me. I purchased that recorder to keep tabs on him, so I would know all the things he wasn't telling me. He especially needed guidance when it came to women, but he didn't always ask me or tell me exactly what was going on with the women in his life. You see, Detective Poole, I loved my son more than anything in the world. That recorder was to help him. That recorder was because I wanted to protect him from the vile women of the world. I had no other choice but to check up on him. I did what any mother would do in my position. I was protecting my child, my baby. And even with that, I failed him." She was choking up. There were no tears, but her eyes looked red and her soft voice had the slightest quiver. "Noah Donovan's mother failed him, detective. Noah Donovan's mother couldn't save him from that crazy, conniving slut Kadee Carlisle."

She reached over to the table, took a tissue, batted the corner of her eyes, then turned back to look at Poole. Her eyes were sharp, still obviously furious. "Does that answer your question, detective?"

Poole swallowed hard. He had mixed feelings about Belle's diatribe. Part of him identified with her sorrow; her last few statements sounded like genuine grief. On the other hand, her story was strange. The way she rationalized violating her son's privacy made him uneasy. It seemed so twisted, and it left him feeling a tad suspicious. He had more questions, many more. The more her story unfolded, the more questions he had. But he was certain if he continued he would only further antagonize her. So, he decided to leave. Gibbs and he could always come back or bring her down to the station if necessary. But he did have one last comment.

"Just one more thing, ma'am. I think it's only fair to warn you that video recording your son without his permission is a felony and carries prison time. If there are any images of nudity or sexually explicit content of him or any of these 'vile women of the world,' as you call them, you will be charged with unlawful surveillance, you can mark my words on that." He then matter-of-factly added, "Sorry for your loss. We'll be in touch."

Belle responded, "I expect you to make sure Kadee Carlisle goes to prison for the rest of her life, detectives. That's what the taxpayers' pay for, for you to put the real criminals away, not to attack innocent family members like me." She closed the door behind them before she even finished her sentence.

Poole and Gibbs walked down the long row of stairs leading to the street and got back into the police car. Their bickering started immediately. They were in disagreement over Belle Donovan. Poole thought she was as crazy as a loon, a total narcissistic type, but not a murderer. He thought she knew something about Kadee Carlisle that she was unwilling to say because it would make her son look bad.

He reminded Gibbs about Noah Donovan's journal entries. "Donovan couldn't stop having sex with Kadee Carlisle even though she threatened to kill him and was afraid of her. Carlisle is a temptress and I think Belle Donovan knows something. Maybe something about Carlisle and her son's sex life that would prove that she killed him, but would also make her son look really bad to the public."

Gibbs wasn't convinced that Belle was innocent. He had a moment in her apartment where he really felt her wrath, a moment where he felt afraid of her. He thought she was capable of murder. His theory was that she was in a jealous rage after Noah Donovan announced that he was going to marry Yvonne Tracy.

"The woman doesn't think like a normal person, Poole. I bet she went over there to talk to him, and when he wouldn't listen to her, she killed him in a rage. Hell, maybe she even thinks it was an accident and is afraid to come forward with the truth. But I think that woman is capable of anything. She definitely had a weird relationship with her son. It's almost like she was in love with him. Jealous rage, I'm telling you, I just have a feeling about it. And we need to obtain a search warrant for her computer. She was recording him. Even though the camera was off, there is a possibility that there was something recorded the night of the murder. In fact, I think we should try to get a warrant to search her entire apartment."

Poole did not agree that Belle was the murderer, still holding steadfast to Kadee Carlisle. He knew recording her son was illegal, and he found it disturbing, calling it "visual incest," but he thought it was a coincidence and unrelated to the killing. "Listen, this happens in these types of investigations, you know that. We start picking through people's private lives and discover all sorts of twisted secrets. But there is absolutely no evidence that she killed him. I don't even think there is enough to get a warrant to search her apartment. She has an alibi, remember. This is a family matter and unlawful surveillance at best. What that woman needs is a good shrink…We should be able to get the warrant for her computer, though, and if there is any footage on there from the night of the murder, I have no doubt it will implicate Carlisle."

"I don't know, Poole. There's just something off about this whole investigation. I feel it."

"For fuck's sake! We can't go to the district attorney with a hunch. We need e-v-i-d-e-n-c-e. And other than her illegal voyeurism, we've got none. Z-e-r-o."

They were going back and forth, both knowing each other well enough to realize they were not going to resolve their differences. They did agree that they would file the paperwork for a search warrant of the computer to see if there was anything on it related to the murder.

Gibbs thought they should talk to Yvonne Tracy again. He wanted to make sure she was telling the truth about their alibi. She would have no reason to lie, particularly given the way Belle talked about her, but he felt strongly enough that he thought it was worth pursuing. They stopped by her office, but the doorman said she wasn't in. They tried her apartment. She wasn't there, either. So Poole called and left her a message asking her to call them back, saying that they had some follow-up questions for her. Then, they headed back to the station.

When they arrived, Gibbs brooded at his desk, still uneasy about their visit with Belle Donovan. Maybe she wasn't the murderer, maybe it was Kadee Carlisle, but there was something so off about her, he really felt that. He decided to do some research. It wouldn't take long before he made another astonishing discovery.

As soon as Poole and Gibbs walked out of her apartment, Belle Donovan slammed her door in a huff, "The audacity!" she said to herself. She could not believe they had the nerve to intrude upon her private life. She went into her bathroom, sat down at her make-up table; her mascara was slightly clumped from tears. She could not have those lashes all stuck together if she had to go down to Paul's office to file a lawsuit against those low-class civil servants. *What a complete atrocity. Give someone a badge and they think they can throw their power around. They are nothing more than glorified babysitters,* she thought as she dabbed just the right amount of crimson along her lips.

Paul Schwartz was her friend and attorney, as well as an occasional sex partner. She wasn't really interested in Paul romantically, but she knew just how to use her grace and allure to charm him. If she had to do the "nasty deed" occasionally to get him to do favors for her, she was fine with that. Although he was horrible in bed, she could stand just about anything for five minutes, which thankfully was about how long he lasted. And in return, Paul did almost anything she wanted.

Paul's phone was ringing. Belle sat with her perfect posture on her couch, one leg crossed daintily over the other waiting for him to answer. She felt she had been the victim of mistreatment by Poole and Gibbs, and she wanted to do something about that, possibly sue them or perhaps the whole department.

The conversation did not go as she expected. Since Paul was her attorney, she knew the conversation was privileged, not that she thought video recording her son was wrong, she just didn't think her private life was public business. She really believed that *they* were the ones who were the unlawful intruders.

So she explained what happened to Paul. They found the recorder, her fingerprints were on it, they could see it was connected to her computer, and the part that really had her perturbed, that they wanted to search through her personal files.

Paul asked her if she was video recording Noah without his consent. To which she responded, "Naturally, Paul. I had to."

"Had to? What do you mean?" he was matter-of-fact, using his attorney voice, as Belle called it.

"Listen, my son was all mixed up. And I knew he was lying to me about the women he was involved with. I had no choice but to keep an eye on him. He should have known better than to be dishonest with his mother. I didn't do anything wrong, Paul. It was done out of concern."

"Look I don't mean to rain on your parade, but it *is* illegal to record someone without their consent."

"But it was his mother who did it. Surely, she had that right, the right to protect her own child."

"Unfortunately, you don't. I'm sorry. If I may ask, what were you filming anyway?"

"Well, I would go into his apartment some days and put it on to see what he was doing on the nights that we weren't together."

"And?"

"And...I don't know Paul...these are silly questions. He was having a lot of sex and lying to his mother about it. I was afraid that he would be manipulated by the hands of some conniving wench who only wanted him for *our* money. I wasn't going to show the recordings to anyone except him. Listen, I didn't call for this. I'm not the one who did something wrong. It's those two detectives whose behavior was inappropriate, offensively so. What can we do about that? I don't need them bothering me with this anymore. I am a grieving mother!" she was trying to control the knot of tears that was causing her voice to tremble.

His voice sounded compassionate when he responded. "I know dear. I'm very sorry that this is happening on top of everything else you are going through. Let me take you to dinner tonight. What do you say, around 7ish? I'll pick you up."

"I'm not sure about dinner tonight, Paul. I'm very tired. And this visit from the detectives has just worn me down. I feel so violated," she said in her most honey-glazed voice.

"I understand. But as I said, and I'm very sorry," he was back in attorney mode, "filming Noah without his consent —and especially filming him and non-consenting women — is a felony. What's on your computer?"

"What difference does it make? Go pull some strings and make sure they don't get access."

"That's going to be difficult Belle. They're probably going to be able to get a search warrant." There was a pause. "Is there anything from the night of the murder? Maybe your recording could actually help the investigation."

"No, I had turned it off a couple of days before. You know what, I think dinner would be a good idea. I should get out of the house."

"Great. I'll pick you up at seven. I'll make sure to cheer you up with the ole Paul charm." He ended in a cheerful tone.

Belle was annoyed, but responded in her sweetest voice. "Sounds lovely. I'll see you then."

When they hung up, Belle was irritated. She did not want the detectives to be able to push her around. She opened her phone book and started going through the names of her hundreds of friends, wondering which one would be the most helpful. She was going to use her sexual appeal to try and seduce Paul into calling his friend Justine Fellows, one of the district judges. But in case that was a dead end, she needed an alternative plan. *No one humiliates Belle Donovan and gets away with it,* she thought.

There was just one thing about the whole recording scenario that bothered her. It wasn't a nagging worry; she was too in control to let anything get her ruffled. It was more of a curiosity. Where was that container that she had left under her son's desk?

Noah hadn't mentioned finding it, and it didn't turn up during the investigation. Surely, he would have said something if he found it. She had left it there to send him the message that mother knows everything, that there is no hiding from mother. She was getting fed up with him not telling her the truth about his life. And try as she might —and lord knows she tried —he just kept concealing things. She had no other choice but to put that little container together, to show him that he couldn't keep secrets from mother.

She wanted him to know that she knew everything he was doing. She placed it perfectly under his desk, right where he usually rested his feet while he was on his computer. Hopefully the message— you can't conceal things from mother — would register.

She knew he was hiding her pictures when women came over. She did not like that. She thought maybe he did it so that the other women wouldn't be threatened by her. It would be hard for those women to feel confident at all if they knew just how gorgeous Noah's mother was. Regardless, she wanted him to know that she knew what he was doing. She felt by putting that black X over one of the photos, he would get the hint.

She knew about Kadee and Yvonne, and she knew that sometimes he was having sex with both of them on the same day. She witnessed that with her own eyes. And she knew that they were not using contraception. That was in very poor judgment. What if both of them got pregnant at the same time? Clearly not having a father figure left him without a clue about these sorts of things. Mother tried to tell him, but he would not listen. She knew about those other whores, too. He was averaging about one slut a week for the last month. And she knew that when he was alone for the night, he masturbated to pornography, which she felt was low class and not the proper behavior for a doctor. Occasional masturbation maybe, but her son seemed to be doing it too frequently, in her opinion, which was really the only opinion that mattered.

She mulled it over for a few minutes, but she soon realized she was never going to be able to figure it out. In any case, it wasn't found at the scene, which was a good thing. And thankfully, she never saved the clips to her hard drive. She would leave it at that, for now. She decided to lie down for a while, suddenly overcome with exhaustion.

CHAPTER 22

Just around the same time that Gibbs was looking for secrets in the tangled life of Annabel Donovan, Yvonne Tracy had arrived at the jail to visit with Kadee. After Alex had left, Kadee remembered that Hailey had also been seeing Dr. Tracy. She knew she couldn't reveal Hailey's confidential information, but she thought maybe she knew the truth about Kadee's alibi. Possibly there was something she could do to help.

Truth be told, Kadee also felt that they had some unresolved business between them. She knew Dr. Tracy didn't owe her the luxury, but she was hoping to explain why she had concealed Noah's real identity. She wanted to apologize. She had no idea how Dr. Tracy felt about it—her—but she imagined learning about Noah and her could not have been easy. Then adding in that Kadee—her former patient/fiancé's girlfriend—allegedly killed him, it must have been almost too much to bear. She just felt awful about the whole thing.

Kadee was hesitant to call; part of her was ashamed to face her. It was bad enough that she had shared all of her ugly thoughts and feelings with Dr. Tracy. But the thought that she was also in a relationship with Noah and that he chose to marry her instead of Kadee left Kadee feeling even more exposed. She almost felt dirty next to her, like she was the worn out slut he used for sex while Yvonne was the unsoiled princess he wanted to marry. She swallowed her pride and made the call anyway. She really needed her help, and she thought she owed her an apology.

Dr. Tracy walked into the small consult. As soon as Kadee saw her, Kadee became choked up. It was a strange feeling, almost as if she were seeing her for the first time. She looked different to Kadee. Before she was the doctor helping Kadee through her problems. Now she was the woman, the other woman, the one who was going to marry the man they both loved. Noah had a secret life, one he kept hidden from Kadee, and Dr. Tracy was part of that life. She took her hand and placed it on her heart. She ached.

Dr. Tracy had cut her hair, too. Instead of gracefully skimming her shoulders, her dark brown hair was cut short, ending right below her ears. It made her look older, Kadee thought, or maybe it was the grief straining her, making her look tired and weary. As soon as she sat down, Kadee started crying. She reached for a tissue and said, "Dr. Tracy, thank you for coming. I'm so, so sorry about Noah."

In her usual calm tone, Yvonne responded, "I'm sorry, too." She took Kadee's hand and squeezed it.

Kadee blew her nose. She then went on to explain why she had used the name Aaron instead of Noah, that she had planned to tell Dr. Tracy the truth, but kept getting sidetracked with all the drama, and that she was sorry for her deception.

Yvonne took her hand again and squeezed it hard, saying, "It's not your fault, Kadee. This is not your fault. I'm sorry, too. I had no idea."

There were a few moments of silence between them. It was a nice type of silence, as each woman knew the other's pain intimately. A tragic, but significant event now bonding them together, as they each shared the other's loss. Yvonne took a deep breath and broke the silence. She asked Kadee what was going on her with her case. She had spoken with Poole and Gibbs and had seen the media coverage, but she wanted to hear about it from her.

Kadee updated her with the details, most of which Yvonne already knew. Then she told her about the blackouts, her fear that she might have killed Noah, her association to the word **terminate,** and her hope that she had been with Hailey. Dr. Tracy was nodding, but she didn't say anything. She just let Kadee talk, almost like they were in a therapy session.

Kadee asked about Hailey's abortion. She was tentative as she continued. Finally she took a deep breath and directly asked her if she knew the truth about her whereabouts on the day of the murder. Did she know if she was with Hailey when she went for her abortion? Kadee acknowledged the ethical dilemma she was placing Dr. Tracy in and that she understood if she needed to maintain Hailey's confidentiality. But she was desperate to know.

Kadee was tearing up. "I know this is unfair to ask you, but I just don't know what else to do. I'm scared. I don't think I'm capable of murder, but not knowing is scary. I just want to know the truth. Even if you can just give me a hint, you know…off the record or something, you know…just so I know for sure." She looked down, wiped her eyes with her hands and bit a cuticle. She looked back at Dr. Tracy and added, "I'm sorry to even ask."

Yvonne was listening, nodding her head, but she was undemonstrative. Kadee was immediately uncomfortable. She was spilling her guts, totally vulnerable and she had no idea what Dr. Tracy was thinking. Of course, that was what it was like much of the time in their therapy sessions, but in the present context, given the extraordinary circumstances, her stoicism made Kadee anxious. She began fidgeting with her fingers, pushing down her cuticles, wondering how Dr. Tracy was going to respond.

Yvonne began nodding her head more quickly, over and over, almost like she was twitching, her short bob bouncing below her ears with each head motion. She finally stopped, rubbed her hands down her arms and began to speak. "I understand, Kadee, I really do, but you're right. Hailey's files and our conversations are both confidential. And it sounds like she probably would not sign a consent form. Maybe you can have your lawyer see if he can have her files subpoenaed."

"OK," she looked down still picking at her fingers. "Is there anything you can say, anything, like a hint or something, that might help me know if I was with Hailey that day?" She buried her face in her hands. "I'm sorry," she was shaking her head. "I shouldn't even ask."

Yvonne was doing the rapid nodding again as she listened to Kadee. "Let's just say… I don't think you'll find what you're looking for in my records."

Kadee blurted out, "So she didn't tell you? It would be just like Hailey to keep it a secret from her therapist. Just like her… top secret abortion mission…" She felt frustrated.

"I'm going to be honest with you. Do I think you killed Noah? I'm not sure, but I really don't think so. Do I think you're capable of murder? Yes, I do. I think everyone is capable of murder. Anyone can hit a point where they just break, where they just absolutely, positively cannot take another second of holding in their feelings, where the rage has been simmering and simmering for way too long, where they have felt hurt and betrayed over and over and over, and they just can't hold back anymore, not for another hour, not for another minute, not for another second, and suddenly…something just snaps. Then it's all over." She put the back of her hands up to her cheeks. They were bright red.

Kadee's eyes were wide as she stared at Dr. Tracy. It was the first time she had ever heard her speak so passionately. Her speech was so fervent. Kadee could feel it. For a second she had a chill.

Yvonne took a long deep breath, sighing before she continued. "So you see, Kadee, I think you could have done it, but I don't think you did. You were obsessed with my fiancé, with Noah." She gave Kadee an uncomfortable smile. "He was stringing you along and stringing you along, and you went from loving him to loving him and hating him. Is that a toxic combination, even a lethal combination? Yes, I believe it to be. Some people have killed for less. But unlike some people, you were able to say how you felt. You were able to put words to those feeling, the pain may have been unbearable and you may have…well, we both know you did…you did think of killing him, but it was a thought and you shared those thoughts. You didn't hold it all in, letting it simmer like a volcano, until one day you just exploded in a violet rage. Nor were you planning and plotting a scheme to kill him, at least not that you shared with me."

She paused for a second to consider. "But even more important, you blamed yourself, not him, for the way you felt, for the dysfunction in your relationship, for not being able to leave — really, for most of the problems the two of you had. You may have been enraged with him, but you didn't blame him, you blamed yourself. And I could be wrong, but it is my personal and professional opinion that your self-blame left you more vulnerable to suicide than homicide. I just don't think you would have killed him without feeling he truly deserved to die and that you had every right to do it." She sat back in her chair and folded her arms.

Kadee looked at Yvonne. It felt strange to be the one listening while Dr. Tracy was doing the talking. But she appreciated everything she said. She trusted Dr. Tracy, so her words were comforting. "Thank you, Dr. Tracy. Thank you."

"Kadee, call me Yvonne."

Kadee smiled, "Thank you, Yvonne."

Yvonne's phone had gone off a few times while they were talking. She checked her messages and said she had to go. Kadee had one more question before she left. Did Yvonne have any idea who else might be responsible for Noah's death?

Yvonne responded, "It's hard to say. I guess it could have been any number of women, any woman who felt betrayed by him, or enraged. There are a lot of very unstable people in the world. Sometimes the most disturbed people come off as stable when you first meet them. Maybe he had a fling or two with some really unhinged woman. Or, it could have been his mother," she laughed. "His mother controlled his life. They had a love-hate relationship. I could totally see her going off the deep end in a rage."

Kadee cocked her head. She couldn't tell if Yvonne was joking or not.

"Let me see if I can find anything out that will help you. I'll come back later in the week. And please call if you need anything." She leaned down and hugged Kadee.

Kadee hugged her back. Yvonne turned to walk out. Right before she left, she turned back, looking at Kadee and said, "I don't want to upset you even more, but I should let you know that they have subpoenaed our session notes. I tried to use your right to confidentiality to protect you, but the court's privilege to know overrides doctor-patient confidences. I *am* very sorry. Thankfully, my official notes aren't very thorough; I keep more extensive notes for myself. And they won't have access to those. But I should tell you that a few of the notes they will get have incriminating content from some of those really difficult sessions when you were describing homicidal fantasies. It doesn't prove anything, Kadee, so please try not to worry too much. I'm sorry I couldn't stop them from having them. I really wish there was more I could do to help you."

Kadee nodded. What could she say? She blamed herself. If she hadn't lied about Noah's name, this never would have happened. Sure, part of her was angry with Yvonne; she should not have told them that she was her patient. *But* they would have found out sooner or later. Kadee continued to remind herself of that to rationalize away the anger she felt toward Yvonne. Her emotions for Yvonne were convoluted, and she was having a hard time sifting through them, particularly since Yvonne might be able to help her in some way.

She was almost more upset with Yvonne for being Noah's fiancée, as though it was Yvonne's fault that Noah chose her instead of Kadee. And what did that mean anyway? He wasn't faithful to Yvonne. He was probably fucking her while Yvonne was out showing off her engagement ring to her friends. But he must have treated Yvonne better than he did her. A woman like Yvonne would never have married the Noah that she was involved with.

Yvonne left, closing the door of the small consult room to leave Kadee alone with the ticking clock that echoed off the bare walls. Every second that ticked by reminded Kadee of her life that was being wasted spent in custody. And of the year of her life she wasted on that manipulative user Noah. She crossed her arms, resting her head in the nook they made. *What a fucked up triangle,* she thought.

Her thoughts shifted as she began to think through some of their sessions. She knew that whatever was in those notes was only going to make things worse for her. She needed to let Alex know. Or maybe he already knew and was afraid to tell her. She was being strong, but she was terrified and he knew that. Of course, she had to realize that Yvonne's therapy notes would eventually be admitted into evidence. It just didn't seem real until Yvonne said it. In fact, nothing about her situation seemed real. *This is not good,* she thought, *this is not good at all. I know I said a few times that I wished he was dead. For the love of God, I hope she didn't write that down.*

Her thoughts moved to Hailey. How could she lie to her on the phone saying Kadee didn't go with her for her abortion? Clearly she was being deceptive. At this point, Kadee was convinced that she went with her and therefore, did not kill Noah. If she could just set aside her reputation for a minute, she could help Kadee out of this mess. Hopefully, Alex's assistant would find something about that day, some concrete evidence that she was with Hailey.

Her thoughts were racing a bit as they shifted again, and she wondered if Yvonne was right. Could Noah's mother have killed him? They had a twisted relationship, but murder her own son? That seemed a bit outrageous, and she was in the business of studying some of the most atypical of human behaviors.

Thoughts about the naked women on those memories sticks entered her mind. Maybe it was some other woman he was sleeping with. Who knows how many woman he was manipulating. She felt nauseous just thinking about it. She reminded herself that she needed to get tested for STDs.

Then she remembered that those memory sticks never surfaced during the search of her apartment. And they had rummaged through her filing cabinet. They weren't there. What did she do with them? It's probably a good thing that they were gone; she didn't need the entire New York City Police Department staring at her vagina while they gathered information for the case against her. And all they proved was that Noah was a sick voyeur who had no respect for women. In fact, the way detective Poole looked at her with such distain, she was certain that he would try to say that the contents of that package gave her even more of a motive. *Thank God they didn't find them,* she thought. She could just imagine the feast the media would have had with them. The headline would probably read: KILLER KADEE, NAKED LADY. *For the love of God, I hope I buried those things somewhere.*

On the other hand, she wondered if maybe they could help her case. If they knew about the other women, it might create some doubt in the court's mind. They certainly demonstrated that there could have been someone else who had a motive. That might help her. She went back and forth, trying to think it through intellectually without letting her dread of having her own video being made public affect her. She didn't have a clue where they were anyway, and they could be on the hard drive of Noah's computer. She decided to tell Alex about it and let him make the decision. He was her attorney, after all.

She hated that she couldn't remember chunks of her life, and perhaps the pieces that she was missing held the answer to what really happened, or maybe not. Either way, once they got their hands on those session notes, she was going down the river unless something miraculous happened before then. Since she didn't believe in divine interventions, she considered any miracle an unlikely possibility. But as she reflected, she decided that maybe tonight was a good time to start praying. She needed all the help she could get.

She looked up at the clock and could feel it ticking in her throat. "Please, clock, shut up already. I can't take anymore!" Kadee dropped to her knees and prayed.

CHAPTER 23

The day was moving along rapidly for Poole and Gibbs. District Attorney Melanie Pearce was asking for the evidence against Kadee Carlisle. She was working on her presentation for Carlisle's indictment and needed all the evidence they had. Poole and Gibbs were also meeting with Carlisle and her attorney, Alex Suarez, the following day. Suarez had called and asked for the meeting. Poole was hoping for a confession, but Suarez explained that there were a few things Carlisle wanted to share about Noah Donovan's life that might help them find the real killer. Of course, they had to follow through, but Poole did not like this pussyfooting around; he wanted her confession — and he wanted it yesterday. He thought she was playing games and wasting their time.

Poole tended to be caustic when he was under pressure. It came in handy when he was interrogating suspects, but it could work to his disadvantage when he wanted something from the person who was on the receiving end of his sharp-tongued comments. Gibbs was busy at his desk digging through the past life of Belle Donovan, and Poole had run out of ways to convince Gibbs that he was wasting time.

Poole grabbed the file Gibbs had buried his head in. "Oh, look. Belle took a class at night school. You did it. You broke the case!" He shouted across the office. "Sheehan! Call the district attorney. Carlisle can go free. We've found our killer."

Gibbs took the file back. "This could go much faster if you helped instead of fighting me."

"We have more important things to do. Like prepare the case against Carlisle. Do this crap on your own time."

"Did you look at the title of the class?" Gibbs handed the paper to Poole, who kept his arms folded. "Just look at it."

Poole kept his arms folded and sneered at him. He finally snatched the paper from Gibbs' hand. He scanned the course title and syllabus.

Gibbs nodded his head. "Designing your own home security and video surveillance system. Setting up an Internet protocol camera. This smacks of the setup we found in Noah Donovan's apartment."

"So what. It only proves she's a snoop. We've got enough to tie the Carlisle woman to the murder. We need to focus on that. We can nab the crazy mother for spying on her son when the Carlisle case is locked down."

"Poole, you do this all the time. You get a scenario locked in your head and you can't let it go. Sometimes your intuition works great. Other times, though, it's just plain tunnel vision. And that's when you miss the good stuff on the periphery."

Poole tossed the night class paperwork back on the file. "That might be, but it doesn't negate the fact that with you on your wild goose chase, I'm the one stuck filling out all the evidentiary documents to file with D.A. Pearce." Poole glared at his partner as he stomped away.

After digging deeper into Belle Donovan's past, Gibbs found something about Dr. Allen Donovan — Belle Donovan's deceased husband, Noah's father — that piqued his interest. The first bit of information described the circumstances surrounding Allen Donovan's death, most of which he already knew from Belle Donovan. When they questioned her about the whereabouts of her husband, she said he had passed away thirty one years ago from a heart attack. It was a sad story, but not of any relevance to their investigation, so they didn't pursue it.

As he continued his exploration, there were a few other leads, but his endeavor was interrupted when Poole waved him over. Yvonne Tracy was there and with her were the notes from her sessions with Carlisle. Gibbs saved his search, and went into the consult room with Poole to meet with her.

Poole already had the file of notes open and was skimming through. Gibbs could see his eyes moving rapidly through the pages as he sat down. He shook the doctor's hand, then asked her again about her alibi. She had dark circles under her eyes; she looked exhausted. She grimaced when Gibbs again asked her about her whereabouts at the time of the murder. And she responded with the same answer she had previously provided: She was with Belle Donovan at the time of the murder.

"I'm not sure what else I can tell you. I wish I knew more." She paused, putting her hands on her cheeks. "These notes… you need to take them for what they are. People talk about all kinds of things in therapy, things that they would never even tell their closest friends. People have fantasies, sometimes violent, sometimes perverted, sometimes…I don't know…everyone has dark thoughts, and it doesn't mean anything other than that they are thoughts. I'm sure you've thought of hitting someone or yelling at someone in a way you would never actually act upon. And maybe you never tell anyone because it's not the most attractive thing to share. People often feel very ashamed of their dark thoughts. So they keep them private. I hear a lot of those thoughts in my sessions. And well…those notes, they just reflect thoughts, nothing more."

Poole looked up and said, "I understand. We need to go through these, but this is a murder investigation and I can already see a few notes that show that Kadee Carlisle wished your fiancé dead. And another here were she talked about thoughts of killing him. These show strong evidence of premeditation."

Yvonne placed her hands on the table as she considered her response. "Like I said, those are just thoughts, fantasies. If I had considered her dangerous, I would have had a duty to warn her potential victim. I never once felt that she was going to act on her feelings. She was enraged, and she felt trapped, but she was talking through her feeling. That's all. Just talking."

Poole gave her a sideways look. "I respect your professional opinion, but taken with all the other evidence against Ms. Carlisle, these notes reflect her culpability. We will look through them and call you if we have more questions. Thank you for coming down."

Poole raised himself off his chair and leaned over to shake Yvonne's hand, when Gibbs asked her another question. "Doctor, under the Tarasoff ruling, you have a duty to warn a potential victim or you could be held liable for their death. No disrespect, but I have to ask, couldn't your protection of Carlisle really be you just trying to cover up your own negligence?"

Yvonne pondered his question. "Yes, I have a duty to give warning if one of my patients makes a threat against a potential victim, but I also have to have a reasonable expectation that they will act on it. The fact that I was not searching for the man that Kadee called Aaron meant that I had no reason to think that she was threatening actual harm. She was venting out some very difficult feelings. That's my professional opinion. Naturally, there's human error. I could have been wrong, but I was not negligent. I never thought Kadee was actually going to hurt anyone."

"Did she ever threaten suicide? You said your fiancé was concerned about this. Is there anything in your notes revealing that possibility?"

"Not exactly. She did blame herself for a lot of things, which often renders people vulnerable to suicidal thoughts and actions. But she never reported that directly. I think she was telling Noah that she was going to kill herself so that he wouldn't leave her. People do that sometimes when they're desperate." She paused. "It's all very sad."

Gibbs eyes lit up. "Do you think it's possible that your fiancé was lying to you about Carlisle's suicide risk? Maybe as an excuse for his continued infidelity?"

The edge of her lips moved slightly downward as she fought off a frown. "I guess it's possible. But I don't think so."

Gibbs looked at Poole indicating that he was done with his questions. He knew Poole was probably salivating as he waited to dig into those session notes.

After Yvonne left, Poole was about to show Gibbs one of the notes when Gibbs'spoke. "Maybe they both did it? Maybe Carlisle and the doctor plotted Donovan's murder together? Maybe they conspired the plan and then the doctor convinced Carlisle to execute it?"

Poole squinted. "I dunno. Sometimes you make my head spin with all of your theories. Does it make sense? Sure, but we would need evidence against the doctor and there isn't any. Either way, Carlisle definitely did the killing. Let's go through these notes, gather the information against Carlisle, and keep the conspiracy theory in the back of our mind. If they did work together, maybe Carlisle will give the doctor up if the state is willing to cut her a deal. One step at a time with this. It's a complicated case and we need to stay focused."

Poole handed Gibbs a file, and they both started going through the pages of confidential information. Gibbs was examining the notes, but his mind was split in three. He was trying to keep the different possibilities compartmentalized, but his rush of ideas was making methodical thinking difficult.

He stopped reading for a few minutes to massage his temples in hope that his thoughts would make sense of this. There was some incriminating content from the sessions, implicating Carlisle. But there was something about the doctor that still felt off to him; a conspiracy made complete sense. He had thought earlier that Donovan's behavior left both women with a strong motive. Then there was the research left unfinished on his computer, exposing the layers of Belle Donovan's past. He wanted to get back to that. Before the notes came, he had felt pretty certain that his research would lead him to the truth.

He wanted to exhaust all of the options in front of him, so he developed a plan. He would look through the notes, help Poole organize the information, then go back to his research and follow it through until he satisfied his intuition. He was determined to know who killed Noah Donovan and he was still not convinced that it was Kadee Carlisle; and if it was, he was not so sure that she acted alone.

Chapter 24

It was a long restless night for Kadee. The previous afternoon, she had spoken with Alex, who informed her that Yvonne Tracy's notes had some damaging content in them and that they were going to hurt her case. It was no shock to her, but hearing it confirmed left her feeling like she had eaten a pound of spoiled meat.

"What are my chances?"

When it came to Kadee, Alex had no poker face. "I'm not going to lie. It could be much better." He watched Kadee's spirit sink. "But don't give up hope. You and I know you're innocent, so that's a start, isn't it?"

"Shit. I'm done for, aren't I? I can't even convince my fair-weather friend Hailey to prove my innocence, how will I convince a jury?"

Alex bolstered his spirit and put his hand against the tempered glass that separated them. He spoke into the visitor phone, Kadee's lifeline to the outside. "I won't give up until I clear your name. I know you. There is no way you could kill someone. I'm going to prove it if it's the last thing I do. Now let's prep for our meeting with Cagney and Lacey."

Kadee laughed at his joke. In a way, Poole and Gibbs did remind her of the female police detective team from the famous 1980's television show.

The day following her meeting with Alex, he and Kadee would sit opposite detectives Poole and Gibbs in an interrogation room. Alex was told that the detectives had numerous questions about Dr. Tracy's session notes with Kadee. Alex forewarned Kadee that it was going to be a difficult conversation. "But don't worry," he added. "I'll be there every step of the way to facilitate your responses. I'll make sure you don't say anything that will further incriminate you."

"OK, I appreciate your support, but no more rose-colored glasses."

Alex gave her a steely look. "It's not good…yet. But we're just in the beginning stages of our investigation, so anything can happen. My assistant is scouring Hudson County and Bergen County law enforcement and Port Authority data bases for images of Hailey driving to or from the abortion clinic. We *will* find something. Stay optimistic. I need you with me on this. OK?"

"Yeah…OK. As long as I know we've got forward momentum, I can keep the faith."

She also told him about the memory sticks she found in Noah's bedroom. She hated admitting to him that there was a video of her dancing naked floating around somewhere. He always saw her as so strong. She despised exposing how foolish and weak she was with Noah. But she felt Alex needed to know. Besides, revealing it to him was nothing compared to if the detectives and the media were to get their hands on it. *There goes my dignity. Again. Will this never end?*

"We all make mistakes. It's OK. I'm not here to judge. I'm here to help. You fell for the wrong guy. I get it." Alex flattened his hand against the glass. And on the opposite side of the glass, Kadee mirrored his hand with hers while he continued. "I made the same error with my ex-wife. We live and learn, and in between we do the best we can. We should tell the detectives about the recordings, even if *we* can't find them. They may be able to locate them on Noah's computer. I know its humiliating. But it does reveal that there are other possible suspects, as well as showing a bit about his true character. This could make his own words from his journal less credible."

Kadee perked up. She was relieved that her decision to tell Alex about the recordings was correct. "OK then. We tell them tomorrow in our meeting."

When they hung up, Kadee was led back to her cell. While she laid on the thin, grossly soiled mattress, she thought about Alex. They were pleasant thoughts and a needed respite from the ruminations about the case, the layers of deception she had been exposed to, and how truly hopeless she felt. She was constantly fighting off visions of herself locked up in prison, labeled a first-degree murderer. She had never contemplated suicide before, but in the privacy of her thoughts, she scared herself by thinking that killing herself was more appealing than being stuck in a cell for the rest of her life.

Alex was like a different person now. Of course it had been fourteen years since they were together, and people usually mature over time. She really liked the person he had become. It did make things a little easier having him there for support, and that sympathetic statement he made really touched her. It's soothing when people can commiserate without judgment. For a millisecond, she wished that she could call him just to hear his voice again. She felt so alone trapped in the emptiness of the cell. It made her feel as though her life was over. Her remaining days might be spent in a hollow shell just like the one she was in now — maybe one that was infinitely worse.

She spent the entire night tossing and turning, breathing into her sheet. The smell of cheap industrial detergent was better than the foul odor that lingered in the murky air of the jail, something like dirty feet, mixed with an awful scented aerosol.

The next morning, Kadee and Alex were brought to the consult room where they would review the details of the case before meeting with Poole and Gibbs. Alex believed the detectives might try to use the information from the therapy sessions to push her into a confession. Although collectively there was a lot of evidence that suggested she may have perpetrated the murder, it was all circumstantial. Since there were no fingerprints or DNA, they most likely wanted something more concrete to offer the district attorney for the arraignment. He also knew that the information they did have still made for a strong case against her should they find even the smallest bit of incriminating evidence.

Meanwhile, the media was in a whirl. Alex's office was receiving calls asking for interviews with Kadee and him. He had his assistant warding them off, but the media outlets were beginning to gather outside the jail. Alex had a real distaste for the way information was generally conveyed to the public, but now with it being personal, he was downright disgusted. They were calling Kadee "The Beautiful Butcher" and "Beautiful but Deadly."

People were all over social media using the trending topic #beautifulbutcher to pass commentary on the case without having their facts straight. It seemed that people had strong opinions already, arguing about it as if it was personal. Alex tried not to read too much on social media, it just enraged him. But when he looked a few times, it seemed that the public was split down the middle.

He asked Kadee for her Facebook password. He wanted to pull her page down. He noticed on Twitter that people had gone to her Facebook page and pulled what they could off of it. They were tweeting and re-tweeting her pictures and posts as if they had the privilege to rummage through her life. She had not even been formally charged yet. Alex understood the passion of expressing strong beliefs; he was an attorney after all. But, he felt real antipathy toward those who made ill-informed statements without attempting to get the actual facts.

Poole and Gibbs came in the room and the air immediately felt heavy. Kadee was doing her best to be strong, but she was feeling pretty hopeless. Poole's demeanor was determined; he wasted no time getting to the nitty-gritty. Poole had one of their files opened before his backside even touched the chair.

"Ms. Carlisle, there is strong evidence of pre-mediation in these session notes—"

JACQUELINE SIMON GUNN

"Everything in that notebook is circumstantial." Alex was not letting anything get misconstrued.

Without losing a beat, Poole picked up where he was interrupted. "In these session notes where you said you wished Noah Donovan was dead. There are also a few where you were actually describing thoughts of killing him."

Gibbs continued the badgering without missing a beat. "Let's face it. This doesn't bode well for you."

"C'mon, Ms. Carlisle," Poole said. "We know you killed him. If you tell the truth now we can help you." Poole paused for effect. "Kadee. This is your last chance to make a deal."

Alex said, "My client is not going to respond to that."

Poole pulled out a few sheets of papers. "Here are two notes that I found particularly interesting. The first is from all the way back in May." He switched his stare-down between Alex and Kadee the entire time he read the session notes. *"Patient reports feeling hopeless and wanting to end her relationship. She describes feeling trapped and unable to leave. She further states that sometimes she wishes he were dead, saying that if he were dead, she would have to move on."*

He paused to punctuate the severity of the statements. "This one is from July. *Patient is becoming increasingly angry. She states that she loves boyfriend, but knows she can't trust him. She describes feeling fragmented and confused. She states that she doesn't remember who she is anymore. She reports that part of her wishes he were dead. Her clinical presentation is growing more agitated. Patient is gaining more access to her aggressive feelings, becoming more able to express them. I may refer her to toxic relationship group for added support. Treatment goal is to help patient separate from the*

290

relationship with boyfriend and to help her understand what keeps her en-gaged in this type of dynamic."

"Those don't show any premeditation" Alex responded. "Ms. Carlisle was in a private therapy session ventilating feelings. That's all."

"I thought you might say that," Poole responded with an edge to his tone. "Here is one from two weeks before the murder.*"Patient has been describing aggressive fantasies toward boyfriend. She states that she feels like killing him. She describes a recurring image of herself standing at his bed holding a knife. We discussed the difference between fantasy and reality. Patient reports that she can distinguish between the two. Therapist asked patient if she had intent or plan to harm boyfriend. Patient responded that she had no intention of killing him, but that the thoughts of doing it were intrusive and both frightened and disturbed her. Continue to access patient's impulse control and help build her strength so she can get out of her situation."*

Kadee felt her heart drop. She knew that last note did not paint her in good light.

Alex said, "She's just expressing feelings. It says right in the note that she reported no intent or plan. If the doctor thought she was going to do something, she would have had a duty to warn the victim. Clearly, she knew that Ms.Carlisle was using the therapy to get her feelings out."

Poole raised his voice. "It says that she felt like killing him, that she had a recurring image of standing over the vic-tim with a knife — which, may I remind you, was the mur-der weapon — and that her thoughts were intrusive. From where I'm sitting, it sounds like she was having homicidal thoughts that were becoming more frequent, that she tried to stop herself at first, but eventually couldn't take it anymore, and decided she had no choice but to kill him." He turned to Kadee, "Isn't that what happened Ms. Carlisle?

"No," Kadee blurted out, trying to swallow the lump of tears that sat burning in her throat.

"Ms. Carlisle, you killed Noah Donovan. We all know you did it. These notes are just more evidence showing that. Do yourself a favor and tell the truth before it's too late."

Alex said, "My client just told you that she did not kill Noah Donovan."

Kadee's whole body was shaky as she felt a wave of adrenaline surge through her. She lost control. "I did not kill Noah! And do you know how I know that…I know that because I know that he didn't deserve to die. I did wish he was dead, and it's true I was having fantasies of killing him. And they were intrusive. I wanted to stop thinking about killing him, but then he would do something that would make me enraged, and the thoughts would just come, even though I didn't want them." Tears poured down her cheeks.

Alex tried to calm her by rubbing her back. "Kadee, don't contin—"

"I loved him. I hated him, too, but I did love him. And he treated me horribly, he used me, and I allowed it. I tried to end it, but he just kept coming over and calling me, and I was getting more and more angry. But through all of that, I still loved him. And it was my fault too. I could have stopped returning his calls or taking his calls or letting him in my apartment. How could I kill him, if it was just as much my fault for staying as it was his fault for continuing on with me? Please. You have to believe me.

Or at least consider who else might have done it. There is a murderer out there that's going to get away with this."

She slouched against the back of her chair, wiped her sweaty palms along her jumper, and stared at the floor, feeling totally drained from her appeal and ashamed of losing control.

They were all gaping at her uncharacteristic outburst. There was silence for a moment as they each tried to regain their footing. Alex spoke first. "My client isn't going to answer any more questions."

Poole shook his head, clearly frustrated. "Thank you for your performance, Ms. Carlisle, but we all know you did this. I gave you a chance to tell the truth. You should have taken it. You can continue to carry on your innocence charade, but it ain't gonna help you once the DA gets her hands on this information."

Gibbs added, "No Ms. Carlisle, are you sure there isn't—"

"Do you know about Noah Donovan's illegal recordings of his many sex partners?" Alex waited for them to catch up.

Poole and Gibbs exchanged looks like they knew something related, but they didn't share. Gibbs leans in. "Go on."

Alex explained about the package under Noah Donovan's desk and the contents on the memory sticks. He told them that Kadee couldn't find the copies, but that there must be evidence on Noah's hard drive that forensics could recover even if Noah had erased them.

Poole looked stunned. Gibbs, on the other hand, looked vindicated. He shot an "I told you so" smirk at Poole. Poole was still for a moment, then he appeared to have a moment of recognition, like whatever had confounded him was figured out.

Alex thought it was a curious response. "What is it, detective?"

Poole got up and said, "Nothing I'd like to discuss at the time, Mr. Suarez. Thank you for the information. We'll be in touch."

Gibbs got up. They both shook Alex's hand and exited.

Poole and Gibbs returned to their desks following the meeting. Gibbs had called to check on the affidavit for the search warrant he filed for permission to investigate Belle Donovan's computer. The information Suarez shared about the contents on those memories sticks had them both astonished. Was Noah Donovan also recording himself? There was nothing in his apartment suggesting he was making videos. The only device used for that, found at the scene, had Belle Donovan's fingerprints on it.

And if Belle Donovan took the recordings, what would motivate her to put them under her son's desk? And the last piece Poole did not like at all: Was there someone else that had motive to kill Noah Donovan? He knew they had to search Belle Donovan's computer for the images. He still did not think it had anything to do with the murder, but it was compelling. Gibbs disagreed; he thought the implications that Mrs. Donovan might be the killer were growing.

Poole reminded him of the substantial amount of evidence against Carlisle. He felt confident that even without the confession, which he didn't think they were going to get after witnessing her outburst, they had enough for an indictment.

Then some squabbling started between the partners. Gibbs thought Carlisle's speech was genuine. He sensed authentic emotion and felt that they needed to pursue other leads at the same time as they were gathering the information against her.

Poole was beside himself. "She's a psychopath. They are always convincing. I don't believe a word she says. That speech was one of the most artful manipulations I've seen in a long time."

"If anyone's crazy, it's you. That was one of the most sincere pleads I've ever seen."

"For fuck's sake, Gibbs, look at the evidence. There is so much of it. That speech was engineered with such skill; she's got you questioning the facts."

"I agree the evidence is pretty overwhelming. But let's be honest. You and I both know it's circumstantial. And until we get hard evidence pointing to Kadee, I'm going to continue following up on other leads."

"Christ. You just called the perp by her first name. She's got you hook, line, and sinker."

It was a difficult day for Kadee. After Alex left, she was alone in her cell for the whole afternoon. She could not stop ruminating over her outburst. She wished she could go back in time and stop herself. If Alex is not able to find an alibi for her, she may have just signed her own guilty verdict.

She felt like the tight cell walls were closing in on her as her thoughts were spinning round and round without reprieve. A few times she was overcome with such a devastating panic that she doubled over, choking, gasping for breath. She felt like she wanted to crawl out of her own skin, but she had nowhere to go. She was locked in.

That last note was incriminating, even Alex said he knew it was damaging as soon as he heard it. The evidence against her was mounting and the arraignment was probably going to result in an indictment. He had hoped it would never get that far, but he was running out of time, and the odds were not in their favor.

Alex was planning to submit an affidavit to see if those files were on Noah's computer. He needed to create doubt; maybe the videos would help with that. If, in fact, he could find them. If not, it was just hearsay — and even worse, the source was facing a first-degree murder charge. True or false, without something tangible, this was going to be a tough sell.

He had one assistant sifting through the life of Noah Donovan to see what they could come up with and another continuing the search for Hailey's alleged abortion road trip. In the meantime, he was sorting through all of the state's evidence and creating arguments to show doubt for each one of them.

He reminded Kadee that they needed to remain hopeful. He believed in the justice system, even though he knew sometimes it failed: guilty people remained free; the innocent were sometimes punished. He had enough faith in it, though, that he felt certain Kadee would be freed from the charges. Or perhaps, Alex Suarez was simply deluding himself for more personal reasons.

Kadee appreciated everything Alex said, and certainly all the time he was spending to help her. However, she was losing hope — rapidly. Whatever optimism she was able to hold onto flew out the window after she heard that last therapy note.

After her dinner, she was allowed to make a phone call. She called Vanessa, and it only made her feel worse. Vanessa was always so positive — it was her natural temperament — but even she sounded gloomy. Kadee knew her too well to be fooled. Despite trying to sound hopeful, Vanessa was just not good at faking it. Kadee could tell that her attempt to be upbeat was a visage; try as she might to be encouraging, the doubt in Vanessa's tone rang clear.

Kadee told her about the therapy notes. Vanessa was silent for just a second too long. Kadee knew that she was thinking the same as she was: "This ain't good."

"It's going to be OK, Kadee. You've got Alex in your corner. And I'm here for you always, no matter what."

"Thank you, Ness. You've always had my back."

"Damn straight. Even on that night when you kicked me out to have sex with Noah. As pissed as I was at you, I was even more pissed at that asshole."

"I truly am sorry. I can't believe I treated you like that."

"Not another word. I redirected it at the asshole that very night, so no anger lingered about for me." Vanessa laughed.

Kadee was silent for a moment. "Huh?"

"Oh my God! I just realized that I never had a chance to tell you because the shit hit the fan right after it happened."

"What shit hit the fan?"

"When Noah was killed. After I left you, I stood outside your apartment and waited for him to come out."

"For what reason?"

"One way or another, I was going to make him leave you alone. I pounced on him as soon as he left you and badgered him all the way back to his apartment. And true to form, before going into his apartment, he told me he would fuck you for as long as you were weak-willed enough to let him. He was a sick fuck. He got what was coming to him."

"Vanessa! No one deserves to be murdered. I can't believe you said that."

"Yeah, well, sometimes people change your views on things."

Kadee did not know how to respond. Vanessa was always the dearest of friends to her. And she was one of the most charitable people she knew. But this was a new side to Vanessa. And she did not like it. This was the kind of behavior that the detectives were convinced Kadee was capable of.

"Kadee? Are you still there?"

Vanessa jarred Kadee from her thoughts. "Yeah. Listen, they're giving me the signal that it's time to hang up."

"Oh. I thought we had like another ten minutes."

"Um… no."

"OK. I guess I'll talk to you soon. I'll try to visit as soon as I can."

"Bye." And Kadee quickly hung up. Thoughts began to swirl about her head. What if? What if the killer was not even on the police radar? What if the killing was for revenge — and it came from out of left field?

As Kadee was led back to her cell, her thoughts got the best of her. What if, she thought, what if… what?

What if Vanessa killed him? Kadee gasped at the thought.

But it's not possible. Is it? Could Vanessa be capable of such an act? Kadee loved her as much as she ever loved anyone, and she did not want to think that it was possible. *But…* what if? Kadee was scaring herself with such dark thoughts about her dear friend. If Vanessa did kill him, would she allow Kadee to take the fall? That did not make sense, since if she had killed Noah, it would have been to protect Kadee. But Vanessa knew where he lived. And she might have even been the last person to see him alive. And she never mentioned any of this to the police.

She had to get all of this out of her head. She would never be able to sleep if this was gnawing at her all night. She had to believe that Vanessa did not report anything to the police because she had no viable information to offer. *But...* she could have provided information about Noah's character. Namely, that he intended to continue fucking Kadee for as long as she would have allowed.

Now Kadee was feeling even more hopeless. She was certain she was going to be charged and convicted, destined to be locked up for the rest of her life.

When Kadee returned to her cell, she stared at the ceiling and started bargaining aloud. "If I am set free, I will never take anything for granted. I will never complain about stupid crap. I miss the stupid crap. I promise I will always appreciate all the important people in my life and I will value every single second of precious freedom I have. I will never EVER take that for granted EVER again. I am a good person. I don't know why this is happening, but I will learn from it. I will. I promise...please... please...I promise..."

She was allowed two books. Alex had brought her *Man's Search for Meaning* by Viktor Frankl. She had read it before, and she re-read the entire book that afternoon. She opened a dog-eared page to a quote that spoke to her. It read: "Everything can be taken from a man but one thing: the last of the human freedoms—to choose one's attitude in any given set of circumstances, to choose one's own way."

It was a testament of wisdom from a courageous and inspiring man who had survived the Nazi concentration camps. She was saying his words over and over in her mind until she could recite the quote from memory. She had to hold on to hope. She had to try her hardest to maintain a decent attitude. Anything was possible at this point. *You cannot give up,* she told herself.

She closed her eyes and imagined that she was lying on the sand along the ocean. She pressed her lids together hard, trying to hold the picture in her mind, letting it envelope her. The sky was cloudless, seemingly infinite, and the shore went on for miles. The open space, the crashing of the waves along the coastline, allowed her to breathe deeper, more evenly. She lay there using her brainpower to keep the image vivid. She was pushing air in and out of her mouth in long inhales and exhales, matching the rhythm of the water meeting the sand. She intermittently repeated Frankl's quote until she finally dozed off.

CHAPTER 25

The next morning, Gibbs was finally able to return to his research on Belle Donovan. The day before had been spent preparing for Carlisle's indictment. He knew there was some pretty convincing evidence against her, but he was becoming more convinced that she was innocent. He definitely did not think she was a psychopath. The problem was that what Poole had established was correct. There was a lot of information pointing toward her. So he felt it was his responsibility to make sure he pursued other potential leads.

He was sipping coffee and digging deeper into the life of Belle Donovan. It was only a few minutes later when he made a disturbing discovery. He shifted in his chair and continued reading as the layers of buried secrets revealed themselves on his computer screen. He stood up and surveyed the office, looking for Poole, but he was nowhere in sight. He continued reading.

At the same time that Gibbs was consumed with unraveling the mysterious life of Annabel Donovan, Poole was approached by a petite attractive woman with curly blond hair and perfectly white teeth. She was wearing large designer sunglasses and she had asked to speak with him privately. They went into a small private office to talk.

After an article confirmed Gibbs suspicion, he printed out the most germane documents and went searching for Poole. Sheehan pointed toward the private office.

Just as Gibbs reached for the door knob, Poole came out. He was rubbing his right temple with his hand and shaking his head. He was notably distressed. Gibbs shifted his focus away from his own discovery to ask Poole what happened. Poole motioned for them to walk back to his desk.

Once at their desks, Poole began speaking in an unusually low voice. It was almost a whisper. Gibbs leaned toward him putting his elbows on the desk straining to hear him. Poole explained that he had just spoken with a friend of Carlisle's, a woman named Hailey Beckham, who alleged that Carlisle was with her on the day of the murder. It was an unusual story, a scandalous story, but Poole thought she might be telling the truth; and that Kadee Carlisle had an alibi.

Poole was going to make a call to confirm her story. He gave Gibbs the details. "She has asked that we keep this as confidential as possible. She said she's concerned about the media exposure."

Gibbs nodded, "OK, we can try, but there's probably not much we can do to protect her from the media."

Poole nodded in agreement. "She says that she was having an affair. She did not want to disclose the name of the man, but she said he was famous, and that they were both married. She got pregnant and went to New Jersey to have an abortion on September 19th. She said Carlisle went with her."

Gibbs said, "Why wouldn't Carlisle tell us that? It doesn't make any sense. If she knew where she was at the time of the murder, why wouldn't she tell us? She's sitting in jail in right now!"

Poole nodded, "I know." He stood up, shifted his belt and sat back down. "Beckham is saying that Carlisle was out of it, on Valium and some other stuff, upset over Donovan and that she didn't really remember going. Beckham knew about the word **terminate** in Carlisle's calendar. She alleged that it was a note that Carlisle left for herself. A note to remind her that she was going with Beckham…to 'terminate' her pregnancy. It seems a little farfetched." He was shaking his head.

Gibbs agreed, "Does seem like she could be covering for Carlisle. But at the same time, I have heard shit much crazier than that. And speaking of which," he held out his hand with the documents, "I've got one right here."

Poole looked at the documents, "What's that?"

Gibbs was just about to speak when Poole cut him off. "Shit. Wait a minute. I forgot this Hailey Beckham is in a rush. She said she wasn't even going to come forward. I have to call the abortion clinic and scan over a picture of her and Carlisle. Apparently she used a fake name to protect her identity. She gave me her picture. I just want to get this shit over with so she can leave."

"If Kadee Carlisle was there, if this Beckham abortion story is true, my money is on Belle Donovan. I have some pretty incriminating evidence right here."

"I dunno. Like I said before, she's crazy, but not *that* crazy. Killing her own kid… She'd have to be psychotic…I dunno."

"Well, she has a history," he waved the documents in front of Poole's face.

"Oh, crap...for fuck's sake, what a crazy day. I don't even have time to take a shit. Let me just make this call."

It was early that morning when Vanessa called Hailey and gave her a piece of her mind. She could not believe that Hailey was turning her back on Kadee, particularly when she held the information that could save her life. After her conversation with Kadee the previous evening, she felt that she had to step in and do everything she could to help her. Vanessa was an even-mannered woman, for the most part, but when she felt something really strongly, she could lose her temper. When she got to that point, her words were not gentle.

She started out the conversation with Hailey politely. But when Hailey mounted her high horse going on and on about reputation, status, her need to be classy, Vanessa was becoming increasingly impatient.

Hailey said, "Vanessa, I don't expect you to understand. You are a quirky writer, a starving artist type; no one cares about how you present yourself. And I know what you're thinking: You're thinking that you come from family money. That may be true, but no one knows who you are and no one seems to care. But I...I...I, on the other hand, have a certain manner I need to uphold. I am a classy woman, that's how people know me, and I would like to keep it that way. I can't expect you to understand."

That pushed Vanessa over the edge. Her usual warm, kind tone turned harsh and cutting. "Hailey, let me tell you something, and I want you to listen very carefully to what I'm saying because if you don't, I am going straight to the media to tell them what you're hiding. At this point, it won't matter if they believe me or not, I am sure it will be released in the paper."

Hailey gasped on the line.

Vanessa ignored her and continued. "Class isn't about money or status, class, Hailey Beckham is about how you treat people. Your whole life is one big fucking paradox. You think you have class because you have money, because you think you have a certain status; but you, my dear, have not one ounce of integrity, not one fucking ounce of class. You can lie to yourself all you want, but I know somewhere buried deep beneath the face you show to the world, I know you know the truth." Vanessa took a deep breath and wiped her thick curly hair off her sweat-soaked forehead.

Hailey was bruised, but she wouldn't let Vanessa know that. "Vanessa, dear, how can you speak about a topic, such as class, when you know nothing about it."

"Whatever, Hailey. Bottom line: This isn't about me or you; it's about Kadee. I hope you do the right thing." She hung up before Hailey could respond.

Hailey was livid, but Vanessa was right. Deep down, in places Hailey tried to pretend didn't exist, she knew Vanessa was right. Hailey had been covering her wounds for years. She had spent so much of her life pretending to be someone she wasn't, that eventually it became who she was. Something about Vanessa's words, or maybe it had to do with the dire circumstances Kadee was in, but something, for the first time, something broke through. Vanessa held up the proverbial mirror, and Hailey did not like what she saw.

After Vanessa hung up on her, she went in the kitchen, ate a whole box of oatmeal raisin cookies, then went into the bathroom to throw up, over and over, until there was nothing but clear fluid coming up. She lay on the floor crying for more than an hour, her blond hair pasted to her head from perspiration and tears. She had so much pain, the tears she shed were from years of tamping down her feelings of emptiness and worthlessness. She spent her entire adult life trying to ignore it, trying to deny it, but in that moment, all of her resistances broke down and the floodgates opened. She cried and cried, and just when she thought she got it all out, she cried some more.

It was an emotional breakthrough for Hailey, and as she got into the shower, she realized that she felt calm. It was a good feeling. As she scrubbed her back with her shower brush, she was smiling. Keeping up the pretense, the amount of energy that went into her masterful self-deception was completely and utterly exhausting. In that moment, right there in the shower, she recognized that she actually felt free. She started scrubbing her back harder as she decided that she had to make things right.

She was a horrible person, and she wanted to change that. She would call Dean, tell him the truth, reveal her indiscretion and hope he forgave her; then she would go down to the station and tell the truth. She would tell them all the truth, herself included. There was a burden lifted— and she felt rejuvenated.

Poole made his call; he scanned the pictures and sent them over to the abortion clinic. He waited on hold for the woman to receive the emailed photos. A few minutes later, she got back on the line and made the confirmation. She remembered Hailey as the woman who had had the abortion on September 19ᵗʰ and Kadee as the friend who escorted her.

He went back into the small office. He took a written statement from Hailey, thanked her and released her.

"Will Kadee be released from custody?" she asked as she was putting her sunglasses on and getting up to leave.

"Yes, ma'am. There is some paperwork that needs to be filed, but yes, she should be released today, or at the latest tomorrow. Thank you again, Mrs. Beckham."

Hailey smiled. It was an authentic smile, revealing all of her perfectly white shiny teeth. It was a defining moment. As she walked out with her head high, she felt a sense of pride she had never felt before.

Just as Hailey was turning the corner out of the office to leave the station, Yvonne Tracy had entered the same hallway and was going toward the office. Hailey didn't notice Yvonne, but Yvonne saw her. She thought of stopping her to say hello and ask if she had come forward with the truth. She decided it might be inappropriate given that Hailey had been a patient. Besides the current circumstances were already convoluted, she didn't want to exacerbate them or make Hailey uncomfortable. She watched her as she disappeared down the hallway and out the door, wondering if she did the right thing. She then entered the office.

When she arrived inside and asked to see Poole and Gibbs, Detective Sheehan informed her that they were in a meeting. He led her into the same small office Hailey had just been in and told her to wait in there. Poole and Gibbs would be with her shortly.

She was anxious while she waited. She was there to disclose a truth she had concealed, and it was a rather uncomfortable situation for her. She played her imaginary piano with her fingers in the air, a Beethoven symphony, as she tried to maintain her composure.

While Yvonne was waiting, Gibbs was in the process of disclosing the scandal surrounding Belle Donovan's secret past. As it turns out, Gibbs had amassed a lot of information. Belle Donovan was the daughter of a minister named Frank Cameron. She grew up an only child, her family lived a modest life in a small town in rural Virginia. From what he could gather, her mother was schizophrenic. When Belle was a young girl, her mother was placed in a psychiatric hospital after she was found wandering through their quiet neighborhood naked.

After that, Belle was raised alone by her father, along with help from some of the ladies in the church, who acted as surrogate mothers. There was no information addressing Frank Cameron's relationship with any of the women. There were a few photos in old newspaper articles of him surrounded by a few women, with Belle at his side. He wondered if her father was having relations with any of the women. He could not be sure, and it probably was not of much relevance. What was clear was that Belle, from a young age, was raised by her father, a single parent.

Belle eventually moved to Boston. Gibbs did not know what brought Belle to Boston from rural Virginia. She was a graduate of Boston College, so he thought maybe she moved to the city to go to college. The next piece of information he had was that Belle Donovan married Dr. Allen Donovan, a well know orthopedic surgeon in Boston, when she was twenty-one. She was working as a nursing assistant at the time. He was fifteen years her senior. Later that same year, she gave birth to their son, Noah.

Ten years later, Allen Donovan died suddenly from a heart attack. There were articles describing some suspicion that Belle had poisoned her husband. His colleagues were in a battle with Belle over performing an autopsy on Allen. He was only forty six and in perfect health. Of course, this sort of tragedy happens. But a friend and colleague knew that Allen was contemplating leaving Belle, who had signed a prenuptial agreement. He was concerned that she had a motive for foul play.

There were legal documents that had been filed by Allen's doctor friends who tried to gain permission to perform the autopsy, but they were denied. The court voted in favor of his wife's wishes, which was that his body not be mutilated by a medical procedure.

There were quite a few newspaper articles implicating Annabel Donovan. One was on the front page calling her the DOCTOR'S WIFE WHO GOT AWAY WITH MURDER. There was one article that described Belle as having a breakdown titled: GUILY DONOVAN BREAKS DOWN. It said that she was placed in a psychiatric hospital. Those records were sealed; they would need a subpoena for them. But he did find an article dated two months later, talking about her release from the "madhouse."

Just three months later, she moved to New York City with her son and all of her late husband's money, purchasing her luxury apartment right on Fifth Avenue along the eastside of Central Park.

When Gibbs finished filling Poole in, his immediate response was, "That doesn't prove she killed her son." He paused for a moment and continued, "It is interesting, though. And with Carlisle's name cleared as our killer, it does make me suspicious."

Gibbs agreed, "Me, too. Especially when you add in the creepy surveillance. Let's bring her in and grill her."

"She's a very smart woman, maybe smart enough to get away with murdering her husband. She's not going to come without her attorney, who is not going to let her say anything without a formal charge against her. And we don't have enough to charge her, especially since she has an alibi."

"What is it with you and her? Normally, you'd be all over this."

"I don't know. But you're right. I just wish we had more direct evidence. All we have is circumstantial at best."

"We have more on Belle Donovan than we did on Kadee Carlisle, and you were fine with that. Listen, she clearly is not a stable woman, between those emails to her son, her stalking him with the video recording, thinking she was helping him and probably placing recordings of the videos of him with other woman under his desk, and now this…a possible murder, a breakdown. C'mon, Poole."

"What's the motive? Jealous rage? Sure it's one of the oldest motives in the book, but a jealous rage from a mother to son, it's a hard one to prove."

Gibbs would not relent. "Listen, you know as well as I that everyone has a breaking point. The more unstable someone is, the less it takes to hit that point."

Poole stood up and adjusted his belt. He started to open the door as he said, "Let's bring her down for questioning. I doubt we'll get much out of her, but let's give it a shot. If that doesn't work, we'll get a warrant to search her apartment. We should have the papers for the search warrant of her computer sometime today. Maybe there is some concrete evidence on there."

"Good plan. I'm going to call her to let her know we'd like her to come in. That should be a pleasant conversation," Gibbs chuckled.

They left the meeting room to place a call to Belle when Sheehan told them Yvonne Tracy was in the other office waiting to speak with them. They went in to meet with her. Poole immediately noticed that she looked more rested than the day before, her skin looked radiant, which he found quite appealing. There was no question that he had a bit of a crush on the doctor.

Yvonne stood up and shook both of their hands. Her cheeks were a bit flushed. This wasn't going to be an easy conversation for her. She had wanted to say something the day before, but lost her nerve. After the conversation about her session notes, she knew she had to come forward. She had been withholding information, possibly compromising their investigation. She was there to tell the truth.

She put her hands up to her cheeks and took a deep breath. "Listen, detectives, I have done something I am very ashamed of and I am here to make things right. I hope I'm not in any trouble."

Poole and Gibbs glanced at each other. It had already been a day filled with surprising revelations; they were unfazed at the possibility of another bomb dropping. Poole leaned toward her, "Go on, Dr. Tracy."

"May I have a glass of water, please," she swallowed hard, pursing her lips.

Poole left the office and came right back with a small bottled water.

There was a moment of quiet as Yvonne sipped the water. Then, she told them a truth. She was not with Belle Donovan on the day of Noah's murder. Poole and Gibbs looked hard at each other.

Poole said, "Please continue."

She went on to explain the difficult conversation between Noah, Belle and her that fateful evening in the restaurant when Noah walked out with Yvonne, abandoning Belle. She told them about Belle threatening Noah to cut him off financially and their follow-up argument where Belle actually said if he married Yvonne, she would never speak to him again.

"You see, detectives, this was the sort of thing she said to Noah all the time. She was always trying to control him and she was usually successful. But I guess...I don't know for sure, but I think this time he had just had it. We were in love, and he wanted to be with me. Belle wouldn't allow that, or at least she tried her best to make him leave me. But this time...this time, he didn't listen." She looked at her hands, then returned her gaze to them. Her eyes were tearing at the corners. "I blame myself for Noah's death. If he didn't choose me over her, over Belle, he would still be alive." She looked down again.

Poole and Gibbs were staring at her. Gibbs asked, "So you're saying Belle Donovan killed her son?"

For a split second, her light blue eyes looked like razors, penetrating through her glasses. Her voice became stern as she said,

"That's exactly what I'm saying. At least, that's what I'm convinced of. I mean, I have no hard proof, but..." She composed herself. "I didn't know what to do when she told me she had no alibi. I mean, she's Noah's mother. At first I felt guilty, like I drove her to it. Noah loved her so much. I thought to myself that he would want me to protect her. I thought Noah would want me to lie for her. I did it for him. It was the last thing I could do for him. But I know now that it was wrong of me. I let Kadee stay in jail when I knew there was a strong possibility, given what I just told you, that she was innocent. I have hurt a lot of people. I feel like a very bad person," she was crying. Yvonne almost never cried, but the tears streamed down her face like a running facet.

Poole wanted clarification. "Did she actually say she killed him? Did she say those words?"

"No...no, detective, she did not." Yvonne removed her glasses, wiping her tears, as she continued. "But I know she was threatening him, saying he would be sorry if he married me. But no, she did not say she killed him. She just said that she was scared because she didn't have an alibi. I asked her where she was, and she said home alone. Belle Donovan is never home alone during the afternoon. She's always busy doing something with someone. In my heart, I knew she was lying."

Gibbs was suspicious for moment. There was something about her vagueness that left him uneasy. "Dr. Tracy, I'm sorry to ask this, but it's standard. Do you have an alibi?"

She was nodding. "Oh, of course Detective, I understand. Yes, I do have an alibi."

Poole chimed in, "And?"

"I was with my ex-husband, Dustin. Dr. Dustin Stone. He knows I'm here. You can call him to confirm. Here's his card." She produced his card from her bag and handed it to Poole. "We hadn't spoken in quite a while, and then I ran into him one day on the street. You know, one of those strange New York coincidences. We had parted on such bad terms. He asked me to a friendly lunch. I figured enough time had passed, so I decided to go. We were in Central Park that day, pretty much all afternoon, sitting underneath a large oak tree right near the zoo."

"We will have to confirm that," Poole said.

"Of course."

"Would you be able to give us a written statement, detailing everything you just told us?" Poole asked.

"Of course, detective. I want to help in any way I can," she looked down again. "I really miss him. This has been difficult." She removed her glasses again, wiping her eyes dry with her hand.

"I'm sorry, doctor," Poole said.

Gibbs chimed in, "Yes, sorry for your loss, Dr. Tracy."

Poole brought Yvonne a small laptop and asked her to type a thorough statement of everything she just told them. She agreed. They left her alone in the small office.

Yvonne was typing slowly while humming the Beethoven symphony. Classical music always helped her from becoming overly emotional. There was something else that she probably should have told the detectives. She had wanted to, but then she just could not do it.

Kadee had mailed Yvonne the contents that were in that container under Noah's desk. The package arrived about a week before the murder. There was a note:

> Dear Dr. Tracy,
> Please hold onto this for me. I can't keep these things in my apartment, it's too upsetting. But I don't want to throw them out, either. I may want to look at them again, at some point in the future, when I'm not so distressed. I know you offered to hold onto them for a while, so I hope you don't mind. I had to get them out of here today. I was about to watch the videos again, and I know that is not a healthy decision. I guess we can talk about it in our session. See you next week.
> Thank You,
> Kadee

Yvonne had placed the package in her locked filing cabinet where she kept all of her patients' confidential information. It wasn't unusual for her to receive requests such as this from her patients. She had a separate drawer where she kept contents just like this: notes, letters, pictures, and various other items that were related to people's therapies, but that they were not yet ready to discuss. Of course she didn't know it at the time, but this package was different.

It was just the day before, after she visited Kadee at the jail, when she decided to go through the contents of the envelope. She knew Noah would never violate someone's privacy with a hidden camera. She wanted to see what exactly was on them. She just knew it was Belle. She had been stalking her own son, the pictures of him and Kadee proved that. She figured that those videos were just another way to intrude upon his life, and attempt to control his every move. She planned to hand the evidence over to the detectives, exposing the truth about Belle, but after she watched the film clips she changed her mind.

Two pairs of the panties were hers. She could hide those from the police. But there were two videos of her, too. She was totally naked in both of them and the angle of the camera offered a near perfect view of her and Noah having sex. One of them had them engaging in oral sex, and the images showed everything. She just couldn't hand those over. She always took sexual intimacy very seriously, and the exposure of their private life was something she just could not handle.

She thought of throwing her own videos out and giving them the rest, but she knew they would look for the originals and that when they found them, the whole department would be watching her and Noah engaging in intimate acts. She assumed Kadee didn't remember, because nothing was mentioned. The detectives did not ask about them. If they asked, maybe she would tell them. She knew they might turn up during the investigation. There was nothing she could do about that, but she did not want to draw their attention to them.

She really wanted to give the memory sticks to the detectives, but she just could not bring herself to do it. Belle had completely and utterly invaded her privacy; the thought of Belle watching Noah and her having sex made her so angry. But Yvonne was good at compartmentalizing her feelings, so she just tucked away her emotions and instead made what felt to be a rational choice.

She would not tell about the films, but she would come forward with the truth about the alibi. That would be enough for them to investigate Belle. She was pretty sure Belle would bury herself after that; her own entitlement would indubitably work against her.

At this point, Poole had done a one-eighty on Belle Donovan. He was now ready to head over to her apartment to arrest her. He had his pre-arrest-salivating look on.

Gibbs halted him momentarily. "I think she's lying, Poole."

Poole threw his hands up in the hair, being purposefully dramatic. "You spent the whole day telling me you suspected Donovan, and now that we have enough for an arrest, you're changing your mind. You can be a real pain in the ass with your hunches, Gibbs. This isn't a Sherlock Holmes episode. This is real life."

"I'm not saying it's not Belle Donovan, I'm just saying we need to cover all of our bases, and the doctor here…" he nodded his head toward the small room where Yvonne was. "The doctor here also had a motive."

"So did Kadee Carlisle, and she didn't do it, either. We can't go chasing Dr. Tracy around just because she might have had a reason to kill Noah Donovan. Besides, she has an alibi. I'm going to call Stone, confirm her story, then I think we should head over to Donovan's."

Gibbs conceded. He knew Poole was right. There was nothing implicating Dr. Tracy, and Belle Donovan no longer had an alibi. If they had to release Kadee Carlisle, someone would have to take her place, and they had a solid feeling who that someone would be. Gibbs wasted no time starting the paperwork for the search warrant they would need.

Chapter 26

Poole and Gibbs went over to the jail to inform Kadee of her release. She had a confirmed alibi and was to be discharged from their custody. She was innocent and free. They were just waiting for the paperwork to go through. They had notified Alex Suarez to pick her up. Poole told her about Hailey's visit, her disclosure of the truth, the confirmation phone call and the arrest of Belle Donovan.

It was a shocking account, Hailey coming forward, risking her own exposure and then Noah's own mother, the killer. Kadee just listened to Poole, hearing the words roll off his tongue. She just kept shaking her head in disbelief. It was an unbelievable story.

When Poole told her that the video recorder found in Noah's apartment was registered to Belle Donovan's computer, her stomach dropped. The memory sticks must have been taken by Belle Donovan. Noah's mother was a voyeur. She was watching them have sex and recording them. She felt violated.

Poole and Gibbs asked for permission to go back into her apartment and search for the missing sticks. Kadee didn't love the idea. She just wanted to put the whole ugly mess behind her, but she said yes. She wanted them to find the truth. They would also search Belle Donovan's computer. They would use all the evidence they could get their hands on in the case against Belle. Without fingerprints or DNA or a confession, they would have to build a strong circumstantial case.

Kadee hugged Poole and Gibbs, crying tears of relief and thanking them over and over. As they left the small conference room the clock was still ticking loudly, but Kadee barely noticed. She was free. She was physically and emotionally free. Alex came to get her a few hours later. It was the middle of the afternoon. He offered to take Kadee for a celebratory lunch, but all she wanted was to go home, call her parents, take a bath, then a nap in her own bed.

They planned for a dinner that evening. Kadee would call Hailey and invite her. She couldn't wait to call Hailey, actually. She wanted to express her gratitude and also take the opportunity to resolve the conflict that had been building between them over the years. And, of course, she would invite Vanessa. Kadee felt awful for postulating that Vanessa might have killed Noah, but she thought it best to never mention it to her. Regardless, she couldn't wait to see them.

It was around the same time that Kadee had just placed her head on her soft, fluffy pillow, ready for a long comfortable nap, that an officer at the jail made a tragic discovery. Annabel Donovan was dead in her cell.

Less than twenty four hours before Belle's demise, Poole and Gibbs had gone over to her apartment and arrested her. It was an awful scene. Not that any arrest is a pleasant site, but Belle, petite as she was, was kicking, screaming and flailing. She was resisting arrest. At one point, she took her small hand, rolled it into a fist, and punched Poole smacking his left eye. She had a large ring on that hand, which was evident by the bandaged cut and swollen pocket of discolored skin around Poole's eye the next morning.

As they made their way out the front door of her building, anonymous spectators were gathering, watching, wondering what happened. Some of her neighbors came out to observe. They watched with jaw dropping stares as their normally reserved, now-handcuffed neighbor was led to a police car, screaming, "I did not kill my son! Let me go! Somebody help me!"

When they got her to the station, she refused to speak without her attorney present. Poole gave her the phone and she made her call; her attorney would be there shortly. While they were waiting, they sat with her and went over all of the evidence they had against her, in particular, her lack of alibi and the statement made by Yvonne Tracy. Poole said, "Mrs. Donovan, we know you did this. If you tell the truth now, maybe we can help you."

Belle just glared at him, saying, "Detective, you have no idea who you're messing with. As soon as I am released, I am going to sue you and your entire department. This is an atrocity, and you will pay heavily. I can promise you that."

But things became worse for Belle when her attorney, Paul Schwartz, arrived, listened to all of the evidence and informed Belle confidentially that things did not look good for her. Belle yelled at him; her mellifluous voice discarded, she was speaking in a harsh tone. "Paul, you are a worthless excuse of a man and an even worse attorney. Take your cheap tie and cheap shoes and get out of here." And with those two venomous sentences, she fired him.

Belle called five more attorneys that day. Each attorney informed her that the mysterious circumstances surrounding her husband's death made the case a challenge. Each also told her that if she didn't accept a plea bargain, the prosecutor would be digging through her past. It was bound to be a humiliating experience. Belle hung up on each one of them. In her mind, she was innocent and she wanted an attorney who was going to fight for her.

Finally on her sixth call, she spoke with Gabrielle Smart, her friend's attorney, who seemed a little more optimistic. She did inform Belle of the extensive media coverage. Given the nature of the alleged charges, the media was being very unforgiving. It was going to make Belle's journey through the legal system all the more challenging. Belle didn't respond to her comment. She was undeniably horrified by the media exposure. They set up a meeting for the next day.

When the officer went to Belle's cell to retrieve her for the appointment with Gabrielle Smart, who was waiting in the small consult room, the officer stopped in her tracks. "Oh shit!" She grabbed her shoulder walkie-talkie. "Code Blue in prisoner holding cell 12." Her voice was shaky and her hand trembled.

As two more female officers came running over, they also stopped frozen in place. The three stared at the small cell. Belle Donovan was hanging in her undergarments from the side of her bed, her head cocked to one side with her city-issued jumper as the noose. The guards exchanged nervous glances. They should have been following suicide-watch protocols, but someone—one of them—dropped the ball. One or all of them was going to catch hell for this in a big way.

They called Poole and Gibbs, who immediately rushed over to the jail to survey the scene. It was unsightly. Poole and Gibbs were shaking their heads as they saw Belle Donovan hanging, her body limp, her eyes open and vacant.

It was hard to understand what she might have been thinking. Of course, she did have a previous hospitalization after her husband's death. Perhaps she made a suicide attempt then, but was unsuccessful. At first, Poole and Gibbs thought it might have been the media exposure that prompted her. Maybe it was too much too fast. Maybe she just did not have the wherewithal to deal with the consequences of her actions.

But then they noticed some paper sticking out from underneath the mattress. Belle Donovan had left a note. Poole pulled the paper out; Gibbs leaned over his shoulder as they both read her last words.

I did kill my husband, Allen Donovan. I poisoned him with Belladonna. He called me beautiful lady during our first years of marriage, so I thought it was a fitting choice of lethality. I added the berries to his cereal the morning of his death. He was threatening to leave me and take his money and my son with him. He left me no other choice. I couldn't have him take Noah. Noah, my son, gave me a reason to live. He was mine, and I was his. It was a love I had never felt before. I could not have that taken away from me.

My son and I were like one person. I was him, and he was me. We were inseparable. It was a bond that could not be broken. Everything I did, I did to protect him. In the end, I couldn't save him from the evils of the world, the vile women, and the seductresses that only wanted to take us away from each other. But I have no regrets. So I leave this world to enter the next and be rejoined with my beloved son for all eternity.

Annabel Donovan

Poole and Gibbs looked at each other, each had a slight shiver. It was a chilling confession. Poole shook his head. Suicide following a murder always unnerved him. It was an unrewarding ending; there was no opportunity for any real justice.

Gibbs wasn't so sure it was a full confession. "She didn't actually say she killed her son, only her husband."

Poole took a deep breath and sighed. "Come on, Gibbs. Sometimes people say things without really saying them. Sometimes you have to read between the lines."

"I don't know. I just have a feeling."

Poole threw his arms up in the air. "For fuck's sake, Gibbs, enough with you and your hunches. You sound like my ex-wife." He gave Gibbs a friendly jab in the shoulder. "Read between the lines, man. She's saying she killed him. Case closed. OK?" He paused for a moment, rubbing his hand over his bald head. "Let's go grab a beer."

"We're still on duty."

"You're getting on my last fucking nerve. One beer. We're off in an hour and a half anyway."

Gibbs nodded, "OK. One beer."

It was an unsettling ending to a complicated story of love, hate and the interweaving of the two, which on occasion ends tragically in murder. It seems paradoxical that what starts as an all-encompassing feeling, bonding people together, creating an atmosphere of intimacy and closeness, can turn so deadly. But just like any human emotion, passion and love are filled with contradictions. And the truth, well the truth turns out to be, in essence, the greatest mystery of all.

It was about a month later when Kadee heard a most intriguing story. It was a fictional story, but like any good fiction, without the need to adjust or conceal the truth, it actually might be the greatest expression of truth.

Chapter 27

Yvonne Tracy had called Kadee to see how she was doing. The two had not spoken since that day in the jail. Yvonne obviously knew of her release, her vindication, and she was glad for Kadee. It was a difficult time for Yvonne as she tried to put the pieces of her life back together. She had taken a personal sabbatical from her clinical work. She was strained and didn't think she could be emotionally present for her patients. She was staying with Dustin for a while. She didn't see them as back together, really. As it turned out, despite his reasons for their divorce, he still loved her; so she was relying on him for support temporarily.

It was a beautiful late October Saturday afternoon. The cool air, the colorful leaves and the angle of the sun all reminded Kadee of that first chance encounter in the coffee shop, the day she met Noah, a year earlier, before he began playing manipulation games with her... and Yvonne... and who knows how many countless other women. She still missed him. Despite how damaging the relationship had been to her psyche and the trauma over her arrest and possible prison sentence, she was able to hold onto the good parts of the relationship.

She learned something, which was the way she chose to look at the emotionally trying events. To make the loss and all that she endured less painful, she gave it meaning. She learned that she possessed the ability to love someone, totally and completely, and now she knew that she wanted to have that in her life. Noah opened her up, and she decided to stay open. This time, she would move a little slower, using better judgment, making sure the relationship had a more solid foundation. Alex and she had been doing just that for the last month, ever since he helped her in her time of need. They were spending time together, becoming reacquainted, enjoying each other. It was… nice.

Kadee was excited to hear from Yvonne. She had wanted to call her, but was hesitant. It was an unusual situation, her being her former therapist and the almost wife of her boyfriend. She was waiting for time to pass. Yvonne relieved her of her indecision when she called and asked if Kadee wanted to meet for an afternoon picnic. When Kadee said yes, Yvonne asked that they meet underneath the large oak tree in Central Park right near the zoo. She gave Kadee the exact landmarks so she could find the tree. Yvonne would have her cell phone, just in case Kadee couldn't find it. Kadee agreed.

Just two days later on that beautiful Saturday, Kadee and Yvonne met underneath the large oak tree. The two hugged, sat on the checkered blanket Yvonne brought. They ate egg salad sandwiches, munched on crackers and berries, and even had a bottle of red wine. They caught each other up on the details of their present lives. They talked about Noah, about missing him, yet feeling free, and about the tragic ending of Belle Donovan. It was surprisingly pleasant.

Yvonne had mentioned her time off from her clinical work. Kadee asked her what she was doing. Yvonne smiled. Her eyes lit up, seeming delighted. "I'm glad you asked." She went in her bag and pulled out a huge chunk of paper. It looked like a dissertation. "I'm writing a book. A novel, actually. It's almost done. The whole experience has been very therapeutic."

"Wow," Kadee smiled wide. "What is it called?"

"It's called *Circle of Betrayal*."

Kadee felt a quick chill run down her back. For a second she was uncomfortable. "Hmm…so what is it about?"

Yvonne smiled. She took her glasses off, shook her short hair, almost like she was an actress stepping into character. Her facial expression looked slightly unfamiliar, too. The way she was holding her mouth, crooked, one side down, the other up, she looked different, strange. And her pupils were a tiny speck, a pinpoint, surrounded by the blue of her irises, giving her a dazed look. It almost looked like she didn't know where she was. Kadee brushed it off as an eccentric writer behavior and waited for her to start talking.

She looked at Kadee with her dazed eyes and began. "It's about a woman, a young woman who wasn't particularly beautiful or particularly talented. She was loved by her parents, but wasn't their favorite. She always did the right things, but she never really got any acknowledgement. She always felt sort of like she was just there, a perpetual wallflower, wanting to blossom but no one to water her. Her brother committed suicide. After he was gone, all her parents ever did was compare her to him. She would never be as good as him, as smart as him, as fun as him or as loved as him. They loved her, but they never really noticed her.

"One day while she's in graduate school, she meets a boy, a man, a young man actually. He pays a lot of attention to her. More attention than anyone ever had before. He notices her. He sees her and she feels alive for the first time, almost like she was a marionette and he her puppeteer bringing her to life. She falls in love. She doesn't just love him; she is totally and completely head-over-heels in love. But he doesn't reciprocate. At first she's angry and hurt, but then she forgives him and they become good friends, the best of friends.

"She moves on with her life, she marries another man. But she never stops thinking, wanting, hoping that this first man will come around. He tells her he's closer to her than anyone else. She believes him. It keeps her going. Finally he starts showing interest in her. He tells her he loves her, he wants to marry her; she is the only one for him. She feels noticed, loved. Finally, she is someone's number one, someone's favorite. She's his favorite.

"But suddenly, all of her dreams are squashed, smashed, when she finds out that he has been involved with another woman, a beautiful woman, a spectacular woman, a woman she wishes she could be, but isn't. She still loves him, but her anger starts simmering, it triggers all of her past disappointments and rejections, all of the times she was pushed aside, made to feel second best, not noticed. All the pent up emotions culminate, and she begins to feel rage. It's a simmering, rage; it seethes, veiled beneath a thin surface, but she ignores it, pushes it aside. She tries to be the good woman, the understanding woman, the forgiving woman. That's who she tries to be.

"But the rage, the rage just keeps seething. It seethes to a point of no return and the tension becomes so unbearable that nothing she tries relieves her. So she decides, even though she tries to talk herself out of it, she decides that this man has to die. As long as he is alive, she will not have one ounce of peace. All of the tension will be gone. She will finally be released from her hell if she eliminates him. He must go; it's the only way out. And he deserves it. He deserves it for the way he has made her feel: invisible, second best, unnoticed.

"She goes to his apartment, her hair pulled all the way back, puts plastic all over her clothing, slips the gloves on, takes the key from under his mat, sneaks in quietly while he's sleeping. Takes a large butcher knife from his kitchen, goes in his bathroom and waits. She makes a noise in the bathroom. She keeps making a noise until he wakes up and she sees him walk in. He notices her. She sees terror in his eyes. She loves him and hates him. It's so painful, she can't take it. The rage comes; she has no control. She stabs him and stabs him and stabs him until he's dead. She stares at his body, the blood pouring from his wounds; she stares and stares until finally, finally she feels free."

Yvonne put her hands up to her cheeks. She was totally flushed, her cheeks were bright red. She picked up her glasses, put them back on and smoothed her hair. She took a deep breath. "So what do you think?"

Kadee had goosebumps. She pulled the sleeves of her sweat-shirt down past her hands and wrapped her arms around her chest. She looked at Yvonne and nodded as she said, "Sounds like the truth."

Yvonne pursed her lips, looking like herself again. She said calmly, "It is."

The two looked into each other's eyes; it was a moment of shared recognition of a truth that was almost too frightening to know. They both stood underneath the large oak tree. Yvonne leaned in and kissed Kadee right on the lips, she backed up, slowly packed up her basket, folded her blanket, turned around and walked away. It was as if nothing happened.

Kadee stood underneath the large oak tree as she watched Yvonne disappear, becoming only an anonymous speck in the crowded park. She stretched, reached for the clouds, inhaled the fresh fall air, then began the walk back to her apartment.

He mind was clear for the first few minutes, then the flood of ideas nearly drowned her. *What?* She said to herself, as she made her way home. It was almost impossible for her to register what she heard. *She killed him? Holy crap, she fucking killed him. No. There's no way Yvonne killed Noah. She was my therapist. I always saw her as so in control of her emotions. I aspired to be as well contained as her. It can't be true.*

But... she said that it was. You said, "Sounds like the truth," and she said, "It is." But why would she tell me? Maybe she figured I deserved to know, or maybe she thought I'd be glad she did it. Did she frame Belle Donovan to rescue me? Is that why she told me? But there is just no way. I just can't believe she snapped like that.

But it's so often the people that seem in control who have that seething rage. But she couldn't have. Should I go to the police? What would I say?

That she wrote a fictional account of the murder? She's smart. She could easily say that it was just fiction, a form of writing therapy. Maybe she told me to stick me in this dilemma. I was "the other woman," maybe she blames me. Was it some sort of subtle mind game threat toward me? Now that's scary. But she didn't seem upset at all. Well, she didn't seem capable of murder, either. Maybe she's a total psychopath. I do not like that thought at all. But she did kill him. I can't even really wrap my head around it.

Isn't Alex taking me to the movies tonight? Right, we are going to dinner and a movie with some of his friends. I should think about that instead. This is too much right now. Maybe I can just pretend I never heard about Yvonne's book.

But… you are not good at denial.

But… it is fiction.

But, but, but…stop thinking. You can re-visit this next week after a little time has passed and you've absorb what was told to you. It was one of the only times in Kadee's life, as far as she could remember, when she wished that she didn't know the truth.

Right before she temporarily buried what she knew somewhere deep in the back of her psyche, she thought, *sometimes the truth is just too hard to hear.* And then as she opened the door to her apartment, she said to herself in a whisper, "and taking someone's life is the ultimate betrayal."

AFTERWORD

Thank you for reading *Circle of Betrayal*. I am always grateful to those who take the time to read my work. I hope you enjoyed your experience.

Although the story is entirely fictional, the content explored is one of my long time interests. As an alumna of John Jay College of Criminal Justice, like Kadee Carlisle, I entered the graduate program in forensic psychology with a curiosity and fascination for what I believe to be one of the most paradoxical crimes: passionate homicide. How does love turn to murder? I couldn't learn enough about it. And the question remained without a satisfactory answer.

My original career ambition was to work for the FBI's Behavioral Science Unit (now the Behavioral Analysis Unit) as a criminal profiler, but I eventually decided to pursue my doctorate in clinical psychology instead. Academics seemed more of a natural fit for me. And so it goes...

I worked in the criminal justice system as a psychotherapist and forensic evaluator for years, picking and probing the psyches of violent offenders, writing papers, evaluating insanity plea acquittals, journaling thoughts, formulating hypotheses.

After finishing my dissertation, then authoring two nonfiction books, and co-authoring two more, I found myself feeling limited in what I could learn. In psychology we conceive an idea, explore, research, hypothesize, write, but we are always looking to find what we set out to look for. In this way, it is somewhat formulaic, or at least it felt that way to me.

So I decided to use my knowledge of psychology and my clinical experience a little differently. I created characters, set a background, let my mind wander freely, allowing the characters to drive the story. I wanted them to provide the answers.

I submerged myself in the inner world of each character, allowing them to guide me through the narrative. They offered me the opportunity to experience firsthand what I was interested in knowing more about. There was love, rage, envy, obsession, risk, chance, loyalty, fear, betrayal, redemption all coalescing. I experienced it *all* as I went through it with each of them; I *knew it* in a way I couldn't possibly have understood it before.

I wasn't even sure who would be responsible for the murder in the beginning; I just gave each character the motivation. They did not disappoint. As the story went on, it became clear who did it and *why*. Each one of them left me fascinated, surprised, disturbed, exhilarated. And I loved every moment with them, even the highly emotional scenes, when I could feel my own heart racing.

In the words of Kadee Carlisle, *"But..."*

The story doesn't end here. My characters are telling me that there is more to explore, to learn, more surprises. So this is the first book of the trilogy, *Close Enough to Kill*. It will go on and I will continue with my exploration of love and passion and the contradictions within. There will be more plot complexities and variations on the theme.

The second book of the trilogy will be out sometime in 2016. No spoilers, but I dare say that this time you just may be privy to the inner dialogue of a murderer.

Thank you again for reading!

ACKNOWLEDGMENTS

From the first few paragraphs, to the hours pounding away at the keyboard, some days until my eyes were blurry and my mind a fog (sorry if we spoke during this time and I wasn't able to provide reasonably sound conversation), to the sleepless nights when the ideas wouldn't relent, to the final edits, this has been such a rewarding experience. I am grateful to many who shared in this process with me! Sure, hard work, discipline and persistence are vital for writers, but having people believe in you, show interest, support your work, well…in my experience this is priceless.

I am eternally grateful (I can't say it enough) to my long-time friend, sounding board, creative collaborator, cheerleader, and brilliant editor, Carlo DeCarlo. Without his ongoing support, belief in my creative abilities and knowledge of fiction writing this book would probably have remained an idea, yet to be written. Thank you! Thank you! Thank you!

To my husband Joseph Gunn for creating another wonderful book cover. And who helped me through some plot hurdles, listened tirelessly to the story as I was writing it (I know it was annoying especially when I was over-caffeinated and started reading you pieces of the book first thing in the morning), and talking me through some moments of doubt. I am so grateful!

To my father, Philip Simon who also listened with an inexhaustible ear and heart as I was creating the story, for reading the drafts, for supporting me and believing in me. I must be the luckiest girl in the world to have such a terrific dad.

Much gratitude to my trusted consultant, James Flanagan, formerly an Assistant Essex County Prosecutor and formerly an Assistant US Attorney, for contributing his knowledge of criminal investigations and the legal system, for taking the time to explain details of the process and for suggesting places I could take creative liberties. I could not have finished the book without your expert advisement.

To all of my readers, Pamela Frank, Melinda Gallagher, Alecia Seliga, Mike Alonzo, Brent Potter and Ellen Neville, who read, re-read, gave significant commentary, brought up important questions, offering ears in which to bounce ideas, my deepest appreciation. Your time, interest and feedback were an invaluable contribution to this process.

About the Author

Jacqueline Simon Gunn, Psy.D. is a clinical psychologist in Manhattan. She is the author of four non-fiction books, including co-authored non-fiction novel, *Bare: Psychotherapy Stripped,* as well as numerous articles relating to psychology, psychotherapy and running. In addition to her clinical work and writing, she is an avid runner. *Circle of Betrayal* is her first work of fiction.

Gunn is currently working on two sequels for her novel, as well as other writing projects.

OTHER BOOKS BY JACQUELINE SIMON GUNN

In the Therapist's Chair

Bare: Psychotherapy Stripped (co-authored with Carlo DeCarlo)

Borderline Personality Disorder: New Perspectives on a Stigmatizing and Overused Diagnosis (co-authored with Brent Potter)

In the Long Run: Reflections from the Road

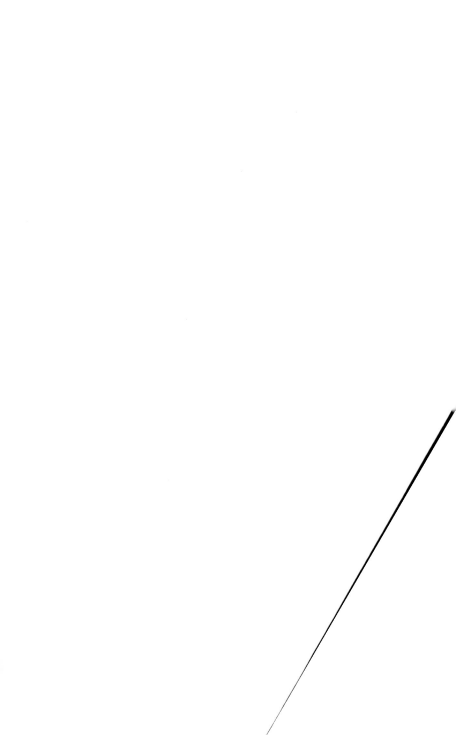

9 781518 788215